INVISIBLE FICTIONS

INVISIBLE FICTIONS

CONTEMPORARY STORIES FROM QUEBEC

EDITED BY GEOFF HANCOCK

ANANSI
TORONTO

This collection copyright © House of Anansi Press Limited, 1987. Introduction and biographical notes, copyright © Geoff Hancock, 1987. The Acknowledgements constitute an extension of this copyright page.

All rights reserved. Except for brief quotation for purposes of review, no part of this publication may be reproduced, transmitted, or stored in any form or by any means without permission from the publisher.

Cover design: Laurel Angeloff.

Translated with assistance from the Canada Council; published with assistance from the Canada Council and the Ontario Arts Council.

Manufactured in Canada for
HOUSE OF ANANSI PRESS LIMITED
35 Britain Street
Toronto, Ontario M5A 1R7
1 2 3 4 5 / 97 96 95 94 93 92 91 90 89 88 87

Canadian Cataloguing in Publication Data

Main entry under title:

Invisible fictions : contemporary stories from Quebec

Translated from French.
ISBN 0-88784-153-8

1. Short stories, Canadian (French) – Translations into English.* 2. Short stories (English) – Translations from French. 3. Short stories, Canadian (French) – Quebec (Province).* 4. Canadian fiction (French) – 20th century.* I. Hancock, Geoff, 1946-

PS8329.5.Q5I58 1987   C843'.01'089714   C87-093244-6
PR9197.32.I58 1987

CONTENTS

GEOFF HANCOCK	INTRODUCTION	9
ROLAND GIGUÈRE	MIROR	17
MADELEINE FERRON	THE WEAKER SEX	35
MARIE-JOSÉ THÉRIAULT	THE THIRTY-FIRST BIRD	45
ANDRÉ CARPENTIER	BIRDY'S FLIGHT	63
YVES THÉRIAULT	NULIAK	83
ALAIN GRANDBOIS	THE THIRTEENTH	89
THOMAS PAVEL	THE PERSIAN MIRROR	107
JACQUES BROSSARD	THE METAMORFALSIS	121
ROCH CARRIER	THE BIRD	149
	STEPS	151
	THE WEDDING	153
	THE INK	157
	THE ROOM	159
LOUIS-PHILIPPE HÉBERT	THE HOTEL	165
	A TEXT CONCERNING STRAWBERRIES	169
MICHEL TREMBLAY	THE HANGED MAN	173
	THE EYE OF THE IDOL	177
	THE GHOST OF DON CARLOS	183
	THE OCTAGONAL ROOM	193

MICHEL DE CELLES	RECURRENCE 199
PAUL PARÉ	FIVE FABLES 207
FRANÇOIS HÉBERT	PROWLING AROUND LITTLE RED RIDING HOOD 217
JEAN FERGUSON	KER, THE GOD KILLER 229
CLAUDE GAUVREAU	THE DREAM OF THE BRIDGE 241
	THE PROPHET IN THE SEA 247
CLAUDE BOISVERT	A SLICE OF NOTHINGNESS 257
	THE PROPHET 261
ELISABETH VONARBURG	COLD BRIDGE 267
PIERRE CHÂTILLON	GHOST ISLAND 299
CLAUDETTE CHARBONNEAU-TISSOT	COMPULSION 315
YOLANDE VILLEMAIRE	IN FRONT OF THE TEMPLE OF LUXOR 329
JACQUES FERRON	THE DEAD COW IN THE CANYON 359
MONIQUE PROULX	ABC 389
CLAIRE DÉ AND ANNE DANDURAND	A METAMORPHOSIS 397
	A CASE STILL OPEN 403
VICTOR-LÉVY BEAULIEU	*from* MONSIEUR MELVILLE 407
NOTES ON CONTRIBUTORS	427
ACKNOWLEDGEMENTS	435

INTRODUCTION

Geoff Hancock

Invisible Fictions: Contemporary Stories from Quebec is not a reassuring collection of *contes*, *recits*, or *nouvelles* in English translation. Readers who look for realistic settings, historical backdrops or sociological character studies will be startled. These stories are fantastic, surreal, gothic and grotesque. The writers do not describe the Quebec you thought you knew. No pea-soupers, no maple syrup, no separatist politics. The St Lawrence River offers no point of entry. You cannot navigate in this place. The geography of these fictions is elsewhere, in that unmapped area Victor Lévy-Beaulieu describes in *Monsieur Melville:* "At the other end of the earth in the country that is invisible because it is Québécois. If you were to come there," he goes on to invite us, "maybe it would become transparent at last."

In this country of fables, dreamscapes, plant and animal transformations, medieval tales made new, time travel and time stoppage, is a textual space where the psyche of a province is contained in words. This world is restricted to the surface of the page. The writers have invented a place that does not exist, but which can liberate the reader. The stories collected here offer us paper worlds which do not necessarily point beyond themselves to a corresponding reality, and the pre-eminent geography is invisible: emotional longings are more precise than any fixed point. Québécois authors write themselves into existence and are transformed, even as their writing raises unsettling questions about the very nature of fiction, of reality and art.

Many of the conventions of Quebec literature were established early: the theme of the New World as an aspect of dream, the idea
of the noble savage, a utopian El Dorado, even the image of the man of the woods, the *coureur du bois*, as an independent and anarchic spirit. The stories in *Invisible Fictions* convey a nostalgia for the failed myth of the past. After 1760, Quebec feared for its survival. As North Americans living under British law but speaking French, Quebeckers showed their tendency toward a literature of resistance. The so-called "Second Conquest", the Rebellion of 1837, led to Lord Durham's report of 1839, with his comment that Quebeckers in fact have no history and no language. A response to this was François Xavier Garneau's three volume *Histoire du Canada*, a masterwork not surpassed for over a century, which established the idea of Canada as a land of two languages and two cultures. Much fiction of the 19th Century emphasized the folklore and legends of the country as a way of establishing a literary identity, and in this way, the supernatural became more than a curiosity of Quebec's literature, it became essential to the tradition.

The contemporary Quebec fantastic story has come to its present form in the twenty-five years since the Quiet Revolution politicized and transformed Quebec society. Quebec writing also came of age at a time when international literary developments included Beckett, Borges, García Marquez, Calvino, Handke, and other writers of "unreality". The literary reviews examined theories as diverse as *Tel Quel*, Russian formalism, the *nouveau roman*, semiotics, feminist criticism, and metafiction. By staying true to its earliest literary past, Quebec writing, when the time came, was able to merge into the modernist mainstream without distorting its own distinctive forms.

While the fantastic tale is universal, with a long international tradition, certain characteristics are unique to Quebec. At the simplest level, these Quebec stories are an extension of the motifs of folklore and the oral tradition which had evolved for centuries in a relatively isolated province surrounded by English-speaking North America. Some of Quebec's literary strength could be said to draw upon the fantastic, macabre and supernatural elements of pre-Conquest literatures of 1760: even Rabelais' *Gargantua and Pantagruel* was inspired by the journals of Quebec's discoverer, Jacques Cartier.

Marvellous fictions are appropriate to a country waiting for miracles. Folklore was used to subvert a society which supports a conservative nationalism, a rigid clerical hierarchy and intellectual censorship. Many of the early motifs of the French North American experience resurfaced in works as diverse as Denys Chabot's *Eldorado on Ice* and the tales of Jacques Ferron and Roch Carrier in the 1960s and 1970s. The writers of a New Quebec had to reinvent their country, and they found that their place could have a heroic centre not on any map or in any particular historical event, but rather in a unique imaginary landscape, self-created and fantastic.

The flowering of such concerns in Quebec literature came after the publication of the 1948 manifesto *Refus Global (Global Refusal)*, a turning point in Quebec intellectual and cultural history. The authors were painters under the leadership of Paul-Emile Borduas, and, later, Jean-Paul Riopelle. They "refused" the repressive examples of official culture, as represented by the Province's long-time premier Maurice Duplessis, the Catholic Church, the landowners and the capitalists. Instead of conservative theocracy, they wanted liberation. They were especially interested in writing that "appeared to be a hybrid or a grotesque, blended by insult, metaphor, and argument." André Breton's manifestoes stimulated their interest in "automatic" writing and painting. *Refus global* also introduced the absurdist "plays" of Claude Gauvreau, impossible to produce on stage and thus included as fiction in this collection. The creation of literature, said Gauvreau, was the opposite of history, which merely led to the rational, whereas creation led to the authentic, the imponderable, the invisible.

By the early 1960s, the so-called "Quiet Revolution" had

transformed Quebec politically. The Liberals had defeated Duplessis' conservative *Union nationale*, the term "French Canadian" was replaced by the less colonial Québécois. The literary world was flooded by the rhetoric of revolution and insurrection; many writers openly supported separation from the rest of Canada; the search for an identity, a history, a place, became intense. For many writers, the language of the search was joual, a non-language, Québécois slang, the French of the slums—another evidence of the attempt to throw over the conventions of the past and invent a new language for a particular place.

By the late Seventies and early Eighties, the political climate was tempered and the aggressive rhetoric of the Sixties was replaced, as Michel Lord puts it, by "a shy beginning of recognition for fantastic short fiction." From two fantastic titles a year, published in 1960, the number jumps to over 100 titles by 40 authors by the end of the 1970s. Virtually every Quebec writer is interested in the fantastic at some point in his or her career. Lord points to an issue of the literary review, *La nouvelle barre du jour*, as ushering in a phase in which the fantastic becomes a predominant mode of the literary imagination in Quebec. In fact the literary magazines and reviews, such as *Lettres Québécois*, *Nuit Blanche*, *Québec-Français*, and many others regularly feature and promote the fantastic form. Nearly a dozen books of short fiction—and two-thirds of them fantastic—are now published in Quebec each year, directed to an avid reading public. Perhaps the popularity of the form is based most solidly on the need of every reader for the elements of fiction: a story told, a story heard.

Where is Quebec, then, in these writings? Denys Chabot entitled his two novels *El Dorado on Ice* and *Moon Country*, and notes that his books pertain "less to those countries one discovers than to those one invents." Ferron writes his tales "from an uncertain country," Gérard Bessette finds Quebec a "pseudo-geographical region," and for Pierre Trottier, Quebec is a "baroque land" where fixed forms of narrative are reinvented or cast aside. The "nada" in Canada becomes "nothing" after the *nada* in Spanish. Quebec writing is full of such negations of place—my country is not a country, it's winter, as the Gilles Vigneault song says: *Mon pays, c'est ne pas un pays, c'est l'hiver*.

With these fictions as a guide, the reader is drawn into a search for a new reality. Quebec novelist Hubert Aquin declared that only the writing of chaos can correspond to a country that makes no sense, that the writer must awaken the reader's consciousness with prose that leads us to the "next episode" in life, the promised revolution. Reproducing "reality" in prose is a highly structured and constrained activity which limits a writer to time, space, and the concrete. But in creating worlds outside the traditional narrative, the symbolic system of language can be challenged. Surrealism is one way, a reinvented or "dreamed" language is another. Many of the stories in this collection escape from public language by deliberately withdrawing into the silent world of animals, or the perceptions of madness, or a sci-fi or prehistoric or Native specialized vocabulary. Pictures are used instead of words, as in Yolande Villemaire's "The Temple of Luxor", and the surface of a given story may seem to read as if decoded from another language, a reminder to us that all language is foreign.

On another level, the imaginative contours of these "invisible" worlds reveal the presence of their exact opposites, the visible real. Surrealism and symbolic writing operate by associative leaps the mind must make, and thus imagery and psychic energy are the controlling principles of "invisible fiction". If English-Canadian writing might be described as horizontal, based on an observing perception, Québécois writing is largely vertical, moving geometrically, outward and inward. This may be why so many of the works here affect us as if they were still-life paintings. Objects are seen at rest, reposing on endless plains, as in Claudette Charbonneau-Tissot's fictional atmospheres of thin air, smooth surfaces, and long shadows. A sharp focus makes the world seem doubly strange, and suggests a hidden, ominous presence in tangible things. In these places, we are hardly surprised to find that strawberries are malevolent, grass comes to us from another dimension, crabs and lobsters move in on human reproduction, and trains bare their teeth. Without corporeal restraints, metamorphosis is the prevailing natural law, as men turn to trees, magicians disappear into the void they have created, and dancing rats in red shoes wait for tourists in a cheap hotel. We always suspected it was like this, somehow.

In a place where history is fluid, the writers are doomed to restructure time past and future. Jean Ferguson and André Carpentier give us "prehistory" in their stories; the absent future is presented by Jacques Brossard and Elisabeth Vonarburg. Many of the new writers are concerned with origins, beginnings. Rootless characters who live bleak lives either take possession, inhabit or find a new territory to carve out. In their urge to escape history, protagonists search out the elemental, the basic, to become one with the earth regenerating itself. By returning to the land, these writers suggest, the Québécois will recover their lost strength and revitalize the invisible country. The move from "culture" to "nature" is meant as a rebirth, not usually a journey into self-annihilation—although sometimes it is hard to be sure of the difference. The entire history of narrative from primitive thought to utopian vision is encapsulated in the Quebec literary imagination today.

French critics speak of a literature of absence, a literature moving towards the silence they describe. Tsevtan Todorov: "The literature of absence is always selfconsciously artificial, always aware of itself as a negativity." A fieldmark for this kind of literature is that the narrator is so often reduced to a rudimentary self and an audience of one, using diaries, asides to the reader, found manuscripts, remembered conversations, and letters to the self which both emphasize isolation and encourage the reader to participate more actively. Sometimes the lonely narrator creates a double, and the plot exposes the compulsions of such a split. In the new Quebec fiction, it is common for a narrator to fall asleep, and dream a self or a landscape out of his or her head. Lacking a social context, the narrators travel, orphans wandering in a world of images trying to find substance in Egypt or ancient Persia or the old French colonial empire. Ronald Sutherland has called the liberating effects of this activity "extra-territoriality", and when the search for territory fails, as it always does—as in the stories of Alain Grandbois—characters turn inward to the search through the chaos of the psyche.

In Quebec writing, it is often a cold search. In stories by Carpentier, Carrier, Tremblay, Hébert, and Charbonneau-Tissot, winter is the eternal season, an incantatory space, a blank which resists being mapped. Its whiteness is a blank sheet, which can liberate us from the social framework, but which tempts us to fill in the blank—or succumb to madness, apathy, or death by freezing. However, against this blank, "other" worlds can be projected, and other languages may take root. There can be a demonic joy in creativity here, a wild humour which gives these fictions a special cutting edge. The theory of the carnivalesque, as defined by Russian critic, Mikhail Bakhtin, seemed to provide an appropriate means for reading Quebec fiction. The carnivalesque is identified by play, odd logic, turnabouts and subversion of order. In the Bakhtinian sense, Quebec has moved from Lent to Carnival. The old moral order is over: incest, homosexuality, and prostitution are celebrated, as an anti-world of black masses, sorcery and dreamed horror is brought in to travesty our everyday society. The story lines are, as Hubert Aquin says, "like equations with many unknowns."

In these fictions the reader must be the double of the narrator, sharing in the equation—because so often the leading character is one whose identity is perilously shifting as we read. Invisible fictions ask us to share in the fantastic restructuring of the world, and to be the accomplices in a pay-as-you-go reading experience, as exhilarating as it can be frustrating. That Quebec should be pre-eminent in the practice of this form is perhaps inevitable, given the accidents of its historical past and the cultural necessities which that past has engendered. Attempting to escape tradition, invisible fictions become an integral part of the tradition. In the best new Quebec writing we are in the company of pioneers, offering us a search for an authentic language, a self-created universe, and hardy characters who live in a space where energy is expanded and where the most pleasure comes when the pure moment of writing can occur.

MIROR

Roland Giguère
translated by Sheila Fischman

I

Miror, seen from the back, had the appearance of a noble chain of mountains; seen from the front he was a forest that had been cleared away, stripped bare by years of domestic struggles.

II

Miror was also a swinging door: one had only to glance at him to see everything within him spread out on the ground, without shame or defence.

III

His shadow was, rather, himself. He had arrived at the state of shadow, he was nothing but a shadow among the nights, a shadow that mingled with his familiar objects, with his slightest gestures, with his thoughts. A memorable shadow.

IV

To draw him out of the dream where he had lived during the dark seasons it would have taken a blast of reality, capable of whitening the darkest nights that he had lived as well as the ones he saw coming.

V

He always came back to what was tearing at him, to the long claws he nourished like a tapeworm and which lacerated his guts in return. Miror patiently awaited the day when he would be able to open his body and shake those claws in the open air.

VI

His house, his dwelling, his prison, his garden, the place which every day saw his head roll along the glowing embers, the place which heard the booming of his heart before the eruption, that sacred and cursed place, was what today is still called the Earth.

VII

Miror possessed, one night in ten, a glass that was transparent but empty, a line with no book, a fish with no hook, and a few memories of green leaves now yellow and brittle, without value, without beauty.

VIII

In his moments of leisure Miror would amuse himself by drawing mirrors. He used the smallest ones to reflect the lines of his hands and destroyed the others as they appeared, for fear they might escape him and go so far as to send back to him the white visage of his solitude.

IX

Miror had one fear among others, a fear that reduced him to the state of a seismograph, a dreadful fear: that one day he would lose the green leaves of a cherry tree he had pressed in the bottom of his pocket.

Miror detested dead leaves. When autumn came, then, he had to take endless detours, walk hundreds of miles, horror-stricken, in order to return to his cell.

All that was obviously only *ideas*, but with such deep roots. . . .

X

He often felt that he was living in a clock; it even happened that he became confused with the mechanism. Then Miror would begin to turn around and cry out the hours like one condemned to death. It could go on for an entire day; at midnight he would collapse, exhausted, unwound like a broken spring. But the final hour was retreating.

XI

He had to retrace his steps a hundred times; still the sea presented its curtain of daggers to him, projecting the image of ruins that haunted his memory: flickering stones of his poor brain drowned in black waters.

Miror's only defence was a minuscule crushed shell whose fragments, however, contained radiating blood.

XII

On a grey and dusty morning Miror set out to climb the mountain. Small lights cast their fires around him, small lights of lost men, dead in the midst of their ascent. A curious obsession, wanting always to go higher ... Miror simply wanted pure air.

XIII

One day Miror picked up a large blank page, spent two long hours bent over his table and wrote:
I am dehydrated. I am running in neutral.

XIV

A small animal continually entered his cell and made him doubt his own words. To forget it Miror took refuge in long and painful silences, but then the animal would howl, howl until Miror, unable to stand any more, began to howl like a dog himself. Twenty times, a hundred times Miror had thrown the little animal out into the night, but he always came back unscathed, more alive even, more formidable than ever.

Animals born at night show white teeth, sharp, ready to bite the softest hands. Very few know this nocturnal fauna; all those who do bear deep scars.

XV

Miror wanted to die struck by the sun in his chest. Thus he often stood at his window bare-chested, motionless, awaiting the fatal stroke.

But never

Never did the sun dare to perforate the chest of a man for fear of reprisals from the heart. An abrupt burst of the alveoli and the sun would be splattered, draped in a murderer's velvet. Miror, however, was born to die in the strobe of bright light, at mid-day.

XVI

When Miror spoke out loud the leaves trembled on the trees and then the snow fell, forming a white ring around his mouth. His words became crystallized. The snow melted only with his silence. Words remained crystallized for a long time and travelled from mouth to mouth like multicoloured butterflies. Each time the leaves trembled, each time it rained, everyone knew that in his dark cell Miror was talking and then they would wait tensely like crystals for a word to keep, a word to repeat.

XVII

He knew.

A drifting ship always runs aground on the tranquil shore of a green isle and through its partly opened side the blue water enters gently, as though it were at home, stretches out in the captain's cabin and sleeps.

Miror knew how sweet it was to drift and the caress of the grateful water. Often he surprised himself tacking in his cell.

XVIII

Strange Miror....
Like his habit of looking into his neighbour's head....

When someone came too close to him, Miror immediately took his head, scalped it and looked for a moment to see how things were going inside: his curiosity satisfied, he would put the cover back nicely, all without the other knowing about it, as quick as a wink.

When night came Miror constructed hypotheses on the various heads he had opened during the day. He calculated, compared, studied them, lingering over one in particular, made a complete synthesis of it, discovered the lowest common denominator, the quotient, the centre of gravity, the spinning-axis, the Q.E.D. Only then did he sleep.

XIX

If it occurred to him to pour some water into the window of a restaurant, it would immediately become an immense aquarium and the people inside would start to swim, looking for the exit. Miror would barricade doors and windows and the temporary swimmers, seeing themselves condemned to swim for life, became resigned, quickly growing accustomed to it and finally regaining their place, not without wondering what kind of madman they were dealing with.

XX

It took a great deal of courage to set out on the journey. Miror did it for a change of air, to be somewhere else. When he arrived in the promised city he was astonished to feel immediately at home. "What's the use of travelling!" he said. As he had no compass and the forest encircled the city and the journey had been made at night, Miror had quite simply described a great circle and, like a boomerang, come back to the starting point: his home town.

He had to begin again.

XXI

When Miror tackled something or someone he always put himself in the skin of the Other.

And so on the day when he tackled a rock. . . . He moved forward like a rock himself, muscles taut, spine stiff, cold, heavy and threatening, in a single block. When they touched there was a horrible detonation immediately followed by debris and thick clouds of smoke. When calm was restored Miror was erect, the rock at his feet. Then he set out to open its side with his pocket-knife, a fine blade: he slit it along its length, delicately. Through the wound—a long, fine slash that bled a little—Miror heard the beating of the rock's inner life: a shuddering of sanguine curtains on the walls, the dull sound of hammers on the cells and the sharp cries of globules paddling vigorously in the veins of quartz and gneiss and mica. Stunned by all the uproar Miror closed the wound, sewed it with a thread of his own blood and went away, disoriented.

XXII

Every time he stared at a stretch of snow Miror would see a family of glaciers suddenly flaming in an enchanting display of rainbows.

XXIII

For relaxation Miror liked to attend his neighbours' domestic struggles, his favourite sport. The spectacles were always very lively, full of the unexpected, of boldness and brutality. Agonizing and exhausting spectacles, for the spectators as much as the gladiators themselves. Miror left these performances in a sweat, troubled, feverish, nervous and fearful.

XXIV

Mills need water. Like all of us Miror had his little mill. The water had just run out. Miror's mill soon began to waste away. It grew pale and every day found it weaker; it was slowly going away. Miror took off like a madman, running in every direction and crying: "Water! Water! Water!" like someone dying of thirst, like a drowning man. ... No one had any water.

When Miror returned, his little mill was no more; there was nothing on the floor but some debris from one gaunt wing.

XXV

Miror had tamed a drop of water. When he spoke it rolled on his lips in time to the rhythm of what he said; at times it would lodge in the corner of his eye and remain there, immobile, until he closed his eyes. When he slept the drop of water whirled around on his forehead, excited by what might be going on behind.

It lived with Miror for a long time, reflecting in turn his joys and his anguish until the day when Miror, having grown ambitious, resolved that he would tame a river. The drop of water was drowned.

XXVI

As for the river, Miror could not succeed in taming it; it burst into his room, turning everything upside down, making the room look like a beach battered by a furious sea. If he went out with his river Miror caused terrible disasters everywhere: his river drowned children, created inundations, spread epidemics. It was a terrible scourge.

From then on the municipality prohibited the domestication of rivers and Miror had to abandon his.

XXVII

If he said "Hello!" to someone the person he addressed would turn around and ask suspiciously, "What do you mean by that?" So Miror often spoke to himself; it was the only way he could say what he wanted without having to give endless useless explanations.

XXVIII

Miror was propped against the wall, the same wall that had always encircled his home, an unscalable Wall of China. A train moved along the horizon (a double horizon that served as rails for his imaginary journeys). Miror suddenly felt like going away. He wrote on the stones of the wall—in big white letters like the ones on the blackboard at school—the names of the countries and cities he wanted to visit; then he loosened several stones and slipped his body through the gap. On the other side was the void or its equivalent: an anemic and cloudy past. ... Miror withdrew, replaced the stones and began again to write on them, not only the names of countries and cities this time but also elaborate drawings with infinitely elaborate details. He drew everything: houses, streets, their inhabitants, even the insides of the houses and the insides of the inhabitants. He spent months like that, drawing the places where he would have liked to live, and he forgot the wall.

XXIX

"You won't go far with your sore feet!" Miror told a stranger who was going along the road. "I know that even with my good feet I've never been able to leave here. Oh! I've tried many times, believe me. I speak from experience, you don't leave here, I'm telling you. ... And I've known people, athletes even, *coureurs de bois*, runners with ants in their legs. ... No indeed! It seems to be fatal: we are here to die, it's not possible to leave here alive. It's like a law of attraction, like an elastic with one end nailed to a table and the table bolted to the ground and the ground congealed. ... Hold on, one day I. ..."

The stranger, already very small, stepped over the line of the horizon and sank and drowned with the sun.

XXX

Miror hurled himself into the Great Crevice. It would have been easy for him to step over it but if he had done that he would not have known what was in the bottom, what lived there. So he rushed into it.

The fall was long and for a moment Miror thought that he would never reach the bottom. He arrived there. He entered the shadow arms first, eyelids dilated, panting. The bottom of the gulf was seen to be paved with tattered hearts on which Miror saw that he was obliged to walk.

He had never felt so heavy in his life; he seemed to be wearing lead boots and every motion that he risked crushed his head as though he were walking on his own body. He stretched out his arms, felt all around him with the strange sensation that he was searching the inner walls of his being. Wanting to see clearly once and for all, he pulled his eyes out of their sockets and cast them ahead of them. Then he realized that he had plunged into his deepest self.

XXXI

During a walk in the forest Miror lost his life. Immediately he began to search wildly for the life he had just lost so foolishly, through simple absent-mindedness. He searched everywhere: each thicket, each fold in the ground, the grass, the sand; and he called for help. Rescue squads went scouting in every direction; raids, reconnaissance flights, torch-light searches were organized. They searched all the animals, questioned them, put them in the bathtub, bludgeoned them, with no result. They laid siege to the forest, sacked and burned it, to no avail: nothing was found.

Miror screamed, hollered, pounded his feet and his fists. Useless to tell him that there was still hope, that a life is not lost forever so easily, that he would find it again one day when he least expected it: Miror would have none of it. He was desperate. "I loved it so much," he cried. "It often caused me pain but I was used to it, we had lived together for so long. . . . We both had our little ways. . . . My little bitch of a life that behaved itself, now it's gone, lost, like that, for nothing. . . . I lost it stupidly, without thinking . . . the way you lose an old tooth or a rusty key . . . I don't know what . . . I don't know what I'll do without it now . . . alone . . . I don't know . . . I don't know."

And he lost his head.

THE WEAKER SEX

Madeleine Ferron
translated by Basil Kingstone

When you saw her get out of the taxi, you were leaning against the big front window of your funeral parlour, the facade of which you remodelled last year. You don't regret having spent a lot of money to give your establishment the opulent appearance of a Victorian house. You had noticed that a new tendency was leading people to get buried sumptuously, a notch higher than their social level and their financial resources. Your practice is in a little middle-income French Canadian mining town.

You are leaning against the window and smoking a menthol cigarette, a habit you adopted a long time ago and which always works. When you come out of your laboratory, as you say, stressing the last word, the flavoured smoke of that cigarette rids you of that persistent smell of a body in formaldehyde.

She has stepped off the sidewalk on the other side of the street and is preparing to cross. You haven't forgotten that you have just put this still young woman's husband in his coffin. Obviously you haven't forgotten, because you are above all a businessman, but you cannot stop memories from opening, waving and quivering, in her wake. You can see again, all the more clearly the closer she comes, the two months you employed her.

She is wearing those shoes with thick rigid soles, created by a sadistic designer who inflicts on liberated women the walk of a Chinese woman of the Ming dynasty. You have always been surprised by the needless difficulties which women in general impose on themselves, and you are amused by the particular example which is coming towards you. She seems to you to be having the same difficulties as an acrobat balancing on his tightrope. She still has that starlet's face that first attracted your attention: hair like lather, lips the colour of strawberry juice, a complexion the shade of cinnamon. You had long since noticed the remarkable air about the young woman, but it was her trade that had led you to hire her. You wanted to give your funeral parlour a modern touch. You had become enthusiastic about the advantages which would accrue from this hairdresser's work and from the combination of your dynamism and her imagination. Unfortunately she never understood the subtlety of your intentions at all. At first it all went very well. It had been agreed that she would come and practise her trade to offer your clients the additional luxury of a last set. It cost you no more, since her services were added to the extras on the final bill. You have always admired the tricks of the soap powder companies: the bit with the free towel in the big boxes, for example. You had not foreseen that your new associate would be dictatorial and arrogant, a behaviour she had acquired from the snobbish clientele who patronized her own beauty parlour. It didn't suit your establishment, the only one for forty miles around, where one was bound to find all classes of society. It took skill, psychology, a discreet method of persuasion—especially with the poor. You well remember the unfortunate incident which opened your eyes. You had just finally sold your last plush coffin, seeming to let yourself be beaten down. Your poor clients were going to the limit of their means. To complete the deceased's appearance, you had only to smooth down her white hair with the palms of your hands. Your hairdresser had insisted that the relatives let her do a special hairstyle—the latest thing, she said—had insisted and grown angry and contemptuous. It was a gross error of judgment and could have had serious consequences. She did not always commit such obvious gaffes, but she always ran that risk, it was worrying and got on your nerves.

The closer she comes, the more you find it regrettable that you had to fire her. On a false but acceptable pretext, of course, protecting pride and safeguarding subsequent relations.

Now she is coming up the steps. You realize that, good Lord! her mourning clothes are black leather; you are delighted to find she is still the same; a marvel at compromise. You go and open the door for her. She comes in, preceded by a heady perfume, followed by the almost inaudible but striking sound of a leather skirt which seems to stretch and breathe with every step.

Now you are embarrassed, and ordinarily you remain so self-assured, even in unlikely situations or difficult circumstances. You always know what note to strike, how far one can or should be condescending or sympathetic. You stand there open-mouthed and simply gesture towards your office. She goes in and sits down, as is her habit, in an uncomfortable and complicated fashion. You have the impression the leather of the skirt is going to split before your eyes. Her knees are together but too far to the left. You feel obliged to rush into conversation, but you haven't been thinking and you have no idea what to say. For the first time in your career as an undertaker you say the wrong thing: "You have a very charming way of wearing mourning." She looks at you in outrage: "I suppose you would have preferred me to mourn in red!" You find she is as unexpected as ever; she still takes unforeseeable detours in order to be right. You know very well that condolences would be in order, but you are embarrassed. You know too well the nature of the marital relations between her and the deceased. She has told you everything. Every time you bent over a corpse together, confidences poured out.

You were delighted. She had a care for detail, a skill with words which transformed an ordinary story into an allusive, lively and lucid account. And so you learned that in the passionate beginning of their married life they had combined their respective trades. A highly plausible partnership, since he was a barber. They had the whole first floor of a big house on the main street of a neighbouring small town. A prime location. The facade had two doors. On the left, under the traditional revolving pole, hung the sign "Razor cut." Her idea, of course.

The right-hand door opened into the antechamber of a salon fit for a marquise. False marble columns, wallpaper with gold flock appliques, Louis XV armchairs made by the cabinet-maker on Saint Alphonse Street, huge mirrors with yellow silk tassels hanging down. On the white wall opposite the door was an enlarged photocopy of an oracular diploma, awarded by a master hair-stylist from Paris who had come to Montreal to give a crash course lasting a week.

It was obvious that the modest red and white revolving pole would soon offend the hairdresser's ambition. Did the breakup of their partnership precede or follow that of their love? It didn't matter, she replied tersely, since both were the result of an incredible misunderstanding. One fine day the barber had loaded his chair with its chrome armrests into a moving van. He had followed it at the wheel of his sports car which he had dreamed of so long and finally bought himself. The dissolution of their company and his marriage freed him at last from the joint savings account which he was mercilessly forced to refloat at the end of every month, even at the cost of doing without food, tobacco and evenings out. Austerity is only acceptable if buoyed up by ambition. In the hairdresser it inspired dreams; in him, it aroused thoughts of suicide.

Did you offer your condolences to the young widow or didn't you? You cannot remember. She is in front of you, squeezed into her leather skirt, and is observing you in perplexity and perhaps amusement. There is that mocking glint in her eyes which means she is in a position of strength. If you offer your condolences twice, you will look ridiculous. If you fail to offer them, you will be caught red-handed; the house rules must be strictly observed, as you constantly tell your employees. So to cut your hesitation short you deferentially suggest: "We should go into the parlour."

You have walked out of your office. Reaching the arched doorway first, she has suppressed a momentary revulsion, it seems to you, and regained self-control.

"Is it to your taste?"

"It's all right," she says, half closing her eyes to get a better view of the overall effect. "It's very good," she adds, in a conspiratorial tone which embarrasses you slightly. "One would never think the coffin isn't solid steel. Nobody will notice. It would have been harder to get away with wood veneer, his family is from the Gaspé."

"My oak coffins are solid oak, you know that."

You are hurt, but she pays no attention to the sharpness in your voice.

"I'm respecting my husband no less with fake steel, since everybody will think it's real!"

This sort of unbelievable statement always bewilders you. You remain silent.

"Can you move the wreath forward and stick it a bit nearer the kneeler?"

You were about to satisfy this reasonable desire; it was normal for the loving wife's floral offering to be prominent.

She has raised her voice:

"How much is the whole job?"

The way she has asked the question, it is like having a gun stuck in your stomach. Ordinarily there is a whole ritual with the very delicate question of the fee. After a few moments' entirely forgivable confusion, you have recovered your composure.

"It's two thousand dollars for everything, including the pallbearers, and the wreath, which is in your name."

She is still standing in the doorway. You were moving closer to her so as to speak more discreetly.

"There's no hurry; I'll wait as long as you want. The first payment will be at your convenience."

"D'you think I need time to pay?" she shoots back arrogantly. She smugly turns her back and goes towards your office.

"Do you have a cheque?" she asks coldly.

She is trying to impress you, that's obvious, but whether for the sake of doing so or for some ulterior motive you cannot make out.

"Times have really changed since our association. I have twice as many customers. And luck is with me," she assures you triumphantly.

"I'm having trouble keeping my clients; they would tend to leave me if I didn't keep working at it all the time."

Your very simple confession, your frank worry, at once influences her strategy. It would be more accurate to say she decides to forget it for the time being.

"Luck is a capricious animal, it reacts especially when it's provoked," she murmurs, leaning over your desk on the palms of her hands. She winks, and with her typical impudence:

"Albert's death was my latest stroke of luck!"

You are speechless and don't answer. She goes straight on:

"When Albert was single he loved auto racing. I noticed his foot had kept its old habit; if there was a space in front of him, he accelerated at once, foot to the floor."

She continues, volubly, aroused by this impromptu confession.

"I had an intuition he might have an accident," she explains with no shame at all. "After our separation, I immediately took out an insurance policy on his life. A big one. Double indemnity in case of accidental death!"

"Not too dumb," you reply, whistling like a cynic, so as not to seem weak and to control the shudder which is making the hair stand up on your arms. She lowers her head modestly.

"There are material advantages which are stupidly lost in our capitalist system for lack of thought and knowledge," she concludes, recovering a more sober dignity.

The deceased's relatives arrived in the late morning, dressed in black, grieving and exhausted. You went to greet them promptly and with sympathy. They reminded you so much of your own family, unassuming and proud. They apologized politely for arriving later than expected. They hadn't allowed for the time they would take to find your funeral parlour. The town had grown so much since the last time they had come here, perhaps fifteen years ago. Of course, they had left the address on the kitchen table.

"I put it there specially so we'd see it," added the mother in embarrassment.

They kissed this strange person whose role, for them, boiled down to her having been Albert's wife. "It's terrible to die in an accident .... Be brave .... These things are sent to try us ...." You were listening to the various voices of this chorus of antiquity as they improvised the lines for the sorrowful widow, not foreseeing that she would grab the solo part. She let out a first sob, followed by a more expressive second one, then several others in a continuing crescendo. Finally the family, deeply touched, saw Albert's wife literally throw herself with outstretched arms across the coffin lid with repeated groans of "Albert" which moved the audience to tears. You went and fetched the now almost regulation double dose of Valium which keeps peace and quiet in your establishment, eliminating the outbursts of tears and despair which used to be inevitable. Albert's wife was thus able to retreat into a silent role, seated impassive and distant in the proffered armchair and not moving. A situation she took undue advantage of. After the first day, her silence proved frustrating for the deceased's relatives. "How did the accident happen?" "What time was it?" "Is it true he was unrecognizable? Half his head torn off? Was Albert's skull empty?" "You never know ... times have changed ...." That is why, at the end of the second day, seeing the widow's obstinate silence, you felt you should satisfy the members of the family. Hardly had you given a few answers when you found yourself surrounded by further questions, and you ended up giving details which normally you keep secret, for example the fact that the doctor was slow in getting to the scene of the accident, arriving long after you. You went into macabre detail: the victim's ear hanging by a thread of bloody skin, his teeth scattered over the floor of the car, the bit of brain on the stiff's right shoulder. You had reached these shameful statements and you were secretly questioning yourself as to how you had come to make so many concessions to your listeners. They were nice relatives who had come up from the Gaspé—that was your excuse, the only one you could admit to yourself, whereas your real motive was to draw their attention to the skill of your work, even if the result was imperfect and your success relative. You had succeeded in forming a handsome face, the features were faithfully reproduced, they were indeed the features of Albert's face, but it wasn't Albert.

"When you're embalming an accident victim, you can guarantee results, as long as you have all the pieces." You let the remark slip out, as if unwillingly. It was the final excuse you had found to explain why your work wasn't perfect.

At the exact moment when your statement was dying away, Albert's wife suddenly started bubbling. A cork had just popped out.

"What? They didn't find all the pieces?"

"Only a few items were missing," you replied, suddenly worried about the possible consequences of your indiscreet remarks, which were surely a breach of professional ethics.

"Well! Were they fed to the fish in the river or dumped in the garbage?"

She stood up, a tragic figure; she was outraged.

"It's a profanation, a sacrilege! We'll see if they can treat a dead man like that! I'll talk to my lawyer .... They may pay dearly for this! I can find out who did it, all right."

She was shaking her fist. For a second you were afraid she would point her finger at you. The relatives, amazed at first, shaken for a moment, had recovered their common sense and were observing Albert's wife warily. This restored your calm and gave you the power to be scandalized in turn at the behaviour of this formidable woman who seemed to be selling her late husband piece by piece and part by part, with a cynicism which surprised even you who lived on death.

Fortunately the three regulation days of tears and exhaustion, grief and boredom came to a decent end, that is to say, custom was respected and no untoward incident threatened to sully the good reputation of your business. The next day, you had not yet finished the inventory of your manifold reactions to your former associate's excessive behaviour. You were still indignant at certain of her attitudes but, even as you speculated on what she might be worth, your feelings towards her were not unmixed with admiration, perhaps qualified but real. You were perplexed and hadn't yet decided how you should judge her. You were leaning against the big front window of your premises, smoking your menthol cigarette—another dead person had come in that morning—when you noticed her crossing the street towards you. She had exchanged her black leather suit for an ensemble which was mainly a startling yellow, and she seemed to you to be moving like the eye of a hurricane, uncontrollable and devastating. She came in as if she owned the place and looked you up and down coldly. You suddenly felt overwhelmed by a sense of inferiority.

"How are you?" she asked.

You felt the clinical tone of her question lay your weakness bare. You tried in vain to call back your self-respect.

She ordered you to sit down so that she could explain her project to you. She had foreseen and figured out everything. She had the necessary capital for the further modernization of your funeral parlour. It would be extraordinary: atmosphere, furnishings, extra services. And definitely very profitable, she said with authority. And why not pleasant as well, she added flirtatiously, with a wink.

At that moment you became a sort of flabby object which you let fall into your chair and which you heard repeating in a choking voice: "No. I don't want to, no thanks, it's impossible."

"Honestly, men have no breadth of vision! All right, live in the past!"

She left at once, and you stayed sitting in your chair laughing helplessly. "The weaker sex!" you kept saying through your laughter, but you were aware you would not always escape danger so easily.

THE THIRTY-FIRST BIRD

Marie-José Thériault
translated by
Luise von Flotow Evans

For Bahâdor, Wahib, Georges and Pierre, for Persia, Egypt, for calamus and ink, and for the thirty birds of Islam.

They made sure that they were really the Simorg and that the Simorg was really the thirty birds. When they looked in the direction of the Simorg they saw that it was in fact the Simorg who was there, and if they cast their glance upon themselves, they saw that they themselves were the Simorg. In fact when they looked in both directions at the same time, they saw that they and the Simorg were one being. This being was

Simorg, and Simorg was this being. ... The birds finally vanished utterly into Simorg; shadow lost itself in the sun, and that is all.

—Farid Uddin 'Attar
Mantic uttair[1]

They say—and only Allah is wiser!—that when Schahrazade had won the heart of King Schahriar with her stories for one thousand and one nights she became his legitimate wife and therefore did not fear for her life. They say too that King Schahriar, having insomnia, continued to ask for new stories. And so it was that there were the first thousand and one nights, then another thousand and one nights, and another thousand and one nights, so that the couple had nights more sleepless than days, until the Inevitable Destroyer of friendships arrived to take Schahrazade away from the love of her King. But long before the tragic day that cast Schahriar forever into a sadness for which there was no cure, on the two-thousand-eight-hundred-and-forty-third night, King Schahriar, having heard Schahrazade's earlier stories with ever-increasing enjoyment, said to her: "Oh, Schahrazade! oh rose-scented lips! how your words delight me! By Allah! what other wonderful tale can you tell me?" And Schahrazade said: "Oh Master, I know of the adventures of a bird whose disdain for good precepts and whose taste for worldly pleasures, led to a rather sad fate." And Schahriar replied: "In truth, I would have preferred a merrier story tonight, but I have no doubt that you will be able to delight me anyway. So if you wish to tell me about this amazing bird, so be it." Schahrazade, after a moment's reflection, began:

---

[1] Muhammed ben Ibrahim Nischapuri, called Farid Uddin 'Attar (ca. 1150-1220), *Le langage des oiseaux* (Mantic uttaïr) translated by Garcin de Tassy (reissue of the 1836 edition), preceded by *Poésie philosophique et religieuse chez les Persans*, Paris, Papyrus, 1982.

The Story of the Thirty-first Bird

I have heard, oh King of time, that in Baghdad there once lived a rich merchant and his daughter, whose name, Ziba, bore witness to her great beauty. In fact, Ziba—which means "beautiful"— had been endowed from birth with a face that even the moon envied for it far surpassed him in its brightness and perfection. Her eyebrows arched evenly and shaded her deep black eyes like a canopy, her lips were two scarlet rubies and when she spoke pearls rolled from her mouth. Silken tresses curled about her shoulders and she moved as daintily and elegantly as a young cypress swaying in the breeze. Besides she had a lively intelligence and a melodious voice: when she wasn't moving men to tears with her songs about the delicious torments of love to the accompaniment of her lute, she could rival the wisest men in the kingdom in knowledge.

Her father tried in vain to marry off this charming creature whose perfect beauty troubled the hearts of many young men. Each suitor would find himself rejected by her, for being too short, or too tall, too thin or too fat, not handsome or rich enough, or lacking in wit or daring. And so the years passed without Ziba finding a husband, and little by little she began to sink into a languor that sullied her beautiful face and wrung heartrending sighs from her.

Her father, the merchant, who till then had accepted his daughter's whims because of his great affection for her, and although very much saddened by the decision he had just taken, felt it was necessary to assert his authority. He had a talk with her.

"My daughter", he said, "the condition that I see you reduced to breaks my heart. For a long time I have allowed you complete freedom in the choice of a husband, but you *won't* relent until all your suitors have been turned away, their heads bowed and their souls filled with sadness, leaving you comfortably alone. What do you expect of marriage that such exemplary young men cannot provide?"

"Father", Ziba replied, "allow me not to reveal my secret which would sadden you even more. Spare me from inflicting this pain on you."

"Am I to understand you wish to continue this isolation that is hardly fitting for a lady of your quality?"

"Alas! father, loneliness weighs heavy upon me, but it is still lighter than the company of a husband who does not touch my heart."

"Daughter, your stubbornness annoys me. Since you refuse to do as I ask for your own good, you force me against my will to command you. And, as I believe that a husband's company will restore your brilliance and your good temper, I charge you to accept immediately the first suitor that my fancy may cause me to present to you."

"Father", replied Ziba, "I must obey you. Let it be so, since you command it. However, whatever the respect I owe you, it seems that I would be submitting no less to your will if I requested one condition."

The merchant, balancing rather uncomfortably between his fatherly duties and the inordinate love he felt for his daughter, had not the strength to refuse Ziba's new whim, and so asked her to relate it to him.

"I will marry whosoever brings me a feather of the bird Simorg. This sovereign bird resides beyond Mount Qaf, and with its light dazzles the perfect souls that enter its court. The road is long and difficult; one must divest oneself of everything, give up everything. The man who, for love of me, goes to find Simorg and brings me back a feather, that man will have a pure soul and to him I will give my heart."

When the merchant heard these words, he was greatly discouraged, for he knew the realm of Simorg to be almost inaccessible, and he also knew that one rarely returned, should one by some unlikely chance arrive there. He tried to make Ziba see reason, but when he realized that she would not abandon her resolve, he consented to her condition.

"Since that is how you respond to my kindness, do as you please. But do me the favour of not entering my presence, so that your sad condition will not move me to tears of grief, for I would rather put an end to your life than see you languish in such a horrible situation."

Although Ziba was very attached to her father and the thought of no longer sharing his company was painful to her, she promised to avoid coming into his presence until the day that some suitor should bring her one of Simorg's feathers; and so they parted, overwhelmed with grief.

To tell about all the merchants, warriors and princes who undertook the perilous journey to Simorg for the favours of beautiful Ziba would take up scores of nights. For the moment it is enough to know that not one of them returned bearing the marvellous gift, that not even one of them was ever heard of again.

After this talk with her father, Ziba retired to her apartments. Seated next to a window that overlooked gardens filled with roses and fountains flowing with pure water which slaked the thirst of a large number of birds, she uttered some words in a low voice, seeming to address herself. Immediately one of the birds left the edge of the fountain he was resting on and came to perch on the hand Ziba held out.

The bird was a magnificent creature. Its long curved feathers sent sparks of silver and gold into the sunlight. His eyes were brighter than precious rubies; jewels decorated his wings and shone in many colours; a crest of pearls and sapphires adorned its head, and its beak was of the finest mother-of-pearl. Ziba spoke to him thus:

"Prince Djalal, Prince Djalal, what is to become of us? The most delicious moments of my life are the ones I spend here in your company without the knowledge of my father. But see how I am smitten since an evil witch deprived me of your kisses! How long, dear heart...."

While speaking these words Schahrazade saw the dawn appearing, and being discreet, she spoke no more. Schahriar, visibly annoyed by this interruption, cried: "Oh, Schahrazade! this is a wonderful story! How anxious I am to hear the reasons for Prince Djalal's metamorphosis!" But Shahrazade replied: "Oh, well-beloved King, that is a very long story and with your permission I would rather tell you first the rest of the one I have already begun." Schahriar approved this wise decision and they went to bed, entwined until broad daylight. Then, King Schahriar got up and attended to his duties the whole day. And then came the two-thousand-eight-hundred-and-forty-fourth night. Schahriar went to find Schahrazade, who said:

"I have heard, oh King, that Ziba said to Prince Djalal: "How long, dear heart, must this metamorphosis last? How many years, or even centuries, must I suffer the grief of not seeing the prince who is so handsome, so attractive, and who has been brought to such a sorry state by an enchantment?"

"Madame", the bird replied, "know how much it pains me not to be able to put an end to the sorcery and how it saddens me to be prevented from showing you the affection that your beauty and charm inspire in me. The most I can do, alas!, is to caress your hand or your cheek with a gentle touch of my beak, when I burn with a passion for you that is so violent it makes me your slave."

"If that is so, Prince Djalal, you will have to find the person who can return you to your original form, otherwise I will call upon death to come to my aid and deliver me from this languor I feel because I cannot delight in your love. Oh, Prince Djalal, I beg you to find a remedy for our affliction!"

"You know, Madame, how many magicians, sorceresses and even dervishes have tried with their potions and prayers to disenchant me without ever being able to give me back my natural form. I'm afraid we will have to give up all hope of seeing me restored to my original state. But even as a bird I will not cease to love you, Madame, nor be faithful to you until death."

"Prince Djalal, I cannot resign myself to that until we have tried everything to solve our dilemma. It was quite easy to get my father to agree to a request I made that I not be forced to marry the first suitor who comes. We still have some time, but we will have to be quick, because I don't know whether my father, pained at being deprived of my company, will not return in a less favourable frame of mind."

"Madame, should we live one hundred lives, I doubt that we would have any other prospect but resignation. Do you know of any magic that could quickly rid me of this enchantment? Oh, pray God I might hope for such great happiness!"

"Prince, if your love is as great as mine, you will not hesitate to submit to my wish that you go beyond Mount Qaf to the court of the bird Simorg. He is an extraordinary king who they say is capable of a thousand wonders and endowed with the greatest powers. I see our last chance in him. Go and find him, Prince Djalal, for love of me, and beg him with all the fervour you are capable of to give you back your shape. Bring me back a feather from his coat too. With this evidence my father will not be able to refuse to give me to you in marriage, and will send for the cadi."

At these words, Djalal could not suppress a flutter of his wings that revealed his fear.

"Oh! dear soul! there is nothing in the world I would not be willing to do for love of you, but this I really cannot. To find Simorg seven perilous valleys have to be crossed. Many have lost their lives there. No one can undertake this journey and hope to return. Don't expose me to such great danger! Allow me rather to be consumed by my love for you here, in the shape of a bird! Whatever difficulties I will be subjected to, they will be less painful than to be forever separated from you!"

"Can it be possible that you love me so little that you are afraid to risk everything for the joy of finally possessing me? Prince Djalal, I could not abide your presence without languishing, and without my love being transformed into contempt at the thought that you did not make every attempt to surmount the obstacles that your metamorphosis has put in the path of our love. Go. And do not return until you have entered the court of Simorg to make your request. Painful as your absence will be, I will suffer it in the hope of soon seeing the valorous and handsome prince who is hidden now beneath this plumage. And if you do not return, if you die on the way, I will let my breath leave me and will join you in another world."

"Madame, I would be undeserving of your love if I did not obey you. I shall go. But I ask of you the favour that your prayers accompany me every day to protect me from all the perils I may encounter as a result of your request. Good bye, Madame. God willing we shall soon be reunited."

They parted with many tears and embraces, and Ziba, leaning at her window, saw Prince Djalal fly off in the direction of the mountains. Her gaze followed the brightly coloured bird whose plumes of gold, silver and precious stones sparkled in the setting sun, until he was no more than a tiny point on the horizon, and later too, when night fell over Persia and the sky was covered with thousands of stars.

***

Djalal travelled all night. He flew over cities and towns, domes and minarets, seraglios, terraces, and huts. Not once did he stop. Below him grassy hills, rocky plateaus, bare plains, now and again a swamp, now and again a desert passed by. The darkness softened shapes, blurred details; there remained only masses and shadows that even the moon's reflections were not able to define. Djalal flew steadily. Fatigue made his wings heavy; thirst tortured his gullet; hunger tormented his belly. But Djalal did not rest on any branch; he drank no water; he did not eat a single berry.

In the morning, when the sun restored their shape to objects, Djalal saw that he was journeying between two high mountains and was at the entrance to a deep valley. When he noticed a bush heavy with grapes at the side of a stream he could no longer resist the hunger that racked him, and he came to earth to take some refreshment. He ate his fill of sweet, juicy berries, but when he leaned over the water to drink, he had a sudden spell of dizziness, doubtless due to excessive fatigue, and fell head first into the stream. He barely had time to cry out "By Allah and the Prophet!" when he realized that the stream flowed not with water but with blood. Horrified, he tried desperately to pull himself onto the bank, but the weight of his gold and silver feathers dragged him toward the bottom. All his concentrated strength allowed him only to keep his head above the surface, not to regain dry land. Weighed down with the fortune he carried on his back he fought for an eternity against this element that now unleashed the violence of a torrent against him. How many minutes did this last? how many hours? weeks? years? Djalal felt the eddies of blood snatch away feathers and gems as he progressed painfully, completely exhausted, in a sort of hypnosis, against the current. Then, one day, when he was no longer expecting it, he felt the bottom beneath his feet; the stream calmed; the blood became water. Djalal was able to touch the bank and fell in exhaustion. He fell asleep and did not wake until much later, perhaps months, perhaps years. The sun was setting behind the mountains, in a green sky. Djalal continued his flight.

He journeyed all night. In the morning when the sun restored their shape to objects, Djalal saw that he was at the entrance to a second valley. No sooner had he set foot in order to recover a little and he saw that he was surrounded on all sides by a wall of fire. "Allah!" he cried, seeing the flames lick at the very sky. "Allah! of what am I guilty that you should send me such a calamity?" But Allah did not deign to respond to his servant, and Djalal only felt his plumage, already spoilt by the torrent of blood, redden and melt in patches, while the gems, freed from their settings, fell to the ground. He tried to fly away, but the flames closed above him like a dome. He decided to move forward taking small steps, but in vain did he look for an opening to escape this devouring inferno. As he proceeded, so did the circle of fire that held him prisoner. How long did this last? how many hours? weeks? years? Djalal continued, feeling his strength lessen, seeing his golden and silver plumes melt, broken by heat, thirst and fatigue. Then, one day, when he was no longer expecting it, he saw the flames part before him. He gathered the energy he had left to thread his way into the passage thus formed, and with a pitiful beating of wings, he succeeded in hoisting himself onto a cliff that overlooked the valley, where he fell asleep. He did not wake until much later, perhaps months, perhaps years. The sun was setting behind the mountains, in a green sky. Djalal continued his flight.

He journeyed all night. In the morning when the sun restored their shape to objects, Djalal saw that he was at the entrance to a third valley. Shrubs laden with fruit attracted Djalal who was famished and needed to eat. But how great was his astonishment when he saw that the fruits which from above had looked like cherries redder than rubies, apricots more yellow than topazes, raisins bluer than sapphires, were in fact eyes that had been torn by the hundreds from birds whose bodies were lying on the ground in two rows. A long moan escaped from his throat at the sight of the lined-up corpses. He wanted to fly away, but a powerful voice prevented him and spoke thus: "Miserable Djalal! How dare you disturb my peace?" At these words the earth trembled and the firmament darkened. Djalal raised his head and realized with a shiver of fear that the whole sky above him was filled by an immense djinn, with shaggy hair and a grimacing face, who held a giant two-edged sword in his hand. There was no hope of escape in that direction. He had to find another way. He moved forward on sagging legs between the rows of birds who had all had their heads cut off at the throat, whose eyeless heads had only two holes deep as wells. Then the djinn, laughing hilariously, struck with his sword and just missed Djalal, but removed the pearls and sapphires in his crest. Djalal continued, all his feathers trembling, while now and again the djinn, with a prodigious laugh, would amputate a gem here, a piece of wing there, a fragment of tail there. How long did this last? how many hours? weeks? years? Then one day when he was no longer expecting it, Djalal noticed the sky grow lighter, the djinn's laugh become more distant, and the blade of his sword miss its target by a little more at each blow. There were fewer decapitated birds and soon not a single one. Djalal did not try to find out by what miracle he had been spared and he continued, sometimes hopping, sometimes fluttering, while the djinn grew feeble, pale, until he was no more than a light smoke at the edge of the sky. After a long moment, Djalal, at the end of his strength, found a cave and fell asleep in it. He did not wake until much later, perhaps months, perhaps years. The sun was setting behind the mountains, in a green sky. Djalal continued his flight.

He journeyed all night. In the morning, when the sun restored their shape to objects, Djalal saw that he was at the entrance to a fourth valley. This valley, where Djalal could not see a single tree, flower, or fruit, shone like a smooth mirror, and its blinding glitter attracted Djalal like a magnet attracts iron. He descended, in twirling arabesques like those that illuminate Al-Koran, swiftly as a falling star, and he burst through the surface of the mirror with a great splatter. Regaining consciousness, he found himself in the middle of an immense and limitless ocean. The horizon was only a wavering line around him. There were no mountains nor shores, no islands, no ports, only this huge expanse of salty water where Djalal floated like a flower petal. Soon the sky, clear until then, was covered with black clouds. Thunder rumbled. Torrential rain began to fall. The wind rose, merciless. Djalal struggled in the centre of this wild storm, amid waves higher than minarets, that knocked him about, whipped him, lacerated him with their crests. Every moment, he thought his end had come and he was surprised that he should survive such torture. How long did this last? how many hours? weeks? years? Djalal fought off the ferocious elements, holding himself on the surface with superhuman effort. Then, one day, when he was no longer expecting it, the tempest calmed and Djalal found that he was very near a sandy bank onto which he managed to drag himself. He let himself fall asleep. He didn't wake until much later, perhaps months, perhaps years. The sun was setting behind the mountains, in a green sky. Djalal continued his flight.

He journeyed all night. In the morning, when the sun restored their shape to objects, Djalal saw that he was at the entrance to a fifth valley. This one shone with pink and yellow reflections of such purity that it seemed to be covered completely in gold. Djalal's curiosity won over his prudence, and he let himself glide down to the ground. No sooner had he landed, than he saw what the trap was: this was not gold, but the finest sand. Djalal was in the middle of a desert, under a torrid sun, the sand burning his feet like hot coals. He tried to fly away, but a violent wind raised before him, behind him and above him whirlwinds of sand that whipped and blinded him. He covered his head with his wings as well as he could and called to Allah the Merciful and Forgiving, begging him to make the storm stop if this were His will. Did Allah hear His servant's prayer? However that may be, after days and days, the storm abated. Djalal, exhausted, dying of thirst, completely worn out and wasted, crawled on one wing, then on the other toward an oasis that he could see in the distance, praying that it not be a mirage. It was a pitiful sight, poor half-dead Djalal dragging himself through the sand leaving behind him the trail of a viper. How long did this last? how many hours? weeks? years? The oasis hardly seemed to come any nearer: sometimes Djalal even thought it was moving away. Then one day when he was no longer expecting it, he felt the shade of a large date palm over his head and a fresh breeze ruffle his feathers. He gathered his last strength to touch the foot of the tree, drank his fill at the well there and fell asleep. He did not wake until much later, perhaps months, perhaps years. The sun was setting behind the mountains, in a green sky. Djalal continued his flight.

He journeyed all night. In the morning, when the sun restored their shape to objects, Djalal saw that he was at the entrance to a sixth valley. A rhythmic song rose from the valley, sung by hundreds of voices like those that recite Al-Koran at communal prayers. Djalal, attracted by these voices, came to rest on the ground. Immediately he was surrounded by dervishes who, stopping their chants, began crying "Ya Allah! Ya Allah" running in all directions and pointing their fingers at Djalal. How great was Djalal's surprise when he suddenly felt himself gripped by powerful hands, lifted off the ground, then thrown, and caught by other hands, then thrown again, and all this to the accompaniment of cries, laughter, curses! He soon realized that he had become the stake in a tournament similar to *bouzkashi*, a barbaric race practised by the nomads of the high plateaus. He had scarcely time to consider this for he was now no more than a tattered rag being pulled, thrown, pummelled. With each flight, with each catch, he lost a few more feathers, and it was in vain that he tried to escape from the dervishes and their cruel game.

How long did this last? how many hours? weeks? years? The dervishes were in a wild frenzy; they abandoned themselves to the tournament with the same fervour that at other times they applied to the making or the chanting of verses from the Book. Then, one day, when he was no longer expecting it, the dervishes ended their game as abruptly as they had begun it, tossed Djalal into a thorn bush, crouched down and returned to their prayers. Djalal detached himself from the thorns that were tearing his skin, and fell asleep exhausted at the foot of the bush. He did not wake until much later, perhaps months, perhaps years. The sun was setting behind the mountains, in a green sky. Djalal continued his flight.

He journeyed all night. In the morning, when the sun restored their shape to objects, Djalal saw that he was at the entrance to the seventh valley. Curious about what this last stage would bring, and emboldened by having survived the six previous tests, he came to rest on the ground. There were fissures everywhere in the earth, and through these fissures acrid black smoke rose and obscured the sky. The air was filled with moans and cries that seemed to come from the very heart of the earth. The trees and bushes, such as there were, looked scorched, their brittle, leafless branches served as perches for thousands of birds of prey with eyes like daggers. Djalal trembled in terror and was rooted to the spot unable either to take a step or to fly away. Suddenly the ground opened under him, enveloped him and closed with a horrendous noise. Djalal let out a shrill cry that resounded for a long time like an echo, then, dazed, he struck his head against something hard and fainted. When he regained consciousness he saw that he was in a huge dark cavern full of graves from which rose the stench of putrefaction, moans, and thick smoke. The smoke took him by the throat and made his eyes fill with tears. The smell of decaying flesh overcame him. The moans deafened him. He wanted to flee from this cave of death and fluttered in all directions, only to come up against damp walls covered with mould. Then, finally, he thought he had found a way out through a long corridor, and he was able to leave far behind him the tortured souls lamenting from the depths of their graves. But now he found himself in opaque darkness where he couldn't discern a single shape, in a crushing silence where he couldn't hear a single sound, in a terrifying void where nothing was apparent, neither wall, smell, lament, nor shadow. "By Allah and the Prophet!" he sighed. "Is it possible that I too am dead? What is this emptiness if not the kingdom of souls?" This thought filled him with dread and he truly feared he had entered the other side of the world. But he said—and this reassured him—"There is no power or strength but in Allah!", for everyone has an allotted time on earth, and when his hour comes, he cannot defer it; and if his hour has not yet come, he has nothing to fear. How long did this last? how many hours? weeks? years? Djalal continued to flutter around blindly, seeing nothing, hearing nothing, smelling nothing, touching nothing, and this activity seemed to him to be eternal. Then, one day, when he was no longer expecting it, he saw, far above him, a tiny opening, where a bit of daylight shone through. Exhausted and half-crazed by his experience in the cave, he exerted a last effort to fly up so high. It was in fact an opening, but so small, so tiny, that he was afraid he would never be able to squeeze through. However, just as the camel passes through the eye of a needle, Djalal managed after great effort and contortions to leave his prison, leaving behind the last of his feathers. When he finally reached the open air, he was no more than a ridiculous carcass of a bird, without his crest or his plumage; he was nothing more than a lump of bare flesh covered in wounds; he was nothing more than a half-starved pale shadow. He fell exhausted where he was and slept. He didn't wake until much later, perhaps months, perhaps years. The sun was rising, brilliant, behind the mountains, in a green sky. A voice made him jump.

"So what's all this! Who are you? Where did you come from? What can I do with a *nothing* like you? Get back where you came from!"

Djalal identified this voice as that of a very noble chamberlain, one of Simorg's officers, dressed in his most beautiful robes of honour. He was standing at the entrance of a shining palace, encrusted with gold, silver and thousands of gems each more precious than the others. Djalal, dazzled by such wealth, felt he was in fact as lowly as a handful of dirt, as insignificant as an ant. He took hold of himself, however, and addressed the chamberlain in these terms:

"My lord, have pity on me who has survived the seven tests! Will Simorg, in his supreme majesty, ignominiously reject me? See how great are the signs of my suffering! Have mercy Sir, for my condition is such that you would not leave your worst enemy thus; do not deprive me of the sight of my king, for I know no other way that might lead me to him!"

And so the chamberlain, taken with Djalal's appeal, opened, one after the other, ninety-nine of the one hundred curtains of light that separated Djalal from Simorg, and Djalal went down the long corridor that led to the throne room. Arrived at this point, he saw that access was blocked not by a curtain as he had expected, but by two curtains side by side: the one-hundredth, which sparkled with millions of ethereal fires, and the one-hundred-and-first, which burnt with a real fire. When Djalal saw that the chamberlain was not opening either one of them, he prostrated himself, kissed the ground seven times and spoke these lines:

I have been searching for a refuge near God from the moment of the break of day,
Against the malice of the beings he created,
Against the ordeal of the darkness of night, when it overtakes us,
Against the evil of the sorceresses who blow on the knots,
Against the spite of those who envy us.[2]

Here the majestic voice of Simorg himself resounded, interrupting this beautiful introduction.

"Miserable one! How dare you claim such good intentions. Don't I know, I who see everything, hear everything, know everything, for what reason you are here? Look at this proud liar! The reasons for your journey are not written in the Al-Koran, and even if you were to recite suras from it until tomorrow you would not convince me of your good faith, because I know all the gestures, all the phrases. Is it not written:

> *We have created man and we know what his soul speaks to his ear; we are nearer to him than his jugular vein.*
> *When the two angels who are charged with collecting the words of man begin their task, one sits at his right, the other at his left.*
> *He utters not a single word without someone there to note it down exactly.*[3]

"Therefore," Simorg continued, "I know that you are not here for love of me, as is the case for the thirty birds that preceded you. Their's were pure intentions. Besides it seems to me that you are rather late ... but I will ignore that slight for you are guilty of a much graver insult. Is it not concupiscence that has brought you here? Lust? Are you not here for love of a woman? Would you dare to deny what I say? Look. Read. All the actions in your life are recorded in this diwân."

And Djalal saw a large square book appear before him that he looked through carefully. He found all the moments of his life recorded there since his birth, including his metamorphosis into a bird, his conversation with Ziba, and his perilous crossing of the seven valleys; everything had been noted in his diwân in letters of gold illuminated with a thousand colours. And he was filled with shame. He said:

"May the curses of the Sky come upon me, oh Simorg! And may my head be covered in ash, and my mouth be filled with dirt, for it is the truth; I am here for the love of Ziba. For this beauty among beauties, for this star among stars, for this rose among roses I came to you to beg you to restore my original form. For I can no longer be deprived of the joys of her love. I am nothing but languor before such beauty, and I melt with desire, I die of despair, not being able to enjoy her caresses. Oh, Simorg, for pity's sake, deliver me from the evil spell which has turned me into a bird! I swear upon my head that I will prostrate myself forever between your hands, and will proclaim your glory until the sky be split in two and the tombs be overturned!"

"Oh heedless pride! Carnal love has made of you a being more base than the last of the crawling insects! You give the name of beauty to what is nothing more than a handful of dirt, and you still want to melt in my light and receive my gifts! Stand back! Go away! You are not worthy of Simorg! You are not even worthy of his shadow! But ... since you have made this long journey ... let it not be in vain. You will have what you deserve, and no more than that."

Simorg then asked his chamberlain to open the one-hundred-and-first curtain to Djalal. This he did. Djalal saw a staggering sight that nailed him in place. A bird, as large as a thousand birds together, and blacker than a thousand black ravens, whose feathers were keener than a two-edged sword and from whose eyes and beak red flames escaped, rose before him and spoke these words:

"Prostrate yourself before Eblis, the hidden Face of Simorg, God of the Shadows, Warrior of the Orient and the Occident, Courser of the Night, Angel of Death, the Second Judge, Master of all Misfortunes! They say that you are not content with your condition? You wish to change it? May it be so!"

At these words, Eblis gave a grotesque laugh and dipping the end of his black wing into a basin of boiling water, he sprinkled it over Djalal, pronouncing these words:

"By virtue of the Magical Names and the Powerful Words, by the Majesty of Eblis, Master of the Magicians, I order you to leave this shape and to take on the one that most resembles your damned soul!"

Immediately Djalal saw himself transformed from the plucked and purulent bird he had been, into a large black raven. While he lamented and bemoaned his new condition, which was even worse than the previous one, Eblis, half-suffocated by his ferocious laughter, said:

"Now you are well-served according to your merit! Return to where you came from! And know that no djinn, no sorceress, no magician can do anything for you. From now on, you are my servant. You are Eblisi Djalal: neither man nor beast, but an agent of the Evil One, the glory of the Devil, a slave of the Shadows, my most beautiful creation!"

Eblisi Djalal quickly looked at Eblis and realized with stupefaction that he himself was indeed Eblis and that Eblis was himself. Already he was getting accustomed to his new shape, quickly acquiring the traits of Eblis whose incarnation he was. He foamed with venom, rage, and evil, beat the air with his black wings and spat fire. Then he vanished utterly into Eblis. Shadow had lost itself in shadow, night into night, and evil into evil. Eblisi Djalal and Eblis were now one being. This being was Eblis, and Eblis was this being. And that is all.

Arrived at the end of her story, Schahrazade was silent, for she saw the dawn breaking. King Schahriar, greatly astonished, said "By Allah! a fitting end for such a shameless bird! And it certainly seems that Allah did not feel compassion for him!" Schahrazade smiled and said: "It certainly is a delightful story but what is it compared to the one I will tell you tomorrow night!" King Schahriar cried: "Indeed I don't see how a story can be more edifying than this one. What could you tell me tomorrow night that would be more captivating than what I have heard to this day?" And Schahrazade replied: "Oh, well beloved King, let me tell you that Eblisi Djalal, dragging his fate like a ball and chain, took the road home, and arrived in Baghdad at the end of a long journey full of adventures, and also saw Ziba again. During the next nights I will tell you of all the misfortune Eblisi Djalal sowed on his path, and of his meeting with Ziba, and of the words they exchanged, and of all the things that happened later." And King Schahriar said in his soul: "Praised be Allah to have given me a wife so eloquent and wise!" Then he took Schahrazade in his arms and they went to bed. When it was day, the king met with his Council and until evening, he proclaimed, governed, rendered justice, and had a few heads cut off. Then he returned to his palace where Schahrazade awaited him. And when it was the two-thousand-eight-hundred-and-forty-fifth night, Schahrazade and Schahriar smiled at each other, and she said . . .

[2] Koran, sura CXIII
[3] Koran, sura L

BIRDY'S FLIGHT

André Carpentier
translated by Michael Bullock

> *Let a Stoic fly dry-eyed to embrace death.*
> —André Chenier

I know in advance that the story I am about to tell from this hospital bed will be judged by some to be far-fetched and unbelievable. So what's the use of relating the facts, you will say? No doubt in order to try to figure out how much treachery a friendship can stand, or perhaps to discern how much vengeance is contained in forgiveness, if this makes any sense. Or else simply to separate the magical from the real, like the yolk from the white. Because if this adventure is imbued with fever and physical disabilities, it is also permeated by the operation of unknown forces and indelible traces of the astounding powers of the mind. This is also called magic, I believe . . .

In reality, in the course of this misadventure, I was wished ill to the point of love and well to the point of fury. My mistake was not to have understood events until too late and motivations until long after the facts. Thus, in a sense, I consider myself as much a victim as the man who died from having wished my destruction.

I, who have always known how to fill my solitude, for once feel alone. I now know that for the last ten years I have only been living for a fraction of myself, whereas I thought I was living for two. And if I think about all that now, it is in memory of what I no longer want to be.

Can you hear me, Drien, where you are now? Listen, this is our story.

***

My name is Charles Perreault, but people call me Birdy Perreault because for a year, that's to say since winter 1937, I've been an airman, a bush pilot. I'm thirty-one and I was born in Montreal, in the Saint-Jacques district.

My vocation as an airman originated in 1935, when the twenty-three planes of Italo Balbo, like a formation of migratory birds from the south, came majestically to rest near Longeuil on a mesmerized and delighted St. Lawrence. I watched this spectacle in the company of my friend Drien, whom I had got to know in 1928 around the time when the De Lorimier stadium was being completed. We met again during the building of the Le Havre bridge; then we struck up an indissoluble friendship— a friendship that will last forever, Drien, I promise you.

In 1935 we were working for the city of Quebec, Drien as a mechanic, I as a roadbuilder. In order to watch the grandiose spectacle of the "landing" of Balbo's hydroplanes, we had skipped work for three days. Three days in which marvellous daydreams swirled above our heads and bound us forever, it seemed, in a common desire to fly up above these dreams and become one with space.

We wanted to become two of those godlike demons who exorcize fear by braving altitude and despising its dangers. We wanted to insult death by defying it to snatch away our *semi-civilized* lives. We read everything on the subject, the aeronautic magazines as well as the novels of Saint-Exupéry and the adventures of airmen in books for boys.

It was in this same spirit that, while Drien was slaving to maintain the presses of the newspaper *La Patrie*, to enable us to survive, I put in the obligatory fifty flying hours, at Saint-Hubert and Kingston, that would qualify me for a pilot's licence.

At the beginning of 1937, in the greatest euphoria and financed by a Quebec lumber merchant, we established our own air transport company.

I shall never forget our first flight as a team, taking off from the dirt runway at Saint-Louis in the old Travel-Air B6000, whose water-cooled ninety horsepower engine drove, at a low rpm, big shiny propellers that sliced through the infinity of the sky.

I can still remember Drien's white face as we landed! Drien, who people were already calling Drien the Mechanic, was a force of nature. Although he was not one of those who don't know fear, he always mastered it. This time, however, the bumping and shaking had shattered his usual calm; and he was forced to admit that during the flight he had feared for his life. The contrary, that is to say indifference, would have been a sign that flying left him cold. Drien was as white as a sheet ... and we were happy.

Little by little, in the course of this first year, we established a reputation all over the Laurentian plateau. Our services were called upon wherever the absence of arterial roads prevented the blood of commerce from circulating. Everywhere we were admired, fêted, fussed over. Drien and I learned that pilots are neither the gods nor the devils, neither the magicians nor the heroes we had hoped to become. But in the eyes of the people of the countryside we were still all of these—the pilot even more than the mechanic, it must be said. The pilot who rubs shoulders with death, who puts his life on the line, and whose skill and coolness daily make the difference between this hazardous life and certain death. I was the hero whose legend always precedes him on every night flight. Whereas Drien, in this situation, looked more like an insignificant, pudgy assistant, a sort of major-domo serving the gears and the gas pump.

To be sure, every time we were given an official reception in one of the villages, I never failed in my speech to share my glory with Drien, my mechanic and friend, stressing his talents, his tenacity and even his bravery. And each time the good natured audience politely applauded this blushing thick-set man who, far from captivating and inspiring dreams and admiration, looked more like an unmarriageable bachelor, retiring and sedentary.

The serious, heavy Drien contrasted with my tall, slim, dishevelled bush pilot image. I know now that this chance dichotomy led to the birth and unconscious growth of aggressive feelings, mixed with friendship and innocence to be sure, but increasing with every trip until they reached fatal proportions. I was really stupid not to have realized this until I ended up in this hospital bed, many days after Drien succumbed to magic.

There's no doubt that another element in this unfortunate antagonism was Carmen's love for me, Carmen the joyful chatterbox the two of us got to know in Quebec, who had waited for me for almost two years. Would anyone have thought that Carmen's love was another reason for Drien to hate me?

Drien, when I leave hospital I shall find the sorcerer and ask him to call up your soul and your voice as he called up the voice of the owl and the moose in the vast igloo of the Land of Cain. You told me almost nothing as we lay side by side in this hospital ward. That went on for days and days and it sowed in me more doubt than certainty.

I shall say to you: Drien, do you remember those long, marvellous days stranded in a village on the coast, waiting for fine weather? We wondered if the human condition, by dint of rending and digging the soil, had not been buried up to its belly in immense quantities of time. We had time to waste, an infinite amount of noisy laziness. The way we lived then, we enjoyed getting up in the morning with our soul languid and our heart restricted; we let our beards grow, we strolled at ease, and watched the frozen horizon; we chatted with the snowstorms, frolicked with the sun and the cold and we cherished the void; we had a brief eternity, dozing amid good food and enjoying the local liquor, as if there had been some trace of a just man in each of us.

Now the hot clamour of my face, as if I were having a little chat with the infinite, barely masks my solitude. I still love you, Drien, like a brother.

***

That morning—I think it was the first of February—there were a few of us in a hangar at the Saint-Louis airport, called Resinwood because of the clumps of resinous trees bordering the runway, waiting for the weather forecast to come true: we had been promised a cold, sunny day without wind.

While some of us were loading our old Travel-Air B6000, equipped with wheels and skis, Drien was making the final adjustments to this simple but robust machine. Others, grouped around the canteen, were holding forth about international politics, weighing up the chances of war and the possibility of an economic revival while slapping their shoulders with their mittens and mixing gin and coffee. Meanwhile Carmen was displaying her nervousness to everyone, almost begging Drien to look after me and telling me over and over again to be careful. Was she talking about aeronautics or morality?

Then, around eight, satisfied with the weather, we set off on one of those long and complicated trips we often made. This one was to take us on the first day to Montmagny, Les Éboulements, flying over Île-aux-Grues and Île-aux-Coudres in case we had to make a forced landing, then to Rivière-du-Loup; on the second day to Trois-Pistoles and Rimouski, where we had more than once cursed the old, dilapidated, badly maintained airport, then to Tadoussac via Île du Bic and Les Escoumins; the third day promised, and in fact turned out to be, more strenuous—and also more dangerous. Loaded to maximum capacity, we had to fly up from Tadoussac to Chicoutimi; a difficult flight at a height of four thousand five hundred feet with a strong west wind that rocked our eggshell like a feather in the wind. Drien and I felt very isolated in our delicate bird above this long, black, deep crevasse bordered by huge, steep mountains covered with an eiderdown of white snow. The Saguenay terrified us at the same time as it filled us with wonder.

At Chicoutimi we had off-loaded our cargo in the grounds of a seminary. But we had to return to Rimouski the same day, still following the upper lip of the Saguenay then crossing the river diagonally, which was quite an adventure in this almost desert landscape with its rugged terrain. We were carrying eight passengers, all of them forestry engineers from the Price company.

The wind was even more violent than on the way out and a light sheet of fog compelled us to veer off our route slightly along the banks of the Sainte-Marguerite river in search of a flight path with some visibility. There were ten of us under a very small sun, suspended like a swarm of trapezists clinging to a timid searchlight. All ten of us were shivering with fear.

In this plane without a headlight, flying desperately towards an airport devoid of landing-lights, it was essential to reach our goal before nightfall. Taking everything into account, it was better to land in grazing-land or an isolated field, taking care to avoid the fences while keeping an eye on them to estimate the depth of the snow, than to try to reach our destination without a stopover and risk a night landing. This compelled us to land the B6000 on Île-Verte and spend the night there.

On the fourth day we took off at dawn in weather even rougher than the day before and reached Rimouski about an hour later. Six engineers deplaned there with obvious relief, while two others who had to continue the flight, on my advice and in agreement with the two government technicians who joined us, decided to put off our departure for the North Coast until the next day, weather permitting.

This also left Drien, who had been calling for it ever since Tadoussac, time to overhaul the B6000's engine and repair some tears in the fuselage.

That evening, while Drien was freezing his fingers palpating the engine, I had to relate some of our adventures and even invent a few to satisfy the audience. I liked to sprinkle my stories with symbolic images, strange characters and disquieting and dramatic elements. And that evening, I must say, beside the fire, drink in hand, I was in particularly good form. I kept coming up with just the right word, the effective phrase, the image that made the listeners catch their breath. For some reason, unknown to me at the time but which I now recognize as a premonition, I portrayed Drien as totally lacking in courage. I credited him only with skill, depicting him as devoid of any quality that might render him fascinating and as being merely unintentionally a figure of fun. I represented the storm, he the fog.

On the fifth day, a little after eight, once we could see that the weather was going to be in our favour, the two engineers from the Price company and the two government technicians took their places gingerly on the hard seats of the Travel-Air with their technical equipment. Only Drien was lacking to enable us to take off on the most difficult leg of our trip. Drien, for the first time since the founding of our little air transport company, had failed to be on time! We looked for him in his hotel, in the hangar, on the runway. He was nowhere to be found. The local men hadn't seen him anywhere since the previous evening, and I couldn't imagine that there was any woman who could have told me more. In my mind, the very name Drien the Mechanic was synonymous with work; it certainly had nothing to do with pleasure and love.

The more time passed the more impatient my four clients became, worrying that every extra minute my mechanic was late was eating into their observation time. So a little before nine, still without news of Drien, I felt obliged to take off without him. It was the first time I had gone up in our B6000 without Drien.

I knew he detested the Land of Cain, but was that reason to desert ... ?

***

I headed towards the coast, almost due north, in the direction of Pointe Betsiamites. After flying over Île Saint-Barnabé we had some thirty miles to fly above a river that would have left us no chance of survival in the case of a forced landing. Countless blocks of ice were dancing lazily beneath the cold belly of the B6000 as though in a vast ballet. They seemed to be defying us and challenging us to dive. We used to call this the white terror. It was not so much that we hated the St. Lawrence ... oh, God no ... nor that we no longer trusted our old Travel-Air—you see, Drien, I'm still talking about *us* as though you had been on the flight—but we knew that one had to dominate the other—and the B6000 was rocking us like a pregnant woman.

Then, to the great relief of the passengers, Pointe Betsiamites finally hove into view. All at once the mood on board grew lighter. We hugged the coast as far as Pointe-aux-Outardes, this time cutting across the Papinachois, the Rosier river, the Raguenau. The coast, blurred with snow, looked like an endless slide frozen into immobility. Here and there mountains rose like huge eggs between the river and the rocky horizon. The sun was gradually thinning the shadows and the streams were pinching their lips. Only the river, which embraced the whole of the right side as far as the horizon, lost in haze, bore witness to the rotation of the planet. We were floating alone above this beige, brown and white immensity, divided by the raised nose of the Travel-Air into two worlds hooked onto two apparently distinct horizons. Because the B6000 was pointing towards God, He who makes the distinction—unless it is we who make it in His name—between that which he calls Good and that which he names Evil. I must have been thinking of Drien, not as of an absence, as was actually the case, but the way people no doubt think of their religious faith, although for my part I have only hope.

Further on rose the great Outardes waterfall, opening onto the inviting, sensual, fine, strong river, dotted with rapids and waterfalls. The four men were arguing vigorously above the high-pitched whine of the engine, sketching the great work of sedimentation, photographing the play of rocks and water, accumulating notes on ... the future. Slowly we plunged into a stretch lit by sunshine and snow where the frost seemed to have laid down in perpetuity all the despairs of the night of time. But within the same picture this heavy vastness afforded hints of great hope to the minds of these visionaries or madmen—I still don't know which—who, perched along with me on a tiny dot in the sky, were gazing at the invisible behind this mass of solitude.

The moment aroused emotions reserved for the intuitive. That is to say, more than the others, as I gazed at the landscape I had to drown my distress at being neither a painter nor a poet. But at the same time, I tried to reason away an anxiety that had gripped me ever since we passed over Île Saint-Barnabé and here grew even more intense, because we were rapidly approaching an area of cotton batting that promptly blotted out the landscape like a white mat imprisoning a virgin canvas.

In a few minutes we were on the edge of a worrying turbulence that gave us the feeling of flying on the spot. So I decided to shorten our route by veering east-south-east towards the Manicouagan river, which we would have to follow on our return after flying over its magnificent lake shaped like a cariboo head. But from that point on things moved fast . . . .

First the plane was enveloped in a heavy snowfall drifting lazily through a thin mist that reduced visibility almost to zero, thereby defeating the purpose of this observation flight.

Then the engine began to misfire, causing my passengers indescribable apprehension. I looked in all directions and at every altitude for a flight path with some visibility, but the inevitable happened. At an altitude of over three thousand feet, and some seventy miles north of Baie-Comeau, the engine lapsed into a dense and persistent silence. Since no one knew the day of our arrival in that new pioneer town, we couldn't hope for any help from that quarter for days. Nor from anyone else.

Oh, I can still hear the dramatic dialogue between the wind and the carcass of the B6000. It was like a trumpet tune accompanied by the roll of drums, all enveloped in a great solemnity intensified by fragments of prayers. Similarly, as we made out bit by bit the jutting menace of the landscape, our cockpit was filled by the shouts of isolated phrases set free from our unconscious by the terror of our approaching end. A woman's name, perhaps, or a child's. Cries for mother ... to God too. Attempts to escape from a bad dream, pinchings of the flesh which at other times the epidermis would have rebelled against but which here, faced with panic, it didn't even notice.

I implored God for a place to make a forced landing. Failing this I would let the wind decide the place where our tomb, in the guise of an airplane, would seek its way to the centre of the earth.

There were five of us in the white night hoping that a too-heavy fruit would let itself be drawn to the ground like a weightless leaf.

I know that at the last moment, thrusting away the hand of fate, I leaned over to the right, as I had to in order to see ahead from this airplane with its nose still pointed above the horizon, and risked a last manoeuvre—to the left!

I wanted to decide—but not to see.

The double vision which then presented itself to me was at one and the same time that of my baptism and that of eternity in its most timeless, most insidious, most indigestible shape. I suddenly knew that I wasn't dead. Death couldn't be so uncomfortable, so agonizing ....

***

When I awoke, grief weighed so heavily on my temples, my body was so stiffened against the pain and cold that my senses refused any expenditure of energy. My distraught mind did not even know who I was. When you come out from what you believed to be death there is a short lapse of time during which you are no one.

To be sure, my memory, shattered by a series of shocks I couldn't even guess at, was neither awake nor concerned about time. Time past, that is. Because I had no memory of myself ... nor of anything else. I don't think I could have taken in the fact that I had been living there for a week and that Montagnais hunters had pulled me out of the B6000 and brought me back to their winter camp. I had become a lump of inert matter. My universe was reduced for the moment to pain and semi-consciousness.

In this state I was aware of several awakenings interspersed with deep black holes into which I plunged. But in this state of despair I fought both against the blackness and against the depth. Until the hole closed —beneath me.

Then I understood that I had been saved, still without recognizing this person, this indefinable me for whom I had been fighting so hard, flaying myself alive in order to live and suffering injury in the struggle against death.

Suddenly I perceived people above me, Montagnais Indians, I learned later, hunters, women and children, neither delighted nor disappointed. Only curious to see that my life had been spared. And in any case, as soon as I showed signs of life, they turned from me to a gentle young girl who had been both my guardian angel and my nurse during those last few days, soothing my fever and delivering me from evil.

Now, when everyone had turned to the young girl, as though in a collective sign of appreciation of her talent—because I don't think they were particularly worried about me—she for her part cast a glance that was at once sad and knowing at another man, an old man, to whose rare powers I wish to bear witness here.

The young woman, then, looked at the old man in a way I cannot forget: in an almost spiteful manner that suddenly reminded me of the way my poor mother looked the day she told my father that Julien, the son of the corner store owner, had fondled her buttocks as she carried the groceries to the car. My father, as though guided by a mixed emotion of vanity and vengeance towards the storekeeper, which he could never have admitted, went and cracked some of the ribs and knocked out some of the teeth of the unfortunate seminarist who later became a sailor. And curiously, this memory reassured me, because it breached the thick fog that filled my brain: all of a sudden I knew who I was.

The old man, yielding to the young woman's proud and, yes, haughty look, went off into the forest and did not return until late in the afternoon with a group of young men. As evening fell in the forest glade, I clearly saw them thrust some twenty rough poles deep in the snow, then tie the tops together in the shape of a cone pointing up into the night and bathed in starlight.

When I woke next day, having recovered some of my strength, the construction had been covered with tanned hides firmly lashed together from the base up to three feet from the top, where the crossed poles formed a crown. And while the hunters and the children were putting the finishing touches to the work, the old man stood with his back to the narrow opening in the wall of the structure. From time to time some of the women or the young men came and spoke a few words to him. Sometimes he showed no reaction; sometimes he nodded agreement.

Then the men came and gave him a collective message to which he immediately acquiesced. Finally—and she was the last to make what seemed to be a vow—the young woman, more modest this time, more retiring too, leaned on the old man's shoulder. The two of them looked at me together and I trembled a little, disquieted by the unknown, weak in the face of the unfamiliar. I felt afraid, certainly, but strange as it may seem not really for myself. I simply felt that something grave was about to take place.

All I can say about the inexplicable ceremony that followed is that I watched it with a complicated feeling of uncertainty, bordering on incredulity and mingled with fever and paralysis. Frequently too, areas of shadow passed before my eyes and blocked out my vision, removing me for long moments from the harsh and suffering reality that was my lot. Although I must confess to a certain fascination.

The young girl was sitting beside me firmly holding my right hand as if I had to swear to something. How I wished I could speak her language and gain some inkling of what lay behind her reassuring enthusiasm! And that of the old man who, crouching in his pointed dwelling, had intoned a kind of prolonged chant that was at once plaintive and ceremonial.

For the first few minutes this chant resembled a call for help. Around the hut, while the children shivered with anguish at the ritual, the men exchanged worried, almost tormented glances, each one seeking from the others a hint of comfort before the sacred powers.

Then the cries of animals rang out from the forest.

It took me some time to understand; later I realized what had been happening.

The truth was that the old man had first called upon the hare spirit, which came almost at once and they both yelped in dialogue with him in the wigwam. At this moment, too, the structure, although firmly planted in the frozen soil, swayed slightly to and fro while the cries of the hare spirit and of the man echoed through the clearing, and certainly also in the woods, as though in harmony. The audience now no longer seemed truly worried or frightened. Some of them even peeped discreetly through the skins.

Later, the yelps faded gently away, leaving only the increasingly melodious calls of the old man. Then, still in harmony with the old man's voice, that is to say standing out very clearly in distinct cries, and accompanied by a growing vibration of the structure of poles firmly anchored in the snow, there resounded the barking of the otter and the mink, then the hooting of the owl and the clucking of the hazel-grouse.

Mingled with these increasingly present, increasingly violent cries, I distinguished the howling of wolves, which made me jump.

Finally, silencing both this multitude and the wolf spirits, the growling of the bear and the magnificent belling of the moose rang out. At this precise moment, everyone seemed more tense, but this tension did not persist. After a minute or two of this conversation with the moose spirit, the sorcerer emerged from his shelter and announced to everyone what appeared to be some very good news.

Without hesitation the men picked up their weapons again and, following the detailed indications of the spirits, plunged into the dense forest that encircled us, followed by the proud, relieved gaze of the women, while the children, and I too, were overcome by amazement. That very afternoon the men returned, their backs and the sledges laden with quarters of moose. Nature had consented to our survival.

But meanwhile . . . .

Meanwhile the old man, obviously a bit more tired, had cloistered himself again in his temple shaped like an arrowhead. This time it was not the cries of animals that burst forth from space, but a multitude of voices as though produced by an echo but softened by time and wind. By fever too, and by the language barrier. Then these voices drew closer, to the tormented delight of the attentive women who now surrounded the hut.

This lasted for several long minutes, amid fear and anxiety. The voices echoed to the four corners of the forest, sometimes in gay little bursts, sometimes in long, grave murmurs.

When the sorcerer emerged from his holy place, casting good and not so good news to left and right, the joyful women hastened to console those struck by misfortune in lucid space—and confused time. Over distance. Yes, the old man had sought, among the sky spirits, for news of faraway relatives and friends in order to distribute to everyone these fragments of love and grief. The intelligence of the blood had mocked at distance.

I scarcely believed my feeble mind as I begged from those around me, cast into despair by the differences of language and race, for some logical, or failing that some magical explanation. A waste of effort! They understood my confusion, but how can you explain colour to a blind man?

Decidedly, all I could do was to amass suppositions, scrape together a semblance of truth and pierce the dense fog of the paranormal with little flashes of deduction.

People will say I'm making it all up, I know. But there are so many signs, so many pieces of evidence. Without counting Drien's death the other day, in his hospital bed—quite close to me and at the same time so far away.

When the women and children dispersed, the old sorcerer went back into the spirit hut and intoned a new chant. At this moment the young woman with the gentle eyes raised my head and supported it on her forearm so that I could better watch the ceremony. At least that's what I thought.

During the first few minutes, in fact, the young woman shook me several times as though to urge me on, to invite me to participate more actively in a ceremony of whose significance I had no inkling.

From time to time she seemed to be reassuring the old man. Then she shook my languid body, inviting me to do something I didn't understand. This lasted for several minutes when suddenly, in a brief instant of indifference, at the very moment when the image of Drien flashed across my mind, simultaneously as an active thought and as a memory, I heard a frightening cry that froze me as it did the young woman.

Then she seemed to be encouraging me. To do what? I didn't know at first, because the cry of fright was immediately transformed into a kind of lament as long as eternity, a change which rendered the voice—how shall I put it—more recognizable. It was Drien's voice, plaintive, suffering. I even believe that I heard my name coming from the spirit lodge and infiltrating into the black and white forest.

Suddenly I rose on my elbows and shouted his name with the little strength left to me. And the lament changed again into a strident cry. I begged the young woman to put an end to this terrible ceremony. She doubtless could not understand my words, but she evidently understood that I wished Drien no ill. But she insisted with a look, pointing out my bandages, miming the crash of the plane.

I understood very well what she was insinuating, but I refused to believe it. Not Drien. Not him, that faithful companion of my follies as of my triumphs. Not Drien . . . . No . . . . It would be too cruel, too unjust. What would be left to me?

The sequel to this episode remains buried in the long days of fever and delirium of which I have retained only a few images. Children bending over me, the old man with the mournful eyes, the frankly saddened young woman, an airman's helmet framing a rather familiar face. Perhaps a voice also, reassuring, and a few words in the language of Duplessis! The delicious sound of an airplane engine and my eardrums crushed by the altitude. The pervasive white and the antiseptic smell of a hospital. The sweet perfume of Carmen and her silky hair on my face. A pain in my arm and a feeling of comfort, calm and peace.

***

The morning after my return to the "civilized world" I was woken by a shaft of sunlight and its fatherly brightness. It warmed my feet. I also had, in this room that was as shiny as a new propeller, the beneficent feeling that the brightness and the whiteness had arranged to meet in my room in order to restore me to life. Behind these limpid windowpanes, like a premature baby in its incubator, I reserved all my energies for the conquest of a new and detestable emotion: despair.

I was hungry and very anxious to see people. And a few minutes after my awakening Carmen came to my bedside, squealing with joy, smearing me lovingly with tears and makeup, drooling on my neck and stammering words of love. To be sure, I couldn't grasp all she was saying, but her warmth did me good.

So much talk gave me the illusion of being a treasure that had been lost and found. It also reminded me of Mother's brooch that I had pinned on the snowman before Christmas and found again in spring. Mother had died in the meantime, so the treasure never left me after that. I could still see the little brooch set with a fire opal pinned to my white scarf tied to the head of the bed.

So much love flowed from Carmen's words that, even if I had had the strength, I could not have answered them. I would simply have embraced her, caressed her and crushed her with pleasure, as if I owed the blonde the life that the brunette had restored to me .... But at the same time my soul also harboured a great deal of friendship. Then, in the flood of her words, a phrase made me jump.

" ... and that's why I asked them to put Drien in the same room as you ...."

I sank even deeper into silence. I had believed him innocent—
or dead.

***

Every morning after that reproduced more or less the same
scenario. I was woken by the action of the sun, Carmen came and
spread her soppy love over me, drowning me in a flood of words I
didn't listen to. I knew I was capable of a great deal of love for her,
but on condition that she left me a little room to breathe—as before. I so much wanted a little silence to be established between
us, like a hyphen. And then there was Drien, who never spoke.

I learned from a doctor that Drien had been struck down by a
mysterious sickness a few days before my return. A nurse talked
to me about multiple contusions such as are sometimes suffered
by victims of a car crash. Another one spoke of respiratory problems. A second doctor mentioned symptoms connected with
brain function. But no one really knew.

In the eyes of some, Drien was simply mad. For others he was
the victim of one of those rare disorders that generally attract
specialists from Montreal or even Boston. An "interesting case"
that would put his doctor on the map.

We spent long afternoons side by side, stretching out in spite
of ourselves—pain. We were living so close to one another that we
could have held hands. But Drien didn't speak to me, didn't look
at me. I called him, I questioned him. All he did was turn his head
away and stare at the horizon. This went on for a week, that's to
say until the day before I was due to leave the hospital.

That evening, at suppertime, Drien started doling out the first
scraps of information, beginning with the cruellest.

"I even screwed up the murder of my best friend . . . ."

I refused to hear him, and when he repeated it I refused to understand. I denied his right to spoil our friendship. Today I
wonder whether I was really so concerned about this friendship,
or if it wasn't the prospect of having to call into question our years

of adventure that repelled me. Or was it simply that unconsciously I couldn't bear the thought of finding myself without a friend?

My heart was reduced to mush.

Between the meal and midnight he drove a multitude of vengeful little rivets into me, each one imprinting a different pain on my body and my mind. I wished Carmen was there to bathe me in her crazy torrent of words. I wished Drien would leave me in peace about his sabotage of the Travel-Air, his horror at having caused me a few superficial injuries that was greater than his repugnance at having killed four innocent people.

From beginning to end, while I kept gluing together the pieces of the ten years of our joint existence, he tore everything to bits like a child envious of a playmate's toy, depicting me as a poseur obsessed with his own superficial personality, an armchair-adventurer. A sort of puppet whose strings he had imagined cutting, because my fame, he said, depended on his clearheadedness, his desperately hard work, while I was having my vanity flattered by a bunch of provincials ready to marvel at any bird in a cage.

He wanted me to curse him, because I think he knew better than I what I would have had to do in order for the magic to put an end to him: I would have to hate him and call down the magician's curse upon him. But I only wanted him to be reproved by God and also by men. That way, I could have supported him in adversity and re-established our original relationship. But all I did was justify everything I had done in the past, everything I had said. And also some of my secret thoughts . . . .

His last words, as the clock struck five, were to tell me to go to another hell than his. After that he said nothing more.

I looked at him and I listened to him sleeping until sunrise. His torso rose regularly, in obedience to some involuntary instinct of self-preservation. I don't know whether he was suffering or whether he was aware of the final battle he was fighting with death. No doubt his spirit was already flying elsewhere—between the azure sheets of the infinite.

His fine arms reddened by the open air rested upon sheets as white as exhausted and melancholy feather-boas. His bandaged hair haloed his face and his head lay there like a mute rock. His covered and slightly bent legs, like tusks detached from some huge pachyderm, suggested, strange as it may seem, emotions connected with resignation and serenity. But on the whole I felt him to be tired of life, bored with himself and disgusted by the rest of the world.

I believe I cried at the sight of his calm silhouette. And above all, I hated him, as he wished. Oh, just for a fraction of a second! But I really hated him. Not for having tried to do away with me. No, merely for having spoiled everything.

I am talking about my ease in living.

Following this instant inadvertently dedicated to hate, I knew that this single thought would bring about Drien's end. The event took place very quickly, as if someone were afraid I might change my mind. It was during the grandiose ceremony of sunrise.

First I observed a play of shadows in the diaphanous curtains which warned me that the spirit of the old sorcerer was still circulating, no doubt at the urging of the attentive young woman, between evil and vengeance. Then, while Drien remained perfectly silent, his countenance inscrutable, I heard the double of his voice uttered by space, a voice that was at first almost plaintive and then gradually changed into a kind of long cry that had the power to kill. I tried to force my fists into my ears, but too late: the magic had already drawn added strength from my instant of hate. The die was cast: Drien's voice was already in a chorus with the chanted spell. The magic had just carried Drien off.

I cried out murder into the night-time in my head while pouring out my truth into the daylight, until I felt my lungs being crushed and my throat squeezed. I told them the enchanter had come and uttered his death-rattle wrapped in Drien's voice. They didn't believe me and kept me with them.

***

Drien. I know your mouth will soon be filled with earthly dust. My wish for you is not to remember us.

At the end of your short life you were inhabited by the soul of an airman, trusting to your lucky star and wishing to crash somewhere else than on the blue orange. But space, when all is said and done, showed you much cruelty, gathering you in slyly and finally committing your cockpit to grass and mud. Poor Drien, who all your life were afraid that death would come and take you on an impulse, without discernment and without letting you grow old into a beautiful death. Even when you were old, I know, you would still have felt yourself too young for death.

The other morning, at the moment when the sun was starting off a new day to be lived, magic death, in the ambiguous shape of an emaciated light, the source of your last voice, came and increased tenfold alongside your sleeping body. And you passed from sleep into death, lying humbly on your spinal column, your soul between the white sheets, your knees close to your heart.

You passed on in the shape of an ear, like an adventurer being born, listening in to magic. A violent, dirty death for a man of your stamp. I pray for you, Drien, now as at the hour of your death.

God above, did you have to love life in order to die like that, your mind distracted by an old dream of revenge, without feeling the cold shadow slipping under the sheets across distance and time?

Drien, I am flying above your dream. It is Birdy telling you.

NULIAK

Yves Thériault
translated by M.G. Hesse

When Napayok saw Ikionak for the first time, he refused to remember that name and baptized her instead with a name which, it seemed to him, suited her better. Of course he said aloud Ikionak, but to himself, he said quite low, to show that this mattered: Nuliak, which means wife.
Wife?
He had only caught a glimpse of her, nothing more, a glimpse. But her hands were strong, her body strong, and her eyes alive. When she smiled, Napayok wanted to spring on two bears, or to catch a bearded seal with his bare hands. He imagined feats. Every evening, for ten days, he dreamed of her. Above all he triumphed in her eyes. A better hunter than the others, he beckoned to the big girl who came to him with her quiet and heavy step.

Nuliak?

But that was his dream.

Outside the Arctic stirred. A wind blew in from the West and whirled all the snow around and buried the banks of the Hudson Bay under an immense mass—whirling, blinding, and sinister.

Safely huddled in his igloo, Napayok composed a song while the winds howled.

> I am the Inuk, armed,
> let the caribou come;
>
> My weapon is ready,
> let the seal come;
>
> The harpoon is pointed,
> let the walrus fear;
>
> My gun is oiled,
> let the bear take care!
>
> I am Napayok, listen, Nuliak,
> I am Napayok.

The mild weather returned, the wind fled, snow fell again. A pale sun appeared on the low horizon and filled the night with grey shadows. Once again Napayok harnessed the dogs, put on his snowshoes and left again.

He visited Tudlik, the wise man of all the land of ice.

"I respect you."

This greeting was accompanied by a handshake.

"The Company Man was looking for you," Tudlik told him. "He asks you to go to his wooden house. He got the radio."

"I'll go," Napayok said.

What had made him think of buying it? The radio could be kept in your pocket, even held in your hand. What if he'd charm Nuliak with it . . . ?

(He didn't mention any name. He was thinking aloud. Tudlik pretended not to hear anything. At the age of seventy Tudlik had learned to wait.)

Because of its transistors this radio is so small.

Napayok could pronounce the foreign word. He had learned it from the Company's White Man. Napayok had remembered it.

"You speak only about this radio," Tudlik said with feigned naïveté.

He knew very well that Napayok wasn't here just as a casual visitor in his hut—a hut of stones roughly joined together by dried clay. What didn't they come here to ask for, from Porungnetuk, as well as from many villages of the area? Knowledge first of all, then prudence, good advice, signs, an indication of ways to be pursued: the wisdom of old age.

"I am twenty years old," Napayok said. "I've called Ikionak my wife. I say Nuliak."

"Good."

Napayok showed his hands.

"My ancestors knew how to fashion ivory, stone."

"And today's people, too."

"Me," Napayok said, "I'm a better hunter than they."

"Yes," Tudlik noted.

"For Nuliak, I want to know how to cut the smooth stone."

"The green stone . . . . They do it for other reasons," Tudlik said. "But you, you are different."

Napayok nodded.

The hut was as big as a man, a lonely, old man. You could take everything in by staying squatted on the cariboo skin that was spread out on the floor. The visitor took up half the empty space before Tudlik and half the doorway. With his hand lifted above him he could reach the roof; with his outstretched hand he could reach the pemmican that hung on the wall; his knee touched the lamp standing on the floor. It was warm here, the air was heavy, the odour rancid. Napayok didn't know the odour of bright and healthy homes; this one was good enough for him and couldn't surprise him.

The odour of a stone hut, of a tent of cariboo skins, of an igloo shelter or a village igloo—familiar, imperative, and necessary. The odour was linked with the dream, it belonged to Nuliak as much as to the husband, it was an ancient heritage.

"They sculpt," Tudlik said, "to please the White Men. Their stone objects are carried throughout the world. But you, you'll sculpt for Ikionak, ... I mean Nuliak."

"Yes."

The old man who had been the teacher of the ancient crafts to so many young people of all tribes along the coast, took from behind him a piece of marbled, sea-green soapstone. He put it on the ground before him and between his knees and those of Napayok.

"I don't think I have anything to teach you," Tudlik said. "Only this: put your hand on the stone, then your other hand. Stay like this for some hours or days if necessary. In each stone fragment there lives the soul of an animal; there lives the soul of a man; there lives the soul of a thing. Soon this soul will pass from the stone and enter into you through the skin of your hands, through the blood of your body. The soul will live with yours; the soul will be with you and for you. And your hands will suddenly seize the cutting tools, and you'll free the stone of all its surplus. What will be born will be the body belonging to this new soul in you, which will travel fast so that it will live in the stone body that has come from you. Do you understand?"

"Yes, I understand."

"Put your hand on the stone," Tudlik repeated closing his eyes. "The work will be born out of itself without you being there for anything except the labour of your hands."

Six days later, having worked the stone, then having polished and repolished it, Napayok went off to Nuliak's igloo.

In his hand the body of stone that was now inhabited by a new soul represented a stocky Inuk with his harpoon poised, who watched a seal rising out of the water before him.

"You are Ikionak," Napayok said to the girl.

It was the first time he had spoken to her.

He put the sculpture before her.

"I looked for the soul of the stone as I was thinking of you," the man said. "This man that represents me came out of it. That's what I offer you."

The girl opened her eyes wide and observed Napayok for a long time.

"I know you," she said.

"I changed your name," answered Napayok. "You are no longer Ikionak. You are Nuliak."

"And I," the girl said after a while, "I knew that you were Napayok. But from now on I'll call you U'i ..."

(U'i means husband, just as Nuliak means wife.)

They stayed a long time like this, looking at each other. Once Ikionak touched with her finger tips the stone body before her. Then she smiled and inclined her head a little.

"U'i," she repeated, like a caress, like a gentle word.

Then Napayok took from his parka a piece of cariboo skin which he had brought so that he might offer it to the girl.

With a serious glance, she took the skin and brought it to her mouth. Slowly, deliberately, she chewed it, as she would have to do throughout her life, so that her husband, their little ones, and the Old People who would seek refuge in the igloo of the new couple would all be dressed warmly.

Later she said:

"From now on I am Nuliak. I've forgotten my name."

Then she went and laid down next to Napayok who had stretched out on the ice bench. Then the man took from his pocket the battery-operated radio and turned it on. And while they loved each other for the first time like a couple, there came from the Great Whale station right up to the silent igloo the voice of Elvis Presley....

THE THIRTEENTH

Alain Grandbois
translated by Larry Shouldice

Five kilometers from Djibouti, in a hollow deep in the fiery sand-dunes, the Ambouli oasis emerges suddenly, like a miracle. There are springs bordered by pink and white oleanders continually in bloom, tufts of greenery mottled with patches of deep shade, hibiscus bushes, cinerarias, date palms, doum palms, and those tall royal palms that thrust their starry heads into the unwavering blue of the sky. There too are the deep, cool huts of the Somalis. The air is soft and light, wafted through with perfume. The men are proud and noble; the women move slowly and gracefully; smiles sparkle on the beautiful black faces of the girls. Everything in Ambouli evokes the very Paradise described by the Prophet.

In the full moon of this particular night, however, demons had been at work in the oasis. Danakil warriors, who had travelled from Obock, were holding a tam-tam, and we had sat watching it right through to the morning. It had begun the previous evening, on the trampled earth square around the huge red fires, with the dull beating of drums. Squatting, the audience marked the rhythm with sharp movements of their heads. The first rows were made up of warriors. The women remained apart, clustered like dark grapes, jangling their heavy copper bracelets in time. Occasionally we would catch a glimpse of their gleaming eyes or teeth. A slow murmur then arose, and was soon transformed into a hoarse, repetitive, breathless chant that was amazingly poignant. And then the dances began.

First of all, one of the Danakil moved away from the warriors and began dancing alone. Then another came to join him, then a third, and then still others. They were tall and naked. Their chests were scored with blue tattoo marks and their elongated skulls were piled high with tufts of hair that had been whitened with lime; the faces below looked twisted and tortured. Their eyes wild and rolling, they would gasp and pant violently, sucking in their stomachs and cheeks. This was the dance of hunger. Other dancers then came to replace them. This was the dance of war. Brandishing spears, daggers and swords, the new dancers howled like madmen, raising and lowering their copper shields which seemed to grow purple with blood in the light of the flames. This went on for hours. Finally, streaming with sweat and staggering like drunks, they moved back into the shadows.

The huge fires glowed red in the night. There was a kind of unreal waiting period, as though time were somehow strangely suspended. Only the drums went on, lashing through the silence and the dark. Then one by one the women, their hips swaying slowly, arranged themselves around the fires. Some of the Danakil came to join them. The moon was sinking into the horizon. The last dance began—the indescribable dance of love. And with it, a diabolical orgy ....

The sky was already light when we left the crazed oasis. The salt-pans along the road to Djibouti shimmered with thousands of soft blue lights, like fresh morning snow in the lands of the North. I left my companions at the entrance to the city, in front of the market. The shouting and howling, the red glow of the fires, the palm wine we had been drinking immoderately, and lack of sleep, had all tired me out; I wanted to shake off the torpor coming over me by walking back to the hotel where I was staying. I dawdled through the market, getting lost, and by the time I found my way again an oblique, implacable sun was already beating down. I walked bare-headed, unconsciously seeking the shade under the awnings. Suddenly someone grabbed me by the shoulders and pushed me into the entrance of a bazaar. "Hey, Sidi, fetch him a pith helmet and a pair of sunglasses!"

As my eyes adjusted to the darkness, I saw before me a tall, skinny fellow with blue eyes and reddish skin. "Here, now don't you think you'd be better to ..."

"I say, mind my own business. Yes. I know. We'll talk about that some other time. Come on then, Sidi, are you asleep?"

He was speaking French with a thick British accent. His voice was strangely hoarse. The Arab came running with a pith helmet and glasses. "Here, Suh, here. That's twenty-two francs, Suh."

"It's 10 francs. Don't give him more than 10 francs. Not a centime more!"

"I won't give him anything at all .... Although I generally pay for the things I buy myself, I'm not in the habit of ... of ..."

I was choking with anger. Like a naughty child caught doing something wrong.

"No more than ten francs. Remember .... They're worse thieves than the Tuareg in the desert .... And do be careful of the sun!"

He burst out laughing and left.

The bar of the Hotel des Arcades, at six o'clock, is the place where the white inhabitants of Djibouti meet—at least the white males. The customs supervisor comes in for a game of cards with the assistant schoolmaster; the pharmacist meets up with the petty officers from ships that are passing through; the postmaster drops by to discuss politics with the Vosikis boys (Vosikis & Co., Import-Export—Commission Agency. *Headquarters:* Djibouti, *French Somaliland. Branch Offices:* Diredawa & Addis Ababa, *Ethiopia*); the chief of police stops in to talk of his love affairs to the managing director of the Bank of Indo-China, (Capital...120,000,000 francs. *Our Djibouti branch provides full banking services);* the minor functionaries from the Governor's Office, whose vanity dictates that they remain aloof from everyone but the garrison officers (who happen to hold them in cordial contempt), come by to drink scotch and soda until it's time to go off to the Club for what they pompously refer to as the Match (for the record I am obliged to note here that the Match is a poor game of baccarat which would be laughed at by even the most timid poker player in the land of Quebec); and finally a swarm of little pickaninnies, shrill, rowdy, blue-black and naked as Adam, as bothersome and persistent as mosquitoes, buzzes around the tables trying to sell their trinkets.

My room happened to be located above the bar. I had tried in vain to get a little rest, but below a certain latitude it's impossible to sleep except at night. And Djibouti is one of the hottest holes in the world. About 4 o'clock, after a discouragingly lukewarm shower, I went down to the bar in the feeble hope of finding a bit of coolness in some drink or other concocted by Papaphilippopopoulos, whose nickname was Papou, for reasons that are not too difficult to understand. Papou, behind his counter, was dripping with sweat. He was small in stature, but enormous, with a cadaverous face as pale as a sickly moon. Whenever he got drunk, he would tell of his "misfortune." His wife had run off with a Copt who was dealing in arms with the dissident tribes in the Hijaz region.

"A eencredeeble woman, thee most beauteefool in thee world .... She must have weighed, no lies, about 160 keelos .... Oh, I hop I am never see her!"

"Would you kill her, Papou?" we would ask him.

"Keel her, so charmeeng, so deeveen, keel her! I would keess thee bottom of her dress and cry pure tears from my soul ... Ah! ..."

Then he would truly start sobbing; huge tears like hot wax would well up in the corners of tiny eyes sunk in the surrounding fat, and would roll down his cheeks, mingling with the sweat and then plopping onto the smooth surface of the counter.

I said to Papou, "I'm thirsty. Give me something to drink, in a tall glass, with lots of ice."

Papou was fanning himself.

"Eet's thee tam-tam. You drunk their feelth. Bad, bad. More bad than thee Yapanese wheesky. All that, good only for speet ...."

He turned his head away and spat.

I asked him, "What do you advise me to drink?"

And then I heard that same hoarse voice from the morning, at the Arab's shop.

"Hello there! Did you sleep well? I didn't. Damned heat. Allow me to buy you a drink; I owe you one ...."

I turned around. The man was laughing. He was stretched out on two rattan chairs, with his feet on a low table, so that he looked inordinately elongated. He continued speaking.

"The tam-tam. The Three Dances. Yes. That's Africa. Yes, but not all of Africa. The Three Dances are only the preliminaries to another little dance, a tiny little dance, actually, which looks like nothing at all, but which is absolutely frightful .... That one's called the Dance of Death."

He exploded in a spasm of hoarse laughter. "Here's what you should drink. Papou, give the gentleman a tall glass, ice, one third scotch, two-thirds milk .... The advantage of this mixture is beyond question, since it allows the imagination to preserve a most tenuous dignity. If the milk is sour, you taste only the whisky, and if the whisky is polluted you taste nothing but the milk...."

"And if the milk is sour, and the whisky polluted?"

"In that case you're completely devoid of imagination, and suffer from moodiness as well. An unfortunate combination in a man engaged in the pursuit of life...."

He held out his hand. "My name is Bill Carlton," he said.

We were on a first-name basis that same evening, and we were together constantly for four days. Bill was waiting for the mail steamer to Aden; I was waiting for a cargo ship that was supposed to take me to Singapore.

Bill was not at all typical of the sort of traveller who goes around the world nestled under the wing of some Cook agency or other. He spoke a dozen languages with the greatest ease. He was highly cultivated and had a prodigious memory. In the back room of a little Armenian café where we spent the hottest hours of the day, he would never tire of reciting, in a sort of interior monologue, aphorisms from Marcus Aurelius, verses from Catullus, odes by Horace, fragments from Livy, the letters of Seneca, Shakespeare's sonnets, poems by Blake, Emily Brontë, Guillaume Apollinaire, St. John Perse or Paul Eluard. I can still see him stretched out on a filthy mat, his eyes half-closed, arms crossed behind his neck, and I can still hear his hoarse, toneless voice droning that wonderful poem by Cendrars:

> *In those days I was in my youth*
> *I was barely sixteen and my childhood was forgotten*
> *I was sixteen thousand leagues from the place of my birth*
> *I was in Moscow, in the city of a thousand and three*
>   *steeples and seven train stations*
> *And my youth was so fiery, so crazed*
> *That my heart in turn burned like the Temple of*
>   *Ephesus or like Red Square in Moscow*
> *With the sun going down...*

He was silent for a moment, his eyes completely closed. Then suddenly: "Hey, Mesrob, ice, and whisky!"

The Armenian, his black servant girl, three blind beggars and ten pickaninnies immediately came running. Usually they all stayed behind the bamboo door, squatting quietly, watching and listening to those strange syllables that fascinated them even if they couldn't understand them, especially the strange voice that would carry them off, through the supreme power of poetry, into the magical realms of music. They would come barging into the room, bustling about, carrying and breaking glasses. The

Armenian would mutter apologies, deliver a round of kicks, and finally everything was served; then they would return behind the doorway and I would see the last of the pickaninnies voluptuously squeezing into the palm of his hand a tiny stolen piece of the precious ice.

Bill drained half his glass in one gulp and looked at me, smiling. Then he started up again, in a silence that you understood was full of expectations and worries (was he going to keep on saying those mysterious words?):

> *Still, I was a very bad poet*
> *I didn't know how to go through to the end*
> *I was hungry*

He would stop only at nightfall, and he filled the Armenian with a sort of respect mixed with terror and fascination, since he was virtually considered a supernatural being.

We would go back to the Hotel des Arcades, where we had adjoining rooms and shared the same veranda. And there until the pale light of dawn we would watch the stars glimmering in the African night.

Although Bill's monologue was virtually inexhaustible, it would have been difficult for any man to show more discretion regarding personal matters. He was extremely reserved, and the stories he told never included any role for himself, not even as an outside or chance observer. He would never say, for instance, "One day when I was in San Luis de Paz," but rather, "One day in San Luis de Paz there was, etc." Still, it was clear that he himself had seen, in San Luis de Paz or another city he would name, a particular woman, murder, riot or tidal wave. I knew nothing about him except his name and that he held the rank of major, that he loved risk, adventure and poetry, and that he had arrived from Addis Ababa and was leaving for Aden. Only on one occasion, the last evening we spent together in Djibouti, he told me, "I've just about spent the last of a small inheritance left to me by an old aunt. I must confess that I abhor unearned money. One must always pay for one's adventures .... My dear old aunt, I was very fond of her .... She lived in a little manor-house in Devonshire, not far from Torquay, on the seacoast. She had been a widow for half a century. Her young husband, immediately upon their return from their honeymoon trip, which they had spent on the Italian Riviera after the fashion of the time, was killed while out riding to the hounds. A bad fall. What does happiness depend on? And life? Well ... they were very much in love with one another. She had brought back a small palm tree from Rapallo, and she planted it in front of the manor under the windows of the master bedroom, so that it would be a reminder of their time of perfect bliss. He had gently teased her about this. He was a lively, handsome lad who was too passionately involved in tasting the joys of life to be able to take any sentimental talisman very seriously .... After the tragedy she withdrew from the world, cloistering herself and not wishing to see anyone. Her palm tree had become the object of her affection. She thought of it constantly, taking enormous care of it, protecting and nurturing it as a mother would her child. The servants claimed to have heard her speaking words of love to it. She neither saw nor thought about anything else. The farmers and fishermen in the area called her the 'Palm Lady,' not in any mocking sense but with a kind of tender affection. The common folk are the only ones left who can recognize genuine love, recognize it and respect it .... In any case, a few years ago the taxes were becoming too heavy and she had to resign herself to putting the manor up for rent. She was crippled with rheumatism and was having heart trouble. Her doctor ordered her to move away from the coast, which she categorically refused. She moved into the gardener's cottage. At great expense, she had the palm tree, which by this time was enormous, dug up and replanted in front of her window. She went on living there for five or six years. In the end she was no longer able to move, but she had her bed placed in front of the window .... She died last winter. Now, on the night she died there was an extraordinarily violent storm, which rarely occurs in that area, and at the very hour of her death the palm tree was struck by lightning ..."

He was no longer speaking but I could still hear the sound of his hoarse voice overlapping the notes of silence. We were stretched out on our lounge chairs. On the veranda the moonlight had painted a large mauve rectangle. Then, with astonishing vehemence, he cried, "But I'm telling the truth! How dare you not believe me! Go on, say you suspect that I'm making it up...."

The moonlight was hitting him in full face. I shrugged. He had had a great deal to drink during the day. He wasn't drunk—I never saw him drunk—but there was a strange little sparkle in the pupils of his eyes and his hands were shaking imperceptibly. Fever, or alcohol? Or both? I knew that he suffered from malaria. Then he began to laugh. "Let's go on down to Papou's," he said.

We went down to Papou's. It was already very late in the night and the bar was deserted. Papou was dozing. Bill asked for whisky and ice. He emptied his glass in one long draught. Then he said to me, "Do you know this poem by Supervielle?"

> *The ladies in black took their violins*
> *So that they could play with their backs to the mirror.*
> *The wind faded away as on the finest days*
> *The better to hear some obscure music.*
> *But almost immediately with immense forgetfulness*
> *The violins went quiet in the ladies' arms*
> *Like a naked child who has fallen asleep*
> *Among the trees.*
> *It seemed that nothing would bring to life again*
> *The stilled bow, the marble violin,*
> *Someone whispered to me: "Only you can do it,*
> *Come right away."*
> *And then it was from the depths of my sleep* ...

Bill immediately finished another glass of alcohol. His hands were shaking and he was laughing as he tossed his head back. I said to him, "You're taking great care of your malaria."

"I say, do you think so?"

Behind the counter, Papou had started dozing again. He was drunk, as he was every night, and he was sobbing unconsciously, which had become a habit for him. He was thinking of the Copt, that his repentant wife had come back to him, that he was kissing the hem of her dress and her bare feet soiled with the dust of the road.

"Yes I think you're in the process of developing a liver big enough to impress the doctors in Harley Street. Of course, if that's what you like ..."

He raised his two large arms in an expression of mock surprise. "So you believe in that, in the existence of the liver! Dear boy. Ah! But, really, the liver exists only in the troubled imagination of a few elderly hypochondriacs."

"Well, some people believe that the number 13 is unlucky, whereas I ..."

He suddenly interrupted me. "Don't talk like that; you've no right to." Two or three times he repeated, "You've no right to, you've no right ...." I thought at first he was joking. His expression had completely changed, however; I could see that same little flame dancing again in the depths of his eyes, and I thought he was really drunk.

He finished several more glasses of whisky. But he remained close-mouthed until we took leave of one another to go back to our rooms.

The next day I was going to see him off on his boat. The heat was like a blazing oven and the light was blinding. The pickaninnies, usually so lively, remained motionless; as if they had all been struck with paralysis, they were crouched in the big squares of purple shade under the awnings. The sea was an immense expanse of molten lead.

Bill jumped nimbly into the little launch that was bobbing at the end of the floating dock—his black freighter was steaming at the entrance to the roadstead—and turned to shake hands with me. "Goodbye, now," he said. "There are a lot of roads in this wide world, but they always end up meeting somewhere. I'm sure we'll see one another again .... And take care of the sun," he added, laughing. And then the launch moved away with a roar of its motor, the stern enveloped in a pall of smelly black smoke.

I sauntered through the big souks until nightfall. Then I dropped by the Armenian's for a coffee, but there was no one behind the bamboo doorway. Bill's departure had broken the spell. I went back to my room, packed my bags, paid my hotel bill and went off to see Papou. It was about eleven o'clock. As on the previous evening the bar was empty, and as on the previous evening Papou was dozing. I offered to buy him a last drink. Papou usually drank absinth which he cut with Geneva gin, a mixture that would kill an ox. "I like my alcohol to taste sometheeng," he would say.

The drink woke him up completely. "So, thee Major ees go! Here, everybody happy. Thee French, thee Eetalians .... They theenk he ees too much dangerous man, that he works for Eengleesh Eentellegence Service. Thee Chief of thee Police was steel talkeeng about eet thees eveneeng. I don't geeve a f.... Eet ees hees country, England .... So .... And also, for me he is good man. He knows for drink and hee knows for talk. Ah! Eef he ever meet my wife, he would know for find thee words wheech breeng her back to me. You know, my wife leave weeth that peeg of a Copt ... "

Large tears were welling up in the corner of his little eyes and rolling down his cheeks. I left the bar.

The following year in Canton, I was with about twenty other whites in the drawing room of the Victoria Hotel, in the centre of the little island of Shameen. We were all trying to while away the hours, some of us playing bridge and others mah-jong. The air was damp and sticky. It had been raining for three days. And for days now Canton had been in an uproar. That very morning (it was March 1, 1934), in far-off Manchukuo, Emperor Kang Teh had been crowned—a coronation imposed by the Nippon Empire according to the "will of Heaven." The Southern Chinese were talking of raising an army and marching against

Chiang Kai-shek, whom they were accusing of making secret deals with the Japanese. They were also accusing the Western powers of treacherous complicity. The city was alive with demonstrations and riots. The little people of Canton, nervous, turbulent and ferociously nationalistic, had once again not forgotten Sun Yat Sen's revolution, the forced concessions that followed, the massacres, the blockade of Hong Kong and the war on imperialism; and once more they were rising up for their ideal of freedom.

The bridges that connected Shameen to the city were closed off with barbed wire. The guard had been increased. The most bizarre rumours were going round, especially that Shameen was to be bombarded in reprisal. We could not leave the island. At regular intervals we would hear the crazy buzzing of airplanes. And that hot, heavy rain that kept falling endlessly ...

Our little group included two elderly Americans connected to the Protestant Mission Office; a young French couple from Saigon; a fat, jolly businessman whose nationality was probably Russian although he was certainly of Jewish origin; and a heavy-set Bavarian Catholic missionary who was blond and balding, with a thick powerful neck. At first people had exchanged anecdotes about Chinese customs, habits and beliefs. Later the talk turned to superstitions, telepathy and mysterious coincidences. It was then that I told the story of the "Palm Lady," and to give my talk the ring of truth I ended by saying that I had heard it straight from the lips of the old lady's nephew, an English Major by the name of Carlton, Bill Carlton ...

Tea was served. I had a good book to read. I excused myself, left the drawing room and was about to enter the stairwell when I felt someone lightly touching my arm. I turned around and saw the Bavarian priest. Smiling, he said to me in a low voice, "Would you excuse me if I took the liberty of giving you a word of advice? I've been living in the Kangting for twenty-five years now. I was here when the first Republic was proclaimed by Dr.

Sun Yat Sen. Since then I've seen a lot of things and witnessed a lot of events .... The Southern Chinese are extremely impulsive creatures. They catch fire like match-sticks. You know as I do the unfortunate circumstances that are keeping us cooped up here in Shameen, and the hotel has a great many domestics. The point of all this is that there are certain names that are probably better not mentioned. The name of Major Carlton, for example .... But forgive me!"

I exclaimed, "Thank you very much, Father ... I am very grateful indeed. But ..." (I was burning with curiosity), "but could you not tell me a little more about Carlton? Surely you must have known him very well?"

"The Major was in Hong Kong at the time of Borodin. There were bloody reprisals on both sides, and ... in any case, a stock of unfortunate events that would be too long to tell of, nor would it serve any purpose since they're all lost in the past now. Of course, my position does not ask me to judge men but rather to try to understand them, and absolve them. I can tell you, however, that I spent some pleasant hours with Major Carlton. He would recite certain lyric poems by Goethe most admirably .... But may I ask what you're reading?"

I was holding Huxley's *Point Counter Point*. He took the book, read the title, and immediately gave it back to me. "The most beautiful book that I know has no author's name on it. It's entitled *The Imitation of Jesus Christ*. Good-bye, my son, and may God bless you."

Several days later I arrived in Macao. The lovely peninsula was in full flower. The captain of the boat that had taken me there wanted to be the first to show me around. He was a good Dutchman, close-mouthed and peace-loving, who must have been approaching sixty. He lived in a charming little pink house on the side of the hill overlooking the city. His wife, of mixed Chinese and Portuguese ancestry, was as graceful and fragile as a flower, her fingers as white as the petals of a daisy. They had no children. Thinking it would please him, she begged him to take a concubine. Her devotion flattered him. His words of protest were awkward and touching. He adored her.

We were having lunch on a rose-ringed terrace. The air was heavy with perfume. The captain, who was going back to his ship, left me at the hotel.

Macao by night looks like a city destined for divine vengeance: all the lights, all the joys, all the shouts, all the vices. Like everyone else, I went off to play fan-tan. The gaming rooms are semicircular and, as in a theatre, there are several levels of balconies. The most important people in the colony remain in the upper circle. In general they are newly rich Chinese merchants or retired generals. Surrounded by their concubines, they nonchalantly smoke pipes of opium while the boy assigned to them lowers the bets in a little wicker basket on a string, lifts up the winnings and keeps track of the game. Like everyone else, I lost, and I left in a very bad mood. The next day the desk clerk at the hotel handed me a letter. The envelope was neither stamped nor dated. "It's a gentleman who left this, two or three weeks, maybe a month ago, I can't remember. I would have given it to you yesterday but I didn't quite catch your name. When I was looking through the guest register this morning ..."

I broke open the envelope and saw first of all the poem by Camoens that begins with this line, *Vasco whose happy sails* .... Bill added, "Neither the ghost of the poet Camoens nor the shade of the great Saint Francis Xavier will welcome you to Macao, which for a hundred years has been irreparably devoted to the sinister workings of the Black Angel .... Above all, be careful of the fan-tan ..."

I saw Bill in Mukden four months later. I was having dinner at the Yamato with a young Chinese doctor. It was a Friday, the thirteenth of July. The Chinese was confiding to me, "Here in Mukden, five years ago, there were sixty-five doctors of my race. Now there are only two of us. And the authorities still tolerate my presence only because I'm in charge of the dermatology clinic at the municipal hospital, because they know I studied in Paris under Saboureau, because they haven't found a replacement for me yet, and last but not least because V.D. has been taking a frightful toll on the new Japanese occupants. Unfortunately doctors are not a special case. They've saddled the businessmen and merchants with such heavy taxes that they're forced out of business; they've absconded with the farmers' crops; the system of education has been completely turned upside down; there isn't a single Chinese left in the public service. We're being picked clean under the pretext of being protected. My family has been living here for three generations. My mother is Manchurian and so is my wife. We'll have to leave the country but where will we go? This 'order' that's being forced on us and talked about everywhere with so much fuss, if it could only have some positive results or some real value for us .... You can see the sabotaging of the railway line yourself! Since spring there have been at least three attacks per week between Mukden and Harbin. They spread the craziest rumours about this; they blame it on the Soviets, the White Russians, the Chinese. Everyone knows perfectly well that it's the bandits on the steppes. If the Japanese really wanted to, they could clean out the steppes in two months. They don't do it so that they can go on justifying their occupation in the eyes of the world. There's certainly no lack of cunning on their part. As if a country without thieves needed watchdogs!"

It was then that Bill noticed us. We had coffee and liqueurs together. Bill seemed in charmingly good humour and was even moved to recite a little Chinese poem by Ho Kin-ming:

> *How quietly the river is murmuring*
> *Tonight, along the banks, your maid-servant is gathering*
>   *orchids.*
> *You, my lord, have left in your junk, carried off by the*
>   *current,*
> *While I, alone, stand motionless at the water's edge!*

When the Chinese doctor had gone, Bill said to me, "I know a little Russian café that serves a vodka worthy of all the dear departed Czars. Come along, we can go there for a nice long chat."

"I'm terribly sorry," I replied, "but I'm leaving in an hour for Harbin."

"You're leaving tonight!"
His hoarse voice sounded surprised.
"I'm leaving this evening at exactly 11:45."
"You're not leaving. I'm going to Harbin myself tomorrow. We can make the trip together."
"I'm sorry, but there's someone meeting me at the station. A chap named Kaufmann, a staff-writer for *Pravda*."
"Well, telephone your Kaufmann to say you can't make it."
"I've already put off meetings with Kaufmann twice in the past week."
"Good, this will make it three. Now call him and say you aren't coming."
I was astonished, and irritated, by the commanding tone of his voice. And yet I did have a strong desire to stay. Bill was one of the most entertaining characters I had ever met. I was about to give in when he suddenly added, slowly and as if with some effort: "One must never set out on a Friday the thirteenth."
I looked at him. His eyes were avoiding me. He went on, as though he were ashamed of what he had said, "It's been five or six days now since the bandits have derailed the train. Don't you think that tonight ..."
At that moment, I really felt pity for him. But I was still too young not to have contempt for pity, and in my silly pride, I replied, "I've made up my mind. And I did promise. I'm leaving tonight. I'll see you at the station." He made no answer and left abruptly. And I didn't see him at the station.

The train rolled through the night with extraordinary smoothness. I didn't wake up until morning. Sunlight was playing on the windows, dissipating the usual dreams. We were heading into an endless gentle steppe. Then came the heat. By noon it had become a furnace.

Kaufmann was at the station. He took me back to his house. His daughter greeted us there and we spent the afternoon together. She was about thirty, with thin lips, broad shoulders and mousey hair; she wrote little short stories that were ferociously Voltairean. At that time I had the blush of youth and a look of innocence about me, and she thought she had fallen instantly in love with me. Kaufmann noticed all this, smiled, and led me off on a tour of the city. We spent the night in cabarets that scarcely lent themselves to the crystallization of pure love. In the very early morning (all along the main street old Russian coachmen were shivering with cold in box-coats that were green with age) we went to the *Pravda* office. Rotary printing presses dating from the time of Marinoni were grinding away. The sleepy foreman handed Kaufmann a dirty slip of paper. "We just received this message from Changchun."

The dispatch announced that the train from Harbin had been sabotaged two hundred kilometers from Mukden and that the bandits had abducted several Chinese and three Europeans. One of the latter was named Major Carlton. God forgive me, but I broke out laughing. Kaufmann looked at me, then said in a slightly pinched tone, "I don't see what you find funny in this piece of news."

I told him about my meeting with Carlton. It was his turn now for a hearty laugh. "This Carlton is an extraordinary fellow. They say that he used to work with Lawrence of Arabia. He's supposed to be one of the best agents in the British Intelligence Service. People talk about his fantastic exploits. He drinks alcohol like a child drinks milk, but he lived for months on the fringes of the Gobi, subsisting on a handful of rice per day. His superstitions have become legendary. He'd far rather have his right hand cut off than eat at a table set for thirteen .... Oh, he'll get out of it! It's not the first time! But the British Consulate will have to pay a heavy ransom if those bloody pirates happen to find out who he is."

Several more months went by. The next year I was in Cannes, at a little nightclub called Le Dolphin. Hildegarde was singing. Her beautiful bare arms were undulating like the neck of a swan.

She was wearing a long white dress and her sad voice reminded one of great lost passions. We were all letting ourselves be lulled by the cheap emotion; heavily nostalgic and a bit facile, it was carrying us helplessly away into the realms of a thousand dreams. Suddenly I saw Bill come in. He went over and leaned on the bar. When Hildegarde had finished singing I walked over to meet him. He was drinking a glass of Vittel water. He looked at me, smiling. "I've discovered the existence of the liver," he said.

We went outside. The night was balmy and we headed towards the Croisette. The sea was surging quietly, with soft little noises like the gentle moaning of a woman.

"I saw Papou, a month ago, in Djibouti. His wife came back to him. He beats her day and night. He accuses her of cheating on him with one of the Vosikis boys. But there are other things going on down there ... Mussolini's planes .... Now it's the Dance of Death for the Danakil ...."

There was a brief silence, and then suddenly he went on, "No doubt you had a good laugh on me, in Mukden. But .... In any case, I want you to know this: I was taken prisoner on the night of the fifteenth. I was freed on the night of the twenty-eighth. You count the days ..."

We sat down by the sea and remained there until dawn, watching the glimmering stars in the beautiful French night.

THE PERSIAN MIRROR

Thomas Pavel
translated by Michael Bullock

As employees of the university were entitled to a considerable reduction in tuition fees, Louis took a course in creative writing. His old essay on *Aloysius Kaspar, which he had translated into English with Barbara's help, had been rejected by the* Journal of Metaphysics *on the grounds that it was too philological while* Germanic Philology *considered it too philosophical. Since leaving France, Louis had not written again to his former thesis adviser, Jean-Paul Dionne. Everything connected with the MA thesis he had embarked upon in Bressac now seemed to him like a bad dream which he had not the least wish to remember. Since he was left with an obscure desire to say something about these experiences, he tried the literary route. On his return from a trip to Vancouver, where he had taken part in the National Librarians' Convention, he started to write the story required for the final course mark. In a few evenings and one weekend he put down on paper the following story, which he called "The Persian Mirror".*

Some time ago, in the neighbourhood of Nanaimo on Vancouver Island, I learned some remarkable details concerning the play of possibilities.

One humid summer evening, when I was driving through the forests of giant firs towards the centre of the island, I heard a persistent and rather loud crackling sound coming from around the left rear wheel. I stopped several times and examined the wheel and the muffler, but I could find no cause for the sound. Being worried about it, I made for the first hotel advertised by the roadside. The hotel, called Lake Y Resort, stood in the depths of the forest at the end of a tortuous private road several miles long. Even though darkness was falling I could see, attached to the hotel sign, a notice saying NOT OPEN. Since the gate was not padlocked I drove on. The hotel was situated at the juncture of the two arms of a Y-shaped alpine lake. The central building looked deserted, but the windows of one of the cabins scattered along the banks of the lake shone into the night. The cabin was occupied by an old Dutchman named Hermann, from whom I learned that the hotel had not been open for years. The owner, Mr Ormond, a wealthy retired geologist living in the British Properties in North Vancouver, wanted nothing to do with it. A clause in an imprudent contract prevented him from selling the establishment. The Dutchman lived on the premises and looked after the place. He understood my problem at once and invited me to spend the night in the cabin. Next day he would phone a garage at Port Alberni.

Next day was a Sunday; the nearest garages were closed. Seeing that I hesitated to drive as far as Parksville for fear of breaking down on the way, the Dutchman suggested I should spend another night at Lake Y. We walked around the property, which comprised the whole lake and the slopes of the surrounding mountains. I was astounded. Several times I asked my host how much this property might be worth, but each time I had to be satisfied with evasive and sometimes even ironic replies, from which it emerged that the owner could not hope to sell the estate except at a derisory price, because in spite of its considerable value the land and buildings were encumbered by such unusual conditions that no reasonable purchaser would invest money in them. I was more and more charmed by the place. I told myself that if the price was really so low, I might perhaps acquire the estate in spite of these mysterious obstacles, which there must certainly be some way of circumventing. The Dutchman, whom I told of my idea, tried in vain to dissuade me. The more my host sought to put me on guard against the inconveniences and even dangers of the region, the more I insisted on being put in touch with the hotel-owner, Mr Ormond. In the end, tired of hedging, Mr Hermann told me straight out that there was no chance of doing a deal. I wanted to know why. After many futile attempts to avoid answering my question, the old Dutchman finally confessed that he was himself involved in the contract that prevented the sale of the hotel.

The contract had been signed many years ago. Soon after arriving in Canada, Mr Hermann had been involved in some sort of business conflict with Mr Ormond. Eventually they reached a compromise which included an undertaking to maintain a thirty-year truce, and also the ceding to Mr Hermann in perpetuity of the enjoyment of the Lake Y property, except by mutual agreement and then only in the event of a renewed conflict after the thirty-year truce. The estate could not be sold except on condition that the sale did not interfere with Mr Hermann's life-interest, an unlikely situation. For his part, Mr Hermann had had to resign himself to living on Vancouver Island, spending most of his time on the banks of Lake Y.

The Dutchman's story did not shake my resolve. I was not displeased by the prospect of having someone to oversee the property in my absence. Mr Hermann seemed to be one of those polished and honest old men whose mere appearance is enough to make people believe that earlier generations respected their ideals better than the present one. My purchase of the property, I assured him, would make no difference to his current way of life. I had no thought of exploiting the property commercially, at least not for the moment, and if I ever tried to do so, it would only be with Mr Hermann's consent and advice . . .

To this proposition—for it was one—the Dutchman replied evasively, arguing that the present owner had never written to or visited him, so that he had got used to living with no thought that the estate belonged to anyone else. A new owner would mean a disturbance he was not prepared to put up with, unless, of course, the purchaser were willing to offer him exactly the same conditions as those he now enjoyed. That would mean, he explained, that the owner undertook never to visit the property, never to send anyone to look at it and that he, Mr Hermann, would retain all rights to it for life.

Somewhat taken aback by this reply, I let the matter drop. It was Mr Hermann who, later and of his own free will, spoke to me of what he called his "secret". For it was not by chance that he had chosen to live on this property and nowhere else. Mr Hermann *needed* this place. He explained the virtues of Lake Y to me in detail. The vast winding valley containing this lake of glacial origin was situated at the epicentre of the most powerful negative magnetic zone in North America. The magnetic effect was intensified even further by the quality of the crystalline quartz of which the rocks were composed. I am not very well up in geology, and I didn't understand these explanations very clearly, but Mr Hermann's tone of voice as he described the lake made an unpleasant impression on me. A little later, when I had learned the Dutchman's "secret", it struck me that he might just as well have been alluding to the magical properties of Y-shaped lakes. The ancient Iranians thought that these lakes communicated with the centre of the world. According to Simon the Magus, the Celestial Tiberiad is this shape. In our own day, the Nootka Indians still believe that the universe emerged from between the arms of such a lake. The very letter Y itself is heavily charged with occult significance: according to certain authors, it represents the three spokes of the cosmic wheel through whose centre passes the great axle that makes the stars turn. According to others—and the two interpretations are not incompatible—this letter, having the reversed shape of a woman with parted legs, represents temptation, desire and the generative energies. It is no coincidence, by the way, that the name Ysolde begins with this letter.

The Dutchman informed me that he was carrying out scientific research and took me to see a laboratory he had set up in the cellar of the main building. Installations that seemed to have served for alchemical procedures were mingled in confusion with electrical appliances with numerous dials and consoles. It was easy to see that Mr Hermann was in the mood to take me into his confidence. When we returned to the cabin I asked him how he had come to the island and what had started him on his investigations. He had to start at the beginning.

He was born in 1912 in Groningen. His father, of German extraction, died when the child was only five. His mother left him in the care of an orphanage and disappeared. Being very gifted, he completed his schooling and won a scholarship to Leyden University, where he enrolled in geology. On the completion of his studies, in 1936, he was taken on by a big international oil company for which he prospected, generally with success.

He travelled a great deal, especially in Europe and the Middle East. Like all his colleagues, it was his habit on his trips to buy useless exotic objects to serve as mementoes of his wanderings. One day, in the souk at Isfahan, a tattered old merchant ushered him into a small windowless room at the back of his shop and, after many salaams and with great circumspection, showed him an ancient mirror framed in pewter and decorated with lapis-lazuli. Contrary to his habit, Mr Hermann's servant and interpreter, a lively adolescent with big black eyes, only translated part of the merchant's hurried, breathless words. After a sentence which the latter hissed with his open left hand raised above his head, the boy turned pale and went out without a word. Later, he stubbornly refused to talk about this episode. Left alone with the merchant, of whose gibberish he understood nothing, Mr Hermann examined the mirror, which he considered beautiful although too small and tarnished to serve any other purpose than to decorate a corner of the wall. They agreed on a price in sign language. The merchant tried to take advantage of the opportunity to sell off a tattered parchment written in unknown characters, but Mr Hermann would have nothing to do with it, which he later regretted. He took the mirror and hung it on his bedroom wall. When his servant saw the object he evinced extreme terror and subsequently, every time his domestic duties compelled him to walk past it, he turned his head away and carefully closed his eyes. Mr Hermann had to dust the mirror himself; the reflecting surface remained greenish but the pewter regained its shine and an inscription became visible finely engraved around the encrusted stones.

A few months later, a friend dropped in to see him. The friend was a professor of ancient history at the University of Leyden and was on his way to the archaeological excavations at Persepolis. Mr Hermann showed him the mirror and the inscription. The historian could not say whether the object was valuable or whether it was junk. But he assured Mr Hermann that, if it was a fake, it was a remarkable piece of work: it displayed all the characteristics of the craft work of the late Sixteenth Century influenced by the calligraphers of Tabriz. As for the inscription, the archaeologist found it very strange. It was written in ancient Persian with Zend characters, which suggested that the craftsman who engraved it must have been a Parsee, which was very uncommon. The text said (roughly): "My name is Birth and Departure. The day of desire pronounces the appropriate words." The archaeologist had no idea what it meant. In order to find out, you would have to go to an expert in the history of magic, he commented. But there could be no doubt that there must have been tablets or a parchment that went with the mirror and contained the magic formulas to which the engraved text referred. The parchment which the merchant had tried to sell along with the mirror! thought Mr Hermann. Next day he went back to the market and tried to find the old merchant, but he lost his way in the maze of narrow, teeming streets and had to return home empty-handed.

Shortly afterwards he was transferred to Egypt, where the company had been prospecting fruitlessly for some years. Although still young, he already enjoyed the confidence of his superiors, who frequently sent him to reach a decision in tricky situations. Thus, following his advice, the company abandoned any further search for oil in the Egyptian desert.

In Cairo he made the acquaintance of an Irish teacher, Margaret Ryan, with whom he fell in love. For a time he imagined he could not live without her. Touched by the young geologist's feelings, Margaret loved him in her turn. Margaret's father, the manager of the local branch of Lloyd's Insurance, supported his daughter's feelings. The two young people spent long evenings on the terrace of the luxurious villa built by Lloyd's at Heliopolis. They held hands and gazed silently into each other's eyes. Unfortunately, Margaret's dream was to return to Ireland, settle there and never again leave her homeland. Moreover, she could not imagine her future husband ever leaving her alone, not even for a few days. This amounted to a refusal to allow Hermann to continue his vagabond profession of geologist. Margaret's father had enough contacts in the financial world of Dublin to find his future son-in-law a quiet and well paid position. But Hermann did not see things that way. At that time his work was his life and nothing could have seemed to him more grotesque than to bury himself somewhere in financial administration, tied to a woman's apron strings. Furthermore, Margaret, a fervent Catholic, insistently demanded that he should be converted. Hermann, who was very proud of being a free thinker, wouldn't hear of it. Thus he was forced to the conclusion that it was impossible for him to marry Margaret. Nevertheless, he loved her more and more deeply and could not spend a single day far from her and her eyes. He postponed a decision as long as he could. However, the report he was making for his company was finished and his superiors sent him on a new mission to Venezuela. He made all the arrangements for his departure, even though he knew very well that he would not be capable of moving away from Margaret and that even if he managed to take the train for Alexandria he would return to his beloved next day to ask for forgiveness and to stay with her. The certainty that his love was stronger than his decisions troubled him intensely. He caught himself cursing his feelings for Margaret and realized that in the depths of his heart he felt a secret, impotent hatred for the beautiful Irishwoman.

A prey to these contradictory emotions, he was walking up and down his room muttering incomprehensible, broken phrases. It was several seconds before his absent-minded gaze, falling on the Persian mirror, discovered that the reflecting surface which was usually opaque and veined with rust, was gradually clearing. For the first time since he bought it, Hermann was able to see himself in the mirror. He scarcely recognized himself. The pale, gloomy face that looked at him was not his own. He passed a hand across his eyes. To his terror, the face in the mirror did not make the same gesture. Hermann winked one eye. The man in the mirror remained impassive, looking at him fixedly. In his eyes could be read severity, a touch of sadness as before a separation and, from time to time, a flash of ferocious irony. Fascinated, Hermann dared not move away from the wall. Nevertheless, he took his eyes off the shining surface and turned his head. The room around him was dark and cool. When his eyes went back to the man in the mirror, the latter was no longer staring at him so intently. Looking slightly absent-minded, even bored, the stranger was turning slowly away. He remained for a moment with his back turned, then made for the depths of the mirror and disappeared. In a few seconds the surface was again submerged in greenish water and rust.

For a moment Hermann was flabbergasted, but he quickly regained his composure. He had only one thought: to leave, to get out as quickly as possible, without saying goodbye to anyone. He interrupted his servants' siesta and told them to pack his things immediately. Before nightfall he was on the train to

Alexandria. The following day he boarded a French boat for Marseilles from where, after a few days' wait, he got a passage on a liner sailing to South America. During the voyage he did not think for one instant of his abandoned matrimonial projects. The files he had to study before arriving in Caracas were so voluminous that he had barely enough time to familiarize himself with his new task. In Caracas several months of desperately hard work awaited him, alleviated by occasional drinking bouts in the company of his colleagues. He was so exhausted by the work that he had to request leave. The tropical climate invited him to rest. He made the acquaintance of a young Panamanian woman of Japanese descent, with whom he had a pleasant adventure. Since his bank account was well stocked he prolonged his leave. He did not remember Margaret until the following year, when he came across her photograph in a back number of an Argentine society magazine. As it had been a poor season for events involving royalty or the film world, the magazine had been forced to fill its pages with less spectacular reports. An article about recent marriages in the oil world starred radiant Texans, a beautiful Venezuelan divorcée and sheiks in burnouses. A few smaller photographs showed couples belonging to the technocratic and financial background, such as the touching marriage of Miss Ryan, the daughter of a leading Irish banker, to a wealthy geologist, a marriage that crowned a tender friendship of more than two years. The photo showed Margaret, moved and happy, beside a young man who looked like Hermann, or at least like Hermann before he left Egypt, since he had meanwhile grown a beard. He showed the photo to his new girlfriend, but she noticed nothing special about it. Nevertheless, several details worried Hermann. According to the magazine, Margaret's friendship with her husband had begun two years before the marriage. Now, this was precisely the time when Hermann had first met the Irish girl. He simply could not believe that she had not been entirely frank with him and had encouraged another suitor at the same time as himself. Of course, he told himself, the information given by the magazine could not be regarded as completely reliable: "two years" might be a misprint or a sentimental exaggeration which ought to read "two months". Or it was even possible, after all, that Margaret had hidden this suitor's existence from him either because she attributed little importance to him, or because she hesitated to make Hermann jealous to no purpose. There remained the fact that the "other" was also a geologist, a rather surprising coincidence. Furthermore, on examining the photograph more closely, Hermann observed on the young husband's left cheek a small blemish close to the angle of the jaw, just where Hermann himself had a similar mark. To check this peculiarity, Hermann shaved his sideburns. The mark was no longer there. He looked for old photos of himself: on the ones he had kept there was nothing to be seen, either because the shot had been taken at the wrong angle or because the picture was too faded and faint to discover such a fine detail. Nevertheless, he was certain that he had had this mark: in secondary school he had put up with a good deal of teasing from his schoolfellows on the subject. Margaret used sometimes to kiss him by the ear, whispering that she liked his birthmark. The thing that made Hermann understand the improbable transformation, however, was the look in the eyes of the newly-wed husband, who was scrutinizing him with the same intensity, the same melancholy and the same ferocity as a year earlier, when he had stared at him from the other side of the Persian mirror.

Thus Hermann realized that through this object he had come into possession of an uncommon power: he could separate himself from his desires by dividing himself into two distinct but very similar beings: one who brought his desire to fruition in the world, the other who, freed from this desire, continued his original trajectory. The question as to which of the two was the real Hermann did not even present itself. It seemed to him obvious that he was the real one himself, the one who, without any break, had all the time had full consciousness of himself. The other could only be a sort of phantom, the materialization of a rejected desire, a being devoid of autonomy and substance.

It immediately occurred to him that the strange faculty he had just discovered he possessed could surely be put to use. If, in fact, every time he was poisoned by a desire, a "sick" Hermann II separated physically from Hermann I and naturally led the life which the latter desired but was unable to put into effect, would this not result in Hermann II being happy and Hermann I cured?

The war caught Hermann at a loose end in Sweden. He learned fresh details concerning the mirror from a Jewish orientalist recently saved from Germany by a Swedish network to which, like everyone else, Hermann subscribed. The scholar informed Hermann that every detail of the mirror, each of the interlacing ornaments decorated with lapis-lazuli, had a precise magic significance and that the rules for using the object depended strictly upon these details. The decoration of each mirror was quite different from that of any other and there were thousands of them. The embellishment played the role of a code in cipher, with the result that, although it bestowed a certain power upon its owner, it became harmless in the hands of others. Very probably the Isfahan merchant's parchment had contained the mirror's code and it was not beyond the bounds of possibility that, with a little leisure and patience, one might have succeeded in interpreting it correctly. That did not mean, however, that one could have used the mirror, for most often these parchments contain errors inserted intentionally, the correction of which was only passed on orally from one owner to the next so as to provide increased protection for their unique property. It was possible that the merchant knew these oral corrections, but Hermann should not regret his failure to obtain them, for very often the long tradition through which they had passed distorted them and filled them with new errors impossible to detect. In short, there was almost no hope of ever being able to employ a Persian mirror according to the rules of the art. In fact, even some Iranian magicians complained of this intolerable situation. The most honest had gone so far as to ask help from modern disciplines, such as comparative philology and the history of religions, in order to re-establish the original formulas. Despite considerable efforts, in which the scholar had himself participated, the humanist sciences had unfortunately been unable to assist the occult sciences. This symptomatic cleft filled the old scholar with the gloomiest presentiments regarding the future of the vast and noble domain of the inexact sciences. But in the final analysis, even if they had possessed an entirely accurate text of the incantations, this would not have solved Hermann's problem, because the power of these Persian mirrors was strictly limited: they could only be used for relatively simple tasks, such as the diagnosis of skin diseases, the prediction of the immediate future (and that only in the presence of the interested party), or the least efficacious kinds of love charms. The operation in which Hermann had been involved could in no way be explained by the ordinary properties of the mirror. It was more probable that the sheet of quartz of which it was composed had inexplicably catalysed enormous forces which alone might have explained such an unusual incident. As to the nature of these forces, the scholar admitted his ignorance and seemed to doubt whether any acceptable explanation existed. He left Hermann perplexed.

Around this time, Hermann became friendly with a young German aristocrat named Dietrich von Rechberg, an attaché at the embassy in Stockholm, whose carefree and eccentric character was in strong contrast to his own. Dietrich was vaguely interested in mineralogy for philosophical reasons. He planned to compose a complete refutation of everything written by Novalis concerning the mineral kingdom. He was interested in Hermann's story above all because it featured the mysterious properties of quartz. He urged his friend to undertake research in this direction. In 1943, when thanks to his family's contacts he became responsible for scientific relations with Sweden, he drafted a long and fantastic report aimed at proving to the German War Ministry that the key to the future and to victory lay hidden in quartz and that if they wished to possess it they must give generous support to the experiments of his friend Hermann. He was the first not to believe his eyes when the grant arrived. The payments, which continued with exemplary regularity until 1945, enabled them to live well and buy the prettiest girls in Stockholm. With part of the money they set up a small laboratory in which they studied, with no startling results, the piezo-electric properties of quartz. It was not until after the war and Dietrich's departure that Hermann believed he could glimpse a way ahead. But he lacked the money to continue his research, and as surly spirits were picking on him because of his friendship with a representative of the Third Reich, he considered it more prudent to emigrate to Canada and change his name.

***

Having reached this point in his story, Louis had to leave Windsor for a week. When he returned he could not recapture his enthusiasm. He re-read the story several times without finding a satisfactory continuation and ending. He had originally intended to make Hermann sink to the lowest levels of society, to show how dangerous it is to distrust one's own feelings. The former geologist moved among thieves and drug traffickers in Halifax and ended up getting three years in prison. Once inside, he almost completely lost his memory. His personality disintegrated to the point of becoming unrecognizable. After being taken in by charitable monks on leaving prison, he was rehabilitated in a Montreal monastery. After a year, believing that he was now capable of earning his living on his own, the monks recommended him for the position of caretaker at a motel in British Columbia. When the undertaking went bankrupt he was allowed to live on the premises, of which he continued to act as caretaker. His disordered imagination invented the conflict with the former owner, Mr Ormond, whom he identified with Margaret's husband. In the underground laboratory Hermann was preparing his revenge.

This over-conventional solution irritated Louis. He tried to reinforce the mythological side of the story. The names Ormond and Hermann recalled Ormuz and Ahriman, the irreconcilable adversaries of Iranian mythology. This went quite well with the Persian origin of the mirror. Louis actually thought of giving

Margaret as a wife to Mr Ormond and provoking a conflict between the two rivals. Instead of going down hill, Hermann could have become a geologist with Ormond's company in Alberta. Discovering that he is serving his own creation (because in Hermann's eyes, Ormond was merely an alter ego, an emanation of his love for Margaret), the Dutchman is seized with rage. The description of the conflict kept quite close to the Iranian myth. (Hence the idea of a truce, introduced at the beginning of the story.)

A third variant emphasized the actual proliferation of possible beings. In his laboratory, Hermann succeeded in constructing a magic mirror of immense power, with whose aid he sent out across the world representatives of his increasingly violent and cruel desires. His creations engendered others and bit by bit the globe was invaded by the spawn of this demiurge. This outcome did not satisfy Louis. Passions capable of engendering their own bearers within our universe was a nice idea, but in the strictest sense of the word, a desire is not realized *until it creates another world, destroying the real universe*. One does not satisfy one's desires by creating one's double, but by destroying everything around one that is opposed to them, in order to establish not another ego, but another cosmos.

One night, during this period of uncertainty, Louis had all sorts of bad dreams.

He saw himself in rags, begging from a richly dressed man who was standing in front of a big house with columns. He was refused alms and driven away. He then dreamed of a beach by the ocean, along which two naked adolescents were running hand in hand, a boy and a girl, their faces marked by fear and shame. Finally, he dreamed of a blind old man who offered him water and whose trembling hands were unable to hold the jug, so that the water spilled over Louis's feet.

The following morning he woke early and said to himself that perhaps it was not up to him to decide whether we live in a world permeable to our desires or not. His story had no end, simply because it could not have one. Reassured by this thought, he gave up the idea of finishing the story and withdrew from the creative writing course.

THE METAMORFALSIS

Jacques Brossard
translated by Basil Kingstone

The Trial

I am the clerk of the court. In other words, mainly a stenographer. But my desk is very fine, with drawers and all. Much better than the other courts, in my opinion. So is our courtroom: very clean white walls, real light, natural air and no dust. The judge's bench is distinctive, it's made of walnut (I think) with ironwork, and reminds me of Spain or Latin America.

Above the bench, hanging on the wall where they used to hang a crucifix, is a great shining round copper tray, Inca work, portraying twelve little gods in bas-relief all around the edge and a big god in the middle bearing the insignia of power. When the judge is seated, the tray looks like a Buddhist halo around his head. But the judge is ageless, tiny and skinny—more Hindu in that respect, though not in any other.

And now here come the judge. Or here comes the judges, if you prefer. I use these forms because the court used to consist of three judges, a presiding judge and two assistants. Now the judge preserves the legal fiction of this trinity by adding, after he has pronounced sentence, "I concur" and "Je suis du même avis."

"Clerk of the court," the judge says, "read the charges. Without flourishes; I don't like flourishes."

"On the night of the 30th to 31st of September, in a room which most of the twelve accused have described incorrectly—"

"Don't try to influence me," says the judge; "stick to the facts."

"—furniture was destroyed, decorations knocked off the wall, and a corpse dragged around in a walnut coffin. Twelve persons who don't know each other and describe in differing terms—"

"I'll be the judge of that," yells the judge. "I get the flesh of the case, you get the bare bones."

"—are separately accused of this crime and this slaughter. They all plead self-defence and claim they don't know each other."

"That's better," says the judge. "Are there no witnesses?"

"Only the accused, your honour. That's the same thing."

"That's my line. Call the first one."

1. A strong, rather thickset man of about forty, brush cut, self-confident, abrupt gestures, brown suit.

"... pale walls, an average-sized room, not much furniture. A fine room your lordship. A huge chest in the middle. To my great surprise, it opened by itself.

"Well, I thought *I* was rich, milord, but I've nothing compared to that treasure chest! It would have scandalized my poor father, who believed in work; a hundred times more than the super-lottery! Enough to dazzle my wife and satisfy even my children forever! Enough to buy fifty per cent plus one of our elected representatives, enough to become prime minister! Oh, judge, if you'd seen that!"

"Don't mix me up in this," says the judge. "Go on. You bore me already."

"In a sea of gold, silver and copper coins from the time of Julius Sneezer, Bill the Conk, Louis XIV the Sin King fund and our own dear Lizzie, there was a hoard of communion cups, ciboria and monstrances of solid gold, studded with medallions and stuffed with hundred-dollar bills. Then there was—"

"I am not a bit interested," says the judge. "You're keeping me waiting. What did you do?"

"Suddenly it all flew into the air, coins, bracelets, communion cups, ciboria, necklaces, hurled in all directions by a muffled explosion. And I could hardly believe my eyes, a big black feller stood up, in a coppery-red turban, but filthy dirty. They're all filthy dirty, your honour, niggers, Indians, Ayrabs, Chinks, the lot of 'em. A huge black feller in a red turban, his arms crossed, with a long scimitar in his left hand, all shining and sparkling. I mean, what would you have done? He looked at me, laughing—"

"—with his white teeth?" the judge asks. "Nothing. I wouldn't have been there. Go on."

"I've never been afraid of anything. I hurled myself at this apparition as if at a scarecrow; he didn't flinch. Then I bravely seized his scimitar and I hit him—oh, I hit him, I hit him! I don't remember what happened after that."

"I do," says the judge, his eyes shining. "Oh, I remember! Lock him up. Next."

2. Eighteen or twenty, hair dyed blonde, very pretty, long fluttering lashes, slim waist, well-filled sweater, elephant pants in chamois leather, a lovely voice, a silver necklace in a striking simple design.

"... a big room with beautiful white walls, such as you see in castles in Spain. And a white rug, thick and comfortable. And engravings, I think. But above all, at the far end, there was a huge trunk, its stained wood and dark ironwork contrasting sharply with the whitewashed walls.

"And from somewhere came a breeze; it smelled good, it smelled fresh like undergrowth in a wood in spring, but with scents of lilac, honeysuckle and jasmine, full of memories of Lake Maggiore and the Riviera. I thought I was dreaming: slowly the lid of the trunk was opening.

"Inside, there was a great round mirror framed in silvergilt, and the glass itself had orange glints. In it I saw first, wavering as if at the bottom of a well, the curtains of a bed with spiral bedposts and a canopy. I recognized a room in the palace of Ferdinand and Isabella at Santiago de Compostela. A very pretty young woman was combing her fair hair in front of the half-open casement and looking at the sky over the Dominican monastery."

"My child," says the judge, "I don't like travelogues, they bore me."

But the witness is miles away. "The sky was cloudless and the sun was sumptuous and liquid as the sound of the flute or clarinet flooded the park at the chateau of Chantilly, splashed and sparkled down the elm trees of the Duke of Illwater and ran off into the green pond where a fair-haired young woman in a very low-cut lilac dress was looking at her reflection.

"Suddenly I heard galloping horses! Horsemen appeared, with red hair and moustaches, wearing mail coats and waving guns like Indians, long hunting rifles inlaid with mother-of-pearl and ivory. They were galloping towards me!

"The mirror suddenly shattered and I screamed, for in the room where I was kneeling on the rug, one of those warriors was standing in front of me, pointing his rifle at me! I was quicker than him, reached for his waist and grabbed his hunting knife—and then I don't remember what happened."

"Pity," said the judge, "that was the best part. Luckily, my child, *I* remember very well. Put her on bread and water. Next."

3. Twenty or twenty-five, rather stupid looking, long sweater, struts and snaps his fingers, an insolent expression, dirty jeans, sometimes fire in his eyes.

"Well, there was this huge trunk at the back of the room, lit by a big red spotlight. Except it wasn't a trunk at all, your honour, there was a super Ferrari sports car in it! Nothing cheapo about it, black and silver, no chrome, aggressive looking and so beautiful it gave you a hard on, your honour! Man, if the gang had been there, we'd have had a real party! They'd have given me anything to be able to use her. And what an engine! Like thunder! Because she started purring. In fact, I think she turned towards me and aimed her two big lit-up glass breasts at my eyes, yellow lights like the spotlight.

"Very beautiful, but she resisted. When I tried to open the door, it was jammed. I pulled, I pushed, I got it open just a crack and it closed on my fingers. So of course I got angry and punched her on the hood. And the hood sprung open and the whole machine started shaking.

"Under the hood, your honour, there was a tangle of barbed wire, as sharp as knives or wolves' teeth. I was good and mad—fooled again! Every time you buy something, they fool you.

"After that, I don't know what I did. Tore out some barbed wire, I think. My hands were all bloody. I broke some windows. I rushed at the doors and started scratching them—"

"I know, I know," says the judge. "You're dumb. Lock him up. Next."

"On second thought," says the judge, "clerk of the court, read the record."

I do so.

"Hm," says the judge. "Not great. They weren't observant and they didn't understand. It isn't like that at all. Still, let's go on, we'll see. Next."

4. Thirty, burning eyes, hair streaming in the wind—except that the windows are shut—square-jawed, leather jacket, bursts of violence in his voice, tendency to clench his fists or hold his arms above his head like torches.

"... not very big, but it's true I never have enough room. On the right-hand wall was a black eagle with wings outspread, by Mathieu, on an old-gold background and across from it were portraits of a jurist and a revolutionary theologian of the 16th century. That I liked.

"In front of me the red setting Sun exploded in anger against the death of the Day. A tall Dais in iron and dark wood stood amid Stormy Gleams, the Sun cast across it the spiral Rays of its flaming Lances, and the Wood and the Iron caught fire like the volcanic Forges, deep in the Earth, of our old Gods." (His thunderous voice calls for capitals.) "Oh, Learned Judge, could you have resisted the dizzying call of that Sun and that Dais?"

"Easily," says the judge. "But you interest me, go on."

"I stepped up onto the platform. Before me the rug became a vast crowd from which, by the power of my gaze, thousands of heads emerged like green diamonds. I raised my arms and preached the truth to them. The red sun spread over them silvergilt rattles, gold coins and omega crosses. They acclaimed me and their tumult seemed to shake the platform. 'Crown him, crown him!' shouted the frenzied crowd. It was my triumph; I would be a minister, ambassador, president, I would be king! I would be a judge, dean, academician, I would be me!"

"Mein Gott!" cries the judge. "Are you thereof certain? Come you to your senses, otherwise will you up locked be! Oh, that like I not; way out in left field are you." He stands up, all excited, then sits down again. "Schnell, schnell! Bystrie, bystrie, okonshaniye! K'wai! Vite!"

"I've finished. The platform moved under my feet, as if it were trying to open. I climbed down. The platform was a lid, like that of a huge trunk, and I saw it open, very slowly. Utter darkness, utter silence. I looked in. Nothing. Just a smell of damp earth. I leaned right in. Then, horror of horrors, Herr Doktor, I felt myself seized, grabbed hold of by three icy hands with bones that tore me!

"I struggled against them, I tried to free myself from the burning hooks of those skeletal hands, from which there now came flashes like needles! I grabbed one of the two right hands, tugged with all my strength—and pulled it off! With this hand of bone and needles, I struck out at the darkness in the trunk, I struck, I struck—My Lord, I forget the rest."

"Good move," says the judge. "It's very unpleasant. Lick him up. Knockst."

5. Unkempt faded chestnut hair, could be sixteen or sixty, long dirty dress with a little faded flower pattern, big jiggling white breasts that are much more alive than her (blue?) eyes, slightly greasy dark circles under her eyes, nostrils breathing hard, sloppy posture, slow movements.

"... bourgeois apartment, much too full of all sorts of furniture, pictures—and books, heaps of books; all very square. A nice rug, though, and quiet. I like it quiet, it's great for Freddy's guitar." (Sixteen then.) "But the big plant at the back of the room, chum, that was something, man—"

"I am not your chum or your man," says the judge. "And pull your dress up before they fall out. All right, now tell me about the plant."

"There was this huge wooden planter, and in the brown earth was this magnificent orange plant growing out of it, like a kinda giant sunflower. And it turned towards me and bent down to me, offering me its heart on long petals. I sat on its soft cushion and felt myself lifted up to the sky, while I stuck my hands in the thick material whose orange and red were beating with intense pulsations." (She stops for breath; she loses it easily.) "Then it gently set me down in the huge planter whose dense luxuriant forest welcomed me at once—"

"Woman," says the judge, "you have fine flowering breasts, but botany bores me."

"Colours and perfumes danced in their pretty pink mist. Man, I felt high!" (Or perhaps "I felt alive," I'm not sure.) "I'd have liked all my buddies to come in me—I mean come with me, into that wood. Near a lake I hung my dress on the spruce branch and lay down naked under an olive tree and rolled around in the moss and nibbled mushrooms." (She hikes her dress up.) "But I felt more and more nervous. I was dying of the heat and sweating so much I had to wipe myself off several times with big banana leaves.

"I'd have liked to sleep but I couldn't stay still and I had to walk. Some heliotropes told me where to go, but they said it wrong, or else I heard it wrong, because I ended up in dense bushes and got lost. When I got out it was dark and I was in a stand of dead trees. Suddenly I heard a crackling behind me—

"Oh sir, what a horrible wood! Branches and twigs and tangled dead limbs" (she is spitting, coughing and gasping for breath) "stood there and jostled each other in the half-dark, cracking and creaking and chattering and sniggering and waving about like strings of bones—they were getting closer and waving their thin sharp hard ends at me, like whips. I screamed. I picked up a big knotty twisted branch off the ground—"

"I know," says the judge. "That's enough. Woman, you're tiresome. Put her on bread and water. Next."

6. Twenty-five, reddish-black moustache and beard and long hair as part of the image, red leather jacket, green velvet corduroy pants, fists on hips, aggressive voice and expression.

"Yes, a bourgeois apartment, but a fine poster by Mathieu and three or four not bad books: a pictorial history of screwing, red thoughts, white negroes—"

"Skip it," says the judge. "We are keeping an eye on that, thank you."

"Anyway, the other books were dull and I had no time to lose. There was this big black trunk at the back of the room, with complicated ironwork like weeping onion jacks and a sort of Japanese flag blushing to rise over it.

"An enormously patriotic trunk, enough to blow up a two-headed government, two headless parliaments, four TV stations, eight major newspapers, sixteen skyscrapers, thirty or more banks and all my alma maters as well—enough to wake up thousands of goddamn finks, sons of bitches of speculators and cowardly politicians, stinking rotten sold-out whores, all those fucking paranoids—"

"Order, order!" says the judge. "You haven't understood a thing. You're talking too much. Get to the point!"

"We're coming to it, comrade."

"I am not your comrade," says the judge sharply. "I'm under surveillance. What about the trunk?"

"—enough to wake up all the dreamers and all the idlers as well! Don't worry, I'm coming to the damn trunk! I didn't even have to blow the lock off; it just suddenly opened by itself.

"I hardly had time to look in it. The whole thing blew up, and me and the room with it, and I went flying among English flags, bankers, guns, boots, butchers—and my father's braces, and skirts and flowers, waving the dress my little sister was wearing the night we found her dead—among people shot or bludgeoned to death, tortured or crucified—with workers, poets and peasants, with judges, comrade—and I was holding my blind girlfriend by the hand and yelling love songs to the bourgeois, the infantrymen, the soldiers in the tanks, the astronauts, shaking my fist at the moon and the—"

"That is not in the least," says the judge, "not in the least how you ended up. You're being ridiculous. Order!"

"—I fell back to earth, your honour, into the open carcass of a half-rotten horse, into the slimy blood of the horsemen and noble lords we had ripped open, into the warm blood of my bosses, my parents, all my comrades—and at last we were going to sleep together in the rich shroud of our earth, our mother conquered forever, we were going to—"

"You are going to do nothing," the judge exclaims, "nothing at all, except conclude. Or I will have you shot."

"In the trunk of my dreams, your honour, there were twelve soldiers armed with bayonets. Twelve sword points at my chest.

But I wasn't having that. I tore off the youngest soldier's bayonet and stuck it in—I don't remember any more."

"I do," says the judge, getting his breath back. "All right, lock him up."

The judge bends down behind the bench; all that can be seen of him is his wig. Then he straightens up, lifts his elbow a couple of times, and clears his throat.

"All right, next."

7. Tall, rather fat, forty-five, suit that tries to be in style, dark glasses, a deceiving appearance of respectability, gesticulates, loud voice.

"It wasn't a trunk, your honour, it was more like a Gothic altar, high and very long, with lancet arches carved into the wood. Yet it wasn't an altar either, it was a big bed with a Polish canopy—"

"I like Polish women," says the judge. "And Russian, Hungarian, Romanian and Czech women." He lifts his elbow.

"A high round canopy, red or orange with flaming fringes. And in that bed, your honour, the most marvellous sight!" He stops, wipes his lips and is silent.

"Well?" says the judge. "The beauty in the bed?"

"Red and white, with a body like a goddess and the most voluptuous freckled skin in the world!"

"That's your opinion," says the judge. He lifts his elbow, drops his glass, curses, opens drawers and slams them shut. "All right, go on."

"She got up very slowly, stood on the bed and stretched out her arms to me. She moved like a great cat, your honour! So supple, and the way she rolled her hips and displayed her body! Under her light rustling nightgown, she was naked and perfumed! A burning, dizzying perfume, enough to turn your head—"

"My head never turns," says the judge. "Straight ahead. I'm reason itself."

"... the fascinating gaze of her green almond eyes, with tints of copper and gold in her irises! And the greedy smile on her full lips like a man-eating beast's! She raised her arms and shed her garment. Ooh! Big bouncy breasts like gourds, with pink daisies ..."

(I lost the thread because I was listening. Sorry.) "Stretched out on top of her, I was learning the secrets of their tender jiggling. Her nipples sat up so nicely when I nibbled them, and they quivered under the vibrations of my fingers, my tongue and my—"

"Hey," says the judge, "you're dwelling on this too much, my friend. Get on with it."

(Carried away.) "An ass whose curves would make you dizzy and get you doing the craziest things! And how they bounced when I slapped them! A slightly wild patch of fur, a bit too tickly, I admit—but what an artist on the flute, regular or transverse—what a greyhound, what a panther!"

"That's enough!" says the judge. "This is a courthouse, not a whorehouse, we deal with cases and not boxes. Don't be telling titty stories to a dignified triboobal."

(Obsessed.) "She was clitoral like no woman Casanova ever had! Suction, friction, squelching, squeezing! The tides of Brittany, the convulsions of Africa, the whirlpools of the Sargasso! And what a mould, what a sheath, what a scabbard! So soft and firm I leapt for joy, and plunged in with all the ardour—"

"Listen," says the judge, "you're abusing my patience. Spare me your fantasies, I am not the least bit interested; I have enough of my own. Cut it short, or you're for the guillotine."

"But your honour, I was climbing, I was rising—"

"Doesn't sound like it to me," says the judge.

"I was climbing staircases, flying over crevasses and valleys, penetrating.... But the best part, your honour, was her fingernails. Oh, marvellous! Very long sharp nails, a virtuoso's with modulations and variations, pauses and crescendos! I shuddered, I panted in bliss, accompanying her on her own quivering keyboard! I have short nails, but my fingertips—"

"I said conclude," says the judge. "At the end you and the redheaded tigress were standing up—"

"Yes, voluptuously embraced, interlaced, intertwined, entangled, encrusted in our hot bodies and her perfumes .... Her nails moved across my back with growing insistence—I felt their thin sharp points scratch me, claw me, furrow me deeper and deeper. She was panting as I had been just before, but now there was a harsh growling tone in her warm voice which began to worry me.

"So, with such strength as I had left, I tore myself free of her arms, I slowly loosened her hands from my body—and then, sir, I saw what she had done! I saw her hooked claws, her paws streaming with my blood, and the thin strips of torn-off skin. Oh, the whore! So—"

"Yes, I know," says the judge. "I knew already. That was an easy one. Lock him up, next."

8. A young woman of twenty-five or thirty, tall and very slender, long dark hair down to her waist, translucent skin, burning eyes but a very gentle expression, slightly nervous movements, a jersey dress, very slim ankles.

"... a marvellous light; the room was light and warm, very sunny, a rug and white walls, books bound in many colours. I felt comfortable there.

"I could have believed I was outdoors and waking up in the mildness of the rising sun among the autumn leaves, in response to their last bright colours. I felt so happy that I closed my eyes and opened my arms ..."

"Young lady," says the judge, "you're very attractive, but I have a lot to do. Wasn't there a trunk?"

(Absent-mindedly.) "Yes, sir, there was a huge trunk, the colour of maple sugar or burned caramel. It was open. I went up to it on tiptoe. It was fabulous.

"In the broad daylight I found in it my picture books, an alphabet from which I learned to love Europe, my black doll with marvellous big eyes, my lopsided teddy bear smiling with all his scars, plastic dolls, doll houses, a magic lantern, a scooter, skipping ropes, glass and agate marbles, a swarthy Spanish dancer, the Little Prince and Prince Eric, tennis balls, a mirror, dice, lots of photos, my first—"

"Young lady," said the judge, "wasn't there a sled?"

(Smiling.) "A toboggan, sir. I didn't recognize it at first. But it was so bright and the snow around me was so white, so pure, so dazzling in the midday sun! The tall pines of the Laurentians were so warmed by it that they silently withheld their shadows and shed their ice. The slope seemed very gentle; I let myself slide down on the toboggan. I didn't see the time pass.

(Worried.) "The sun was red in the brief twilight. And I saw this very tall dark man; he was wearing a fur coat as dark as his beard and he was coming towards me, very slowly. He was looking at me. I didn't move. I felt I had been waiting for him since the beginning of the world, and I gave him a welcoming smile ..."

"I don't like sentimentality," said the judge. "Spare me the next scene, young lady, and get to the point."

(Her apparent fragility fascinates me. In fact, it distracted me. I pick up the thread:)

"... and fell on my back, my arms half folded over my hips. I hurt my head. I managed to kneel; sharp-edged stones just showed through the snow, and around one of them the snow was soaking up little droplets of blood. Sharp-edged stones and thick tree roots. Trees I couldn't see, no doubt torn out long ago. Why had they torn them out? And why hadn't they removed the stones?"

"I don't know, young lady," the judge yawns.

"I took a root, sir, and tried to raise one of the stones. The root was brown and speckled with russet and—"

"Yes, I know," says the judge. "Except that it wasn't a stone and it wasn't a root, it was—but what's the use? I'm putting you on bread and water, young lady. Next."

The accused leaves the dock singing to herself, "Some day a day will come, When everyone will be in love, Someone has always loved us, always will, We'll wait until That day when we'll all love each other, Till the end of the world." Her voice fades away.

The judge bursts out laughing: "You won't be there, my pretty child. But I will. Quick, next!"

9. Fifty, stooped, great worries, heavy eyebrows knit in a frown, takes offence very easily, a fairly well-cut but crumpled dark suit.

"The room was dark, your honour, and suffocating with the dark wood of its bookshelves and furniture. And with this huge iron trunk that filled it, like a completely closed, windowless, impenetrable cell. But it wasn't silent. Through the keyhole I heard groans in which anger was mixed with pleasure and pain. I tried to open it."

"Why?" asked the judge. "Never mind. Go on."

"I was walking away from it when I heard the sharp click of the lid springing open. And I saw this horrible dishevelled woman rise up out of it."

"Nothing else?" asked the judge.

"No, there was nothing else in the box at all. In fact, now I think about it, there was no longer anything else in the room. Save stifling velvet curtains black with blood—and thousands of motionless insects—"

"No kidding," says the judge. "And the woman?"

"She was horrible, your honour. And yet her face was young and pretty, very delicate, with fine light-coloured eyes. But their brightness absorbed me like ice and I felt petrified by them. Her naked body was obscene—obscene and attractive at the same time. Oh, it was horrible!" (He grimaces with pain.) "She arched her back, threw back her pretty head, put her hands on her hips, offered me her shining filthy belly, and opened herself with both hands—"

"You're no fun," says the judge. "I detest any kind of emotion. I dislike sufferings I don't know. And I don't like other people's suffering if it's no fun for me. Conclude."

"Very well, your honour. She straightened up and once again fixed her eyes like dead crystals on me. She threw things at me, books, crucifixes and rosaries, old derby hats, an umbrella ripped by its spokes, a picture of Saint Francis, old yellowing photos and a strange rag of dirty wool crawling with bugs and which twitched. She started to snigger as she came up to me and I saw her long sharp teeth—"

"As if literature was not enough," says the judge, "now you drag in the movies. You bore me to tears. How did it end?"

"I hurled myself at her, your honour, and I shook her like an old patched quilt on top of the trunk, I bent her over it with one hand, I took the umbrella in the other and with its scratched and battered point—"

"That'll do," says the judge, "that'll do. I know all that. Lock him up. Next."

"On second thought," says the judge, "clerk of the court, read the last three depositions."

I do so.

"Worse and worse. The more they pretend to grow old, the less they change. They understand even less than before. The wondering dark-haired woman was attractive, but she didn't understand anything either. Still, instead of plain bread and water, put her on barley bread and spring water. And don't pull her fingernails out. Next."

10. Forty-five, elegant goatee beard, inclining towards ash blond, navy blue pinstripe suit of a very fashionable cut, very vigorous forehead, slightly absent-minded gaze, alternatively smiling and mischievous or pompous and mannered.

"... lot of books, but mostly novels and memoirs; I saw very few philosophers and there were several gaps in the classics. No Livy, Paul Bourget or Krishnamurti. Obviously he hasn't read them all, and no doubt he just looks through the art books. A fairly good set of engravings after Hans Holbein the Elder's Dance Macabre, a little Goya of a man bound and torn by chains, but not very good quality prints—"

"I am not in the least interested in such details," says the judge. "Apart from the engravings and the books, didn't you see anything? A walnut trunk or a copper tray, for example?"

"Certainly, milord, a most remarkable trunk. I would like to own the original, provided I could better establish—At first I thought it was a lockable bookcase, such as forbidden books were kept in, in the 16th or 18th centuries. Then it seemed to be a huge sarcophagus from the Spanish Golden Age. It glowed redly in the Delacroix light of a great Indian copper tray, no doubt hammered out at the beginning of the last century by the stocky Chibcha of the plain of Boyaca—"

"I doubt it," said the judge. "What about the trunk?"

"A sheer wonder! It suddenly opened under the pressure of a dazzling firework display whose red, orange, blue and green rockets drew in the sky of that infinite room flaming portraits of gods and madonnas, acrobats and noble lords with thin goatees, shepherdesses and naked odalisques, all chatting, dreaming, praying, living and suffering, forever, among Corinthian columns, in Gothic palaces and in the countryside around Rome, under spinning suns which would soon swallow up the universe dissolved by their light to burst into myriads of cubes or spirals or great gestures—"

"You're getting carried away," says the judge. "Where did the fireworks come from?"

(Slightly confused.) "From a great reception, milord." (Recovering his confidence.) "Vast white drawing rooms resplendent with Venetian glass chandeliers streaming with red gold and brilliantly reflected in basins carved in the form of shells from marble with ivory gleams—vast drawing-rooms filled with a rising tide of sound that took its rhythm from the counterpoints of concertos for harpsichord or saxophone, viola da gamba or sighs and tape-recorder."

"My!" says the judge. "And what were you doing there?"

"Without being bored by anyone, I wandered among the guests at this great fancy dress ball; I saw Haydn chatting to Fra Angelico, Ronsard and Corot, the sprightly Cepe-ee Bach talking to Claudel, I heard Shakespeare and Beethoven and

Michelangelo thunder, drowning the sudden outbursts from Malraux and Leibniz—"

"That's enough, that's enough," says the judge. "I don't know those people. What's more I don't want to know them. I cannot stand people telling me what I don't know. I know everything. You're cheating."

(Provocatively.) "Hamlet, the host, had my nose in words, words.... Our hostesses were charming young women, among whom I think I recognized Natasha Rostov, Helen of Troy, Diane de Poitiers, Catherine Deneuve, Mathilde de la Mole, Marina Vlady—"

"Stop it, stop it," says the judge. "Will you stop it. You can't catch me like that. You know perfectly well you're cheating! What about the Harpies? And the Megaera and the Sirens? And the Medusa and the Gorgons? Get on with it. What was in the next room?"

"There was Saint Vincent de Paul, Jesus of Nazareth, Spartacus, Mahatma Gandhi, Joan of Arc, Saint Francis of Assisi, and Camilo Torres and Che Guevara—"

"No, no," says the judge, "not in that room darn it, it was closed. In the other one."

"But I saw in the light of their Spirit—"

"You saw nothing," says the judge, "nothing at all. And I don't want to hear any more about philosophers or saints or musicians or writers or scientists or women or heroes or workers." He wipes his brow, shivering, then composes himself and puts on a Voltaire smile.

"In the other room, on the right, what was there? Look well," says the judge, "or I will have your eyes put out, your tongue cut out, your ears cut off and your brain removed."

"There were two groups, your lordship, your honour. There was Attila and Genghis Khan at the head of one group, there was Ubu, there was Hitler and—"

"Right," says the judge, "exactly. You needn't go on. I know that list, it's very long. And what did you do in there?"

"They had iron bars in their hands. I seized one and hit them—I hit them, oh, I hit them furiously, the way I used to hit the dead trees, the rotten stumps from which all the poisoned mushrooms grew in the forests of my childhood, I stove in their foreheads and their chests, I spattered their brains and their hearts and I drank their warm blood as it spurted all over me, I—I—I—"

"Exactly," says the judge. "There we are. Very good. Lock him up. Next."

The witness clings to the rail of the dock. "No, I will not be locked up. No, by Leonardo and Johann Sebastian, I will not be locked up."

"What, what?" says the judge, "what? Want to be pigheaded, do you, want to fill up and swell up your head with other people's? That's very ugly, proud sir, in fact it's stupid and absolutely grotesque. I don't know any of them; and I condemn you to silence. Guards, take away this conceited madman and disembrain him. Then give him a shave, and later we'll hang his corpse."

Three guards seize the witness. He struggles furiously. He is dragged off yelling his litany:

"Abelard, Akhnaton, Alighieri, Altdorfer, Althusser, Anaxagoras, Andromache, Aquin, Archimedes, Archipenko, Aurobindo, Averroes, Avicenna, Bach, Bach, Bach, Bach...." His voice fades away.

"Adolph Hitler," says the judge, "Agrippina, Amherst, Attila, Ali Baba, Alleluia!" He laughs heartily.

11. A brown-eyed blonde, tall and slender, very beautiful, perfectly oval face, an expressive, intense, deep gaze, the serenity of the Khmer, stands straight, a blue silk sari with a gold border.

"... a very large luminous room, the light dazzling yet warm, both pure and full of sun. At the back of this huge room, high above me, I saw the magnificent splendour of the rose window whose fires of ruby, topaz, sapphire and amethyst were so strong one could feel them vibrate in the clear liquid depth of the glass."

"Lovely lady," says the judge, "that's all very beautiful, but what about the trunk?"

(Continuing.) "Lit by the rose window, there was a little boat woven of bronze-coloured straw and bound with thin strips of ebony. I stepped into it ..."
(Her eyes shine. I look at her and stop listening. Sorry.) "... I was rising towards the great red sun whose warmth, whose pulsations and intensity penetrated my body and soul, towards the zenith of love and the world, and my wondering gaze contemplated his blinding explosion in the mist of tears of my life, I stretched out my arms in his welcoming flames and felt the burning energy spread through me, the sparks which made me fruitful until my flesh and spirit expanded to their utmost, until all my being unfolded in the other and by the other, and I wished to be set afire and melt and cease to exist in the splendour and ecstasy of his heat, his life, his love and—"
"Whoa, whoa!" cries the judge. "Fair lady, there is no communion. Your boat caught fire in the coppery sun." (He coughs.) "The end, tell me the end. Usher, shake her."
The usher gently shakes her.
"Oh! I felt burned until it hurt, I put my hands on my heart and my belly, I bent and bowed under the sword strokes, I was blinded by the flames from my burning boat, by the smoke and embers of my fall, by the darkness, now wrapped around me and stifling me, by—"
"That's better," says the judge. "Come on now, be brave, we're nearly there."
(Downcast.) "I was lying on the floor of a room impregnated with shadow and with the damp smell of half-burned green wood. Before me there was an open trunk, and in that trunk—"
"Yes?" says the judge, full of concern. "Fair lady, what was in the trunk?"
"That skinny lifeless arm hanging out" (I think of the murdered Marat in his bath), "that wrinkled haggard face, that grinning mouth—and the eyes—the incandescent eyes—" (She hesitates.) "Their burned irises still burned with the embers of their visions.... Smoking ashes where little flowering rubies budded, velvety roses with warm orange and raspberry scents, half-withered tulips in which the life of a spark already throbbed, the promise of a bird the colour of love and blood—"

"No," says the judge. "No. There was no spark. Fair lady, I beg of you, please don't start again. The golden-winged bird died of my sorrow and the purple of his soul made the roses groan."

He wipes his brow and shivers a little.

"Fair lady, what of your children's blood in our trenches of hatred? and the ashes of our deserts in your gardens of dead thoughts? and the icy flame of our fountains—of our fountains—" He coughs, and his teeth chatter.

(Regaining control of himself.) "Fair lady," says the judge, "fair lady who saw me so badly, I condemn you. To unleavened bread and clear water I condemn you. Next, next and let us be done with it!"

"And yet," says the accused as she leaves the dock, "like light in a shadow, I will live in you till the end of the world." The judge doesn't hear her.

12. Lean, pepper and salt, steel-rimmed glasses, grey suit, a twitch in one eye, thin lips, drawn features.

"Liars, idiots, impotent, obsessed. Religion is dead, sir, and the Spirit is dying. Dreamers, visionaries, sir. There was nothing in that room. Nothing, I swear it, I assure you. Save a shadow drawn on the colourless wall by a smoky candle, and piles of books. Sexual obsessions, religious obsessions. Religion is dead and the Spirit is dying. There was nothing, sir. Nothing at all."

"Brother," says the judge, "you interest me. In fact, you're the first witness who really does. But you're not right either. Not quite. Try and remember. Before that vague and uncertain shadow disappeared, what was there? Look well."

The witness is silent.

The judge stands up. He climbs on his chair and from there onto the bench, and stiffly stretches out his arms toward the accused. He's grown thinner; his forearms are scrawny and his hands almost transparent, with thin muscle ridges. He waves his arms in the air, sniggers a little and points at the accused his two needle-studded leather index fingers, which are attached to his hands by steel threads. I hear his joints crack.

"Well?" the judge asks. "Speak! Tell me, tell them! We know each other well, why should we be silent? Before the shadow—"
The witness is silent.
The judge climbs down off the bench and sits down. "Dry bread and no water."
"You're all lying," the accused shouts. They silence him. He is led out chanting, "Nothing, Nothing, Born of Nothing, You in Nothing, Nothing in me, I am Nothing, Nothing from Nothing, Born of Nothing...." His voice fades away.

"It doesn't make sense," says the judge. He stands up. "Tomorrow we examine the facts at the scene of the crime." He sits down. "Accused, stand up; first I will pronounce sentence. It will be brief and send you far. Yes?"

"Your honour," says the usher timidly, "the clerk of the court has in his file weighty documentation on the motivations and psychosocial situations of the accused. Perhaps we might—"

"Out of the question," says the judge. "I'm not a bit interested in what they are. I have to go by the book. And even more by what I know. The clerk of the court can play with his paper if he wants to. He gets the flesh of the accused, I get their skeletons."

(To the accused, huddled in the hallway outside the court): "Accused, stand up straight. This is my sentence. You will live together in *ménages à trois* for twenty years, but first of all your fingernails will be pulled out. I leave it to Mr Sartrass to arrange you in your little rooms with No Exit. I suggest the businessman and the auto fan share the lovely mystic (No. 11), the pornophiliac and the misogynist have the tender girl lost in wonder (No. 8), the world leader and the terrorist get the narcissistic globe-trotter (No. 2), and the civilized man and the rationalist bunk with the crazy gardener (No. 5). But Sartrass may have a better idea.

"After which," says the judge, "you will be put to mor" (legal term for death), "then beheaded with a falsis" (legal term for a scythe), "then your remains will be incinerated with a meta as physical as we can make." (Meta is a solid fuel which burns and leaves no ash.) "Falsis, mor, meta! Meta, mor, falsis! *Je concours*, I concur, *je suis du même avis!*"

The judge dances a solo tango around the bench, waves his arms in the air some more, and does a string of pirouettes. He's still very agile for his age. Then he sits down and wipes his brow.

(Under his breath.) "I'm very tired," says the judge. "I'm exhausted, I can't go on, I'd like to stop. I've been working for five thousand years, I haven't slept for five hundred. 'How my heart is sad and weary.'" (He smiles.) "Oh, how I wish . . . how I wish I could—" A fit of coughing chokes him; his teeth chatter again; he shakes, bows his head and puts his hands, with their leather index fingers, over his eyes.

He raises his head but closes his eyes at once. "All right," says the judge, "till tomorrow. I've done a good day's work. So have you. We've all done a good day's work. We can be proud of ourselves. Tomorrow we'll reconstitute the facts, sum up and conclude." He opens his eyes and smiles wearily.

Then he trots out of the room, with very agile movements. He seems young and old at the same time.

The Next Day

(a) The facts
Enter the judge. He has grown even older (but it isn't the first time); his skin is wrinkled, his mouth is shaking a bit. His hands and forearms are even bonier than yesterday, but his leather fingers and their needles have been freshly polished.

The Spanish chair, with its tall back and its emerald green leather, seems to delight him. He looks around the room. His eyes light up with extraordinary youth—I see a crystal childhood flash in them. He closes his eyes and seems to daydream a moment. Gives a sudden start. Opens them—and I shudder. In the chalky white face, the irises now have the dull glow of a jelly of pomegranates melted in their embers. He shakes. Calms himself. The gleam fades from his gaze.

"Clerk of the court," says the judge, "write: 'Twenty feet by fifteen. Walls milky white or chalk white depending on whether they are in the light or the shade. A Moroccan rug of alternating white and olive-green rectangles with a star or diamond pattern, six feet by nine. The windows behind me, six feet by four. Green curtains in ribbed velvet hung on wooden rings.' Didn't anybody notice those curtains?" (The ninth witness and me, your honour, but I don't say so; I'm writing.)
"Bookshelves of red cedar stained cork colour. For list of books see appendix. A Mexican trunk of stained walnut, with ironwork, four feet by—"
I've stopped writing, your honour. I am not the least bit interested; these details bore me. Your Reality bores me; why should it be better than theirs, however mediocre or incomplete? And aren't you yourself lying? Aren't you my reality? Suppose you haven't understood anything? Your Reason bores me.
Your honour, your eyes are beautiful when you're sad; they speak of your childhood. Was it in Altamira, Akkad or Abydos? or Karnak, Haruppa or Mycenae? or was it in Ville-Marie? Flee from your dreams; they will pursue you into the hereafter of this room and your courts. You will come back eternally to flee from them; eternally they will pursue you. Don't you know that, you who know everything?
Your honour, I refuse to let my dreams be stolen. Poor as they are, it will be better to give them to everybody and watch them join with the dreams of others. None of us can ever be a witness of what is. Nobody will ever be able to describe what he sees. But over the thousands of years our visions will become one.
Our visions will become flesh, your honour, flesh and blood. You will condemn us, but thereby you will be condemned. But we will be reborn like you, eternally. We will invade your parliaments, your offices, your laboratories, your universities. Our visions will become your thoughts, our hearts will feed your blood, our dreams will be your resurrection. You will rediscover your childhood and all—"
"Usher," says the judge, "where are the condemned people? Wake up the damn stenographer; his dreams will be our ruin. I swear he thinks he's a clerk of the court!"

The twelve witnesses enter and line up at the back of the room, in front of the trunk and the red tray.

"In this common place, repeat after me," says the judge.

They repeat, "It isn't a trunk carried away in the white boats of a Giotto theatre it isn't the planter drawn up by the clawed blondness of your suns it is nothing it is nothing it is snow in spring and love in war it isn't the mirror with the countless fires of power it is our children sliding into the arms of your gods of copper and stars—"

"It's none of that," says the judge, "none of that; be quiet. It isn't my sarcophagus nor my sun in decline, it isn't my cradle nor the morning of my thousandth childhood. You are preventing me from seeing, you are hiding the back of the room, you are blocking my sunlight.

"And you aren't my twelve witnesses," the judge cries. "You aren't my twelve accused! What is this comedy? Usher, where are my condemned people? Where is the lovely lady of the sun, the attractive girl of the snow, where are the masks of justice and power, where are my escapes? Usher! Clerk! I can hardly see you, I don't know you!"

"And we can't see you," say the witnesses.

And I don't recognize you either, your honour. Are you our judge of yesterday?

"Usher," the judge yells, "clear the court! Everybody out! I want to be alone—alone with you," says the judge, pointing at me. "Dirty clerk!"

The Execution

The room was empty. The judge stood up, went to the back of it, leapt on the trunk and turned towards me. He had grown even skinnier, but he was pot-bellied like a child; his frail legs hardly supported him, the chapped skin of his face was wrinkled and cracking, his forehead was round and bare, and his great wild eyes were draining of blood which slowly reddened the tendons of his neck; his chin receded under his toothless mouth; his hands were pink and crumpled. But the two leather index fingers still bristled with needles, and in each hand he held by the point a sharp quill pen dyed purple—my pens.

Jumping up and down on the trunk, the judge raised his arms high, then forward, and pointed his skinny forearms at my neck, weaving two sharpened, deadly, already bloody quills. My word, he thought he was a banderillero and I was a bull!

The judge tapped his foot on the trunk, trying to get the old rhythm of the kill. With his two already streaming quills, he aimed for the carotid arteries on either side of my slightly hoarse throat, in the crook of the shoulders. He pretended to leap. I pushed the rug back with my right foot, hunched my shoulders and lowered my head, foaming slightly at the mouth, and I charged the matador; two can play at that game, your honour. But when I felt the points of the quills scratch my skin, I suddenly stopped.

"Come on, clerk," said the judge, "don't keep me waiting! Quick, quick, our copper sun is numbing my brain. Quick, since it is written. Be brave! Quick, quick!"

He straightened up, waving his quills. I tore them from his hands and stabbed him through the heart.

None of his thirteen wounds bled. For a long time now, he has been bleeding less and less when he dies.

I lifted him in my arms like a child. The hidden mechanism worked, the trunk opened of itself. I carefully laid my new corpse in it.

As happens every time, the red sun poured over him, through the mouths of our twelve copper gods, twelve streams of liquid rubies and fire. They burned his flesh and freed his skeleton. Then the god-king in the middle shed from his little emerald eyes gleams of meadows, lakes and mountains.

The trunk filled little by little with a yellowish liquid. The frail bones huddled in it and slowly crossed its arms till the next episode. I closed the trunk and the thirteen gods went back to sleep.

Thus he died for the five thousandth time less one. And how much longer do I have left to live?

Epilogues

(a)

Alone in my study, I look at this Mexican trunk and this Chibcha tray. Old memories . . . .

Didn't I shut the trunk just now, after taking this notebook out? It's slightly open now. Impossible. I don't like that one bit; I think it just very slowly opened a little more. Let me check.

To make absolutely certain, I went and opened it a little farther. Nothing in there. But I left all my notebooks in it. Complete darkness. I put my hand in, to feel the bottom. Then—

Just like back in my childhood, my throat went dry, I couldn't cry out. The trap closed on my fear. Two icy bony little hands latched onto my right hand like steel clamps. My whole body was shivering and shaking, my teeth were chattering. Reality, death, was winning.

I tried to free my right hand with my left. I pulled, my strength increased tenfold by fear and determination to get free. Bit by bit the skeletal forearms appeared, sea-green, in the blackness of the trunk. Then metallic tints. And the very vague shape of that tiny face with its gaping expression, slowly turning towards me.

I yelled, "Not me, not me! You're dreaming, it's all false!" A faint voice murmured in the bottom of the trunk: "What about your death?" "False, false, false!" I shouted. "No, no," the feeble voice replied. "The falsis, the scythe. The scythe is very true. In fact, it's the only thing that *is* true."

Then I shook and pulled and punched those two horrible icy bony hands which would not let go of me. I hit—hit—hit—

I want to forget the rest. It will come back soon enough.

(b)

I am sitting at my study table. I have sharpened my pencils and laid out my pens. The morning sun is flooding in behind me, lighting up the white walls, setting fire to the multicoloured bouquets of my books and giving a warm glow to the red copper of the Chibcha tray from Colombia whose bigheaded god is trying so comically to hold the mythical insignia of his power upright.

In a moment I will phone Micaela. On this last day of fall, we will take a walk on top of Mount Royal and, in a thicket flooded with light, look together at the last explosions of purple and gold which are for us the threat of winter and the hope of spring. And our memories will carry us back towards the youth of the sun.

Quiet, quiet, says death, you're disturbing my sleep.

Let us enjoy our silence, Micaela. Wouldn't we be better off being silent together and no longer writing? Tomorrow, Micaela, we have to be back before the court of upright icy reality.

For the time being, I am alone and sheltered. I will stop blackening these sheets of paper. They will join the thousands of others, in my Bottom Drawer of notes, memories, illusions, our calls, our cries, our dreams. There in that walnut trunk at the back of my study.

THE BIRD

Roch Carrier
translated by Sheila Fischman

One day a swallow came to announce the arrival of spring. Its flight was joyous, its soul filled with delight at what was to come. Then it bumped its head against a wall of wind and fell into the middle of the square.

The next day was extraordinarily cold. Cars refused to start. The river was covered with ice. Streets were deserted. People who were brave enough to go outside were forced back in by the piercing cold.

Headlines lyrically described its fierceness. The newspapers were distributed all over town, but no one bought them.

The radio announced that such a cold had never appeared before in the meteorological records. It recommended caution.

Buses stayed in the garage and trains in the station, iron beasts huddled together, numb. Traffic lights at deserted intersections stalled on red.

The radio recommended extreme caution.

In houses, people eating breakfast were as happy as schoolchildren given a surprise holiday. You could hear a small dry sound like singing crystal: a fine dusting of ice had covered the coffee. The bread on the plates had hardened.

The radio announced that dozens of vagrants had been found on the air vents of the subway, frozen.

Electric lights went out. Faces, walls, everything was permeated with the sombre colour of the sky.

The radio announced that a troop of soldiers ordered to march around the town had perished.

People were bundled up in sweaters, coats, blankets. Houses crackled. Windows shattered.

The radio, which had been broadcasting soft music, was suddenly silent.

Little by little the flames ceased dancing in the chimneys. They stopped moving altogether, congealed there with a livid appearance like melted wax. You could touch it. It made a sound like crumpling paper. Children tore off bits of it and put them in their mouths. The taste was like cold tea.

Some people still felt the urge to speak. But they could no longer be heard. The sound stuck to their lips. Their mouths had become stiffened rings.

Those whose eyelids were not sealed observed a strange phenomenon: in the walls there was no longer any plaster or stones or bricks or wood. Everything was ice. Those who could still move touched it. It gave off heat like a woman's body. They crept along the translucent walls.

Their flesh became transparent. Their hearts could be seen, motionless red fish. Eventually, their bodies crumbled with a tinkling sound.

Then nothing more happened. But a small red flower was quivering in the middle of the public square.

STEPS

Roch Carrier
translated by Sheila Fischman

One evening a man returns to his house. In the place where he left his family that morning he now sees nothing but snow, mute and without memory. He is certain, though, that he has not lost his way. The man knows of a neighbouring village too. He cannot find it. It is covered by snow that seems eternal.

The sun does not set that day and it will not set again. How long has the man been wandering in the snow? Because of the endless day he cannot tell. He cannot even judge the time by his fatigue, because fatigue does not overcome him. He is not hungry; breathing alone nourishes him.

The snow is flat, rough, lifeless. He advances on a smooth plaster sea. The white surface on which he walks is an immense shell that contains the universe. Man has been rejected from it.

He has never lived in another land. He recognizes neither path nor animals nor houses. Everything has crumbled into a white dust that cannot be distinguished from the snow. Around him, nothing moves, nothing stirs or breathes or blooms or dies.

Now and then the man turns around. The snow is always the same.

Then, suddenly, footprints appear. Is he crossing his own tracks? He approaches them, comparing the print with his own feet. It is very tiny. Then there must be a woman alive too. He utters a great cry of joy that falls like a pebble in the sea.

The man follows the tracks. His gaze never leaves them. He clings to the woman's little footprints as to a rope that is stretched very taut. He walks for days, going faster and faster. His steps become more and more impatient. He hurries toward the woman at the end of the footprints in the snow.

Farther away the woman's prints are shallower. Her footfall is lighter. The traces are less precise. The man slows down. He is afraid of confusing the tracks. Soon the woman barely marks the snow, like a bird. Then there is nothing. The snow is implacably virgin.

The man turns around. He notices that the snow now resists the mark of his steps. He brings his foot down hard. The snow has become white rock.

He refuses to venture further.

Is that not his village over there? He runs. He wishes he had the legs of legendary giants.

His village is perfumed with flowers, musical with birdsong and children's cries. Arms embrace him lovingly. He is invited to eat. The bread is hot, the soup is steaming.

The man refuses. He leaves.

Since his return, he has been wandering through the village and the neighboring fields, his eyes riveted to the ground as though he were trying to read a precious sign.

THE WEDDING

Roch Carrier
translated by Sheila Fischman

Martine would have scorned a thousand castles, and all the balls that might take place in them, for a single little daisy from Didier. She never looked out her window without wishing to see him and her wish was often granted: a great part of Didier's life was spent trying to be as close as possible to Martine. No one in the village was as happy as they, and no one envied them.

How many farmers went through their fields in search of a lost cow, how many fishermen fell asleep to the song of the river, not knowing that near by, behind a curtain of rushes, there was being performed the simple liturgy of two people who refuse to be two!

And so it was astonishing when the word went round that Martine was expecting a child. Martine was dumfounded, Didier was confused. He went away, going off toward the city in search of money. Obviously, he did not return.

The child was born. Waiting for the child and waiting for Didier were to some degree mixed up together. The birth of the child was a little like Didier's return.

Although she grew accustomed to the child's presence, Martine began once again to hope for her lover's return. She knew he would agree to come back only when he had made his fortune. Then he would lodge his family in a house that Martine would decorate with little daisies to prolong their youth.

Alas! She had to be reconciled to wait for Didier no longer.

A very large stone building stood nearby, inhabited by women whose faces disappeared beneath intricate white headdresses. Martine entrusted her child to them.

The old nun who received her took the child and clasped it tightly to her bosom, which the black fabric did not flatten altogether. Then she opened a reinforced door and disappeared. Martine could hear nothing but the sound of doors that creaked, one after the other, each one farther away. Finally, everything was quiet except for a few muffled steps that glided down the corridor, as silent as a viper. Martine suddenly had the impression that she had not experienced her love or her long wait or her heavy months of solitude. That road—painful but happy—was erased like a chalk mark.

Martine felt light-hearted when she left the building, as if she were going to meet Didier under some musical tree, in a field where their love would add its light to the wheat. Had Didier really left her? Had he not arranged a rendezvous in one of their usual hiding places? No. Martine was dreaming. An old, bent nun, the eldest of the community, drew up silently and asked, "Are you ready?"

Martine was ready for anything. She followed the nun. Behind them, other nuns in their complicated black robes formed a cortege. Martine, infinitely sad, listened to their hymns. The old nun walked rapidly. Martine could hear her panting. The cortege followed the road for a long way, then turned off in the direction of a flat grey field, at the end of which was the slanting sky. Now Martine saw nothing but the grass bending evenly beneath the wind that had risen with a voice like that of the nuns.

She would have sworn that heaven was covered with the same grass. The wind twisted the robes and made them blacker. This atmosphere was drawn out for several minutes, several hours perhaps. As the cortege advanced, the grass became higher. It came up to the nuns' knees, then their thighs; it reached their waists, touched their faces and finally covered them entirely. Then the leader gestured them to stop.

They had come to a river of black water. The nuns, who had walked in two parallel rows, separated and lined up along the river, giving Martine two great black wings. At an order from the eldest, the women in black brought their left hands to their belts and, with their right hands, moving as one, they broke their rosaries. The old nun gathered them up and tied them, then Martine let them bind her arms, hands, legs and feet.

All this time the nuns had been singing their hymns. The eldest ordered them to be silent and said, "Look carefully at this water which has cast a veil over the truth."

The sibylline phrase appeared very simple to Martine and it did not cause her any anxiety. She merely looked at the place the old nun was pointing to. She was not astonished to see Didier in a black suit, rising to the surface, his limbs tied like her own. He smiled at her. The old nun gave Martine a motherly push and the current carried her gently along. One by one the nuns let themselves fall into the river after her. Their gowns were indistinguishable from the black water. They were smiling. The cortege formed perfectly parallel lines. Carried along on the water and the silence, they passed through the shadow without disturbing it, slipped beneath the leafy arches without frightening the birds and moved toward—what?

The ceremony had taken place far away, very far. However, the child of Martine and Didier had followed it with a troubled eye. She watched her mother pass beneath her window and recognized her, even though the water had brought her hair down over her face. She recognized her father whom she had never seen. She remembered kisses she had never received from him, and piggyback rides she had never taken. She repeated words he had never taught her. Her father and mother smiled at her, she answered them and they were illuminated by an extraordinary happiness. She watched them go farther away with the water, followed by eighty old women who reflected an identical happiness.

When she could no longer see them, a key turned in her door.

"My daughter," said a soft voice, "life is awaiting you."

The child of Martine and Didier emerged from her dungeon. She was a young girl, pretty, and her body had borrowed its movements from a flame. She wanted to smile. But her lips were dead.

THE INK

Roch Carrier
translated by Sheila Fischman

On Sunday they signed the peace treaty. One of the generals initialled all the clauses. Was he too solemn? Was he nervous? His pen caught in the parchment and spluttered.
    The general looked at the stains on his fingers. Helpless, he watched the blob of ink spread across the page. Slowly the parchment drank up the ink. The general was escorted to the wash basin, but the ink resisted water. He came back to distribute handshakes, proud that peace had been signed.
    The stain had spread. Half the parchment was blackened. Signatures and part of the text of the treaty were flooded with ink. Soon the entire parchment was black.
    When the time came to close the buildings, the stain had spread beyond the limits of the document and was pursuing its proud course onto the table. The caretaker closed the shutters,

bolted the door, clumped down ten corridors and headed for the bistro.

When he arrived on Monday the stain had taken possession of the rugs, the walls, the ceiling. It had asserted its presence on the chandeliers and windows. The panic-stricken caretaker closed the door and barricaded it. To no avail. The ink crept down the length of the corridors and slid beneath the doors. No brush, no soap proved effective at barring its passage. By evening it had seeped into the building's most secret corners.

The fire-brigade, police, the army, ditch-diggers and dam builders were called out. They circled the building. The ink triumphed over their unanimous dedication and initiative. After taking on the streets of the town, it took over the parks, tinted the water in the fountains and changed the colour of the chestnut trees and their leaves.

As the stain spread it became more ravenous. By Tuesday not a single house had been spared. The black ink even crowned the tall cathedral spire. The entire town seemed to have been steeped in a huge inkwell.

On Wednesday news from neighbouring towns announced that the ink was drawing near. The wheat in the fields was stained with black and so was the grass. The animals' feet were beginning to blacken. The ink was climbing up the foundations of the houses. The stain spread with the speed of a hurricane. That day, the black fury completed its occupation of the entire country.

On Thursday it crossed the borders. The invasion began. Patriots declared war on the invader. Nations joined together, the better to tear each other apart: fires, bombardments, explosions, blood.

On Friday: fires, bombardments, explosions, blood.

Pitiless, the ink extended its empire. Its shadow hovered over ten countries. Soon the sea would give in too. Fighting became futile. But they continued for a while—for the sake of honour. It was on Saturday, very late, that the cease-fire was ordered.

The peace treaty was signed the following Sunday. One of the generals initialled all the clauses. Was he too solemn? Was he nervous? His pen caught in the parchment and spluttered.

THE ROOM

Roch Carrier
translated by Sheila Fischman

This evening Strelinik takes possession of an attractive room, number 38. It has two windows, one opening onto a cherry tree that is flowering so gloriously it makes you want to run to the four corners of the town distributing its blossoms to young girls. The other window offers Strelinik an azure domain.

Strelinik arranges each object in the place that will belong to it. He lies down on his bed and abandons himself to the pleasure of breathing. There are no pipes groaning in the walls. The smell of fresh paint is as precious to him as all the perfumes in the world. His coffee, in its imitation porcelain cup, contains more happiness than a sea. All the room lacks is a flower. Strelinik goes out to look for one, closing the door with exaggerated care. The slightest jolt would break the spell of the evening's enchantment.

Strelinik goes out, walking through the streets as though the whole town were his room. He buys a pretty hoya, then comes home.

Pulling the sheet over him, Strelinik recalls his childhood: it was a happy one and he considers it improper to think about it. This evening he is happy, so happy he dares not fall asleep. But he is already asleep.

Dawn has yielded to day when Strelinik is drawn from his sleep by the insistent, distant rumbling of a machine he cannot identify. What an uproar! Will he never have peace? Covering his ears with his hands is useless. The muffled grinding is pitiless. When daylight has finally chased the dawn, the light hurts him. The scales of night have barely been removed from his eyes. Has he dreamed? Has he really been importuned? Despite the fact that gears are already turning in the town, there is a silken silence in his room.

That evening Strelinik comes home and takes off his work clothes. He does not intend to go out. His room has the privilege of a delicious shade, the sort one does not leave on certain feverishly sunny days. As he takes a fresh shirt from a hanger, a very fine dust is released. The shirt, however, is clean. His desk is covered with a fine coating of dust. It has made its way into the sheets as well, and onto the window sills. Each step he takes grates on the floor because of the gritty dust. The windows have been shut, the door as well. How has the dust found its way into clothes in drawers and between the pages of books?

It is painful to accept this other kind of night. Finally, exhausted, he sleeps—or rather, he forgets to think about the fact that he is not asleep. Such was his rest. He is barely dozing when from far away—but not so far as the previous night—a machine goes into action, its teeth biting into bedrock. The bitter taste of his meal rises to his mouth. He opens a window. The street glistens, smooth, in the electric light. Nothing disturbs the quiet of the neighbourhood. The night is breathing: one could lay his head against its bosom. Inside, mechanisms groan on the axles of the invisible machine. The building is about to awaken.

Strelinik is overcome by guilt. He goes back to bed, disappears under the covers, suffocating, then uncovers his head and swears, imploring all the gods to make him deaf. When he awakens, exhausted, he watches the hand of the clock move toward the precise, inevitable point where the alarm will sound and penetrate his skull like an axe. He waits, following the minute-hand so attentively that the noise of the machine no longer torments him. He sleeps, and the alarm clangs.

Strelinik gets up, all his muscles tense. He is standing in wet, muddy earth that covers the floor. Time is pressing. He cannot be held up by what has happened: one doesn't explain one's lateness by saying there was mud on the bedroom floor. He dresses hastily. He breakfasts on coffee, a well-deserved luxury after such an awakening. The concierge looks at the stranger with disdain. Every step has left a sticky residue, as though he has been walking on a muddy path.

After work, Strelinik brushes his shoes, waxes and shines them, cursing "that dirt that seems to want to swallow you up," as he puts it. His fellow-workers are amused. Who can make sense of these foreigners? They're so full of mystery.

Despite his fatigue, exhausted in fact, as he has been several times before when he had to sell body and soul to keep from starving to death, Strelinik decides to walk home. He contrives to delay the moment when he must set foot inside the door to his room. What more can happen to him? He will move on Sunday. No, this very night. What catastrophe will greet him? How is he to explain the mud? Will dust come oozing out of him like water from a leaky earthenware jar? This is impossible.

The concierge is waiting in front of the house. She peers at his shoes and tells him, "We're doing a little work in your room. Sorry to disturb you."

Strelinik's furniture—his bed, his trunks with their flowered covers, the chest—all has been put outside on the landing. Furiously, he turns the doorknob. The door is slightly ajar. Something is blocking it. Pushing, he manages to get inside. A tremendous mechanical din makes the floor vibrate like the skin of a drum. From a thousand places at once rams are battering against the walls of his room, saws are scraping against rusty nails. He trips, imagining suddenly that a steel machine is biting at his throat. He shouts, falls, gets up again, finds the switch and turns on the light. Strelinik refuses to believe what he sees, though his eyes are wide open.

The floor of his room has been smashed: a gulf opens at his feet, illuminated by hundreds, by thousands of electric torches, and the immense mouth is howling. He is too weak to stand. He kneels. At the bottom of the gulf, ants that are men scurry among frenzied trucks. Dozens of backhoes are stamping, bulldozers are creeping, pick-hammers are marking time. Hoists, scaffolding, ladders and mine cars slither about like reptiles. Strelinik drags himself onto the landing. A woman takes pity on him. He hears her say, "Poor stranger .... He's so young."

Strelinik makes his way to the stairs. He complains to the concierge. Before he has opened his mouth, she begins. "Read clause twelve in your lease. The tenant can claim no damages from the landlord for deprivation or reduction of occupation of the premises rented for reason of repairs that the lessor will have performed on the premises rented or in any other part of the said building."

On the floor below his, he is overcome by guilt. The uproar must be causing a commotion in the room under his as well. He stops outside the door, hesitating, then finally knocks. A woman opens it: rather old, smiling, her eyes bright.

"I live up above you," Strelinik stammers, "there," pointing, "up there, above you. ..."

"Yes, I know."

"I want to apologize for the noise that ... the noise which ..."

"You are too kind, sir; in fact, just this evening I was complimenting the concierge for finding such a quiet lodger."

"I'm sorry."

Strelinik goes up to his room. He enters fearfully. All is calm. The machines are silent. Nothing is moving. He listens. He moves his hand toward the light switch and presses it.

At first he sees nothing. His eyes are closed, as if he were blind. Then, gradually, he dares to open them. Like one great lamp, the town is all lit up: frenzied neon signs, street lights, windows of houses and stores, headlights and crisscrossed streets. Strelinik turns abruptly. To leave. There is no door, no walls. His hands seek them, in vain. Once again Strelinik has lost his way in an unknown street, a strange town.

He is famished. He knows too well the muzzle of the invisible dog that pursues him every time he comes to a new town. Strelinik is used to this terrible ritual. As he has done every time, he will roam the town; he will walk until his strength gives out.

The town resembles all the towns he has ever seen: walls smelling of urine, illegible names, streets that recall some memory, store-windows containing things he has no right to desire, forbidden doors.

His distress is lightened for a moment by the memory of a room, his last room, number 38, where he was happy one night. As he walks, the town seems to blur, to evaporate and vanish around him. The sound of a horn, the screech of a tire, bring him back to the hard reality of concrete. A burst of light lashes his face, a pedestrian nudges his elbow. The town, quite real around him, sticks to him as his flesh clings to his bones.

Strelinik has walked so much that his legs refuse to bend. His shoes pinch his toes. A sign in a window advertises a room for rent. He can go no further. He rings the bell. The door opens, he is given a key and he drags himself up several flights of stairs. He seeks the door to his room, turns the key, enters and falls asleep. He sleeps for a long time. Two days perhaps. His sleep is a true journey into nothingness, a peace that is too profound.

Finally opening his eyes, returning to life, he sees neither ceiling nor walls. He is outside. The air is mauve. Strelinik advances cautiously. Broken beams loom up here and there amid stones and plaster. An old cinder is smoking in the wind. There are no streets. It is a town and Strelinik is in the center of a squalid pile of building material. He steps on it and slips. The town shatters like a glass that has been dropped. Strelinik's mind is blank. All his attention is focussed on not getting hurt and not scraping his hands as he trips.

The ruins are endless. The walls, the roofs in shreds, lie scattered like sticky rags.

Suddenly an object catches his eye: a door standing upright among the debris, held in place by its frame.

Strelinik remembers that door. All doors look ridiculously alike, but he does remember this one. In his glaucous memory it stirs up waves another door would not have wakened. He pushes it and it moves noisily on its hinges. On the other side, Strelinik recognizes his room, his pretty room 38, with its smell of fresh paint and its gay curtains.

On a little table across from a window his pretty hoya plant stands painfully erect.

"The poor thing must be thirsty," says Strelinik, hanging up his jacket.

He pours some wine into the hoya's pot and fills his own glass.

On the other side of the window, in trees that look like an old woman's hands, the sap begins to sing.

THE HOTEL

Louis-Philippe Hébert
translated by Alberto Manguel

In the great hall with the marble floor is a double staircase that rises from the centre, immediately forks and, halfway along, reaches both sides of the room, and then joins again on the next floor. Or rather there where the next floor should be, because there is no such thing as a next floor, and the staircase ends against a solid wall. A glass slide, oval and slightly concave lengthwise, stretches in between the double line of steps and ends on the floor in the shape of an armchair, also made of glass; the slide is the magnificent extension of the armchair's back. Two rats, some six or seven feet high, stand on their hind legs half-way up the stairs, their forelegs crossed over the red gala uniform whose front flaps only cover the torsos, and whose tails only cover part of the backs. The rats tap their stiletto heels against the slabs of the stairs, but nothing in their gestures indicates a willingness to either mount or redescend the remaining stairs: the shoes that make them seem so much taller make it difficult for them to fall back on their hind legs when changing steps; they are happy simply spinning around in order to adopt one of two positions when facing their partners: either back to back or face to face. These movements do not alternate; frequently they perform a full circle and then resume their previous position. Their movements are precisely coordinated and, much to the astonishment of visitors, there are never any changes, any new combinations such as when (this would be easy to imagine), after a slight distraction, the first rat might appear with his back turned unable to see that the other was in fact facing him; there would at least be a slight hesitation, enough for the second one to change his position. Up to this day, this has never been noticed. The two rats are, no doubt, two most accomplished performers. The hotel owes its fame partly to this daily folklorical demonstration, and partly to its architecture, especially to the style in which the rooms have been set. In the whole of the building there are no corridors: the rooms, separated from one another, communicate only through the hall. They hang suspended at different heights above the immense space of the ground floor. The rooms are reached by private elevators; the stout black leather tubes which contain not only the electric cables but also the water pipes and the drains, and which lead to the rooms, have been left bare, as well as the iron cables and the pulleys. The double staircase, of such imposing aspect, and the slide which reflects the many ascents and descents, serve different purposes: the former, with its white treads and black risers, is used as an altimeter; the latter, under the light that comes from the windows, as a giant screen. Windows opening towards the inside (there are at least two per room) allow one to admire at any given moment, either the steps, or the reflection of the elevating device: the traveller, even if he were dead drunk, would immediately realize his position in the building. He would lie down again, somewhat relieved at the idea that both the staircase and the slide are two useless constructions (for show only) and that the dancing rats cannot use them to climb up to him. And this is the other aspect of these unexpected constructions, not entirely innocent of symbolism: during the night, the rats, falling back into their animal habits, free from bonds of clothing as well as from the training, run all over the place, evidently in search of prey. Because of their size, it would not be surprising if they were to attack the clients. But the elevators can only be controlled from inside. Once the client is in bed, the elevators remain flush with the top floor, their doors matching perfectly the doors of the rooms. It is not uncommon for a traveller, stopping here for the first time and faithfully following the advice of a more experienced client, to spend the night awake, half wary, half reassured, watching the movements of the rats turning round and round, hungrier and hungrier, more and more savage, until, just before dawn, they turn on their own mates. This is the wilder aspect of their dance. Sometimes the townspeople ("for old times' sake" is their excuse) come here to spend the night. To tell the truth, the hotel had not been conceived to entertain foreign visitors. To depend on tourism in a land like ours would certainly mean bankruptcy in whatever trade. This explains, perhaps, why the staff responsible for acting as rats is so badly paid. The heat, underneath the tight-fitting costumes, soon reaches unbearable degrees. And yet there is never a dearth of volunteers, and, as someone who has volunteered a good number of times, I assure you that if the sensation of being safely perched can become agreeable, that of letting loose one's animal instincts, moaning deep within oneself, is even more exalting. Perhaps this is largely due to the dance that must be performed in one place during the day—this exceedingly demanding dance whose steps are regulated and marked by a deliberately broken rhythm. Also the thrill of seeing throughout the day one's "victims" barely ten feet away, of knowing that one could, were darkness suddenly to fall, leap on them, tear them apart and devour them, without being accused, on the following morning, of any criminal act, adds to the joy of being disguised, unknown among one's countrymen. The infrequent total solar eclipses on record have provoked murderous assaults. For the time being, I dance. But I know that in three hours the owner of the hotel, deep inside the large, solitary armchair—this almost royal presence at the foot of the stairs who reassures the one-night visitors—will have fallen asleep, twirling his moustache. His scarcely audible snoring will be picked up by my rat's ears—so much more sensitive than the human ones they deftly cover .... I hear them pierce the monotonous breathing, that regular and scarcely obvious heaving of the chest trapped within a too tight jacket. And as the jolts of my steps and of those of my partner become more and more synchronized, as our taps slowly resemble the comforting tic-toc of a clock, their sound leads the owner deeper and deeper into sleep. Almost all the elevators are now up high. The last rays of the sun outside, and the peculiar light that continues to shine in here a little after sunset, guide the last clients towards their rooms. From time to time the stretched-out *wheee* of an upwards journey gives me butterflies in the stomach. But why do the owner's eyes acquire that almond shape? Books are closed. The main door is barred. How can his nails dig into his fingers to the rhythm of his breathing? The dull slamming of a door, the nervous coming and going in the rooms, the muffled exit of the daytime staff, nothing wakes him. Are we under the spell of the peaceful echo that has overcome the hotel's silence, that we continue to make a few last stereotyped movements, even after the time has come? The snoring, which acquires more and more the quality of purring, acts upon us in an even more alluring way, even more perhaps than our heels tapping above his slumber. Who knows if the owner has not had trap openings set underneath the beds, if he has not decided to send us, down the slide, one of tonight's guests? And finally, why would there be talk of disappearances in the town? Of a recent scarcity of dancers? Unimportant questions like these spring to our mind seconds before the sign is given, to frighten us and distract us, to chase away from our overheated brains the mad dream that a client will once send down the elevator to us, or decide himself to come down. Because tonight, I feel it in my bones, no one will be able to sleep: it shall be a beautiful spectacle, bloody and loud, just as the owner likes them.

A TEXT CONCERNING STRAWBERRIES

Louis-Philippe Hébert
translated by Alberto Manguel

I am continuously under the impression of having written a text concerning strawberries. A rather short prose piece, two, maybe three pages long, but exact and concise. I mean a text concerning nothing but strawberries. A seasonal text, sort of rosy. And far from sad. Something about them made me choke with laughter, something I can't quite remember. No doubt a certain way of handling them. Or the way the whole body waddles when we come near them. A dance? No, there was no mention of that, at least not clearly. Did it, in a word, allude to the legs? This detail— like all others— escapes me. The text, which certainly exists, has the answer, I am sure, and I continue to look for it among my drafts and notes. Reading in order to find it—to find at least the source for so long-lasting a feeling—the sentences escape me: I am forced to follow them the wrong way round, with a red pencil. What a hell of a job on half-torn pages! Exhausting, sometimes.

Suddenly I ask myself if I truly ever wrote it. A similar confusion is apparent in my eyes when, excitedly talking about it to friends, I am not capable of giving them the slightest idea of the text. Or when I see the word strawberry, on its own, lost on a piece of paper, on a blank page or on a page framed with doodles, next to the phone. Had I jotted it down not to forget it? And the numbers? Useless precaution: knowing the importance I attach to it, I would surely not forget it before actually coming across it.

The meaning of this lost text fascinates me. Did I mean that everything, even the very words of the text itself, could have the juicy quality of strawberries, or even *be* strawberries? How could I put it? The text should be somewhat like a piece of candy. Of course one would see in it more than just sweetness. What I would call the strawberry seen from the inside, a class with four-and-twenty desks in it, twenty-one tender hands taking down dictation, dictation coming from a voice, its back turned, and we are unable to see the heart-shaped lips; or an old brick school with a green roof, in summer, seen from the road. In the brown playground, is there a star stuck like a blade of grass onto a red marble? Or seen from a hole as big as a fist held in readiness nearby. And there I drift away. These are certainly not the words I used.

The fact of having often thought about it, and always under identical circumstances (remembering having written it rather than intending to write it) has created in me a kind of habit. This habit must have the characteristics of the text, seeing that it constantly drags me back to it. It would not occur to me that, for instance, I had written a text on the raspberry or the blueberry. At least not in so resolute a manner. I have never been able to disregard the ridiculous side of these two fruits; even today when I think of them, by chance, in a field or shoved away in a type-face box, I feel an urge to deride them and insist on the box: wood, plastic or cardboard—what delightful possibilities! Otherwise I try to enlarge the dimensions of the field, the blue sky, to escape. The strawberry has a different effect on me. It seems more serious. In considering it—I say somewhere in the text—we touch upon dramatic matters. Perhaps I use a less passionate expression. But I find it hard to believe that it could only be funny, and nothing more. The strawberry, for me, has too much of a *déjà vu*. A kind or irresistible adventure. And the red, the yellow and the green.

Sometimes, when I have barely finished placing the final sentence, a verbless but colourful sentence, placing the commas and the full stop, I hold my breath and sail immediately back to the beginning; I look for the strawberries and find instead all sorts of words. But none that resembles the strawberry or even hints at it. Amnesia has nothing to do with this. I believe that, in the same way that the idea of the strawberry skims over my friends, I cannot lay my hands on the text upon my back. A certain life-style, a methodical life-style, would allow me to have the strawberries always in front of me, never behind my back. To find that textual moral code would be beyond my capacity. Because, pursued by everything concerning the strawberries and above all by the purloined text, I cannot presume to find it any longer. Unless I can point at a few demonstrative lines, I will soon be lost.

I will never be able to write, or rewrite, a text concerning strawberries, except perhaps when I am old and so convinced that I have already written it, that one evening quite suddenly I will dictate to my secretary that text, word for word, without ever having learnt it.

THE HANGED MAN

Michel Tremblay
translated by Michael Bullock

In my country, when someone kills his neighbour they hang him. It's stupid, but that's the way it is. It's in the laws.

My job is to watch over the hanged. In the prison where I work, a hanged man isn't taken down as soon as he is dead. No, he is left hanging all night and it's my job to watch over him until sunrise.

I'm not required to weep, but I do weep all the same.

***

I knew very well this hanged man wasn't going to be an ordinary hanged man. Unlike all the condemned men I had seen up to then, this one didn't seem to be afraid. He didn't smile, but his eyes didn't betray any fear. He looked at the gallows coldly, whereas the other condemned men almost unfailingly go into shock when they see it. Yes, I felt that this hanged man wouldn't be an ordinary hanged man.

***

When the trapdoor opened and the rope stretched taut with a dry sound, I felt something move in my belly.

The hanged man didn't struggle. All those I had seen till this one had twisted about, swinging at the end of the rope with their knees drawn up. But this one didn't move.

He didn't die immediately. You could hear him trying to breathe .... But he didn't move. He didn't move at all. We looked at each other, the hangman, the prison governor and I, wrinkling our foreheads. This lasted a few minutes; then, suddenly, the hanged man let out a long yell that sounded to me like the huge laughter of a madman. The hangman said that was the end.

The hanged man quivered. His body seemed to lengthen a little. Then, nothing more.

But I was sure he had laughed.

***

I was alone with the hanged man who had laughed. I couldn't stop myself from looking at him. He seemed to have grown longer still. And that hood I have always hated! That hood which hides everything but lets you imagine everything! I never see the faces of the hanged, but I guess what they're like and I think that's even worse.

All the lights had been put out and the little nightlight over the door had been lit.

How black it was and how afraid I was of this hanged man. In spite of myself, around two in the morning, I dozed off. I was woken—I couldn't say just when—by a low sound, like a sigh. Was it me who had sighed like that? It must have been me, I was alone. I had probably sighed in my sleep and my sigh had woken me.

Instinctively, I turned my eyes towards the hanged man. He had moved! He had made a quarter turn and now he was facing me. It wasn't the first time this had happened. It was due to the rope, I knew that perfectly well. But all the same I couldn't help trembling. And that sigh. That sigh which I wasn't certain had come out of my mouth.

I called myself a double-dyed idiot and got up to walk around a bit. As soon as I had turned my back on the hanged man, I heard the sigh again. I was quite sure this time that it wasn't me who had sighed. I didn't dare turn round. I felt my legs turn to water and my throat dry up. I heard two or three more sighs, which soon changed into breathing, first very uneven, then more regular. I was absolutely certain the hanged man was breathing and I thought I was going to faint.

At last I turned round, trembling all over. The dead man was moving. He was swinging, almost imperceptibly, at the end of his rope. And he was breathing more and more strongly. I got as far away from him as I could, taking refuge in a corner of the big room.

I shall never forget the horrible spectacle that followed. The hanged man had been breathing for about five minutes, when he started to laugh. He suddenly stopped breathing loudly and began to laugh softly. It wasn't a demoniacal, or even a cynical, laugh; it was simply the laugh of someone who is wildly amused. His laughter quickly grew louder and soon the hanged man was roaring with laughter, fit to burst his sides. He was swinging more and more violently ... laughing ... laughing ...

I was sitting on the ground, my two arms squeezed to my stomach, and I was crying.

The dead man was swinging so violently that at one moment his feet almost touched the ceiling. This went on for several minutes. Minutes of pure terror for me. Suddenly the rope broke and I let out a loud cry. The hanged man hit the ground with a thud. His head came off and rolled over to my feet. I jumped up and ran for the door.

***

When the caretaker, the prison governor and I returned to the room, the body was still there, stretched out in a corner; but we couldn't find the dead man's head. It was never found.

THE EYE OF THE IDOL

Michel Tremblay
translated by Michael Bullock

I have only recently returned from that far-off country called Paganka, where the blue men hunt the terrible hyena-bird, an enormous and terrifying monster that attacks the flocks and sometimes even humans; and where the women never cut their hair.

I had crossed half the earth before reaching that accursed country. After a very difficult journey lasting four months across savannahs and forests I finally came to Keabour, the capital of the country, situated in the midst of virgin forest. To tell the truth, Keabour is not even a town but at most a village of four or five hundred inhabitants, where the most rudimentary commodities and the most elementary laws of decency are still unknown. What struck me most on arriving in Keabour was the strange appearance of the blue women.

There is no more astonishing sight than these blue females with their long mop of hair, who look more like tangled spindles than women. The oldest drag behind them hair several feet long which they never wash and which ends up looking like dry dung.

After arriving in Keabour, I enquired as to the whereabouts of the temple of M'ghara, the aim of my journey. But no one seemed to know. However, M'ghara is the god of the country and I had often heard tell of the loathsome sacrifices offered to him in the temple by the inhabitants of Paganka. People even talked about human sacrifices, but nothing had ever been proved.

After three days I finally discovered an old man who, for a few bottles of liquor, agreed to sell me the secret of his people, on the grounds that he was not risking much because he was very old and was going to die in any case. It is a fact that death was the punishment for revealing the secret of the location of the temple of M'ghara. At least that is what the old man told me and I saw later that he had not been lying.

So I set out next day at dawn, mounted on a mule, in the direction of the Mountain With No Summit that can be seen from Keabour. The journey was very difficult because I had to hide every time I met an inhabitant of the country and also because of the ferocious beasts, the reptiles and the voracious insects that populate the jungle.

During the fourth night of my journey towards the Mountain With No Summit I was woken by the sound of a tom-tom very close by. I did not sleep for the rest of the night and the tom-tom did not stop until sunrise.

That day I reached the temple of M'ghara.

***

In the centre of a clearing rose a very ugly building that looked like a beehive and was built of a material which I recognized as graft, a brownish metal much used by the inhabitants of Paganka but of absolutely no value. I was very disappointed by the poverty-stricken appearance of the temple of M'ghara. Had I travelled across half the globe and risked my life countless times in order to discover such a wretched looking temple? I approached the building with chagrin and ascended the few steps leading to the portico. I was about to enter when I was startled by a cry behind me.

An altar had been set up close to the temple and upon this altar were stretched the old man who had shown me the way and an old woman whose hair had been cut off. The old man was already dead, but the woman was still alive and even had the strength to groan. I went up to the altar and bent over the woman. She opened her eyes and began to yell when she saw me. "Accursed be thou, stranger," she cried. "You have reached your goal but see what has happened to my husband and me. Soon the hyena-birds will come to take us to M'ghara, the terrible god with the six arms. And all because of you. Supreme shame, my own children cut off my hair before all the inhabitants of Keabour and spat in my face and in my husband's face. The high priest himself thrust the knife into my husband's chest and he only left me alive so that I should see the hyena-birds coming. I am dying because of my husband's sacrilege, that is the law of Paganka. But I curse Paganka and its laws. I curse its inhabitants. And I curse you, who have come so far in order to seize the eye of the idol with the six arms. Many have come before you, but none has ever got so far. May the curse of M'ghara be upon you. Beware of the eye, it . . . ." The old woman suddenly stopped speaking and her eyes were fixed upon a dot moving in the sky above us. "Already," she whispered. "They are already here." She closed her eyes and moved no more. The dot came closer and closer and when it was close enough for me to make out its shape, I saw that it was a bird with the head of a hyena that was making towards us, croaking horribly. I ran to the temple and entered the portico. I saw with horror that the temple had no doors—doors are unknown in Paganka—and I hid behind one of the pillars of graft supporting the roof. From my hiding place I could see what was happening outside the temple without being seen.

After two or three minutes, the hyena-bird landed beside the altar and went up to the two bodies. It sniffed at them for a few moments, then it screeched. There was a flapping of wings and a second hyena-bird joined the first. For a long time they sniffed at the two bodies without making up their minds to seize them. Suddenly they both raised their heads at the same time and looked in my direction. They had certainly sensed my presence, because they approached the temple and mounted the steps. But they stopped in the portico and contented themselves with looking at me—from their present position they could see me easily. Something seemed to be preventing them from entering the temple and this saved me. After looking at me malevolently for several long minutes, they returned to the altar. Then they each seized a body and soared up into the sky. I heard the old woman cry out. I came out of the temple to watch the hyena-birds fly away. They disappeared behind a large rock on the Mountain With No Summit.

***

The idol was also made of graft. It was very old and almost falling in ruins. If I had not been so exhausted by the long journey and the many adventures that had happened to me before reaching the temple of M'ghara, I should have laughed at the ridiculous situation in which I found myself. I had crossed half the world to find an idol that had absolutely no value. I had spent my entire fortune—very small, it is true—in the hope of discovering an infinitely greater one and now found myself, after months of exertion and privation, before a kind of six-armed monster that wasn't worth ten cents, that was grimacing at me and seemed to be mocking my discomfiture.

I was completely discouraged. I sat down at the foot of the idol, rested my head on one of its knees and would have started crying like a girl if a thought had not suddenly crossed my mind.

The old woman who had just been carried off by the hyena-bird had talked about the "eye of the idol". She had said that I had come to get the "eye of the idol". I raised my head and looked at M'ghara's one eye. There was nothing special about it. As big as a fist, it seemed to be made of graft like the rest of the statue. So why should the woman have attached so much importance to it? Stirred by a vain hope, I rose and climbed up onto the statue's knee. Using its arms like a ladder, I climbed right up to M'ghara's head. I was very much afraid the idol might collapse under my weight, but something at the back of my mind told me it was worth risking my life one last time.

I sat on the idol's shoulder and began to examine the eye. I quickly saw that it was not really made of graft. A thick layer of this metal covered a material that seemed very hard. I scratched the surface of the eye and a few bits of metal came away. Then I had a very clear impression that something was going on inside the statue. I felt a sort of shiver run through the whole idol and one of its arms moved. I told myself that the idol was probably having difficulty supporting my weight and that this movement of the arm was not dangerous. So I continued scratching and at the end of five minutes the whole layer of graft had come off. I moved closer to the eye and almost choked with surprise and joy. I had before my eyes the biggest diamond you can imagine. Finer and bigger than any I had ever seen in my life. Two seconds later, my knife was out of my pocket and I was beginning to scratch around the eye to loosen it. But the idol began to tremble from its metal entrails. I began to feel really afraid and started scratching even more vigorously so as to finish my task as quickly as possible. At the first blow of the knife, M'ghara's head moved from left to right and one of its arms stretched out towards the sky. I was seized with panic and struck the eye with all my strength. The idol doubled up and uttered a yell of pain. I almost slipped off M'ghara's shoulders, but I managed to put one arm round his neck and remained suspended, my body up against his chest. Then I noticed that the idol was breathing.

The idol stopped moving. I climbed up onto its shoulders again. The diamond was almost completely loosened and I told myself that one more well placed blow with the knife would free it. But I hesitated. Wouldn't the idol start groaning and struggling again? But had it really groaned? Had I really felt the beating of its heart, or had I been the victim of my imagination?

I suddenly raised my arm and drove the knife one more time into M'ghara's eye. As soon as the diamond was completely detached, the idol stood up straight and put two of its hands to the wound, crying out. Its head struck the roof of the temple and the jolt nearly made me fall. But I managed to hang on to a pendant M'ghara wore in his ear. The idol began running this way and that through the temple, knocking into the pillars, falling to its knees, rising again and starting to run madly around again, yelling. Suddenly, one of its arms seized me and threw me down on the ground at the foot of a pillar. Half dazed, I got up and ran from the temple.

I ran for several minutes and finally collapsed under a tree. After resting for a few moments, I decided to take out the diamond, which I had hidden under my shirt, and look at it. Oh, I shall always remember the horror of that fateful moment! When I plunged my hand into my shirt, I cried out with disgust. I took out from beneath my clothes a huge, bloody eye, a horrible, viscous thing, that looked at me through a trickle of coagulated blood.

THE GHOST OF DON CARLOS

Michel Tremblay
translated by Michael Bullock

My Uncle Ivan was famous. Everyone knew him, but no one ever talked about him in public. My Uncle Ivan was a spiritualist. People said he was able to communicate with the souls of the dead, thanks to a gift that some Hindu princess had once given him. In fact, my uncle really did possess this gift. In my childhood—my uncle disappeared when I was barely fifteen—I was present at some very extraordinary séances.

Having lost my parents when I was very young, I was taken in, taught about life and cherished by my Uncle Ivan. In spite of all the horrors told about him—for example, that he was a man who respected neither law nor religion—my Uncle Ivan was an admirable man in every way.

A very learned man, he was the best teacher imaginable. He was able to explain the most complicated things in a very simple, very clear manner, which enabled me, with the intelligence and few talents God had given me, to make pretty rapid progress in every area and, above all, in the field of science.

My uncle always refused to talk to me about his gift. When I broached the subject he got angry (his angers were terrible) and told me that he would never, absolutely never disclose his secrets to me. I can still hear him shout: "You want to become a medium, like me? Poor, poor child, you don't know what awaits you. You will never become a medium. I shall always refuse to pass on my gift to you, because that's what you want, isn't it? I love you far too much. I love you far too much."

Every Friday evening—why Friday I don't know—a group of six to a dozen people would invade the parlour of our house and my uncle would invoke the spirits. I have seen truly magic things happen during these extraordinary séances. I have seen women faint when they saw their husband, their son or their mother appear before them. I have seen otherwise very brave men get up and leave the house uttering groans of terror because someone, a dead person from the other world, had touched them. I have even seen a woman in tears passionately embrace the image of her deceased husband. But the most frightening, the most horrible and terrifying thing I ever saw in that accursed parlour was the ghost of Don Carlos.

***

One day Isabella del Mancio, one of the richest and, it was said, one of the most beautiful women in Spain, came to visit our little country. Polished gentleman that he was, our Prime Minister had prepared a splendid dinner in honour of this noble lady. Unfortunately for him, my Uncle Ivan was invited to the banquet. My Uncle Ivan, despite the fact that he was, as I have said, an admirable man, was not at all sociable. He really wasn't made to live in society. His reputation for being unsociable was well founded.

My uncle preferred the company of his books and, I can say so without false modesty, my company to that of those "intolerable aristocrats", as he used to call them. Therefore he was not at all pleased to receive the Prime Minister's invitation. "You ought to feel flattered," I told him, "that a prime minister invites you to dine in the company of the most beautiful woman in Spain." My Uncle Ivan smiled and said gently: "The most beautiful woman in Spain, my boy, is not Isabella del Mancio. The most beautiful woman in Spain ...." My uncle closed his eyes and said in a low voice: "I will show her to you one day."

My Uncle Ivan declined the invitation, pleading a severe migraine.

But Isabella del Mancio was crazy about spiritualism. She had heard of my Uncle Ivan and was absolutely determined to make his acquaintance. When she saw that my uncle was not present at the banquet given in her honour she was very annoyed.

Immediately after dinner she demanded that the "sick man" should be sent for. "I have travelled thousands of miles to meet this medium" (here the Prime Minister was somewhat offended); "I finally get to this miserable country and I'm told this gentleman doesn't want to see me on the pretext that he has a severe migraine. Don't people know how to live in this country?"

My Uncle Ivan refused categorically to come to the Prime Minister's house. However, he agreed to invite Isabella del Mancio to the spiritualist séance the following Friday. That evening, before going to bed, my Uncle Ivan made a strange remark. "I hope," he said, "this Isabella del Mancio doesn't know about the ghost of Don Carlos."

***

The first thing Isabella del Mancio talked about the following Friday was the ghost of Don Carlos.

***

My uncle paled and his cheek muscles quivered, in him always a sign of intense nervousness. Isabella del Mancio noticed it. This ghost must be very terrible to make my Uncle Ivan turn pale! But I shall try to report as faithfully as possible the conversation which then took place between Isabella del Mancio and my uncle.

"I see," she said, "that Don Carlos' reputation is well established. All the mediums seem to know him and all of them refuse to have dealings with him. But I dare hope that you, who are perhaps the most ... "

"I beg you, madam," cut in my uncle, "not to ask me ... "

"But Don Carlos can't be so terrible."

"Yes, madam, he is."

"How can you know? Have you seen him?"

"I have seen him. And even if I had not seen him I should still refuse to contact him. The name of Don Carlos is taboo in the domain of spiritualism. One can only make him appear once and .... As you said just now, all the mediums know him, but none will have anything to do with him."

"Then how is it that you have seen him?"

"That would be too long a story to tell. Besides, I prefer to forget it. Or at least, I should like to try. Because you cannot forget Don Carlos when you have seen him, even if it was only once in your life."

"Tell me what he is like, at least."

"I beg you, madam, if you continue to ask questions I shall get annoyed."

Isabella let the matter drop. The séance began and was not a great success. Isabella del Mancio had taken part in an incredible number of séances of this sort and nothing could interest her any more, nothing except the ghost of Don Carlos. My Uncle Ivan could see this clearly and seemed to be prey to great anxiety during the whole evening. The séance ended with the appearance of the soul of Isabella's father. But Isabella didn't even speak to her father; she had seen him so many times since his death that she had nothing more to say to him.

Before the guests left, I saw my uncle go up to the Spanish woman and ask her something. Large beads of sweat were running down his forehead and his voice was weak.

Isabella smiled and came and sat next to me, on a big divan close to the fireplace. "Your uncle seems very much on edge," she said to me teasingly. I felt that something horrible was going to happen because of this woman. That was when I began to hate her.

When everyone had left, my Uncle Ivan joined us on the divan. He took the hands of the beautiful Spanish woman between his own. "I can show the ghost of Don Carlos, if you wish," he said. "I am old now and spiritualism is beginning to bore me. You see, Don Carlos' ghost is the last thing a medium can call up. When he receives his gift, the medium undertakes to communicate with this ghost once in his life, and he is obliged to keep his promise. Afterwards, everything is finished for him."

I thought at that moment that a medium lost his gift when he called up Don Carlos' ghost .... Oh, if I had only known! If I had only known!

"My career is drawing to a close," continued my uncle, "and I have decided this evening to crown it by calling up the ghost of Don Carlos. I have insisted on doing it in secret, because you cannot show Don Carlos' ghost to just anyone. You have to have tremendously strong nerves. If you wish to see Don Carlos, you shall see him. But I warn you: what you see will be terrifying." And Isabella burst out laughing. "Nothing can frighten me," she said. "Not even the devil in person!"

I tried to dissuade my uncle from carrying out his plan, but in vain. It was no use my telling him it would be a pity to lose his gift on account of a rather too beautiful Spanish woman who wouldn't even thank him. Nothing had any effect. "The time has come for me to call up Don Carlos," he replied.

Isabella del Mancio seemed very happy at the prospect of being able at last to contemplate the famous ghost of Don Carlos. What did the price of this apparition matter to her? "I've been hearing about him for so long." And a smile flitted across her sensual lips. "They say he's very handsome."

"No," cried my Uncle Ivan, "Don Carlos is not handsome!"

***

My Uncle Ivan told me to put out all the lights in the house and close all the doors and windows. We lived in an enormous house by the sea, a big isolated house that might have been three or four hundred years old. "When you come back to the parlour," he said, "shut the door behind you, put out all the lights except the one above the round table, and hide in the darkest corner of the room. Whatever you do, don't show yourself. Under no circumstances, understand? Under no circumstances!!"

When I came back to the parlour, my Uncle Ivan was standing in the middle of the room looking at the huge mirror hanging above the fireplace. "That's the way Don Carlos will come," he said at last.

Isabella started to laugh (all that woman could do was laugh!) and declared that she absolutely must buy the mirror when it was all over. "I want to take Don Carlos away with me," she declared. My uncle looked at her severely. "When you have seen Don Carlos," he said, "you certainly won't want to take him away with you."

I hid behind a curtain, in a very dark corner of the room, while my Uncle Ivan and Isabella sat down at the round table. "Before we begin," whispered my uncle, "I must warn you of one thing. Don Carlos must not know that we are here. Don Carlos must not see us. When you see him, don't make a sound. Above all, don't speak."

"What a pity," exclaimed Isabella throwing back her head. "When I wanted to seduce your ghost."

How I hated that woman. How I hated her.

My uncle spread out his hands on the round table and told the Spanish woman to join her fingers to his. Then he uttered some words that I didn't understand and that Isabella seemed to find very funny. I saw her laughing as she watched my uncle recite his incantations. If I had been able at that moment to foresee what was going to happen, I should have killed Isabella del Mancio and I should have saved my Uncle Ivan.

***

To begin with, all I heard was a slight, almost imperceptible sound that seemed to come from above the fireplace. My Uncle Ivan leaned towards Isabella and whispered: "Don't look at the mirror immediately. I shall tell you when you can look." Isabella turned away her head, but I continued to look in the direction of the mirror. The same low sound was repeated several times over and a soft orange light suddenly lit up the mirror. My uncle continued to mumble incoherent words. He did not look in the direction of the mirror either. But I looked.

Suddenly my Uncle Ivan jumped up and threw himself on me like a madman. "Don't look at the mirror," he cried. "Don't look at the mirror. He might kill you. Don Carlos might kill you."

At the same instant, a terrifying noise filled the room and the mirror was smashed in pieces. A violent gust of wind lifted the curtains while a piercing whistle rent my ears. "Disaster," cried my Uncle Ivan. "The mirror is broken! Don Carlos won't be able to leave!"

A long trail of bluish smoke was hanging in the middle of the room. "He is already here," said my Uncle Ivan. "Whatever you do, don't make a sound. Under no circumstances." He went and sat down in his chair, under the lighted chandelier, beside Isabella del Mancio. Isabella seemed to be enjoying herself mightily.

The trail of smoke eddied in the room to form a long spiral starting from the ceiling and ending on the floor. The spiral swirled faster and faster. There was a sound like the whistling of a hurricane that came closer every second. At a certain moment, the trail of smoke spun round so fast that it was no longer visible.

It had become a sort of transparent blue light. Then I heard the most fearsome neigh it is possible to imagine. It sounded at one and the same time like the cry of an animal and the noise of thunder.

Within the bluish light, the vague shape of a white horse was moving. It was a magnificent animal with an extremely long mane and a superb tail. "What a fine horse," whispered Isabella del Mancio.

"Keep quiet," replied my uncle. "Do you want to bring disaster upon us?"

The horse neighed again and began to trot around the parlour. It circled the room two or three times, then went and stood in the blue light again. Then it raised its head towards the ceiling and neighed quite softly.

Then there appeared the most extraordinary and the most repulsive being it has ever been given to a human being to see. It was not a man, it was a veritable Titan. Seated on the horse, Don Carlos appeared even bigger than he must be in reality. His head almost touched the ceiling. I had never seen such an ugly face or such a vicious expression. I cannot describe here the horror this giant inspired in me. He was ugly, with an almost unbearable ugliness, and his extraordinary size added still further to this ugliness. He gazed around him as though looking for something that he couldn't find. His forehead was creased and he seemed angry. He dismounted from his horse and circled the room, as the horse had done before.

Isabella del Mancio was no longer laughing. She was extremely pale and clutched my Uncle Ivan's shoulders.

Don Carlos seemed to be more and more furious. He remounted his horse. The horse walked slowly towards the mirror. But suddenly Isabella rose and approached the horse. Neither my uncle nor I could suppress a cry of amazement. We cried out just as Isabella touched the horse with the tips of her fingers. The horse reared up as if a hand of fire had touched it. Don Carlos turned towards Isabella, seemed to see her for the first time and bent down to her. He looked her straight in the eyes. Isabella seemed to be hypnotized by his look and did not move. Don Carlos took off his right glove and placed his hand on Isabella's face. His nails sank into the young woman's flesh and, as Isabella screamed with pain, five trickles of blood ran down her face.

Unable to restrain himself, my Uncle Ivan threw himself upon Isabella del Mancio. He tried with all his strength to snatch her from the ghost's clutches, but to no avail. Then he ran to the fireplace, picked up an enormous candlestick and struck Don Carlos on the left arm. Don Carlos opened his mouth, but no sound came out. Finally he let go of poor Isabella, who collapsed on the floor. A few shreds of flesh remained clinging to Don Carlos' nails. My uncle dropped the candlestick, shouting: "Run! Run, before it's too late! Don Carlos has seen us! We're lost! ... No, there's one chance. Open the window wide. Don Carlos will think it's the mirror and jump through it."

Meanwhile, Don Carlos, who had dismounted from his horse, had gone to the mirror and observed that it was broken. He turned slowly and looked at my uncle, still holding his left arm. "Quick, hurry," cried my uncle.

I rushed to the nearest window and threw it open. The wind blew into the room and frightened Don Carlos' horse. The animal seemed incredibly frightened. It began running about the room in all directions, knocking everything over as it passed. Don Carlos seized it by the mane and climbed onto it. My uncle had squeezed up against the wall to avoid the horse, "Run! Run! Don Carlos is angry! Nothing can stop him now! The mirror is broken! Don Carlos cannot leave!"

Then I watched the most horrible sight of my life. An atrocious vision that has left in me an infinite vertigo of sorrow and horror. Don Carlos' horse galloped about the room in all directions while his master kept turning round in order not to lose sight of my Uncle Ivan. My uncle ran to avoid being trampled on by the maddened beast. The crushed and bleeding body of Isabella del Mancio lay by the fireplace. I was hidden behind my curtain and could not move, paralysed by all the horrors I was seeing.

At a certain moment, the horse passed very close to my Uncle Ivan. Don Carlos bent down, picked him up and laid him across his saddle, in front of the pommel. I let out a great yell and hurled myself at the animal. But it was too late. Don Carlos had seen the window and his horse was already through it. "Goodbye," cried my uncle. "I loved you too much ...."

Next day, in the village, a fisherman swore he had seen a horse galloping on the sea. Two men were on the horse. One seemed to be very tall. The other was not moving. He seemed to be dead.

THE OCTAGONAL ROOM

Michel Tremblay
translated by Michael Bullock

As soon as he had returned from his trip around the world, Frederick invited me to dine with him in order, as he put it, to re-establish a friendship unfortunately interrupted during his trip. I had not seen Frederick for three years and I was very surprised to observe how much he had changed since his departure. This was no longer the joyful, carefree Frederick I had always known; it was a dejected, nervous, pale man; a man who had aged, too. His temples were already beginning to turn grey and wrinkles furrowed his brow and each side of his nose. This was no longer the same man at all.

The first thing Frederick said when he saw me was: "You haven't changed. You haven't changed at all in three years. Aren't you ever going to grow old?" I didn't know what to reply. I didn't want to tell him he had aged a great deal and that he looked ten years older than his real age. "I know," he said after an embarrassing silence, "I've aged a great deal. You won't recognize me, you'll see. This three-year journey, all the countries I have been to, have completely transformed me. I have a lot to tell you. After dinner I'll show you my treasures." But he didn't sound very sincere and his smile was forced.

I examined him attentively during the meal and observed that he was nervous, worried to a surprising degree. He kept looking in the direction of the dining-room door and didn't listen to half I said to him. He seemed to be waiting for someone or something. Nevertheless, he forced himself to be gay; but his expression betrayed anguish and I wondered what could be frightening him so much. Because he was afraid, I was sure of that. By the end of the meal, he was trembling and sweat was pouring down his forehead. He had unbuttoned the collar of his shirt and his hands were in constant movement, running from one glass to another, from the table-cloth to his dripping forehead.

When we left the dining-room, he was in such a state of nerves that he could scarcely keep upright.

When he had shut the library door behind us, he rushed towards me, begging me to save him, to deliver him from the frightful things that were pursuing him everywhere and ceaselessly tormenting him. I didn't understand a word he was saying and was obliged to shake him violently in order to calm him down a bit. "What's the matter with you?" I asked when he had quietened down. "Are you ill? I can't make head or tail of what you've been telling me. Explain more clearly." Frederick had sat down in an armchair and seemed to have aged by another ten years. "It's terrible," he said finally. "Sometimes I have the impression that everything that is happening to me doesn't really exist and that I'm mad. But these things are real and I can't get rid of them."

"But what things?" I asked. "What things?"

"You'll know soon," replied Frederick. "I can feel they're going to come. I didn't think they would come today; that's why I invited you to dinner. But during the meal I heard them behind the door of the octagonal room—that's the room in which they've taken refuge since my return—and I'm sure they're getting ready to throw themselves upon me as soon as my will is too weak to fight them."

I thought Frederick had gone mad. What were these things he was talking about and why had they taken refuge in the octagonal room?

I rose and made for the door.

"Where are you going?" asked Frederick.

"To the octagonal room," I replied.

"No, no, don't go! Don't open the door of that room! Even more of them would come and they would kill me."

"But who are 'they'? What are they? You must tell me, Frederick. I must know, if you want me to help you."

"You wouldn't believe me if I told you what they were. When you've seen them you'll believe me. Don't go into the octagonal room. They will come here. You will see them. If you don't open the door of the octagonal room, they won't all come. But if you open the door, thousands of them, millions of them, will be able to escape."

Frederick had risen. He was shouting like a madman, gesticulating and almost running about the room. "You must be imagining those things," I told him as I opened the library door. "Come with me to the octagonal room. You'll see there's nothing there. That's the only way to free yourself from these hallucinations."

"No, don't go, I beg you! You'll regret it."

He followed me as I made for the octagonal room, trying to pull me back by the shoulders or by the jacket. I gave him a push and he collapsed on the carpet of the corridor sobbing. He was in a paroxysm of madness and was screaming like someone being tortured. "You'll be sorry! You will be responsible for my death! You will be my murderer! If you open that door, you will kill me!"

When I came to the octagonal room, which was at the end of the ground-floor corridor, I put an ear to the door. I didn't hear anything. Everything was silent in the room.

The octagonal room, so-called because of its eight walls and also because of the octagonal shape of all the furniture and all the objects in it, was my friend's grandparents' room. One day Frederick's grandmother, who had been a very eccentric, very strange woman, had decided to build a room which was octagonal in shape and in which would be placed an octagonal bed and octagonal furniture and accessories. She had lived very happily in this room and had committed suicide there at the age of eighty.

"I can't hear anything," I told Frederick, who had risen and was standing in the middle of the corridor, his eyes popping out of his head. "There's nothing out of the ordinary in that room."

I quickly opened the door. Frederick yelled with fear and rushed into the library, shutting the door behind him.

There was nothing suspicious in the octagonal room. But the room really was strange. I had never entered it without feeling ill at ease. I had always had the impression that this room had been the work of a deranged mind. Nevertheless, Frederick had sworn that his grandmother had never been mad. What astonished me most when I entered this room was the window. This eight-sided window looked like a ship's porthole and I was always surprised to see a garden with trees and flowers when I looked out.

I poked about everywhere, looking ... I didn't really know what for. I found nothing. The octagonal room was completely inoffensive. I went out of the room, leaving the door open, and made for the library. I found Frederick almost unconscious in an armchair. "There's nothing in the room," I told him. "You must be imagining these things. You should see a doctor."

"Shut the door," whispered my friend. "That will delay them a few moments."

I shut the door and went up to Frederick. "You must tell me everything," I said gently. "I may be able to help you when I know. Tell me everything."

But Frederick refused to explain everything. He only told me these things had been following him ever since he left Africa, attacking him almost every day. "They haven't succeeded in killing me yet because they never attack in very large numbers. I've managed to kill thousands of them, but others come to replace the ones I kill, bigger ones, fiercer ones. The day they all come .... When I got home yesterday, they settled in the octagonal room. They are sure to have multiplied during the night. They made a terrible noise in the octagonal room ... all night long ... a terrible noise. But they haven't come out of the octagonal room. This morning I didn't hear them anymore. Then I thought they would leave me in peace for a day or two as they sometimes do. But you opened the door for them. They will come. Oh, they will come and kill me!"

No sooner had he uttered these words than I heard an odd noise in the corridor. Frederick had heard it too. He took my hand and said: "There they are! Goodbye, my friend. This time a very large number of them will come and kill me. Do you hear them? They have come out of the octagonal room and are making for us!"

I rose and was about to look into the corridor, but Frederick looked at me so beseechingly that I hadn't the courage to oppose him.

The noise was growing louder every second until it became deafening. It was a strange noise, like that made by millions of tiny feet and tiny mouths. It was as though a countless number of tiny creatures were walking in the corridor, bumping into each other, pushing each other to get somewhere as fast as possible ... I don't know where. There was a cracking sound as though someone were crushing tons of woodlice or other tiny insects. And this hideous clicking was growing constantly louder, coming closer and closer to the library. Frederick and I were watching the door and we were afraid. I was beginning to believe what my friend had told me.

Suddenly Frederick jumped up from his chair crying: "Look! Some of them are slipping under the door!" It was no good my looking in the direction in which my friend was pointing; I saw nothing. I only heard the horrible noise coming from the corridor. "I don't see anything," I shouted to my friend, my nerves on edge. "Yes, yes, look, they're coming towards you! Squeeze up against the wall, they'll reach you, they're quite close to you!" But I couldn't see anything! I couldn't see anything! I started yelling with fear and squeezed up against the wall.

Frederick began to run around the room. He kept slapping himself all over, as though to crush things clinging to his clothes. But there was nothing on Frederick's clothes. And that damned noise was getting louder and louder.

The library door, although it was of massive oak suddenly began to give way under the terrific pressure of things I couldn't see. The wood cracked; the hinges were torn off. Suddenly it caved in and a wave of noise flooded the room. Frederick was no longer screaming. He seemed to be under attack by millions of creatures that were devouring him. He fell back under the pressure of these invisible creatures and began to scream again. "My mouth is full of them. My eyes are full of them. They're eating me up. You have killed me! You have killed me!"

I shut my eyes when the noise reached its peak.

RECURRENCE

Michel de Celles
translated by Basil Kingstone

At the end of the huge laboratory, the great glass cylinder rose like a bluish pillar towards the vault hollowed out of the living rock. It was topped by a hemispherical dome, with no break or line between it and the vertical shaft; the apparatus looked like a gigantic test-tube set upside down on the tiled floor. At the bottom, slightly above the floor, was the entrance, a door, also of glass, but set in a heavy metal frame, like an elongated oval porthole, a geometrical vagina in the side of the erect phallus.

Naked, H(n) stepped out of the translucent column through the narrow opening, his skin streaming with the organic fluids which had regenerated him. He rubbed his eyes, half opened them, still squinting, and walked like an automaton towards the living area. He took a short shower to rinse off, after which pulsating waves of air wrapped around him and dried him and massaged and rubbed him. All trace of sleepiness gone, he took a one-piece combination garment from a locker and put it on. Supple boots were built into it. He had only to do up an almost invisible zipper, and he was dressed in perfect comfort in the universal synthetic material invented at the end of the millennium, in the style which had become standard for the next generation.

Thus revived and suited up, H(n) looked around the great room, lit by an ash-white diffuse artificial light, at the consoles, the instruments and the tubes of the automated equipment.

Near the cylinder, panels of lights lit up and went out in turn, apparently at random. The calm rhythm of their twinkling indicated that the master computer was in control of the laboratory, and that the underground reactor was inexhaustibly providing the required energy. Luminous dials and numerical counters gave clear and reassuring readings. Clocks silently told the time in various time zones, and one told star time; without them, time would have seemed to be standing still. Only the barely audible hiss of the air conditioning wove a light rustling net around the ample silence; the air, continually recycled, none of it drawn from outside, contained a fixed percentage of negative ions, the optimum humidity, and a small proportion of vegetable exhalations from the hydroponic tanks.

After his brief reconnaissance, H(n) turned on his heels.

At the far end, the room narrowed into a dark corridor, its ceiling lower than the vault. It was ten metres long and ended in a wall of tinted glass.

The dull light which came through this wide window drew H(n). He strode firmly towards it.

In the gloom, at the entrance to the corridor, he glanced at the oval pod standing against the wall, as if delicately set down on the tiles, its axis horizontal.

Inside it the Follower lay asleep. Under the half-shell of one-way glass which was the lid of this egg-shaped sarcophagus, he was breathing regularly, looking peaceful, protected from light and sound, supported as if in a womb by the warm liquid under the taut supple film of material he lay on. Sometimes one eyelid stirred almost imperceptibly; he was probably dreaming, having passed the first stage of sleep where fatigue had weighed on him like a leaden shroud.

H(n) recognized his familiar features and his impersonal air, which bothered and annoyed him. He didn't try to understand why; he walked straight over to the big window.

Despite the thickness of the glass, which had withstood the force of the explosions, despite its old-gold tint, due to the metallothermic treatment to prevent penetration by nuclear radiation, he could see, down in the plain, the silhouette of the Metropolis, now a pathetic lifeless model. Some of the skyscrapers still stood and reflected brief flashes of light as the sun climbed towards noon.

How many months had it been since the Cataclysm? It all seemed so long ago. First, the radio and TV stations had given fifteen minutes' warning; the surveillance satellites had just detected a swarm of ballistic missiles leaving their launching pads on the other continent. Interception and retaliatory missiles had been launched at once. Then radar screens had filled with a cloud of fluorescent insects moving slowly in a solemn courtship dance, couples mating then disappearing, others avoiding each other at the last moment with an unexpected graceful darting motion. Next, on the horizon, flashes that blinded you despite the tinted glass: hedgehopping missiles had avoided the radar net and the laser cannon. Now neutron bombs were frying the city and the suburbs. The same dazzling spectacle could be seen throughout the country, it was learned later.

In the following hours and for a few days, the strident voices on radio and TV had borne witness to the planet-wide panic and disorder. Those who had escaped the intense radiation, being far from big cities or in some area the generals had overlooked, had tried to flee. Panic on the highways, soon blocked by hulks of cars, fighting and murder around looted food stores. And where was there to go? Radioactive fallout spread everywhere. One by one the voices fell silent in the middle of a last heroic, useless, horrible eyewitness report, and the pictures went black during a final commentary by a hollow-eyed dying journalist.

But no invaders had come; the enemy had suffered the same destruction and slaughter.

In the foreground, just outside the solid glass curtain, the ground sloped down gently for a little way, rocky and dotted with scrawny tufts of grass and a few mountain flowers, as far as the precipice which dropped towards the plain. It all seemed greyish brown. An effect of lingering radiation or the tinted glass?

H(n) noticed a butterfly, apparently colourless, but still visiting flowers. It was the first animal life he remembered seeing for a long time. Had the chrysalis suffered a strange mutation, even though insects resist radiation? He felt nostalgic for a moment, remembering his former colleagues. They had almost all decided, soon after the explosions and although it was most unwise, to go and help their families in the city. None of them had come back. On the other hand, a few weeks later, a little group of unknown survivors, in rags, mostly women, already wasting away, at the cost of who knows what wanderings, had come and pressed their gaunt faces against the thick dark glass. Had they seen him in his shelter, deciding after a cold analysis of their chances of survival (nil) and in view of the disastrous consequences for the laboratory if he let them in, that the only rational act was to leave them to their fate? After a few hours they had all gone away. He tried to dispel the image of women with desirable bodies, lifeless eyes and heads bald in patches.

H(n) remembered all these events clearly, but in a strange way, as if he were not sure he had experienced them himself. An overwhelming vision in his memory, the fire day had left a lurking gut fear, like an archetypal anguish inherited from ancestors long gone, reincarnated in him before he came out of the cylinder and its warm wet soundproof atmosphere like an amniotic fluid.

He went back to the central control panel, unconcerned about the Follower who was still asleep.

For, despite the time that had passed since he had been isolated in the laboratory, he had, oddly enough, not felt really bored, as if he hadn't yet had time to be. At most he regretted being idle and unable to use the vast knowledge he was convinced he possessed.

The scientific equipment was functioning automatically, without the least irregularity. The readings he took on the control sensors, to satisfy his conscience, showed nothing unusual, none of the apparatus needed to be corrected or adjusted.

"So what am I here for? Of what use is this waiting, out of reach of the ancient madness of my race? Shall I ever see again decontaminated, fit, likeable human beings? At any rate somebody other than this dull Follower, always asleep, stupidly dreaming."

Then suddenly H(n) had the Idea!

He would make a copy of himself, a brother, someone worth talking to, by cloning. What could be simpler than doing a biopsy on himself, on the end of his index finger for example, isolating a living cell, since he had all the equipment: scalpel, electron microscope and slides. Then he would only have to induce that cell to multiply by constant division, making sure that the new cells, which would soon be increasing at a dizzying rate, were controlled, that they formed structures, that the differentiations were properly ordered, so that the specialized organs of the future living being were correctly formed. In short, from the matrix cell to an embryo, from that to a fetus, to a baby, to a complete adult man, following a compressed chronology, by providing an exceptionally appropriate environment. He was sure he could do it. With the help of the reactor and its energy flow, regulated by the computer, the translucent-walled cylinder, the giant womb, would produce within itself the vital processes which would lead to a copy of himself, perfect in its form and with all his genetic information.

"In fact, I will do better than that! To this double, whose brain will be a clean slate before he steps out into the world, I will give my own knowledge and my life experience, by infusing them directly into his conscious and his unconscious. The remote control arms in the cylinder will embrace the figure of bone and muscle; electrodes will touch his temple; drills finer than a hair will bore through his skull down to the brain matter. From the computer, billions of bits of information will be diffused in the cortex, flood through the circumvolutions, activate myriads of synapses, and be stored in the infinity of neurons. All the knowledge previously transferred from my intelligence into artificial memories, anyhow, all the data accumulated in these banks, will transform my Fellow-creature into an all-knowing Superman. A stupendous achievement! A paradoxical reversal, Man creating a God in his own likeness!"

H(n) set to work with feverish concentration. The taking of tissue from his finger, the separation of a typical cell, the verification of its chromosomes, were easy to do with the microscope and its automatic accessories. He put the specimen in a protective lubricant and, through the oblong opening at the base of the glass column, introduced into the enormous womb the vase containing the tiny seed of his future twin.

Now he faced the most difficult step: to devise the brilliant computer programme to maintain inside the tube the conditions favourable for gestation. An exciting arduous task, which took hours, but when he finished it he was full of confidence.

Before unleashing the proliferation of cells, however, there remained the problem of providing them with the right nutrition, in the exact proportions required to constitute the new being. To identify, collect and measure them would take many more hours. Did he have the courage? The ambition of making his Promethean dream reality, his haste to see his creation completed, inspired him with a simple striking final solution: the body of the sleeping man.

It contained all the needed elements in exactly the right quantities. The Creator did not need to have scruples, even if the Follower had to die to yield up his constituent elements. Besides he would live again, wouldn't he, identical in all his molecules even though they would be assembled in a different order—and what's more, he would be perfected.

Without further hesitation, H(n) fetched a hypodermic and ran and gave a final anaesthetic to the man resting unawares in the plastic cocoon.

It was an easy matter to undress him and take off his helmet, plugged into the pod, which had regularized his brain waves by transmitting them to the computer. It took one last great effort to carry the body to the digestor, in which the flesh would be skinned, the fat melted, the organs dissected and the skeleton ground up. The resulting sludge would be mechanically stirred, then would macerate to distil a nutritious liquid, which would be injected into the cylindrical reservoir and vaporize in that closed world where, under fluctuating pressure, with the temperature sometimes ice-cold and sometimes stifling, with electric sparks arcing from terminals, primordial life would be born amid damp turbulent ionized gases, as if on the surface of a new planet. He had masterfully planned the unfolding of a compressed but inexorable Genesis, which would culminate the next morning in the appearance of the flawless Adam.

In his excitement, while he had been carefully carrying out his many tasks, H(n) had not noticed time passing. The big dark window, a black gulf at the end of the corridor, told him that night had long since fallen. He felt proud of his work, but also exhausted, and impatient. But it would be many hours yet before his creation saw the light of day. Meanwhile he should rest. Besides, his sleeping hours would be put to good use. He had planned the operations so that during that time the prodigious knowledge in his mind and the invincible power of his creative will would be fed into the computer. He lay down on the warm flexible bed where the Follower had been lying. He put on the helmet, lined with a close-woven net of ultra-sensitive antennae, and closed the bubble lid, thus establishing contact with the inflexible mineral programmed brain.

He fell asleep at once.

***

At the end of the laboratory the glass cylinder rose like a pillar towards the vault.

Naked, H(n+1) stepped out of it through the door at the base, his skin streaming with the organic fluids which had regenerated him. After he had rinsed off in a shower, pulsating waves of air dried him; then he put on a one-piece combination garment.

Looking around the great room and its apparatus, he was drawn by the light to the wide window, and walked over to it.

On the way, he glanced at the pod where the Follower was sleeping, with his familiar features.

Despite the thickness and the tint of the glass, he could see, down in the plain, the lifeless Metropolis.

When was the Cataclysm?

$H(n+1)$ went back to the control panel, unconcerned about the Follower who was still asleep. Idleness weighed heavily on him; he felt useless and alone.

Then suddenly he had the Idea.

He set to work with feverish concentration ....

***

At the end of the laboratory, the cylinder.
Naked, $H(n+2)$, streaming ....

FIVE FABLES

Paul Paré
translated by Basil Kingstone

Man Has Descended From the Tree

For some time I had been huddled up in the fourth finger of a horsehair glove, bashing my spine against the underside of the table. It is a worthwhile exercise and everything comes to him who stretches far enough to reach himself. Reach out and touch yourself.

It's a funny thing. Odd, strange. It happened strangely, all at once. I was listening to weird music—perhaps the tape recorder wasn't working properly—composed of, on the one hand, the passacaglia in C minor (by JSB, of course) and on the other the fourth verse of Titelouze's "Ave Maria Stella"; the two tunes, one forwards and one backwards, joined together, took on the exact harsh shape of the fourth finger of the horsehair glove. It's strange and I can hear no better for it.

On the table, at the same time, if things can happen at the same time, my eye unwound a hundred and fifty metres of black thread, as it said on the reel, and my eye, the same one, unwound itself for a hundred and fifty metres at the same time, without being surprised, without my even thinking of the surprise that results. It's the first time that's happened. I used to have to count the metres one by one to find out how many there were and make sure there was no break. Sometimes I would skip ten or twenty, like years taken off the life of the client of a sanatorium who doesn't know what to do with his health.

To begin with I didn't believe the bit about the thread, the reel of thread, but at the same time it left me pretty unstrung. In the end I don't know, I suppose that's how it happens, I suppose the thread of the idea, the thin thread of the idea, has an idea. And I followed the thread.

Having followed the thread, I found myself in loam, something between clay and sand. All I had to do was grow. At least, if I'd asked anyone, that's what they'd have said. Grow. Without taking root too deeply. Come planting-out time, every little rootlet counts. If one or two are missing, it's riskier. So I decided to take root, but not to overdo it, just enough so that a fresh smell of humus could be detected on the soles of my feet.

I looked at everything with fresh eyes. At dandelion height at first; seldom did I look above the knee. Beyond that, the red jasmines have the crusty bread which waits to satisfy the appetites of birds.

I didn't rush, I was in no hurry. I knew this loam had taken a liking to me, that it was nurturing me with nitrogen and would do so as long as I had the common sense to grow. How one manages to do that, is another question.

When I got to be the size of a tree—maybe a bread-fruit tree, maybe an arbutus—I was very tired. My roots were shot.

***

It's cold up here. That was the first thought that came into my mind. And yet my feet were sweating.

A chill is never comfortable, but it's the best way to make situations change when they are too stable. I could see a long way ahead, of course, since I was up high. Miles and miles of horizon, and kilometres too, for that was the time when the two systems crossed and nobody knew where they were. People were shivering at thirty degrees, and at the same time sweat was pouring down their faces. A chill and a fever.

We had to invent a counter-system to survive.

It was at this moment of the bark that she came. The crust was nice and golden, she could see at once that I was a bread-fruit tree. And I said to her, Don't slice it, tear off a piece; the crust will grow back.

I don't think I have to tell you that it isn't easy to explain. Because it isn't easy to understand. In fact it can't be understood.

I don't need to climb on a chair to see a few strips of horizon farther. And sometimes I'm so completely cramped that I have trouble freeing myself from the bark to see the colour of my skin. Inside, inside the inside, I manage to squint so often that I see myself upside down twice before I see myself right side up.

And yet she manages to gently part the bark without it hurting and touches the crumb with one or two fingers.

Then I am overcome by a strange undefinable sensation, and I take heart and grow a bit more—but only in thickness, and very discreetly, so as not to frighten the birds.

***

One day needles started growing on me. On a pine tree they're normal. On a bread-fruit tree they're pretty, maybe even decorative, but they really don't add anything.

So I shook myself.

***

As a rust-coloured carpet they're much better. It feels good underfoot. Feet can get a foothold. Me too, when it isn't too windy, I manage to bend over that far so as to enjoy it. But I often ache all over when I straighten up, and from then on I'm not very straight. To tell the truth, I never was. But that's all right, you get used to it.

Often she comes and lies down close by. I shake off even more needles, they always fall from the top. I shake off needles till they cover her completely. And then I puff a bit so as to uncover her face. And so as to smile. Just smile. I can do more than that: I can burst out laughing, guffaw at any moment including the wrong one, snicker discreetly, sometimes giggle, but I prefer to smile.

***

It was a bit later that I undertook to pull my roots out of the ground. One by one. Cautiously. How shall I put it? As if to walk without being seen.

All these precautions were unnecessary. I could have gotten loose with one pull, for the loam had remained soft. But I wanted to discover the meaning of this slowness to come out, this lingering birth.

To begin with it's surprising. You tend to put your feet back in the same holes, until you realize what it means to have feet. First one, that's the hardest step, then two. You can do it if you look down, and we know everything comes from below. And then you look just ahead of you. Once you start, you do it pretty well.

But the important thing is not to blink, even in bright sunlight, because then you're lost. You lose the thread. And you can never be sure of finding on your table a hundred and fifty metres of black thread to wind up with one glance.

***

I have neither the strength nor the desire to believe that I ever had feet subtle enough to free themselves from the root-holes of a tree; if I had come out of a tree, I might have wanted to stay in it. Until they chopped me down to analyse me. Even if I ended up as matchwood, or digging scraps out of hollow teeth. But that never happens, and I defy anyone to come out of a tree without getting splinters deep in his guts.

Cause and Effect

It all started when they awarded him the Nobel Prize for the silent majority, to thank him for not having written anything at all. He accepted graciously and didn't give a speech, thinking, "Since they're honouring me for keeping quiet...." But people can't always keep their mouths shut, and when he'd had enough he sat on a little pot and started laying like a cow. Soon the little pot was too small and he made do with squatting at the top of a slope. Everybody except the illiterate realized what was going on: you can't refuse a Nobel prizewinner the right to express himself, in fact you have to publish his writings and record the slightest twitches of his brain.

Soon the bookstores and the libraries were bulging with fat volumes; the janitors and garbage trucks couldn't keep up. They also had to hire extra firemen to put out all the overheated paper which threatened to set the world on fire. Clandestine presses ran day and night, whole forests were chopped down.

When he stood up, they thought he was done, but he just went and squatted on top of a mountain, admittedly not a very high one. And when he stood up again, they wondered what he would think of this time. He hadn't much choice. There wasn't a sheet of paper left on this side of the earth, the real writers were tearing their hair out, the bald ones were tearing the hairs out of their armpits, the playwrights were writing "the show must go on" everywhere, on rags, on their neighbours' backs, on ministers' shirt fronts, on bar tables and on their own cuffs.

A sigh of relief arose when he stood up with his pants firmly zipped and belted. The flood had stopped. But now he started talking; he talked for days and days, weeks, months, without stopping, remembering by heart everything he had written. Luckily, when the word is made flesh, you can always cover your ears. Only the booksellers were in despair for a moment; some of them jumped in the river, others opened butcher's shops. Words are wasted on a hungry man, they say, and they're right, the butchers made a mint. Only a few purists missed the good old days when paper didn't smell of blood.

As for the speaker, he kept on talking, talking, until they decided to isolate him. They took him up a high mountain, persuading him that from that height he would capture more people's interest, and they set up a whole battery of dummy microphones in front of him, and told him, "Don't eat them all at once, there won't be any more." But he was very hungry and getting hungrier, and as he rocked back and forth he started to eat some of the mikes, till there were none left. After which he went on talking, to himself, and they didn't hesitate to say he'd gone mad; but they didn't know, they were just talking, and they didn't want to know, because then they'd have had to look after him, hire specialists, and charter ships to satisfy his slightest whims. But alone on his mountain, he started yelling so loud they could hear him from one sunrise to the other. They couldn't sleep anymore, even with ear-plugs. It's true that the shopkeepers who sold ear-plugs made a mint. However, there aren't many of those and that wasn't much help. As you can see, there is no end to this dangerous story, and we'd better stop while we still have our health.

Autopsy of an Incident

Only after a very long pause for thought did he start moving, painfully, sideways. For those who aren't expecting it, thought often looks like a rudimentary form of stupidity, but of course that's only an appearance. He moved in little hops, each time after a pause of varying length, sometimes a second or two, sometimes an hour or a month.

In this frame of mind he attempted to cross the street. He began by saying he was sorry, by which he meant that it was no fault of his and it might take a while. At the start of this movement nobody paid attention, it was morning and there wasn't much traffic. It was when the first car ran over him that the whole thing really began.

The driver got out of his car, which was as long as two hearses and red with misplaced pride, and started to hurl abuse at him: "You filthy bastard, why don't you look where you're going, you nearly dented my car, look what you've done." In fact there wasn't a mark on it, or on the driver, but there you are, people like to take advantage of the situation, and the driver added, "You won't get away with this, you goddam hooligan, you'll pay for all the damage." And as further proof of his statement, he started kicking him. At that moment he raised his head slightly, painfully, then slowly lowered it, thus indicating either that he was ashamed of what he'd done, or else that he was prepared to pay his debt to society, the supreme price if necessary, as long as he was allowed to go on his way. The driver calmed down a little and tucked his visiting card in his victim's braces; then he got back in his car, which must not have been badly damaged by the disaster, because it took off at once.

He, after lying motionless for what seemed to us a very long time, gave a little jump sideways. Thinking he was pretty clever, he immediately did it again, without thinking, and landed heavily on the right foot of a fat lady, lilac-coloured above, fuchsia below and crimson overall, who was crossing the street at that moment. She uttered a cry of indignation and began to reel off, in a style which did not square with her clothing at all, a string of insane expressions which were hard to take: "You filthy crab, you filthy maggot, watch where you're putting your belly, you're ruining my shoes." In fact, he was only resting on the toe of one shoe, but she obviously intended to get a new pair out of this. She pulled her foot back so sharply that he rolled to one side and had all the trouble in Ulster to resume a decent position, because at that moment his greenish belly could be seen and it wasn't very pretty. He looked sideways at the lady and said polite things, a little muffled at first, but then clearly audible: "I'm so sorry, madam, I deeply regret having offended you, you are infinitely kind, and I firmly intend not to do it again." It was a well-known formula most likely to obtain mercy, but the fat lady completely ignored these pacifying words and yelled, "You filthy little bastard, you won't get to do it again, you are going to jail. Did you see that? He tried to pinch my ass!"

It wasn't true, but everyone pretended they had seen it, and the street started to echo with curses as rare and huge as blue whales.

He was no bigger than a fly. He summoned all his strength, but it didn't all answer the call. Even so, he managed to jump twice as far as usual. People yelled, "Look out, he's trying to get away...follow that man...don't lose sight of him...hey, the bastard nearly got away down that sewer grating...a spy? no sir, he's worse than that, he's a rabble rouser...a revolutionary... he tried to stir up public opinion...he was preparing to overthrow the government...luckily they're keeping an eye on him...look under his belly...he's got bombs hidden there... look out, he'll blow us all up!"

This flood of words didn't seem to surprise him in the least. He was wondering how he came to be the object of so much attention. Just at that moment, in other words just as he started to smile, the police cars arrived, and the fire trucks, and the riot squad; helicopters buzzed the street; from the other direction tanks came rolling, raising clouds of dust, their guns pointed at that thing lying humbly on the pavement two inches from a sewer grating.

From that moment on, the whole incident took place too fast to take notes. It seems he exploded in the middle of the street, splattering people with a thick blue blood. A first cannon shot was fired at the people who were wiping themselves, then another, then the helicopters sprayed the streets with deadly fire.... Details at eleven or tomorrow....

Timbuctoo, Timbuctoo

I didn't want to listen to myself till I was done trembling.
In Timbuctoo there are big black trains with teeth, which grab travellers and chew off their ears. It is important to protect yourself against this. I was wearing a transistorized headphone radio and listening to light music.
At nightfall the train set off, leaving a lot of blood behind it on the tracks. In the dark you can't see it too much. You had to know, or have lost one or two ears. I was sitting on a filthy hassock between a snivelling old woman and a man who chewed bits of tobacco and spat out of the window at the cows. He seldom missed. When there weren't any cows he spat anywhere and sometimes farther than that. It did no harm.
Soon afterwards, or at least it seemed to me we hadn't been going for very long, the train stopped. Depart midnight, arrive midnight. In perfect safety. Destination Timbuctoo. Funny thing, we'd gone in both directions all night.
These things happen.
But we have to start again tonight, the train is still hungry.

It Can't Be Any Different

He cannot understand how anyone can fail to see how obvious it is. But it seems to him that facts are facts and you just have to look at them to see it. "I'd as soon tell you right away," he repeats for the hundredth time, "that's how it is and it can't be any different." "Different from what?" he is asked for the hundred-and-first time. "Different than it is," he feels like answering.
If he is told, "Make an effort to be pleasant," he answers unpleasantly, "If it means an effort on my part I won't find it pleasant, I can feel it, it can't be any different."
All right, it's up to you if you want to make life hard for your-

self! And if he isn't offered caviar for breakfast, he just says, "I was born to live on bread, I never had any luck." He can't understand why there isn't caviar for breakfast every morning. He's told constantly, "People don't like it every morning, they get tired of it, believe me." He invariably answers, "Speak for yourself, I never had it every morning, and I'd like to know what this luxury you choke on tastes like."

One day this remark is thrown in his face, like garbage: "You can never behave the same way as everybody else." He is most indignant: "Sure, and if I behaved like everybody else, I'd soon be told I was only capable of imitating other people." And he adds, "It can't be any different, my way of behaving is the only right one, because it's the only way that suits me."

"All right," he's told, "do as you like, but in future you'll be the only one who thinks like that and you'll be the first to be bored and utterly lonely." "No," he says, "that can't be, I'll never be the only one to think the way I do, because as soon as I've said all I think, since I didn't invent it, there'll be at least two of us who think that way, and I won't be alone at all, there'll be lots of us till the end of time."

He can't understand how anyone can doubt his word, because it's all he has, or so he believes. He can't understand how he can be suspected of calling on words that don't completely reflect his thought. "It's impossible," he observes, "there is always a traitor among us, and you can never be sure of having correctly expressed what you felt, because often at the moment you express it you don't feel it at all, that's how it is and it can't be any different, I've often experienced it myself and you should believe what I say even if I'm liable to deceive you."

People shrug their shoulders because it's all they have to shrug, but he's turned away and doesn't feel the deeply wounding reaction through his heavy overcoat of wildcat fur. Suddenly he turns around and says without a smile: "I really can't understand why you can't understand that you've had it."

The next day it was pouring down rain and nobody thought to wonder why, they were too used to his bad temper. He himself didn't say, but thought, "It's a waste of time, if I tell them they certainly won't understand."

PROWLING AROUND LITTLE RED RIDING HOOD

François Hébert
translated by Basil Kingstone

In memory of C.

The Toad on the Hearth

When Little Red Riding Hood found out that her grandmother had a sister, but that nobody talked about her, her curiosity was aroused. She went into the forest and a woodcutter told her that her great-aunt must be a hundred years old and lived in a castle which was hard to get at and was that way. She went in the direction he pointed and finally saw two high towers above the trees. All around the castle there were brambles, but they parted to let the young visitor through. When she reached the big front door a cat hissed. She rang the bell. A pallid servant opened it and led her to the bedside of the old woman, who was muttering incoherent things: "he didn't come" and "what a nightmare!" and "you're a horrible little boy," which was false as everybody knows, since Little Red Riding Hood was a little girl, the prettiest in the kingdom. The old woman was certainly crazy, and that might explain why at home nobody talked about her. In a vase there was a bouquet of brambles.

"All children are a disaster," said the great-aunt.

"Didn't you have any?" asked Little Red Riding Hood naively, just wanting to leave.

"Only him!" replied the old woman, looking with a grimace at a toad on the cold hearth.

"Pick him up," she added, "warm him, he's cold."

When Little Red Riding Hood touched it, she got a very sharp burning sensation in her hand, as if she had grasped an ember. She cried out, and at the same moment the old woman breathed her last. In the hearth the fire flared up. Little Red Riding Hood set the cake she had brought on the dead woman's bedside table and left. She pricked her knee while struggling through the wall of brambles around the castle. Despite the doctors' efforts, the wound never healed.

"One day you'll understand it all," said her father when she told him her adventure.

"Tomorrow?"

"Later than that."

"When I'm twelve?"

"Later than that."

"When I'm grown up?"

"Later than that."

"When I'm old?"

"Later than that."

"In a hundred years' time, then?"

"You might say that."

The Little Black Thistle

When Little Red Riding Hood came into her grandmother's house, she was horrified by her dark complexion, her piercing eyes, her fleshless ears, her deep wrinkles. She went into the kitchen and got a knife, and pow! she stuck it into the old woman's side. A gloomy howl was heard, that you could have taken for a wolf's. The old woman was dead.

Little Red Riding Hood went home and told the horrible story to her mother, who started crying.

"She was going to die anyway," protested the child, who couldn't understand her mother crying.

"When you're old like your mother," the child added, "I'll kill you, too, because I love you."

Since her mother was still crying, she explained:

"I don't want to grow old. Or die. Do you understand, mommy?"

"No."

"Killing somebody is like picking a flower."

"You're a little black thistle."

"You're my mother; you made me this way."

"Your father will punish you."

Little Red Riding Hood fled into the forest, where she lived like her friends the wolves.

Who Eats Who?

He was a wolf, yes, big, grey, lithe, and with that cold fire in his eyes, that unwavering metallic gaze which was frightening. There was no mistaking it. But also, and grandmother knew it, this wolf she was talking to had two souls: one active and pitiless, a wild beast's soul, and the other a victim's, passive and a bit simple. Grandmother's practised eye had noticed that this wolf wasn't like the others; he was really a wolf in wolf's clothing. A strange disguise! You really couldn't confuse him with any other animal! A whole wolf in fact, with his two skins, the real one and the false one. Which of the two was real and which was false? The first or the second, the inside one or the outside one? That was the trap, and grandmother, being double herself, knew it very well. She had seen the wolf coming.

Grandmother's house looked like its occupant, so much so that without exaggeration you could call her house her second body; and when she let the wolf in, knowing what she was doing, the animal was so to speak *eaten by the house*. The wolf, yes! The eater was eaten! At least, one of the two was. If in the last act the other wolf, the one that survived, ate the second grandmother, the smaller one, that happened in the house—in other words in the mouth of the first grandmother, the bigger one. You can't trust houses.

Imagine, then, in the last act, Little Red Riding Hood coming into this stage with multiple walls; anyone that notoriously innocent will be chewed up by so many pairs of jaws. I wonder which is best: being eaten by a mere wolf; or being swallowed by the grandmother who ate him and being in her belly with the wolf, already half-digested; or being snapped up by a wolf in whose mouth you could still see, in the back of his throat, your grandmother's feet being crunched up.

Never Talk to a Talking Wolf

I'm not sure how wolves die, but I don't suppose their buddies put them in coffins and bury them. They aren't put in the ground, they make their own way down into it, slowly, as the seasons pass. Or else the earth rises up to them, surrounding them, making a discreet tumulus for each of them, not marked by a cross. Among wolves death is without ceremony. But once it happened that a wolf was buried differently.

After talking to this wolf, Little Red Riding Hood met a woodcutter and told him her conversation with the animal. The man warned her:

"Never talk to a talking wolf. Only harm can come of it. Go home."

She did. She ate the cake she was taking to her grandmother and slowly walked home. She lied to her mother about her visit to her grandmother. And the wolf was fooled.

As in the old story, the wolf got into the old woman's house by the well-known trick and ate her. He put on her nightgown and took her place in the bed. And he waited. He waited a very long time, but Little Red Riding Hood never came. Being obstinate, he waited so long that he lost a great deal of weight and then died of hunger. The woodcutter, passing by one day, decided to say hello to the grandmother. When he knocked and got no answer, he used his axe to break down the locked door. He saw that Little Red Riding Hood's grandmother was dead. The family was notified. The old lady was buried according to the local rites. Little Red Riding Hood cried. Since old age and death often make people unrecognizable, it didn't occur to anybody that, rather than the old lady, they might be putting a wolf in the coffin. Certainly they couldn't tell once the lid was nailed down.

The Cake

Mother took out of the oven the most superb cake, beautifully golden, and entrusted it to Little Red Riding Hood to take to her grandmother. The sun had disappeared, the sky was grey. The child went out. Snow started falling.

"It looks like ashes," said mother, parting the curtains to watch her daughter go.

Not far from the mill the little girl fell down, chilled and exhausted. She died, froze, became harder than stone.

"What luck!" thought the wolf when he saw the child.

The poor creature hadn't eaten for three days, since he'd swallowed grandmother. But when he tried to bite into the arm of the frozen Little Red Riding Hood, he broke a tooth. He tried to bite the other arm and lost another tooth. He tried several times to take a mouthful. No use. One by one his teeth fell out in the snow. Finally he had to make do with the cake.

From the mill, the miller watched the first snowflakes of winter falling. They seemed to him big and steel-hard, falling on the forest furiously and pell-mell, like little desperate cogwheels not knowing what to grind. But soon it all settled, and the whole forest was under a great white, hard, flat millstone.

The Story of the Little Pot of Butter

The historian Michelet, who is almost as reliable as story-tellers, declares that little spirits (goblins, imps, will-o'-the-wisps) are fond of butter and like to hide in it. Don't ask me how! People talk a lot about the cake that Little Red Riding Hood took to her grandmother, but they forget that the child also took her a pot of butter. Now in a fairy-tale everything counts. And they say our young heroine's family lived in a village. Maybe. Personally, I may be wrong, but I doubt it, because you are never aware of neighbours. You also get the impression that these people lived alone, isolated, imprisoned in places that were dangerous if not downright hostile. In other words, in the forest. And so we may legitimately wonder where the pot of butter came from, since a fairy story has to provide all the answers to all possible questions.

The day before the fateful day, a wandering merchant had come by and sold that butter to Little Red Riding Hood's mother. The merchant, although he had a splendid coach pulled by four magnificent white horses, was out of breath, because he had been running behind the coach.

"Why don't you ride in your coach?" mother asked him.

"Oh, madam, I can't, I'm only a merchant, I'm not the king—"

"But it's your coach, isn't it?"

"No, madam, *I* belong to *it*. The butter is the coachman."

The man is crazy, thought the good lady, and anybody would have reacted the same way, wouldn't they? Having precious little time to waste, and since she happened to need butter, enchanted or not, she asked the merchant to sell her the little pot of butter, which, as if to confirm the madman's incredible statements, was perched on the coachman's seat.

"I will ask you for a kiss in exchange, madam, which is real gold, madam, and don't talk to me about the stuff other people call real gold, that vulgar heavy metal, which is only symbolic, because let me tell you, madam, that contrary to popular belief everything that glitters *is* gold, madam, and . . . ."

Out of compassion for the poor chatterbox, she paid the asking price. She got the butter and the strange coach went on its way. But that night a horrible chancre grew on her upper lip. Since she wasn't a *completely* rational human being, superstition triumphed and made her blame this evil spell on that damned pot of butter. From her bed, with the sheet up over her, at dawn, she gave her daughter the little pot, telling her to take it to her own mother, with a cake.

"And be quick!" she begged her.

We know the rest: the wolf fooled Little Red Riding Hood and ate her. And her mother's chancre also disappeared. When her husband, who was a woodcutter, came back from a very long stay in distant forests, he found her as beautiful as before; he never knew she had a chancre, or even a little girl by him. That same night she conceived another one. I won't say they lived happily ever afterwards, but just that other things happened to them.

Even a Dead Wolf Is to Be Feared

"A doll!" said her father, watching Little Red Riding Hood leave the house, with the cake and the pot of butter for her grandmother.

"Don't call her that," said her mother.

"What, can't you see that *she isn't natural,* she's as fake as a three-dollar bill? Nothing happens to her that hasn't been foreseen. Her whole life is a game whose rules are dictated by the Powers."

"And what about your life?" asked his wife. It was a good question.

"Yes, of course, and yours, and your very words, and everything, absolutely everything, the village, its inhabitants, even the forest, whose disorder is only a higher order."

The fire was dying on the hearth. The father was filling his pipe, the mother was spinning. Outside the wind was blowing and the leaves falling.

"Our little girl's going to meet the wolf," said the father.

"What are you saying?"

"A wolf who will have eaten your mother."

"What?"

"And then he'll get your daughter."

"I think you've gone crazy."

A little later Little Red Riding Hood came home, still carrying the goodies intended for her grandmother. She announced to her parents that the old lady was dead.

"You see!" said her father. "Eaten by the wolf!"

"No," said his daughter. "I met the wolf. A woodcutter had just split his head open with an axe."

"Grandmother must have just died of old age," said mother, crying.

"But there's blood on your hand," said father.

"I touched the wolf; I wanted to pet him."

A few days later, the village doctor was sent for to look at Little Red Riding Hood, who had come down with leukemia and, foreseeably, died of it in a few weeks.

The Logic of the Fairies

A lot of people don't believe there are such creatures as fairies. Neither good nor bad fairies are much worried about such people; when they have to intervene in their lives, they do so

completely unobtrusively, which leads me to think they respect their prejudices. As for those who talk about them a lot, I think fairies hesitate to interfere in their business, probably for fear of being misunderstood. The logic of the fairies is often beyond us.
There were two fairies in the forest. One said to the wolf:
"Go that way, friend, you'll find something to eat."
The other said to Little Red Riding Hood:
"Go straight ahead, little girl. And mind the wolf! And don't play with the butterflies!"
Now the butterflies were obviously bewitched; they had been sent there to fool the innocent girl. And things happened as the story tells us. One fairy happened to be cleverer than the other, suggesting to the wolf that he should disguise himself as a little girl to fool the grandmother, then as grandmother to fool the little girl.

But why all this complication? And I can't decide which of the two fairies, the good one or the bad one, had previously persuaded Little Red Riding Hood's father to disguise himself as a wolf, or why, unless so that, after so many subterfuges, he could commit incest and cannibalism.

Disappointment

The mother said to her daughter:
"Take this cake to your father. He's in the forest and hasn't eaten for three days."
The man had just chopped down a big tree and was busy lopping its branches off when Little Red Riding Hood found him.
"Thanks," said the father to his daughter, and he ate the cake.
Hidden behind a bush, the wolf was watching the scene. He was starving, too, and he sobbed inwardly. How deplorably dull it all was! Alas, he could not possibly attack an armed woodcutter. He was being left nothing but shavings! In his desperation he bit one paw.

The Wolf's Remorse

When Christ came back to earth, he came across the wolf who had just eaten Little Red Riding Hood. Stunned at seeing him, the wolf exclaimed:

"You again? On my property? You'll spoil my digestion. Go back up to your father's. This is the North, don't you know that? I'm the god here. You've landed in the wrong place. Go back to your palm trees!"

Whereupon the vision disappeared, and the wolf wondered if he'd really met Christ, or had been seeing things.

"Is my digestion upset? Might I be feeling guilty? Have I made a mistake? I think I'm going crazy!"

Remorse was tormenting him. He went home and gave his eldest cub a gift, asking him to take it to Little Red Riding Hood's mother. It was the little red hood. The cub took it and went into the forest, where he met a boy gathering hazel-nuts.

"Shut your eyes," said the boy (who was Little Red Riding Hood's brother), "and open your mouth, and I'll give you a hazel-nut."

The cub obeyed, and from behind his back the boy produced a big dagger and sunk it into the animal's heart, which bled for three days.

In the Dark

It was as black in the wolf's belly as in an ink-well. Little Red Riding Hood (you couldn't even tell she was red, if you didn't know) was very afraid and didn't know what to do. It was sticky and unpleasant in there, not to mention that grandmother took up a lot of room and kept on groaning. Finally she pulled herself together and made up her mind.

"I'm going to bite the wolf. I'm going to eat him from inside."

She took a bite. It was hard and stringy and tasted awful.

"What's going on?" wondered the wolf, surprised at having so much trouble digesting such a succulent meal.

The second mouthful was easier to tear out of the wolf's stomach wall, but no more enjoyable.

"Ooh, ow!" moaned the wolf.

"You eat, too," the child said to her grandmother, who found the idea good, if not pleasant.

Since the wolf was still in grandmother's house and she had some indigestion remedies, he grabbed a bottle and swallowed the last two pills in it. When they got to his stomach, Little Red Riding Hood grabbed them, swallowed one and gave the other to her grandmother. This helped them to finish eating the horrible wolf. They ate him up so completely that in the end only his skin was left.

He was dead, but because grandmother and Little Red Riding Hood were moving around inside him, he seemed to be alive, and so when the hunter arrived and found him in the old woman's house, not knowing the animal had eaten her, he stuck his knife in him. Luckily the blade passed between the two prisoners and didn't hurt either of them. Little Red Riding Hood carefully pulled the knife into the wolf, took it by the handle and cut an opening in the skin, then stepped out, to the hunter's great surprise.

"Come on, grandmother!"

"No, my child, I'm dead tired."

And so saying, she died. Her hour had come; whether the wolf had eaten her or not, the outcome would have been the same.

Old Crimson Riding Hood

Having finished knitting the hood for her granddaughter, grandmother thought it was so fine she decided to keep it for herself. The child came to see her anyway, with a cake and a little pot of butter, but the old lady didn't touch them.

"How well that hood suits you, grandmother!" said the little girl, who didn't think so at all but wanted to be polite, as her mother had advised her to.

"All the better to look like you," said the old woman, looking at herself in the mirror and thinking she had become young again.

But she was fooling herself; the hood didn't make her look more beautiful, in fact the exact opposite. She looked ridiculous, and that's why the people in the village called her Old Crimson Riding Hood.

History has lost track of her, but we may suppose that she either died soon afterwards or went completely crazy. Some say that the old woman gave the child her old, frayed, grey shawl, which the little girl accepted, and that then, on her way home, she met the wolf. He asked her where she was going.

"Home," she said simply.

"Can I come with you?"

"Sure," she said, adding under her breath, "if you can."

Whereupon she threw the shawl over the wolf, who got so tangled up in it that he probably still hasn't gotten free.

Epilogue

Shreds of Little Red Riding Hood's flesh were still stuck between the wolf's teeth when he met a fox who was selling toothbrushes. The wolf bought one. It was deadly, poisoned with nightshade.

KER, THE GOD KILLER

Jean Ferguson
translated by Basil Kingstone

Ker had killed a god; everybody in the tribe of the Saved knew it.

"Ker has killed a god," said the old people.

"Ker has killed a god," said the younger ones, who sighed and turned away at the same time, in a gesture of despair which revealed the terror Ker's recent act inspired in them.

The story didn't go back very far. One sunrise when Ker went into the woods, he saw coming down from the sky a sort of big bubble in which he could make out silhouettes, and heard an unbearable buzzing, as if all the swarms of wild wasps in his country had been stirred up at the same time. The transparent globe rose and flew like a bird; it could hang in the air for many breaths, and when it came close to the ground Ker and the people of the tribe saw a cloud of fine dust go up.

Ker hid in a bush to see what would happen. Then extraordinary beings came out of the bubble, wearing skins that covered their whole body.

Ker had never seen anything like it in his life.

Even their hands were covered in a black skin, so supple that it exactly took the form of their fingers.

Ker had been quick to understand. He was in the presence of gods from the sky, from up there, astonishing gods with pieces of wood in their hands which emitted great brief bursts of flames that burned the leaves on the trees and twisted the young stems.

Ker was afraid, but he went closer.

"The gods are dressed like the trees of the forest," he said to himself, "and that proves they created them."

And he watched them for a very long time. He saw them spread out and listened to them talking a strange language containing many more sounds than he had ever heard. He didn't understand the gods' language, and he severely doubted its value, for if ever a god spoke to him he would at once plumb the depth of Ker's ignorance and perhaps tire of him.

Then, when the gods were tired of making fire with their black sticks, they sat in a circle on the ground and brought out big bags of supple skin, so extraordinarily supple that Ker wondered if he wasn't dreaming wide awake. They took from these bags big round things which shone brightly in the sun. Ker saw clearly that they shone like the surface of patches of water does sometimes, in broad sunlight. Then he was worried, wondering if those shining things would set fire to the forest. But the gods took off the end of the shining things, a sort of little circle they threw down beside them, and they started eating bits from the shiny things—to the great amazement of Ker, who for so many suns had hunted animals everywhere and dug up roots to eat, ever since the world had been turned to glass and the stones made crumbly. The old men of the tribe had told him many times that in the days when man was good on the earth there were all sorts of marvellous things. Doors that opened without your having to do anything except walk towards them. The huts in those days were thousands of times bigger than the huts the tribe built today. Ker knew this, the old ones had told him so. And he wondered why the earth was not as before. And he was very surprised when sometimes he found in the ground big pieces of shiny metal which in former times had been used to build paths across rivers, or so said the wise old men who knew much more than him. But he had trouble imagining how paths could be made of metal, of this shiny metal, to cross rivers, for he never found a path across a river, he swam across them. He had learned since the suns of his childhood to tell bad rivers, the ones you come out of with your hair falling out, the skin peeling off your face, and wounds leaking pus all over your body. Ker knew those bad rivers; a terrible god lived in them, a god called Atomus. Ker didn't know what the word Atomus meant, but the old ones had told him that in the water lived the god Radi-Atomus.

And the wise men of the tribe sometimes uttered strange prayers at the water's edge. They said, "Don't come back, god Radi-Atomus! Don't come back. We don't want you in our clear water anymore, we don't want you anymore."

And Ker had grown used to not going too far, only to the sterile lands where you found very polished hard stones which broke in your hand. He didn't know how that had happened, but the old ones had told him about it one sun's end around the communal fire, and he had felt his limbs shake at the mere description of those dreadful disasters which had devastated the world. He couldn't understand, he didn't know. The old ones knew.

Ker looked at the gods in their transparent ball, transparent like the rocks beyond the frontiers of his village and his country. Ker knew he could walk across his country in three full suns. Ker knew his country was called Oasis. Ker knew that beyond it there was nothing anymore, there was the destroyed world, the sterile world, the frightening world of death. Ker knew that nobody knew the limit of that world, where it ended.

Ker looked at the gods unweariedly. Yet he was afraid, very afraid that the gods might approach him. He didn't want the gods to come towards him. He knew full well that if the gods came towards him, they might burn him with their fire sticks which made so much noise. He was afraid, shaking behind his bush. He shook even more when he noticed that all the men of the tribe had abandoned him. He was worried, but he didn't dare leave for fear of making too much noise. He was afraid, shaking in every limb, that the gods might discover him. Ker looked at the gods.

But the gods piled into their big bird as transparent as water and, with a noise Ker's ears could not stand, went back towards the stars. He was so surprised that he prayed to the god Sun to send his brother gods back again, so he could go on examining them for a long time. Ker was afraid, to be sure, but he also liked danger. He was young. He had a liking for new things. Life made him inquisitive, and that was why he wanted to observe the gods again, in the hope of stealing some of their dangerous secrets from them. For where the gods had fallen, many suns later, grew a sweetish-tasting plant which made you happy and gave you pleasant sleep. Perhaps the gods had wished to show by this sign their desire to make men happy.

In the limited circle where the gods had been, strange plants grew which gave you relief. Ground and mixed with goat's milk and wild honey, they caused a happy numbness in all one's limbs after the long and wearisome hunting. A plant with a perfect sweet taste.

Ker knew the gods could do anything.

He knew it was the gods who had left these seeds for his tribe, to make life easy and sweet.

He wanted the world to be as beautiful as that of the gods, who did not hunt and yet had food.

Many suns later the gods came back. First there was a great buzzing over the horizon, than a shadow over the sun. Ker didn't see them arrive. He was sleeping in his hut to avoid the oppressive dampness of the high sun in the first season. But the cries of fear of the people of his tribe woke him up, and he stopped his ears against the piercing buzz of the gods' bird which was the colour of water. They didn't fly over the huts of the tribe. Ker and his brothers walked for a good half a sun before seeing them in the middle of a clearing. Hidden among the trees, Ker and the others watched the gods' behaviour with immense surprise. By magic, from a little square of skin, big rectangular huts arose, their walls so soft that they rippled in the wind.

And what was even more surprising, when darkness came, the gods did not light a fire like the people of the tribe, but from a long round object they produced light, such an intense light that Ker had to shut his eyes when he looked towards it.

The gods seemed to be settled in for a long time, for several suns and several darknesses passed and they didn't leave. They never came towards the tribe's village. Perhaps because they were too busy collecting pebbles. Sometimes they took out a round tree trunk and stuck it into the ground with a deafening noise. The thing seemed to make holes, for the gods would bend over the ground. And Ker burned with impatience for them to leave so he could see the mystery of these navels close up.

Ker and the men continued their patient watch. They didn't know why they stayed there, relieving each other constantly. Soon the women complained they hadn't enough to eat. And the men went back to hunting. Ker alone spent many suns in the neighbourhood of where the gods were staying, sometimes even forgetting to eat.

And yet almost nothing happened. The gods continued to talk among themselves in their strange language, to make holes and to eat without hunting. For a while Ker really doubted whether they needed to eat. Late one darkness he saw them squatting around their magic fire, and he heard them laughing. Ker felt his heart swell with joy at the thought that the gods also laughed; that way they seemed closer to him.

Then Ker grew weary, and at dew one sun he came back to his people. He was looked at with curiosity, and when he washed in the river he understood why. He had grown thin and his eyes shone feverishly. The world he was coming back from was not that of the other members of the tribe. Ker restrained his impatient desire to go back again and returned to hunting like all the others. But like an old burn, the desire to go back near the gods would suddenly come over him.

Ker hardly paid attention anymore to Kaniana, the girl he wanted the most among all those of the tribe. As a result he noticed that she avoided him. And, feeling weary, he took the only decision which really mattered: to go back to the place where the gods lived. Ker was scared to death they might have gone back up to the stars while he was away.

The gods were still there, in the same place, talking and laughing, going about their strange business.

Then, as was to be expected after so many suns, they reduced their huts to little squares and picked up their round objects. Ker understood with sorrow that they were going back into the sky, and it made him feel very bitter, he couldn't really have said why.

Then he saw a young god leave the group and come towards him. Full of gratitude, Ker decided he wouldn't run away even if he couldn't speak the gods' language. He would show himself to indicate his good intentions. But his nervousness increased as the divine being came nearer. He could hear the leaves and pebbles move under the supple boots.

Then Ker showed himself.

And he was in front of the most beautiful, the most desirable being he had ever seen. At the first glance Ker saw the god was not hairy like him; all his skin was white and probably even softer than that of women.

The god seemed very greatly surprised. He took a sudden step backwards and pointed a little black stick at Ker. They watched each other for a long time, and Ker was extremely disappointed that the god didn't beckon to him to come forward, in fact, didn't seem very pleased by this chance meeting. Every time Ker took a step towards him, he raised his black stick and looked worriedly over his shoulder.

Then Ker decided on one great gamble. He began to advance resolutely towards the young god, who became much more frightened and let out a yell. At the same time Ker felt a tear and a burn in his shoulder, and knew that the stick had spat fire. The god began to run towards the others, but he was forgetting that Ker was young, too, and ran well. He soon caught up with him and embraced him. He did it as delicately as possible, and the god struggled. Ker realized he had no strength, and he also realized the god's skin was fresher than any skin he had ever touched, softer too, softer even than a child's. The god didn't seem to appreciate Ker's attentions, in fact he seemed very afraid. Ker put his hands on the god's penis, and noticed with surprise that it wasn't much different from his own, except it was smaller.

All this time Ker had felt a great disgust rising in him. So the gods were not as powerful as the chief wise man of the tribe had always claimed. So the gods were built like Ker, only smaller and less developed. A caricature of a man, with more powerful weapons, of course, but Ker told himself that if he had the square of skin to put up a hut, the black stick and the mighty fire, he would have been a god, too.

HE WOULD HAVE BEEN THE EQUAL OF A GOD!

This discovery surprised Ker so much that he nearly let go of the young god. Something broke in him, the mighty hunter, he knew he wanted to let drops of water fall from his eyes, like women and children when they felt great pain. He felt afraid of no longer believing in the gods!

Then he felt the god's breath. It was fresh and sweet despite its jerkiness. Then Ker was seized with desire for the young god. He caressed him through his supple green skin. He wanted to reassure him and tell him that he, Ker, wished him no harm. Suddenly the god pointed the black stick at his head. Ker, remembering the burn in his shoulder, twisted it towards the god's chest. There was a noise like a dry branch breaking, and a strange, penetrating, nauseating smell rose to his nostrils.

Over the heart, blood spread across the garment which had been pierced by a small hole. The god looked at Ker intently. He sighed and, with his eyes still open, he fell onto the hairy chest. Ker thought he was dead, but he rejected this idea in horror, for the gods could not die. Despite the blood flowing down his body, Ker warmed him for a long time, because he was becoming cold. Ker hoped that he would decide to move, that he would struggle again, but nothing of the sort happened. And, in the grip of fury, Ker held the god more tightly against him.

He only came out of his torpor when he heard distant cries and great holes of magic light stabbed the air all around him, for it was dark.

Regretfully Ker dropped the young god's already cold body. When he stood up he felt a terrible pain in his shoulder, and at the same time he realized he was shivering. Like a furtive animal, he slunk into some thick bushes.

The gods soon came nearer with their portable fires. They looked for a long time, and every time a stick of light hit his bush, Ker closed his eyes, his forehead soaked in sweat. A god suddenly stumbled over the inert body. He gave a shout. The others ran up. Then Ker was profoundly surprised. Instead of wailing, as happened when a hunter died in the tribe, the gods stood in a circle around their fellow-god, making no movement and saying not a word. They stayed like that for a long time. Then, still without a word, they took the young god's body away.

The sun was already high in the sky when Ker woke up. At the same time the stabbing pain in his shoulder came back, and he had trouble standing up. First he went to the place where the gods had lived. There was nothing left, except a large number of perfectly round little burrows.

No doubt the gods had gone back to the stars.

A little to one side, Ker saw the ground had been freshly dug, and he understood that that was where the young god lay buried.

Ker was too weak, he had to return to the tribe, but he promised himself he would come back.

For many suns he had no strength and no desire to live. He was well looked after by the women, who could not make his wound out. He couldn't have explained it himself. Being young and strong, in time he completely recovered. He was left with only a stiffness in the shoulder and a little round scar.

He hadn't breathed a word of his adventure to the tribe.

Many suns later, the village was aroused by the shouts of a group of hunters. They had been to the spot where the gods had stayed, and they had seen a frightening, incomprehensible thing. The rain had washed away the soil where the young god was buried, and an utterly astonishing sight had appeared before their amazed eyes. Enshrined in a block of material as clear as water, the young god lay, perfectly preserved. And the hunters had decided to bring him to the chief wise man for an explanation.

Ker felt a long shudder at the sight of the young god, who hadn't changed at all since the sun of his death. At most he looked a little more tired. Ker touched the hard translucent block, thinking the young god's body had kept the same warmth he had felt in it. But the material was cool and only grew warm where he touched it. The young god still had the same wound in his chest.

The chief wise man at once had a hut built, and on a carefully dressed stone the young god in his translucent tomb was laid out to be worshipped. The women loved him even though he was dead, for he was handsome. Sometimes at night they dreamed he was making love to them. As for the men, they loved him for other reasons, especially because he was a god come down from the stars.

Then the chief wise man summoned the tribe and spoke for a long time. Ker listened to him. The chief wise man praised the marvellous stone which was preserving the god's life.

But then Ker stood up and told of the young god's death. There was great sadness in the whole tribe as they listened to his story. The death of a god was an immense sacrilege, which required sacrifices, or else the angry gods would come back and destroy the tribe.

Then the chief wise man spoke again. He described the destruction of the world, which the tribe of the Saved had escaped. In the sky there had been a terrifying noise of thunder, and the land had moved in huge waves like those of the sea. The tribe of the Saved had climbed a mountain which seemed higher than the others. Then it had rained for a long time, too long. Many nights, for there were no more suns.

After a very long time the waters of the flood had begun to go down. Little by little the earth had been uncovered. And the Saved had howled with astonishment, for the known world no longer existed. There was nothing of the former world in the tangle of twisted trees, their branches greasy, dirty and damp and full of seaweed in which monstrous fish had been caught and were dying. The Saved were sick to their stomachs with disgust and horror. From the bottom of their hearts they were sorry they had offended a powerful god whose vengeance had almost wiped them out.

Where the fresh girls had gathered fruit of delightful colours and tastes, now great slimy octopuses waved their arms, looking for any sort of prey. And in the distant plain everything had disappeared, the landscape, the huts, the paths, everything. Instead there were swarms of filthy giant crabs, whose immense stench came on the wind to the weakened discouraged people. They stayed inside their caves to escape the world below. And they hoped for the sun, but it didn't come, and even the stars had fled into the depths of the sky.

The people remained on the mountain for a long time, but hunger drove them down to the sticky plain full of lurking dangers. Far off they saw the sea, a sea with muddied stinking water; they no longer felt like going and washing in it.

They dragged themselves feebly across the plain inhabited by the crabs and the slimy octopuses, which they had no choice but to kill in order to eat. But the sickly taste of that flesh made them vomit. Then they grazed on the young moss which was beginning to occupy the hollows in the dead trees. They were very hungry despite their despair.

The sun still did not appear. Sometimes, however, a pink glow appeared on the horizon and stayed there a while. The Saved would cry out in hope and feel their hearts leap in their chests, but this joy was short-lived, for soon the glow dimmed and vanished again, leaving the people plunged in the darkness with its smell of decay.

Then, unannounced, the stars came back, and not long after that a pale sun also appeared, killing the crabs and the filthy octopuses with its pale rays, to the great relief of the whole tribe. Finally the people felt their bodies being warmed. They made their way down to the sea, which had become clear and salty again.

The angered gods had forgiven men, who could once more begin to live.

Ker listened to the chief wise man's story, and he realized that the gods had had nothing to do with any of it, since despite their power they died like men. Ker's atheism scandalized the chief wise man. Before the whole tribe, he stepped forward and said:

"You are drawing down the vengeance of the gods upon our heads! Ker, you do not belong among us anymore. Go! We don't want to see you anymore, we don't want to see you anymore! Ker, leave the land of the Saved!"

Then Ker turned towards Kaniana, but she looked at him as if she had never seen him before. She refused to take his hand.

"You are sacrilegious, Ker! It's impossible—you have killed a god—why do you want me to marry you? I'm afraid. I don't want to marry you, Ker."

Ker, in despair, left the tribe and the village. From a long way off he took a last look at the village, and he realized he would never go back there again. He brushed drops of water from his cheeks.

He walked for two suns, then he built a hiding place so well disguised that nobody would ever discover it, not even the gods.

Now that there were no longer men around him, Ker dreamt, and his dreams were always on the same sad subject: the dead young god. He talked to him, he explained to him that he hadn't wanted him to die. But the god didn't open his mouth, he sighed and looked at Ker, and the red stain on his chest kept growing.

Ker was horrified by what was going on in his head. He would have liked to run away from himself so as to forget.

In the time of darkness, seized by sudden anguish, Ker would come out of his hiding place and look up rather worriedly at the sky full of lights. He revolted inwardly and imagined building a ladder to go and put those lights out, one by one, so that the gods could no longer find their way. He wondered from between which lights the gods would come and destroy him, and he often listened, suddenly thinking he could hear a noise like a swarm of wasps, heralding their arrival. But the suns passed, Ker kept an exact account of them, and nothing happened.

Ker finally issued a challenge to the gods. He went and lived where they had set up their camp when they had stayed in Ker's country. Perhaps they had no desire to return, for they didn't show themselves at all.

Late one sun, the hunters of the tribes of the Saved found Ker lifeless. They buried him face downwards to win the gods' mercy.

They named the place the land of Ka In, that is, of the god-killer.

THE DREAM OF THE BRIDGE

Claude Gauvreau
translated by Ray Ellenwood

A black bridge at night. There is no noise, only a faint sound of water running. The bridge glistens in the half-light as if after a rain. It is feebly lit by old-fashioned street lamps which flicker.
   The bridge breathes deeply in the peace and pure air of the night. Then a young man of about thirty enters. He has a short beard and is dressed in the traditional romantic cape. He moves to the railing and stretches out his arms into the night.
   THE DARK MAN: I will go out into the tongue of the night. I shall become an eddy of night like the juice of a headlight. Ingratitude is the vermilion princess of the earth.
   He climbs over the railing of the bridge and jumps. But, in the middle of his fall, he stops, suspended in space, one leg in the air, his arms flung wide, like an image immobilized on a cinema

screen. He remains there in the half-light like a sketched shadow.

A light goes on in the window of a house invisible in the distance. It stays there for hours, motionless. At last, the square of light becomes obsessive, as if it had coagulated. The eye begins to see it as drapery. Later, it seems to be moving as if in a current of air. Then a warrior with a lance passes through this drapery and begins to run as fast as he can in the light. He runs and runs. Having arrived at the bridge, he goes out onto it. He spreads his legs, he spreads his arms, he stretches greedily, he flexes his muscles, he snickers with self-satisfaction. Suddenly he hurls his lance at the dark man suspended in space. The dark man turns completely red. The lance is hollow inside and at both ends. The red flows into the lance through the end planted in the dark man and pours out through the other end. The red drips, drop by drop, from the free end. The warrior holds his hands under the end where the red is dripping and collects it all. The warrior avidly drinks all the red that fell into his hands.

THE WARRIOR: Ah! Ah! Ah! Ah! Ah!
He leaps like some barbaric dancer.
The night doesn't tell all. The night is discreet.
It doesn't tell about the languor that falls from virginal bellies.
It doesn't tell about the ecstasies of men full of rhythms vaulted with mad gestures.
It doesn't tell about the carnages of mauve eyes. It doesn't tell about the alcoholic sperms. It doesn't tell about warriors of dreams with their drunkenness and wild instincts.
It doesn't tell about the mauves and the bottle greens of painters in the harness of lost Poles.
It doesn't tell about Cain, it doesn't tell about Helen.
The sinuous shadows carriers of fits of coughing. Green libations like the water of an aquarium.
Ah! Ah! Ah! Ah! Ah!
Men think life is dead when they sleep.
Bald-headed drips slip into naivete holding their precious testicles in their hand.
I left with my brother, with the uncorseted ladies, with the breasts like strawberry juice, with the white arms like ostrich

plumes, I left in the settings of nocturnal dawns, I steered the ruddy thighs, I brandished the sparkling wines of sixteen-year-old muses.

Foreheads without vicious pates spread out on the banks among sands and crustaceans, sick brutes didn't see any of it.

I live, I do, I ransom the day-less time.

He tears his lance from the dark man and thrusts it with all his might into the light. He makes a hole which he digs at with his hands. With all his might, he blows into the middle of the light. Two little elves, one male, one female, come out of the light through the hole. Their faces are green. They begin to play on the light.

MALE ELF: Lady elf, you are kind.

FEMALE ELF: Here comes the cool of the starless night.

WARRIOR: I thirst to embrace evil with its hundred red eyelids. I am a vagabond.

FEMALE ELF: My ankles are thin.

MALE ELF: Listen to the water seeding itself with chassis of crystal.

The male elf kisses the female.

The warrior winks to himself and accompanies it with a sadistic smile. Stealthily, without attracting the attention of the elves, he climbs back up into the light and starts to run. He runs, he runs. Arriving at the drapery, he turns around and laughs heartily, ferociously, while watching the elves playing in the light. He passes through the drapery and disappears; meanwhile, the light goes out and the elves, their support pulled out from under them, fall onto the bridge.

FEMALE ELF: Oh! I hurt myself. I fell a long way. Ah! there's no more light!

MALE ELF: No, there's no more light. No more light!

FEMALE ELF: Mister elf, we're on a bridge. Mister elf, our feet are on a river. I feel like fishing.

MALE ELF: Ah! mother elf, how can we do that?

The female elf begins to turn round and round, endlessly. She turns and turns. A long thread of water like a snake comes out of the river and begins to turn with her, around her. The more she turns, the more the thread of water solidifies. It becomes like a whip or a rope. She takes it in her hands and she stops turning.

FEMALE ELF: Now I have my fishing line.

They throw one end of the thread of water into the river and, both holding onto the other end, they begin to fish.

MALE ELF: Ah! you're sweet. The world is sweet. The night of the bridge is for the eye what tin is for the ear. We are rowing in the clear water of charm.

FEMALE ELF: You're right, mister elf. Oh! did you feel it?

MALE ELF: Pull, mother elf!

The elves have felt a tug at the end of the thread of water. They pull the thread of water from the river. At the end of the thread of water wrapped around her waist is a girl all dressed in white whose eyes are closed and whose arms lie along her body as if she were a corpse. Her inhuman whiteness glints like coral. The elves, ecstatic, look at her in silence. They pull on the thread of water and hoist the girl as high as the bridge, but before they can grab her she slips out of the thread of water and falls back into the river.

MALE ELF: Ah! Oh!

She fell. She's with the fishes.

The night-time magpies have been silent for months. They made their nest in my ear and for nobody else. Now I know why. I have understood ever since the dawn came like a mirage into the reach of my breath. I will die with my arms extended, my fingers extended.

FEMALE ELF: She was beautiful. She was beautiful as the luminous promise of barley sugar.

MALE ELF: Oh! Watch out!

They hear footsteps. The elves hide behind the bridge rail. A young man and a young woman, both dressed in raincoats, go by. The young man has a brush cut.

THE COUPLE: The night is calm.

They disappear.

The elves come back to the same spot and start to fish again with the thread of water.

MALE ELF: Let's speak less than the twitterings of dwarf corollas.

Something tugs on the thread of water. The elves pull it from the river. The white girl is attached to it by her waist. They pull her up, but the moment they are about to get their hands on her, she once again falls back into the river.
MALE ELF: Ah! Ah! Fumes of form sublime far from the love-quenched eunuchs!
Far! Always too far! Always inaccessible!
FEMALE ELF: I feel like crying.
MALE ELF: Oh! Ah! too slack a possession!
The elf throws the thread of water far from him. One end falls into the right hand of the dark man. The other end falls in the river. The dark man, suspended in space, never having moved, fishes. Right away a weight is attached to the thread of water and, while the dark man remains immobile, the other end comes out of the river and rises towards him. The white girl is attached to it. She rises towards the dark man and comes to rest lying across his breast, without making a move or lifting an eyelid. Anyway, perhaps she is not made of flesh, or maybe she is dead. She lies on the breast of the dark man.
FEMALE ELF: Did you see that, mister elf?
MALE ELF: Oh! Oh! Boiling globe for butterfly!
Suddenly the elf leaps and hangs onto the foot of the dark man.
MALE ELF: Made it.
He climbs as far as the dark man's waist and is just about to touch the white girl lying on his breast when the dark man continues his fall, dragging the elf and the white girl with him. All three fall in the river.
FEMALE ELF: Ah! Mister elf, mister elf!
Come back, mister elf! Elf lost in the moonlips!
She begins to turn round and round. She turns, she turns. Faster. A thread of water, out of the river, begins to turn with her and solidifies. She takes it in her hands and feverishly begins to fish.
FEMALE ELF: Herds of wild beasts lost in the grassless Poles. I am the shadows on the glacial whiteness. Light in the cadaverous *quilicot* trees. Elf lost in bottomless faith. Elf, come

back to me. Elf, let my line catch you. I'm all alone. Oh! Oh! The moving streetlamps!

She fishes, she fishes, she fishes. Time passes. She fishes. Night is over, day comes on. Then we realize that the female elf is no longer an elf but an old fisherman, plainly dressed, almost a transient. Something tugs on the end of his line. He pulls it out of the water. His fish hook is caught in a romantic cape. Placidly, he unhooks the cape and throws it back into the river. He baits his hook again and continues to fish tranquilly.

THE PROPHET IN THE SEA

Claude Gauvreau
translated by Ray Ellenwood

A man is standing on the shore. He is Louis Chir de Houppelande.

LOUIS: Is it a dog swimming? No, it's the sea swell.

My grandfather sleeps. I can hear him being silent. Dreams of dead men in the incommensurable arch.

The invisible yellow arch where creation stretches out motionless.

My illusory grandfather in the deceitful configurations of nocturnal forests.

The man who writhes in pain in the forest and waves his arms flinging fear, it's a tree.

The immobile tree who welcomes the conscientious robber in the silence is an atrocious man riddled with resentment.

In the shadow-covered forest man and tree merge, one is no more distinct than the other. And I can no longer tell which of the two is speaking.

The frothing gland will jump up at the end of the world.

The gland of life.

The gland of indiscernible lives.

Where is the one-armed silence?

The hushed with the lovely sly black eyes?

A strangled, desperate, distant voice comes from the water.

THE VOICE: Louis! Louis!

LOUIS: Is that my grandfather's voice calling me on the other side of time and space?

THE VOICE: *(hoarse, desperate)* Louis!

LOUIS: I can't see a thing, but are the unexpected and the incomprehensible so frightening?

A thin trunk of an uprooted tree with two branches twisted together like crossed arms, covered with knots, floats on the water.

LOUIS: Lady Edwige will come from the water, said the epileptic madman. Lady Edwige came from my sheets all perfumed with love. And now an old tree trunk comes from the water and it is not Lady Edwige.

My illusory grandfather who was entirely imaginary said to me, all the same, that I should beware of madness.

Crazy tree trunk, you're making liars out of your brothers.

Arms.

Scrawny and symbolic arms.

Louis bends down and touches one of the two branches on the trunk.

THE VOICE: *(emerging painfully from the branch)* Louis!

Louis, frightened, lurches backwards and runs away.

THE VOICE: *(more and more feeble)* My brother!

Louis stops. After a moment, he runs towards the tree trunk, wades into the water and seizes its branches. The branches writhe painfully, as if in spasms.

LOUIS: Ah! Speak.

You must speak.

How is it that you're the man I always knew?

You are the one with rubber paws in dreams.

Have pity on me who ate lemons for their juice because the colour of the waves was killing me.

The discipline of the waves was making me vomit.

One of the branches writhes horribly and then becomes a man's hand, scrawny and pale.

On his knees in the water, his hands on the tree trunk, terrified and ecstatic, Louis cannot run away and does not want to.

THE VOICE: *(barely perceptible)* Touch me, Louis. End my exile.

The branches wave and ring like little bells.

LOUIS: Exile. Exile.

The hut produces perplexity.

Yellow, red or green, wood or thyme, human reminiscences float in the air.

The forehead worn by a cloud drips with fraternal understanding.

A cloud oozes pink and a sumptuous forehead charged with lightning sent to me by the grandfather.

Wood, wood! is that what you want to hear me say?

THE VOICE: Touch me! All over!

Louis runs his hands all over the tree trunk.

LOUIS: There you are. There you are. Calm down.

The tree trunk moves painfully, its bark quivers, and all this agitation produces a kind of mutation. On the trunk above the branches, a human mouth appears very distinctly. Only the mouth can be clearly seen. Everywhere else, suggestions of human traits appear on the bark, as if they were roughly sculpted: a thin nose, small eyes, hollow cheeks, long hair, a beard, and all the rest of the body. One finger grows distinctly on the end of a branch, the others are barely discernible.

THE MOUTH: Louis, I'm beginning to see you, my flesh is coming out of the shadows. I can't see you clearly. My human flesh is filled with bits of tree. Touch me, Louis.

Louis runs his hands over the tree trunk. But he stops because, as he rubs the tree trunk and the bark changes more and more to flesh, Louis' hands are transformed into the shape of tree branches.

LOUIS: *(holding out his hands)* What is this? My hands are turning into tree branches.

THE MOUTH: Trees are born as they die.

The tree's message is the long hoot of an owl on a quiet night, a procession of lemon juice shouting for the unblemished blast, a climate of red and white carnival trumpets, the tree's message is equilibrium, the song of duration.

To die as if to be born.

To sing with its beauty, to be silent with its perpetuity.

Louis, take my place, I called you like a dying man in a cave. Die like a tree is born, because I can't. The blast is not my word.

I must speak with my mouth. For I am a prophet. Will you take my place? Otherwise, I will go back into the shadows that have fallen over my mouth ever since the sweat of the sky mixed with the sun.

Louis Chir de Houppelande, I called to you, will you take my place?

Louis stares straight ahead and does not reply.

Long, long did the petrified prophet wait.

A tree that sings without howling, that summons without pointing a finger.

I am a prophet and my heart howls, my breast begs.

I am a prophet petrified in endless expectation ever since the prophets grew silent.

Tree and man merge. Be the tree, I will be the man.

Because the time of the prophets is coming again.

The silence withered and died one quiet morning without our noticing it. But the memory of angry days leaped in my drowsy breast and I recognized the sap of words by its taste.

Sacred love that ferments and the need to cry out.

The awakening was born from lugubrious silence. A voice came to me, a new voice, and a name to call out.

A new voice that only one name could hear, a new voice like a thin, weakening trickle, the raucous whine of a dog dying of thirst, and one name only, came to me by instinct, the name of Louis Chir de Houppelande.

You alone could hear me, Louis.

Someone is calling me and I must reply.
Words dance in my throat:
The sifting andante auscultates the bertate Edjé oh Mène.
Here is the grapefroon to polish the cycle.
The streetlamps with watered paste carp about a profound schism between the elements of life until the deltas are exhausted.
And the earth, beaten like a meticulous crossbow, profuses the arabesque of the pinned horn the picardy yellow.
Communally bundled the seals break into groups, simplify themselves with heat and burning thirst.
The vestige of the eeled gullible of a published and forbidden ketone excites the murat awning and the blood spurts from the energetic and jerky espousal.
Starting from nothing or from nil tottering, my ascetic cult makes the mutation waddle lancinatingly. There shirt-tail, the sneezal prismatic jungle.
Shortage of brine or inflation of armour, the how to know suppurates from timid, hesitating languorousnesses. The bill-hook bath will flow over these indecisions. Frivolous council that begins at the sugary and digestible border of the frontispieces from angoulême.
The desperate man with eyes of a winter night, with glints of crime hesitant for a second, with the incrusts of undecided oscillations like a pure white dromedary hump, watches my frantic incantations with empty eyebrows.
Tenth inquest, the brief reigns herein of the mistouflous anvil will cause the hegemony of the thirty deons to be divided at the heart. Slow slow separated.
Halt.
What do you say, Louis Chir de Houppelande? Will you take my place?

Louis signals yes with his hand.

Louis touches the tree trunk with his hands and his arms. The prophet's body becomes more and more clearly perceptible as the substance of the tree disappears. At the same time, Louis' flesh is transforming into the trunk of a tree. A solo flute is heard playing during this transformation.

LOUIS: Am I doing it properly?

THE PROPHET: You're doing well, my brother.

The entire tree trunk must be transformed into the body of the prophet and Louis' body must be transformed into the tree trunk, with one exception: one of the prophet's legs will remain wood and one of Louis' legs will remain human flesh.

THE PROPHET: My brother! My brother! I have my body back again. You are my brother!

Louis' head is beginning to change into wood.

LOUIS: *(having trouble speaking)* I did all I could. Now let me say goodbye to you. These are the last words of Louis Chir de Houppelande. Adieu, Adieu. Don't forget the happy man who used his wings to fly but never left the earth. You'll see me again in the water.

THE PROPHET: Yes, my brother. Since that's what you would naturally want.

Louis rubs his bark against the prophet's body and the prophet becomes totally human except for his leg. The prophet is very thin, with little piercing eyes: he looks famished and inspired. Having become a tree trunk, except for his leg, Louis loses his balance and falls to the ground on his side. The prophet begins to walk about.

THE PROPHET: Oh! It's great to walk. I am among men. I am going to touch men.

He stops and looks at his tree leg.

My walk is not perfect. Look, Louis, I've still got one wooden leg. I am incomplete, my brother; and you, you're monstrous.

The prophet picks Louis up and holds him in his arms. With great effort, leaning against the prophet, Louis raises his human leg and rubs it against the tree leg of the prophet. He rubs with increasing effort. Louis' human leg and the prophet's tree leg do not transform.

THE PROPHET: It's no use, brother.

We'll carry our past like a packsack.

So be it.

The prophet takes a few steps, holding Louis in his arms.

I'll get used to it.

He stops.
Louis, do you want me to put you back in the water?
Louis signals yes with his branches.
Even with your flesh leg?
All right. Adieu, brother.
He throws Louis into the water.
Drifting a little, Louis floats on the surface of the water with his branches swaying.
THE PROPHET: At last the earth breathes.

The marble and the caves gluttonously shrink or multiply their bodies tenfold for the vision of mankind.

I make contact with the earth. And the turquoise mirror where the crumb of hidden treasure pants wantonly.

With Louis Chir de Houppelande injected in my arm, the robust shoot will be born like a butterfly in the vermilion daylight.

Louis, Louis, you are hung on the cross and your heart glows violently on the edge of my eyelid like a crescent moon.

Louis, Louis, your hacked body prances in my mouth between my teeth, and will come out my lips like a trumpet, a flood of words with immortal brass pennants.

I am come from the shadows and I present myself to the world with my mouth.

The little blue flower beside the road and the immense sun encumbered by its weight are fabricated under the same transparent globe.

Knots on bark are frogs' eyes, flat rocks are disguised as tambourines, as if for a celebration. Because I am coming.

I am coming.

With my mouth.

Three small children enter running, each pushing a hoop with a piece of wood. As they pass in front of the prophet, each stick breaks against its hoop.

THE THREE LITTLE CHILDREN: *(crying)* I broke my stick!

THE PROPHET: Children, children, don't cry. You can always find another stick.

THE THREE LITTLE CHILDREN: Not a stick like the one I had!

THE PROPHET: Sure you can. Look. Here are some pieces of wood like the ones you had. All you have to do is cut them out.
He shows them his tree leg.
THE THREE LITTLE CHILDREN: Oh! He's right, I see a piece of wood just like mine. It's wonderful. I didn't think there was another piece of wood like mine anywhere.
THE PROPHET: Take them, children, take them, they're yours.
Each of the three little children takes a knife from his pocket and begins to cut a piece of wood from the prophet's tree leg. Suffering terribly, the prophet puts his face in his hands to stop from crying out.
THE THREE LITTLE CHILDREN: Oh! thank you, sir. This stick is just like the one I had. It's wonderful.
The prophet extends his tree leg and the three little children sit on it.
THE PROPHET: The vision clings stragglingly.
Corollas of wheat indicate the entry of the mounts.
I saw the entry coming.
The entry of princes covered with golden piggybanks and mahogany castanets.
The ambrosia to keep quiet.
The dance of the dunes ascended like a mutilated tuque. The dawn loaded with pearls.
I have seen satin pillars encircled with overhanging checkerboards telling lies.
The triumph engendering will not be enough to exhaust the worlds.
Steel worlds where the nervous tulip floats above the sinister overlap.
Arms.
The lead spider in the sulphur whirlwind reflects in grey.
Do not let the dying wheat die.
Do not let the hand sleep while it is being born.
The very high vision of birth.
The ringed palms and the palmate bars indicate the luducrus possession like a gloved sign on the lower lip of the dawn.
The entire tunic will cause the redemption of the cockscomb.

We will insufflate the slate which is afraid of a determination new to the crackled objective.

The famine manifested by tiles will be tinted and the ardent fusion will grow simultaneous on an infinite plan.

The river bank condensed into a lowly ruby will burn with a warning fire.

And when a red-fringed galley above yellow reefs crowned with weeds raises its exigence, austere trees will grow pale as monks and fade away like a rainbow in a cloud.

The hoar-frost farandole will sculpt the lofty morning with green instruments.

A savoury nose pulling an impersonal head like a sled will come to juggle love across the verdigris cockroaches.

Childhood crumbles away from the circular and fringed cradle. Warm and iridescent thrush whose left wing hangs inert.

The glorious childhood of the tunnel where gusts of swallows haunted the monastic propellers comes back to me in memory at this moment.

The dough and the basket come back at a gallop.

Dangerous emerald it can not dissolve from soldered clans of blithe humus.

Consolidated hunger will be anointed with the diadem of ennobled winter.

In the dreamed tumor of chequered cherz that the powder of dawn carries off.

A blond hand leaves a humid trace and swallowed pity comes back with a start.

The golden belts will camp around the princess like a torrid deer petrified in ice.

And the hands will be of olive-coloured sugar.

And the beige drawings in new-year boxes.

The oak-plantation seeded circularly with umbel up to the pinnacle takes a sounding of it.

The passion to knead two-handed the leg of the isolated winter fire.

And then smelt-coloured salivas will come hanging from sheets too dull. And the salient circumflex accents with pale green bends wearing the guimpes of a sad harlequin.

From the consumptive steer will come the four-dimensional rose and the father's sigh. The colour of the haunted and sedented circus.

The rejoicing of the ball accelerated to carnival rhythm by the orange silk stockings and the shovel with joyous little bells winking in its violet furrow.

The head with the price set on it, memory of a boiled prune, will speak without a palpable word.

That will be the prophecy.

Shapes of Chinese houses will slip wordlessly into the twilight.

The blue beard flies in the wind. Comic children juggle twopenny loaves of bread.

And glory droops.

The pastoral rock, smoking with golden dust, insinuates that the dazzling eagle will be a metal engine.

The mauve princess on her tomb smiles.

And the star bleats.

And the circulation is limpid as a thin stream of cream.

The nut-crackers sleep.

And the flushed cheek explores a false dimple.

The sleepy miracle plods along covered over with veils and waves under a deadened moon.

A child's hand is about to reach to touch the shiny object.

Thus the breeze will plaster itself on the atmosphere with sparks from a tulip.

The light will fall from the keg.

As he speaks, the three little children listen with rapt attention; beards exactly like the prophet's beard begin to grow on the sticks that the children hold. Meanwhile Louis, floating in the sea, approves with movements of his branches.

In the sky, a human silhouette, transparent and fluid, looking as if it were suspended on a ladder, says: 'I'm thirsty.'

A SLICE OF NOTHINGNESS

Claude Boisvert
translated by Michael Bullock

It was really wild. Nothing like him had ever been seen around here. I mean Dr Flamel, as he liked to be called. Seeing him on the stage, doing one amazing trick after the other, you couldn't doubt that he had reached a level where he had almost no equal. He was surely one of the world's great magicians.

Dr Flamel let the burst of applause that had followed his last number die down and then, with a low bow to his audience, he asked them to pay the utmost attention during the next few minutes. He was about to produce the most marvellous, the most amazing phenomenon a magician could bring into being.

"Ladies and gentlemen, I am going to create before your eyes, from nothing, a slice of nothingness. What's that, you ask? I couldn't exactly tell you, since I don't know myself. All I can say is that I can guarantee that what I am about to make is real and verifiable. It is the negation of matter. Not emptiness, not air, not the mere absence of anything. The absolute negative. Total nothingness. That, ladies and gentlemen, is what you are about to see."

He emphasized these words with a theatrical gesture, before turning to his left where, only a few feet away, an indefinable black column could be seen gradually forming. It was atrocious and fascinating, attractive and repulsive. It was impossible to take your eyes off it and at the same time you would have liked to run away as fast as your legs would carry you, so as to avoid seeing the unprecedented vision that was growing clearer and clearer. A column of a deeper black than the blackest night, which seemed to have some consistency and which moved, which undulated within very strict limits: you could feel it trying, like waves beating against the jagged edges of a cliff, to break the chains, the invisible barriers imposed upon it by the magician.

A half-approving, half-sceptical murmur greeted the appearance of the column.

"There you are, ladies and gentlemen. You see before you the irrefutable proof of the power, the ascendancy of mind over matter. For I have done more than transform matter—something any mind with some training can accomplish. In this slice of nothingness matter has been completely, irreversibly annihilated, until I decide to restore its usual appearance, to reconstitute it. No, it is not a vulgar conjuring trick, but a verifiable counter-reality. I have transformed the particles of the surrounding air into nothingness, that is to say I have deprived them of their materiality. Better, within this restricted space I have denied matter the right to exist. At this point it no longer exists. If there is anyone in the audience who wishes to check the truth of my assertion, let him not hesitate to step up onto the stage. But I must clearly state that I accept no responsibility for what might happen if anyone tries to ... I myself have never yet risked entering my column of nothingness and, believing what I believe, I never shall. Because if matter, in a smaller proportion, were to enter into conflict with its negation I believe it would instantly disintegrate. To a certain extent this can be demonstrated. I ... Ah, there is a gentleman who is coming forward and no doubt wants ... Noooo! Whatever you do, keep away from the column! Come, give me your hat. Right. Now watch carefully, ladies and gentlemen, and you will see what I mean."

And the hat flew into the air, described an arc and, coming into contact with the black column, disappeared with a strange and disturbing whistle, disappeared forever, claimed the magician.

"There. Any living being who rashly played about with the column would suffer the same fate," he announced triumphantly. "Your attention, ladies and gentlemen," he went on once the thunder of applause had somewhat died down, "if there are any professional journalists among you, they can stay after the performance. I am entirely ready to answer, for the benefit"—and he swelled with pride—"for the benefit of posterity, the many questions which my slice of nothingness may give rise to. Thank you."

Looking down from the height of a scarcely disguised contempt for the small fry occupying the hall, he strode across the stage, confident of the effect he had produced.

The spectators gradually dispersed.

Responding to his invitation, several people remained in their places after the majority of the audience had left.

"Professor," someone called out, "can we photograph your slice of nothingness?"

"By all means! Go ahead, please go ahead."

"Maestro," began someone else, "does the column have to remain in one place all the time? Or could you move it to the centre of the stage?"

And the column, impelled by his brain, did indeed move into the centre of the stage.

"Professor, would you please stand in front of the column for a photograph? That's it. Don't move—or rather, move a little to the left, right, now back a bit and ... Hey, look out, can't you see I'm trying to take a photograph?"

The speaker swore roundly at a person of the feminine sex, nice looking too, who had just bumped into him as she ran toward the stage.

"Jerk! Rotten pig!" she yelled at the magician, who, having undoubtedly recognized her, changed his whole demeanor as he replied:

"Not here, Germaine, please. We can settle our problems at home."

The journalists and photographers were jubilant. Flashes went off non-stop. They wanted to catch this unique scene as it happened in order to reproduce it in tomorrow's gossip columns. But the woman Germaine went on:

"Be sure of that, pig! You're worried about your reputation, eh? Well, what about my reputation, I suppose that doesn't matter? You couldn't care less. I know the whole thing, liar. Filthy liar! You pretend to be going to see your agent—and what about that bitch, that whore you keep in Paris? Did you think I was going to put up with that?"

Red with anger, she advanced threateningly toward the magician, whose face now changed colour, assuming a ghastly tint midway between violet and mauve.

"Germaine, calm down, please, no scandal."

The flashes continued to flare in an infernal rhythm. The atrocious black column still stood proudly in the background, providing an exceptional setting for this family quarrel.

"No scandal, no scandal, take that, jerk!"

And she slapped his face with a skill that was very revealing. It was probably not the first blow of its kind she had delivered.

A white mark on the professor's cheek showed where the blow had landed. As he staggered back, enraged, he yelled: "You'll pay for that, you bitch." But before she could strike again, he stumbled into the slice of nothingness and disappeared into it, forever ...

So be it.

THE PROPHET

Claude Boisvert
translated by Michael Bullock

It was a truly wonderful period.

Every day, thousands of pilgrims came from every corner of the known world, with their little bundle on their back, to see and hear the prophet. And the prophet performed wonders, feeding the multitude physically and spiritually with incredible miracles. He had only to look a blind man in the eyes for him to recover his sight or run and buy glasses. By simply touching a paralytic with his finger he was able to persuade him to get up and walk.

This was a being who was at the very least extraordinary.

Someone who had undoubtedly penetrated inner secrets that other human beings were incapable of exploring. But, above all, his theories amazed the multitudes and put them in a state of delirium.

He brought a message of peace, love and hope. And who, among these suffering people who received nothing from life but misery, could afford to ignore such restorative words?

And from day to day an immense tranquillity shone from the prophet's face as he passed across hills and through valleys delivering his message. And the multitude of worshippers grew ever larger, so that now he moved from place to place with an army of people who put all their faith in the new horizon that he sketched for them with sweeping parables, prophecies and mystic balm.

He handled words as a fairy handles her magic wand.

His fame grew and grew.

Now there was not a single individual in any way capable of lending an ear (at that distant era people were willing to lend absolutely anything) who had not heard him speak, and always favourably.

Oh, there were certainly some who worried and kept a vigilant watch. Naturally there were people of bad faith who, having a social order and a social standing to protect, tried to put a spoke in his wheel—but since he always went on foot... But so long as the danger was not too great, not too evident, they were careful not to do anything, or they dared not do anything too openly. And after all, there was a beneficial side to his activities, a side that was useful to those in power: his teachings helped them to keep the people in that state of blind servitude which, at all times, has been the most reliable ally of any authority.

And, especially in that primitive epoch when the means at the disposal of the authorities were relatively limited, it was good to be able to tell oneself that, in the last analysis, the people were being muzzled by a fellow who had come from the people. That so long as this illuminee brought them his portion of hope the people, that barometer of power, would remain satisfied and would ask nothing more.

All the same, there's a limit to everything. And a tolerant power—or so they thought in those far-off times—is already a declining power. So power reacted.

And once they began to watch him more closely, they suspected him of planning violence and plotting to seize power by devious means. So they mobilized everyone they could find in the way of linguistic analysts and experts throughout the Roman world and brought them at great expense and by every means of transport known at that time—roller skates, water skis, kites, ox carts, horses, teleportation, wings of ignorance and of faith etc.— to this region of Galilee where the prophet continued to pour out his good words over a people that was more and more entranced. And the make-up artists of the whole Roman Empire—the USA of the day—worked miracles in disguising doughty scholars and learned personages as beggars, as pilgrims, in a word as spy pilgrims who infiltrated without drum or trumpet—what could they have done with such instruments anyway?—into the horde of admirers.

And every evening, poring over texts which honorary secretaries—power never lacks devoted minions—had typed out during the day (texts of speeches delivered by our prophet the previous day and conscientiously recorded), our eggheads strove to pinpoint the key word, to decipher the code that would finally enable the State to take action against this individual who, as time passed, was giving the authorities more and more of a scare.

"Suppose things get out of hand, Herod? Eh? What am I to do? ... What? You're joking! My Swiss bank account! An irreproachable civil servant like me? Do you hear: irreproachable! But what about you?"

"Me?"

"Yes, you, if I may say ..."

"Careful, Pilate. There are some things I won't tolerate."

"But you're accusing me—all right, forget it. But don't imagine your nice little private business with the Gulf has gone unnoticed and ..."

"Pilate, I forbid you ..."

"Okay, okay, forget it—but that doesn't solve our problem."

"Right, yes, okay, we're getting off the point. Let's get back to it."

So the prophet innocently and tirelessly travelled the highways of Galilee preaching the gospel. And his countless listeners were joined every day by an increasingly impressive horde of other human beings seeking comfort in the words of the Master.

But among these, as we have said, were concealed traitors, experts in the pay of the Roman Empire. Who produced powerful analyses, who ventured to elaborate super-academic theories in an attempt to pierce the armour of this dangerous seer. Some of them, carrying the joke a bit far, even declared: "He is a luminous seer." In fact the prophet constantly went about with a kind of aureole around his head, an aura which all the photographers took pleasure in capturing on film (we mention this object solely in the interest of historical accuracy, anxious as we are not to leave the reader in ignorance of any detail that might assist him in grasping the importance of the crucial moment which we feel being born at the tip of our pen).

At night the Roman soldiers massed around the crowd that they had been following during the day, making themselves as invisible as possible (disguising themselves as signposts, deserts, oases etc.). They were not keen to provoke a massacre, at least not yet, not before being sure they were not mistaken. What a scandal it would have been if they had embarked on a systematic repression of a mere flash in the pan! Neither Pilate nor Herod wanted to play the role of Don Quixote before he had been thought of. It would have turned the whole of history topsy-turvy.

But as time passed, they became convinced that they had to act, to act quickly and at any price. Because the star in this brilliant performance, who could be seen slowly appearing on the horizon, never let up and day by day collected his harvest of new citizens who forgot everything in order to devote themselves to listening. And he spoke well. God, how well he spoke!

Open-mouthed the followers followed, the soldiers hid and the spies spied. And parables sprang forth, fine parables, so fine they took your breath away. There were even some spies, we have been told, who forgot themselves as they listened to him. They decided to follow him and note down his words. They became the scribes who transcribed in manuscripts the sayings which the Messiah (as he was sometimes called) uttered in all innocence. There was even one who scrupulously transmitted to us the parable of a sea that became bio-negative. We know this account today under the name of the Dead Sea Scrolls.

But time was passing.

And even if the reports that came in regularly to the Roman leaders dealt above all with love, or with the eternal life the revolutionary kept talking about, they didn't want to allow a situation to continue indefinitely that placed all the region's social and economic structures in jeopardy. So they decided to reinforce the security measures and to be ready in case .... The famous anti-riot brigades were massed in the immediate neighbourhood with instructions to intervene the moment the imperial order was threatened.

One morning, before the assembled faithful who had barely emerged from a marvellous sleep filled with paradisiac dreams into which each one transposed his dearest desires, imagining that the miracle-worker would be able to fulfil them, he began to speak. And his aura appeared even brighter than usual. He was in great form.

He harangued his troops with his usual zest and the people, hanging on his lips, sweated with desire and hope. The strong, well-modulated voice vibrated as it reached the thousands of straining ears. No one was too far away to hear. And the words made a strange sound, as if the surrounding air itself was communicating with the Master.

Then, when the famous and unforgettable "Croak and multiply" rang out, the pilgrims, all the pilgrims, touched by grace, no doubt inhabited by the faith that moves mountains and won over by the power of persuasion that could be glimpsed through the vibrations inherent in the words that had just burst forth, with a praiseworthy unanimity were instantaneously changed into crows. Thousands and thousands of black wings began to beat the earth—there was nothing left for the pariahs, the unbelievers, the soldiers who were watching events out of the corner of their eye, to do but pick up the revolutionary who, henceforth, preached in the desert.

COLD BRIDGE

Elisabeth Vonarburg
translated by Jane Brierley

Run. China walls, plastic floor, steel doors. Silence. Your flight is soundless in the deserted corridors, but the echo of your pursuers is equally silent. Run. Stop. Listen. Is someone really after you? Did they think what happened up there could be a diversionary tactic? Perhaps they stopped at the shattered bodies. Run. The corridor dog-legs; now it's a long, straight line under an iceberg of light, translucent and diffuse, with doors (you no longer open them; they only reveal labyrinthine machinery) and further, identical corridors running into this empty artery. All deserted. Perhaps they're being evacuated as you approach? Perhaps the others are following your flight through invisible eyes studded in the white sky of the corridors? They'll take you when they want you. Why are you running?

You stop, lean on the smooth mirror of a door which you don't open; back and shoulders first, then you turn around, forehead, nose, lips, chin, small circles of condensation blur the metal and immediately disappear. As at each halt, you feel the heat of running dissipate quickly, and the cold of the underground passage grips you like a vice. Your chest hurts, the glacial air slices your throat, and the knapsack straps cut into your shoulders . . . .

You remember. The bomb.

Your life—are you running for your life? But you sacrificed it to destroy the Bridge. (*"And when he had crossed the bridge, phantoms came to meet him,"* to welcome another phantom, an empty shell, empty of even a message. The message is imprinted on the body; in the skull there is only one image: the other side of the Bridge; and on the other side this image is erased and replaced by the image of yet another side. The humanoid form transmits itself—an envelope of tattooed skin that is the message—across the stars, once, twice, ten times, until the mindless brain collapses, worn away by too many erasures. Then the protein baths, and the brownish cubes that will no doubt feed future messengers in the prisons . . . .) Remember, it's to destroy all this that you must run. You mustn't run blindly like a scared animal; you must follow the signs as they taught you: the direction to follow is shown by the lightning-crossed circle.

You start running again. You know where you're going, all right. You're going to do your duty. In reality, you know you have no choice; did you ever? If you consciously follow the signs, it's to forget you're going to die. You're called Kathryn Rhymer, you're a Rebel, and you're going to die.

Now that you're running with your brain, all is clear; a path emerges in the labyrinth and you know what's behind the doors: the maintenance machinery for the Generator. The corridors haven't been evacuated. Only maintenance men come through here; the Bridge engineers, like the zombie messengers, descend by the central elevator.

It's getting colder, the heart of the labyrinth is close: yes, an armoured door at the end of the corridor. Shut. But it's only a door; they never thought anyone would come by the underground passages. So many commandos have been pulverized as they attacked the Tower . . . . That was before the Rebels discovered the truth: the Bridge isn't in the Generator Tower; it's buried in the ground. The zombies don't leave in the light of day.

You place the charge, take cover, trip the detonator; pass through the door clutching your weapon and stepping over bloodsoaked bodies. Ears deafened by the explosion, you see the survivors' lips moving but hear no words. You keep them covered as you destroy the elevator controls, the communications system. Then, with a wide, circular sweep, you mow down the engineers. As the last one crumples, your hearing returns and you can savour the renewed silence.

You look around; you hadn't imagined the Bridge like this. The room is vast, lined with flashing consoles, screens where geometric shapes are still moving—numbers or pulsating waves—machines humming subliminally, a world of inhuman half-life, clean, orderly, tranquilizing. You almost regret the turmoil caused by the explosion, the bleeding bodies on the white floor. In the centre of the room is an enormous metallic sphere, like a gleaming fruit in its corolla of cables and tubes, a machine connected by these cables and tubes to other machines: *this* is the Bridge. The light throws off a distorted vision of the room from its rounded flanks: the shattered wall, the scattered bodies, and you in the foreground, an enormous, fish-eyed, batrachian head separated from a miniature trunk; when you lift your head higher you see that a lip is bleeding. You wipe the blood, your grotesque reflection moves in the sphere, you turn away. The bomb must be placed.

But first the door to the underground passage must be blocked. You spend a futile minute straining your muscles against a heavy console panel loosened by the explosion, then shrug your shoulders. One becomes stupid, living with men. You lift your weapon, melt whatever still holds the panel to the wall; it collapses across the hole. Now the bomb. There are four of them, in fact: one for the computer bank, one for the control panel, two for the sphere. You watch your hands as they go about their work; they're steady. To die .... All is quiet; the bombs click onto the bottom of the sphere, the root that gives it life and force to send beings torn from themselves into the stars. The Bridge, the immobile Bridge, the Cold Bridge .... To descend to the depths, to the heart of absolute zero, and in the instant of total cessation to flash across space powered by the irrepressible impetus of the mind, drawing with it the body's subordinated matter. Power, freedom ... the stars.

And one must die?

Your hand stops on the timer. You remember that you shrugged when they told you, "This is the timer. Forty-five seconds to take cover." You didn't need this self-deception. Did they still take you for a woman? You knew perfectly well that if you succeeded, it would be a one-way street: penetrate, kill, and die.

Must one really die?

A groan, a gurgle, a body that rises and falls back. You go over to the man; he opens his eyes.

"Does the Bridge function automatically?"

The authority in your voice cuts through his stupor, wrings a mechanical "yes" from him.

"How does the sphere open?"

The red button; then the zombie is placed inside, naked, and the machine does the rest: puts it to sleep, ascepticizes, chills, colder, still colder .... And as it reaches the threshold where time and motion cease, the zombie bursts out of time and space, floats beyond the universe, *as the Spirit of God moved upon the face of the Biblical waters primeval* .... But it has no spirit save that which has been accorded it, its omniscience has a nose-ring drawing it toward the destination that fills its brain, emptied of all other images; and the zombie awakes in another machine.

But the traveller whose brain has not been erased—no one knows where he regains consciousness. The first cold travellers have never been found. *"The omniscience of the will, freed from time and space...."* Of course they've never been found. Of

course the Praesidium confiscated the Bridge to turn it into an instrument of power, to keep the Neo-Earths in subjection . . . . The Bridge, that creator of Gods, turned into a galactic telex! How they must fear it, those miserable little men who make a galaxy tremble . . . .
    Die? When one can be God?
    You let the timer drop, tear off your clothes, press the red button, and the metal womb opens to reccive you.
    To be God. The last.

It's warm, salty, red; it fills your mouth, nose, eyes, it's water, you're drowning.
    You thrash arms, legs, in the vitreous, pinkish dusk, your feet touch the bottom, a viscous cloud envelops you, but you rise, break through the surface skin. Overwhelming light and a furious roaring fills your ears. Your eyes burn and the water is disgustingly tepid and sticky, but it carries you forward in a gigantic wave. Blinking, your throat full of salty phlegm, you glimpse a beach; then the wave unfurls, breaks over you, flattens you on the sand. Half-dead, you crawl forward, uttering small cries that stick in your throat . . . . You move from damp to hot sand that scrapes your skin raw, but you want to get away from the roaring water and you keep on crawling until you reach the shade. Then you lift your head: monstrous rocks, chaotically piled, devouring the sky. It's cold in the shadows, it is (BE GOD) cold. You clutch at your knees, push your heels against your buttocks; pressing your chin down you smell the bitter odour of water and sand already hardening into a shell.
    Hunger rouses you, an invading emptiness that must be filled. The gloom has dispersed, the sky is a burning mirror. You stir, the sand on your skin flakes off, you're on hands and knees, finally you stand. You squint: colours at the end of the beach. You leave your prints on the fiery sand that forces aching legs to move faster, break into a run; the colours are getting nearer, bringing a fresh smell. (TO BE.)

Plants high as trees, bushes big as mountains, your miniature shadow lost in their shade. A spring that is a waterfall, a pond-lake of calm, blue water bordered by reed-poplars. You tumble into its coolness; the sand, salt and blood slide off your skin in murky puffs. You drink. (GOD.) Your belly clamours for more. You grab a plant taller than you, sink your teeth in, but the flesh is rubbery and unyielding. Tears run into your mouth, open to emit a thin, tremulous scream; half-blinded you stagger to the water's edge.

Suddenly the smell of honey fills your nostrils, your mouth; saliva almost chokes you; eyes half-shut, you follow the promise of food until you encounter an orifice near the ground, a fleshy blossom with its corolla spread wide; the smell of honey floats almost visibly around it. You walk on it, enter it; a roseate glow filters through the throbbing, petals with their tiny red veins, and under your bruised feet the ground is soft, pliable. You penetrate deeper into the warm cavern with its pulpy creases, move toward the source of the honey: a bouquet of pistils crowned with gold; the gold melts on your tongue (TO BE?) as, drawing the pistils toward you with both hands, you let yourself slip to the ground, lying on your back with eyes closed; and the flower closes over you.

Warmth. Silence. Peace. Interminable periods of sleep, panic-filled wakings quickly tranquilized as the pistils bend toward your mouth. A slow movement rocks you back and forth. The muffled music of the wind cradles the flower. Peace. Silence. Warmth. (GOD?)

The earth lifts under you, the warm, rosy gloom splits with an angry snap. The flower shudders. You try to grasp the pistils, but they dodge. You jump and bounce, each bounce bringing you nearer the gash; the flower shakes itself, shakes you, tosses you out and snaps shut, a hermetic shell. Screaming, you hammer the petals with your fists, break your nails clawing at them, then crumple to the ground, sobbing until sleep overtakes you.

You waken to darkness, pull the curtain of hair back from your eyes. Why is it so long? Your fingernails are long too; some are torn, leaving blood coagulated at the fingertips. You're not cold, but you hug yourself—and unfold your arms in a panic. You look at your body in the half-light, feel it, incredulous: soft flesh, no muscles! Horrified, you seize the rolls of fat in your hands, feel them quiver slightly after you let go.

Time. A lot of time must have passed. Hair and nails keep growing on corpses, but the dead don't get fat; that reassures you. You look around: it's dark because night is falling. You raise your head: coloured lights in unfamiliar designs span the sky. You drop to your knees, your head still thrown back. You've crossed the Bridge! A wave of intense jubilation brings you to your feet, you stride along the shore enraptured, eyes heavenward.

The uncomfortable tossing of your breasts stops you. Also an empty feeling in the stomach. Eat. The flower? It's closed. The water laps against the lakeshore. Perhaps there are fish. It's already too dark. Try the plants instead. You forage around, disconcerted by the disproportionate size of everything. Have you shrunk? If not, are there animals as big as the plants? You listen, alarmed; night sounds surround you: rustling, fluttering, clicking, murmuring, crackling—is it the wind moving, or living things? A cluster of large yellow fruit hangs from a bush in the shadow. You tear one off, sniff it, touch it with the tip of your tongue. Sugary. Are there sugary-tasting poisons? You can't be sure here, on the other side (which side?) of the Bridge. Live or die, it's up to you to choose. You eat one fruit, another, the whole bunch. Live and learn. All's fair in love and war. Nothing venture nothing have.

Now a place to sleep. Nothing devoured you while you slept beside the flower. Perhaps tonight? Perhaps not. You plunge into the grass-high moss in the underbrush, make a hole, and curl up in it. Find clothing, explore. Tomorrow. And make a calendar.

Tomorrow. Today. The berries didn't poison you; you eat others and drink from the lake. Searching along the water's edge, you find a long, sharp splinter of rock. You twist grass around the larger end, braid a belt with other grasses, feel less naked, try to forget how your soft belly jiggles. And how hunger is telling you that the yellow fruit is not enough.

Today. Three weeks later (notches on a leaf). From morning to night you swim in circles in the lake to restore your muscles and forget your hunger. You've discovered no fish, and fruit is hard to find. But you haven't left the area to explore further; you sit on the shoreline and watch the flower from a distance while contriving a better grip for your knife.

It's moving, opening again.

You stand up, dropping the knife, run toward the flower, grateful tears in your eyes .... But a small, long-bodied animal, half otter, half lizard, enters the warm, pink cavern first. You arrive to see the flower closing on it. You rush up to the flower, press your ear against the pulpy membrane, hear confused sounds, feel muffled shocks as though the small animal were struggling; you try to force the petals apart, you want to see what's happening, but see nothing. (SHE SAID: "THE BUMBLEBEE IS ATTRACTED BY THE NECTAR, FLIES AROUND THE FLOWER, COMES TO REST, GORGES ITSELF AND DEPARTS. AND THE FLOWER BRINGS FORTH FRUIT." SHE DIED AS SHE HAD LIVED, HER BELLY SWOLLEN. YOU HAD NOT CALLED HER "MOTHER" FOR A LONG TIME.) You recoil, trembling with rage and disgust, run to get your knife, return to plunge it into the obscene corolla—but it's already opening. The honey smell has disappeared, the tiny animal goes off cringing, exhausted, covered with gold-coloured stains. You enter hesitantly: the flower seems dead. You look at the empty, ravaged pistils, lift the weapon in your hand and slash the pink flesh, adding a gash where others are visible. A whitish liquid begins to ooze out. Aghast, you turn and run, still holding the knife, not stopping until the familiar landmarks have disappeared.

Now you find yourself in an unknown part of the forest. Here the plants are normal in size and you feel less appalled, slow down. Trees reign supreme here. Their trunks rise straight and smooth in the light-spattered shade; lace-leafed bushes skirt their swelling roots. Shapes, colours, smells—nothing on your Earth with its meagre, scarred vegetation has prepared you for this, but something in you responds to the majestic luxuriance of the foliage, the unimpeded upward thrust of the ordered trunks toward the sky. A murmuring silence laps about the living pillars, a gentle stirring through the forest sea, a calm, deep sea where one cannot drown. You advance amid the soaring trunks, feeling yourself drawn with them toward the sky; your head spins a little. Now you face the forest king: a tree so tall, so great, so spreading, so thickly crowned that you must have been answering its call without realizing it. You throw your head back; it's not enough: you have to lie on the ground to see the whole tree. It holds the forest by its roots, perhaps the whole continent (is it a continent?), so long are they, so strong, so gnarled. Among its hanging boughs, hundreds of birds sing. A cabin perched in its branches would be a good shelter. But the branches are too high, the trunk too smooth, too wide; you try jumping up several times, but your fingers slip despite your efforts. (HE SAID: "I DON'T LIKE BEING KISSED." YOU PUT YOUR ARMS AROUND HIS NECK AND HE TURNED HIS HEAD AWAY. YOU TRIED TO CLIMB UP ON HIS KNEES AND HE SHOOK YOU OFF, MUTTERING. WHEN HE DIED, YOU DIDN'T HEAR ABOUT IT RIGHT AWAY. YOU HOPE IT KILLED HIM TO LEARN THAT HIS DAUGHTER HAD JOINED THE REBELS.) You braid a rope out of creepers, weighting it with a stone, successfully throwing it over a branch; you tie it to the trunk and begin to climb. Three metres up you're already feeling weak, but you keep on, hands and feet bleeding. You reach the first limb in a tangle of leaves and branches; the birds take wing noisily like a sudden sweep of wind, invisible, and a menacing snarl reverberates close by. The leaves part, and a white shape appears.

Long, slim, almost sinuous, it crouches in a position that seems strange to you. You expected a feline of some kind, and this isn't really a feline: the white fur is short, the front legs articulated like arms, and the long back legs drawn up but splayed on either side of the haunches. When the truly feline length of the body isn't visible, it might be some sort of frog. But the round head with the ears laid back, the circular eyes with vertical pupils . . . the snarl issuing between pointed teeth . . . the claws tearing at the bark . . . . You recover your reflexes in time, and the beast leaps just as you slide the length of the cord, palms on fire. You grab your knife, press your back against the trunk, heart beating; you're sure you're going to die, your whole pain-scorched body is crying out to lie down and let the beast rip you apart. . . . But it hasn't followed you. Your heartbeat slows; again you think of the shelter to be gained in the branches and move off with frequent backward glances. This beast must come down to eat or drink.

You take cover behind another tree and wait. At last the beast leaves the tree. It doesn't jump, but descends awkwardly, limbs clinging tightly to the trunk. It goes off at a jolting gait, half running, half jumping. It's not slim, it's thin; an unhealthy specimen, perhaps? Already you imagine how you'll trap it.

More notches on the leaf. The beast is sleeping in its cage. You found it hanging from a branch, half strangled in your snare, and were wondering how to kill it when it made a strange movement: its front paws gripped the rope clumsily, as though feeling for the knot, and you noticed the long, articulated fingers. You undid the rope and the beast fell to the ground. Knocked unconscious by the fall and lying on its side, it seemed inoffensive, pitiful. You tied it up and went off to build a cage. Now your shelter is in the fork of the large branch, and the beast lives in the cage on the ground. Sometimes it stands and grips the bars, shaking them as it snarls, but wearily, soon lying down again, its large, dull eyes fixed on the tree from which you have banished it.

The plump, oblong fruit on the tree has turned out to be more nourishing than the yellow berries by the lake; from top to bottom, above and below, you explore the tree looking for fruit, hugging the round branches; your body has become hard and tough, deeply brown from the sun which you soak up lying along the highest branches, close to the clouds. To come down again you sometimes grab a flexible branch and let yourself fall twenty metres, breathless but proud of your strength and agility; and when you finish gathering fruit, you feed the beast and tease it.

This evening it's pacing up and down the cage, responding to your teasing with strange, sharp cries, more pleading than angry. Vexed, you throw some fruit through the bars and go off. A stifled mewling makes you turn back toward the cage: the beast is lying on its back, shaking convulsively. ... You rush over to it, not seeing very well in the dusk. The sound is not one of pain; you recognize it, but don't understand. You look closer. The forepaws are holding one of the long, smooth fruits from the tree, pushing it back and forth over the almost hairless belly where six pink nipples stand up violently; the movement accelerates, the pelvis lifts spasmodically, and the fruit disappears into the hidden vagina that has just dilated. The beast ... it ... she ... gives a single cry that ends in a sigh, quivers a little, and lies still. One forepaw rests across the breastbone, the other holds the glistening fruit into which the beast has sunk her teeth.

That night while the beast tosses and turns, groaning at the wounds inflicted by your knife to punish her, you find yourself unable to get to sleep. The tree-fruit you'll eat tomorrow morning sits in a bowl made from a husk. The night is warm and clammy, its noises coming and going as the starlight pierces the swaying foliage. First you rest your hands on your chest, then draw them back, startled by the excited stirring of the skin beneath your cool fingers. A ray of moonlight, lambent, liquid, illuminates the fruit. How long and smooth the fruit is, how well it fits in the hollow of your palm, how quickly it warms to the touch.... You place the other hand on your belly, feel the muscles tighten; you brush the short hairs just below your navel, imagine the weight of the fruit on your abdomen and how good it would be to be touched and not feel that you were doing the touching. You lift the fruit ... and hurl it down on the cage, hurl all the fruit. Some must hit the beast: she moans. Tomorrow you'll make weapons, go hunting.

Tomorrow brings a lowering sky, turning the forest to stone beneath a grey, glutinous light. All is silent. You spend the day looking for wood for a bow and arrow, while the clouds become heavier, gathering noiselessly across the sky as though self-propelled; not a breath of wind moves in the forest and the leaves hang listlessly. The beast sleeps fitfully and you look away each time your eyes are drawn in her direction. Toward evening you hear the first distant rumbling, and a pale light bathes the forest as the last bit of open sky is engulfed by the clouds. The beast has wakened and whimpers softly. You shout at her to stop, but the very sound of your own voice terrifies you. You climb back up your tree and lie down to await the first drops.

It comes soon: a confused murmur that lifts the foliage briefly, and an instant later howling demons loose themselves upon the forest. You feel the branch beneath you pitch like a ship and streams of water break over you as the wind penetrates the fragile walls of your shelter, tearing them away. Lightning illuminates the sky, continuous thunder rolls over the forest, and you hug the glistening trunk, blinded by the rain. Below, the beast screams and shakes the bars; the storm has maddened her, she'll do herself more harm. You climb downward, the rope swinging dangerously, threatening to smash you against the trunk; as you prepare to jump to the ground, a tremendous crash rips through the air around you, an unbearable light closes your eyes, and your muscles contract in a spasm of electricity. You fall on the grass far from the tree, body-hair standing on end, skin tingling, heart pounding.

The tree bursts into flame and splits in two.

The cage catches fire too, but less violently, the rain half-smothering the flames. You pull the limp beast from beneath the debris, grab her around the waist, and drag her under a thick bush. Her left foreleg is broken, her left eye burned; black scorch-marks give her fur the look of a spotted leopard, but she's still breathing.

The tree—your tree—is on fire, split in two.

You don't build another cage. You nurse the beast for days on end, watching her rest on her back, hindlegs extended straight out, forelegs folded on her chest, rolling her head from left to right in a curiously human movement. When she opens the eye spared by the lightning, she follows your every movement, staring fixedly. You help her drink, eat, and watch as she stretches her long, articulated fingers to grasp the food and carry it to her mouth with increasing frequency. When she takes her first steps, she's standing upright, supported on your arm. Once she becomes stronger, she helps you build a cabin that is more solid than the precarious lean-to that has sheltered you during her convalescence. One day, you see her tie a knot to rope two trunks together.

That evening you both eat game roasted on the fire that you've guarded jealously since the heavens gave it to you. The beast is afraid of the fire and keeps her distance, but is quite willing to eat cooked meat. The game was some kind of rabbit—female, fecund; you threw the young in the rubbish hole. You're very weary, lightheaded, body almost floating with fatigue; you lie down on your couch in front of the flickering flames; huddling to concentrate the heat on your taut belly, you let the muscles relax a little in the warmth. Cheek resting on your hand, you watch the blood-red shimmer of firelight on the skin of your thighs and on the fluffy bush of pubic hair. It's two months or more since you crossed the Bridge. Suddenly it occurs to you that you haven't had a period since your arrival; has the journey made you sterile?

A feeling of incomprehensible anguish clutches at you. What does it matter? You are doubtless the only one of your kind here. A quite unpredictable distress fills you, and a sob rises from your gut to your throat; gripping your crotch with both hands, you turn on your stomach, arms between your thighs, panting, head thrown back, mouth distended, tongue protruding, hands kneading, clawing, wanting to tear your flesh; frustrating spasms convulse you, bringing forth pleasureless cries.

Flesh touches you; it's not yours. The beast is kneeling beside you, on your shoulder she places a . . . hand, the skin warm and dry. Turning your head you see her face close to yours; the retractile claws are sheathed, the tips of the . . . fingers caress your arm up and down. You scrutinize the feline mask, the single eye, the thin lips strangely curled back, looking for a human expression that isn't there, that has never been there; a violent twitching shakes you, startling the paw resting on you and making the claws instinctively emerge halfway from their sheath. The beast recoils, drops to the ground and crawls to its litter. In the long moments before sleep comes, you see the fluid light of the fire reflected in her staring eye each time you look her way.

Under your care, the beast has regained her strength, although she limps a little when she drops to her four feet. Upright, she's as tall as you, and her gracile muscles ripple the thickening fur—no doubt a sign of winter's approach. You no longer fear her, and yet when you discover fresh tracks in the mud and she looks back at you with ears flattened, teeth bared, hackles raised, you're afraid for a brief instant. You force yourself to stay still, look steadily into her one eye, and finally she moves off unwillingly, so that you can examine the tracks at close quarters.

They're bootmarks; no animal would leave tracks like that. You begin to follow the trail, heart beating, hands tightened on the shaft of your spear. Behind you the beast growls but doesn't move; you tell her to come, walk on without waiting. In three bounds the beast is in front of you, snarling and blocking the trail with her four feet planted in the mud. You threaten her with your spear, giving her a light tap while speaking in an irritated tone; for a moment you think she's going to leap at you, but she goes off, head lowered, and disappears into the undergrowth, deaf to your calls. You hesitate to follow the path without her, but the tracks are very recent. ... You shrug and resume the trail.

It takes you to the edge of the forest among numerous trees similar to the one destroyed by the storm, but smaller. Autumn has quenched the colours and the empty fruit husks cover the ground, occasionally crunching beneath your calloused feet. On the harder soil the trail fades and you stop to peer at the earth; a rustle in the branches makes you look up—and a cold, dry mass is pinning you to the ground, wrapping itself around your shoulders as a gaping mouth opens very near your face. You struggle in vain as the coils of the snake tighten and a red veil passes before your eyes .... A roar, a jolt; the constriction loosens and you roll away. The confused mass of entwined coils and claws relaxes abruptly, and the snake slithers off between the leaves as the beast pursues it briefly, flailing viciously. Your breath comes painfully, something in your chest is broken; for an instant you see the beast's inscrutable mask bending over you, then she turns her head to listen to something and disappears from your field of vision. You try to lift yourself to see what's happening, but your curiosity and fear remain imprisoned in your brain, unable to reach your muscles. From far away you hear sounds of someone approaching; from still farther you feel someone touching you. Then you're too far away.

The first word spoken, you knew, was his name: "Rirk." That was how it sounded. You replied in a broken voice with your name,"Kathryn." He repeated "Katri" with a sort of hiss at the end, and you closed your eyes again, carrying into your sleep a triangular face, green eyes, a large mouth, pointed ears and a shock of curly hair.

Rirk is still near you when you awake in the warm room. It is Rirk who responds to your first attempts to communicate, who begins to teach you the language of the Marrous. The first lesson deals with the gender of names: all are neuter; they become feminine if you're speaking, masculine if it's Rirk. The masculine and feminine of a name can be very different, the connection almost unrecognizable, because it's more than a change of suffix: a whole way of looking at things is involved.

When he thinks you've sufficiently mastered the basic root words and grammar, Rirk presents you to the assembled villagers like a newborn infant, and for the first time you see other Marrous. Apart from the eyes, all of them green with slit vertical pupils, their physiques vary considerably, particularly as to colour: some have pale skins, others brown; there are some completely black, and others with bizarre colouring that resembles spots or stripes, caused by the down covering their skin. (When Rirk comes into the room on a sunny day with the light behind him, his legs, naked arms and leonine head are outlined in a coppery nimbus.) But when you try to ask whether the village hierarchy depends on the play of colours, you have great difficulty making Rirk understand what you mean. There are words for "competence," "experience" (the root is the same as that for the word "voyage," as you point out to Rirk, who bares his small teeth in an approving smile), and these qualities imply that their possessor has a kind of authority, some sort of power. But Rirk's explanations seem to show that only personal skills are involved, ones that apply to the various details of daily life and have no authority over others, except in special circumstances. The idea of an abstract power, unconnected with any particular situation, doesn't seem to exist. There is no word for "leader." Is there no leader? "Rora leads the hunt," says Rirk; her mate, Mnar', leads the fishing, and others manage the cooking and carpentry.... "Lead" means "teach," and this word comes from the root for "live" and "show." There is no word for "command," but there are an infinity of words for "ask": one adds the root for "request" to the name of the beneficiary—for example, the intimate "to-request-for-me-from-you," or the more formal "to-request-for-so-and-so" or "for-such-and-such." But there is no imperative; the strongest verb, "to-request-for-life" is the equivalent. But the difference is obvious: it's a far cry from "to command."

After a few days you are surprised to find that, although you have asked a great many questions, Rirk has asked none. "Your questions are our answers," he says with a slight smile. You turn away, dissatisfied; who do these savages think they are? You look at the village, the large houses of well-squared timber with their chimneys smoking in the cold air; Rirk, standing motionless beside you, attentive and quiet in his clothes of intricately woven and richly coloured wool, is no savage; you know it. All at once your memory fills with flashing weapons, gigantic towers of steel and glass, an infinite multiplicity of machines in the labyrinthine entrails of your far-off world . . . .

And the metal sphere buried in the heart of the underground passage, and the Bridge buried in the heart of coldness.

You shiver, hugging yourself, and for the first time really ask, "Where am I?"

Today, while you're on the hill overlooking the village, the first snow begins to fall. The children come out of the houses, rolling over each other, jumping at the snowflakes, laughing and shouting. You admire the grace and height of their leaps, the supple play of their friendly battles; seen from afar, one would think it was a brood of playful kittens. . . . Something snaps behind you; the beast is there, staring at you with her single eye; she flees, hobbling, before you can move. But you do not speak of it in the village; you don't want to speak of either the lake or the forest.

From now on, each time you walk a little distance from the village, you feel that an eye is following you; you don't know whether you're afraid; perhaps you pity the beast, thinking of winter; they've told you it gets very cold in the forest. When she shows herself to you again, you make small, reassuring noises, signal her with your hands. . . . She bounds toward you, seizes you with her forepaws, tries to carry you off. But you're stronger than she (she's thin and clumsy, as on that first day) and it's you who drag her to the village when you see that her claws stay sheathed; she's afraid, moaning more than she snarls.

The pounding of feet: three Marrous come upon the scene; they're going to help you. Instead they grab your arms, making you let go of the beast who breaks away instantly. In response to your irritated questions they shake their heads. "We-request-you-for-her to let her go."

"But she'll die this winter!"

"We-request-you-for-her to let her go."

The four of you go back down to the village. In the fresh snow, paths between houses already intersect. You think of the beast: touching her has established a bond; you think of the beast alone in the forest. You tell Rirk that she isn't dangerous, that you will vouch for her good conduct in the village (difficult to say this in what little you know of the Marrou language: one can only be responsible for oneself). But Rirk also says, "We-request-you-for-her to let her go." You get angry, tell Rirk that he is cruel. "She'll die for certain in the village. She has a chance of survival in the forest," he says. You don't understand; he leans toward you, rests a warm, dry hand on your arm; this is the first time that you have seen his eyes so close. "We-request-you-for-her to let her go."

A feeling of melancholy spreads over the village—over the adults, at least, for the children continue to play and learn without appearing upset. That evening Rirk takes you to Rora and Mnar'. Other people arrive, one after another. Soon the whole village is squeezing into the large room: about a hundred men, women and children, jammed together. The meeting doesn't appear to have been organized; it's as though, floating in one current, all the isolated debris of a river were washing into the same backwater. Men, women, and children. You look among the small groups that have formed, talking in low tones as they drink hot broth: no teenagers. It's the first time you've noticed it. "Where are the young people?" you ask Rirk. He points to the children. "No, the...." There is no word for teenagers.

"Those over twelve," you conclude lamely. Rirk looks at you for a moment, his expression serious, then says, "They're in the forest, by the lake, or near the sea."

The beast is the oldest daughter of Rora and Mnar'. "She wasn't able to leave her tree," says Rirk. But the tree was destroyed by lightning! Without having intended it, here you are telling them about your encounter with the beast, about your life in the forest. At the end of your tale, Rirk repeats, "She wasn't able to leave her tree." You feel that you must not be speaking of the same thing.

At about the age of twelve, the young leave. They are not forced to; it's not a period of ritual initiation imposed by the adults as a group, but a normal phase in the evolution of the Marrous. The youngsters become increasingly silent around the age of twelve, keeping away from the community more and more until one day they leave the village completely behind. They go as far as the red sea and then return in slow stages, skirting the lake and traversing the forest. Sometimes they come back quickly, sometimes very slowly; and sometimes, somewhere beside the sea, along the lake, or in the forest, the fingernails become claws, the downy hair becomes fur, and the youngster falls on all fours, never to return to the village. Shreds of rational explanations jostle in your brain: "puberty ... regression ... recessive genes...." But what has all this to do with the sea, the lake, or the forest? "We're made of the same substance," says Rora. "They resemble us, and we resemble them. We speak to them with their voice, battle with them to wear out our dreams. When all the primal dreams have been lived, we return to the village as Marrous. There are some who cannot pass through the stage of living these dreams."

And the beast is the oldest daughter of Rora and Mnar'. You don't understand. It takes you a long time—the whole winter, with its snowdrifts and long watches in the night, its slow-paced life. First, however, you have to fully grasp the intricacies of the Marrou language; at times you spend entire nights without saying a word while your hosts converse insatiably about vocabulary, grammar, pronunciation, history, folklore, religion, scientific knowledge that you never suspected they knew, indulging in interminable discussions of some incomprehensible nuance of meaning in some poem, song, treatise, novel, that all seem to have sucked in with their mothers' milk (or fathers'? Here men breastfeed ...). Driven to self-appraisal by your blank expression, the Marrous reveal themselves to you over this long winter. It is then that, listening to their conversations, watching the way they move or stand—or perhaps, simply seeing them as they are, because your eye is no longer caught by superficial resemblances—you finally glimpse the fact that the Marrous are profoundly, irremediably different, and that you come from some other place.

But why? And why HERE?

Now it's Rirk and Rora, Mnar' and the others who look at you, asking, "Where have you come from? Who are you?"

For a long time you say nothing because you don't know where to begin. Then, in words not made to express such memories, you try to explain: "Automatic ships flying at enormous speeds link the Neo-Earths. But man cannot survive these journeys; only his semen can be transported without the cost eating into profit. This is how the Neo-Earths were colonized. But for our planet to maintain its power and continue forcing them to divert their resources to an Earth bled dry, there must be some means of rapid communication, more rapid than the automatic ships. The means has been found: the Bridge with its zombie messengers." How can you explain this?

Strangely enough, they quickly grasp the idea of ships, colonization of far-off planets, even of technology capable of creating the Bridge; you are amazed, although during the winter you had become aware that this Marrou village was only a minute part of a complex and multiform organization, a halting-place, not a primitive community closed in upon itself, as your cultural reflexes had suggested to you. What they seem to have difficulty understanding is the way in which human societies function—or rather—finally you get it—they don't comprehend the inward nature of humans from Earth, their intimate being. You try to repeat what the ideologists of the Revolution have taught you, but the Marrous stop you: "Yes, yes, it's important to know who produces and who consumes and how it's done; but we request-you-for-our-information to tell us why?"

At this you are confronted with your own question: why are you here among the Marrous and not somewhere else? Rirk must sense your distress. "We-request-you-for-yourself-and-for-us to tell us about the Bridge."

The Bridge. The messengers who are the message. The immobile but instantaneous journey into the cold. As you talk, your hosts exchange knowing looks. What have you said? What have they understood? "It is the image imposed on their mind that carries the travellers to the other side of the Bridge," says Rora conclusively. The others nod. "But I wasn't a zombie!" you want to shout. And yet you say nothing; you don't want to consider the question in front of the Marrous. You might perhaps have to recount in detail how you came to cross the Bridge, the expression on the face of the engineer when you raised your weapon after interrogating him. What else could you do? You had no choice. You were Kathryn Rhymer, a Rebel; your acts were mapped out by others.

But why were you a Rebel? Who was Kathryn Rhymer? You really don't want to ask yourself this, and ask instead why you chose to try the Bridge rather than die for the Revolution.

TO BE GOD. THE LAST. Yes, you remember well. But instead of being God, floating by the force of your will, liberated from Time and Space over the face of the universe, you awakened in the red sea waters of the Marrous.

"The sea of the Marrous is one of your dreams," says Rora; "the Bridge sent you toward it." You protest. You never dreamed of such things, there is nothing like this in your mind. "What do you call your mind?" asks Mnar'. You try to explain the meaning of consciousness, will, free will, words that don't exist in the language of the Marrous. Mnar' looks at Rirk, who looks at Rora. "You have forgotten your shadow," she says, "your desires, hates, dreams, that which drives the young people toward the sea, the lake, the forest." You shrug your shoulders violently; you aren't a young Marrou. "But the Bridge sends you where your mind desires, if your mind hasn't been erased," says Rora, "as the sea, the lake, or the forest force our young people to journey through themselves until they get to the villages, if they can."

You shrug again, but say nothing. You don't like this interpretation; don't like recalling what you've seen, what you've done in the sea, beside the lake, or in the forest. And yet you saw and did these things. What happened to you? The shock of the journey. ... A natural drug in the air or water, in the flower nectar, in the tree fruit. ... Anything rather than think that. ... Anything rather than admit ....

Things are going badly with you now, very badly. You ask no more questions and avoid all who might ask you any. You have left Rirk's dwelling and installed yourself on the hill overlooking the village. You think continually of the world you have left, bent on nostalgia, knowing it's a lie: you were nothing, you had nothing back there that you could possibly regret not having here. Kathryn Rhymer. At times Kathryn Rhymer revolts you; at others you feel she never existed. She never realized she didn't exist. Her combats, sacrifices, killings: pipe-dreams, phantoms.... The struggle against tyranny for justice, freedom, humanity—there was no solid kernel of identity to respond to such truths, providing her life with illumination. Instead they supplied the decor, the props for the show that Kathryn Rhymer put on for herself before a mirror. But the mirror lacked quicksilver; behind it, feeding greedily on the spectacle, were the pipe-dreams, phantoms, and lies that pulled the strings of Kathryn Rhymer.

You look at the village below. You compare it to the grim images that you carry with you always. Is it possible that you are here, that this village, this planet, exist?

AND WHAT IF THEY DON'T EXIST? What if they had

never existed before the cold closed over you? What if, in that transfiguring moment when you were God, the devil within you had created them out of nothing to cross over with you? Yes, the Bridge creates Gods, but the shadow of the Gods follows behind, mocking as he goes. The first cold voyagers remained prisoners of their own god-like creation. But not you, no, not you! Swollen with enormous power, you stand above the village, above the hills, above this miserable clump of soil that owes you life, and you intone, "BEGONE!"

Neither lightning nor thunder strikes. The village is still there.

Then it is a dream. You're floating in some inconceivable space beyond the Bridge, prisoner of one of the traitorous dreams that prowl through your brain. To wake. HOW TO WAKE?

Only one way: one doesn't die in a dream. Sleep is too near to death to admit competition. You recall dreadful nightmares in which death threatened you . . . then, always just as it was about to strike, you opened your eyes in bed, soaked in sweat but safe. . . . The merest attempt to kill you, and you would waken.

You turn toward your hut and notice a figure climbing the hill path: Rirk. Quick, quick, you must wake. You rummage in your things looking for a knife. Here. Ah! the blade hasn't much edge but the point is sharp. You remember confusedly something about Japan, you take the knife in your two hands, quick, quick, steps coming nearer . . . .

You barely have time to prick your belly a little. Rirk appears, snatches the knife; you try to grab it from him, screaming that you want to waken, but he half-stifles you, says your name, and all at once he is no longer holding you to save you from yourself: he presses you against him. You grasp his crop of hair to push him away, shouting, "Animal! Animal!" He tears your clothing, throws you on the ground, drives himself into you with a savage grunting . . . .

No. Your clothes are intact. Rirk is no longer holding you. He has tears in his eyes. You look at him, incredulous. Because someone feels cheated of the scene that didn't take place.

Someone. . . . You?

Yes, yes. You. And someone is happy because of Rirk's tears and the way he stepped back. You, yes, you.

You stretch out your hand, touch his moist cheek. Is this a dream?

Now you can make love.

***

This morning, a large group of Marrous arrives in the village: some twenty adults, thirty children. The children are ten, eleven years old. The adults are their parents and counsellors. You get ready to return to the interior with Rirk and the others. Now you know the purpose of the villages: they watch over the threshold of the Marrous' ancestral memory. In endless circulation, the future and the past exchange places. You look at the shouting children fanning out on the meeting ground, at the young Marrous, their fur scarred by the forest, the sea, or the lake, ready to leave, ready to return. You know them all now, you've seen them all arrive, thin but triumphant. T'rri who limps because of his encounter with a beast, An'r with a necklace of shells snatched from the red sea, M'rim clothed in scored bark, the slender Garri carrying a tiny shoot from a lake flower in a wooden bowl filled with earth . . . you know them. They know you less well, but smile at you as you glance over them, looking for Rirk in the crowd.

Rirk is looking at you; the new arrivals are looking at you. They say nothing. Somewhat surprised and disturbed, you come toward them; the counsellors cross and uncross their long, slim fingers. Rirk takes a step toward you, then stops.

There is a woman in Aïgna where the new arrivals come from—a woman who resembles you. An Earthling? Their eyes are hesitant. Yes, an Earthling. She appeared one day, naked and starved, in a village of the North, ten years ago. Since then she has lived in Aïgna. Aïgna is the western continent, the most developed. The woman's name? They hesitate again. She has given herself one in the Marrou language, and this is what they call her: Am'maïeta, the-several-times-born. *Has the Bridge not been destroyed on Earth, then?* You're surprised by the thought. This happened ten years ago, after all. *The several-times-born.* A zombie that had. . . . *Impossible.* Nothing can revive a mind destroyed. *An experiment?* But brain-intact messengers had not been sent for decades. Or perhaps a clandestine experiment, on one of the Neo-Earths?

You stop biting your lip, astounded: what does it matter to you? What do you care about Earth, the Bridge, even this woman? You've found your place: it is among the Marrous, the only possible refuge for you in the universe, the only peace.

But the questions won't go away. *Who is she? What is she doing? How did she get here? Why here* . . . .

How is she like me?

Is peace so fragile, then? You're filled with anger against this stranger; what right has she to disturb you? But before you're even aware of it, you hear yourself asking, "How do you get to Aïgna?" The feeling that this doesn't surprise Rirk and his companions irritates you, but at the same time strengthens your spontaneous resolve, which you now assert as a conscious decision.

"The shortest way is across the red sea," says the oldest counsellor.

"It's rather dangerous at this season," says Rirk, eyes lowered. "It would be better to go around it with us through the inland territories . . . ."

No, no, the fastest way will be best. They've taught you how to sail.

"Do you want me to go with you?" Rirk asks again.

He lifts his head at the very moment that you, frowning after an instant's hesitation, answer, "No." He smiles at you; he never thought you would say anything else.

Nothing about the journey remains in your memory, except that it was long and that you often found the solitude hard to bear. Of the dangers encountered, storms, currents, marine monsters, days without rain or wind, starless nights, nothing is left but the vague feeling that all this was normal, that you have always done what you must. You have done what you must, because here you are in Aïgna, watching the countryside slip by on each side of the mirror-bright highway along which your sailsled is running (the wind is almost always blowing in Aïgna; when it isn't the sun shines to power the photocells). You smile at the remembrance of your first "civilized" disdain for the Marrous. No towering cities of steel here, no mechanical multitudes colliding against a backdrop of plastic and glass: you can see rivers, hills, and fields that have been tamed or cultivated for a very long time. Although the towns that you pass are always disguised as villages—a very loose, aerated urban network—you can clearly recognize the surrounding factories, mines, quarries, and industrial zones. The Marrous are familiar with sweat and dust, but not their whole life through: they don't die from it.

Your attention should be focused on all these things, you reflect with vexation, not on this woman whom you're moving toward, who works in one of the planet's most advanced research centres and is the equal of the greatest Marrou scientists, so you have been told. Who is she? What is she doing? What sent her to your planet? among your Marrous? On the boat you often had time to ponder this, without getting any very clear idea of what was and is driving you onward. Curiosity? Fear *(fear)?* What can she teach you that you want to know? Is there something you want to know? And yet you were sure you'd forgotten Earth. When Rirk sometimes said to you, "An isolated human being is not a human being"—(he used the phrase, "An isolated *Marrou*" ... that's the meaning of the word "Marrou")—you didn't understand. Weren't you among human beings? But this woman is like you. Yes, an Earthling and a woman. ... All right, she's like you. So what? You don't need her; she doesn't need you. What will you say to her? *(But she came by the Bridge. Intact, like you.)*

The research centre at Taltugun resembles a garden, a zoo without cages, a hardware store, a family boarding-house, and as an afterthought, a research centre; but without white coats, identity cards, military uniforms or NO ENTRY signs on the outside. It also serves as a school, a reception centre for travellers, a theatre and a city hall, if you understood properly the explanation of the young Marrou who took charge of you when you asked him the way. He leads you up spiral staircases, through corridors, past halls, shops, cafeterias, gardens, and warehouses, with an assurance born of long familiarity. Without noticing it, in fact, you pass from the town to the research centre, which is almost indistinguishable from the other buildings that form the downtown area. Through half-open doors you see Marrous busy with machines and efficient-looking instruments; you feel somewhat dizzy, your heart beats a little faster, waiting for the moment when your guide will show you a different figure, will say, "There she is." You continue on your way, reaching another part of the Centre. Then something changes. After passing three or four Marrous, you realize they are looking at you with interest, although not with surprise. Someone smiles at you as at an old acquaintance, saying something to your guide in an unfamiliar accent that forces you to decipher what you hear. What he's said is: "Another one, eh?"

Your guide goes through a door; you stop, ready to draw back. Cold. A large, round room, a metallic sphere with cable arms folded about its belly. . . . Time seems to stand still, and then you sense a new presence at your side. You turn your head.

You are looking at yourself. You are looking at me.

Grey hair among the black curls; wrinkles on the forehead where you have none yet; an expression that reveals knowledge of things about which you are ignorant; ten years more in the sag of cheek and shoulder. But my eyes are on a level with yours; your beauty spot is on my left cheekbone.

For me, your arrival has long been heralded. How hard your mouth is; and have you smiled so little that no wrinkles crease your eyes? And this sharp freshness, this slim, nervous body beneath the travelling clothes. No, I'm sure I was never like that, even ten years ago.

You tear your eyes away from my face, grit your teeth, step stiffly toward the centre of the room.

"You've helped them build a Bridge."

Isn't there an accusation in your voice?

"Yes. They can't travel like this. The Bridge doesn't work for them. But I want to go home."

I would have protested—I did protest, when they suggested this to me after their repeated failures with the Bridge; you, however, stand quite still, trying to sort out the questions that surface. You want to keep control of the situation. You don't say "Why?" You say, "How?" although with a slight shrug.

"It takes a great deal of training, and one has to have made the first voyage blindly, as we did. To be purged. But it is possible to have some control over the journey."

You turn around, look at me again, slowly, deliberately. You don't try to deny what your eyes show you. You are stronger than I. ... No, that's not it; you haven't the same weaknesses. You say, "You're called Kathryn Rhymer, aren't you?"

Have you already understood where the Bridge is taking us?

"I've chosen another name."

A slight smile; your reflexes are also quicker than mine.

"The several-times-born. How many times?"

It's not really a question. In the face of my silence, your smile widens, a tooth-filled smile that doesn't reach the eyes. It isn't the first time; I ought to be used to it, but it's still too much for me.

"Are we going to be enemies?"

I recognize the lip bitten on the inside, the eyelids blinking over eyes that try to look away. The smile slips, returns, not so stiff. Humour? Already?

"Not now."

Yes, you have passed through the forest. You have yet to cross the Bridge—really cross it.

What's needed now is time. Time for you to stop looking away when I talk to you, time for you to stop watching me furtively when you think I'm not looking, time for you to stop automatically touching yourself when you see our reflections side by side in the mirror. Time is needed before you are willing to ask me real questions, not questions that are ammunition disguised as smiles. You've learned enough from the Marrous to stop on the brink of the latter, but you don't yet know enough to formulate the first. While you remain silent, therefore, I talk to you, cautiously, trying to remember the first time I met myself in another universe.

I tell you where I came from, of that Kathryn Rhymer in that universe—the first woman to win the Nobel physics prize since Marie Curie, but there's no Marie Curie in your universe. I remember especially the belly of my own mother, always flat, and the demanding tenderness of my own father; the days spent in the trees being a boy; other days spent learning from books with desperate eagerness, in order to be the best one day. And the few evenings passed in self-deceiving contempt, watching others being together; the afternoons in the streets at rush hour, just to be jostled, touched, touching. I remember the day that I tried the Bridge.

The Bridge. My work, my child of the cold. They tried to dissuade me, but what could they do against my will? I made it, I knew its workings better than anyone. We were sure that the other team had begun experiments with human subjects, so far without success. Were we going to let ourselves be beaten so near the goal? The monkeys used in the first trials rematerialized in their cages; I would be able to transfer myself to a chosen target—post-hypnotic conditioning would guarantee it. Only three-quarters of the monkeys reappeared? But science is an adventure, gentlemen! Live and learn. All's fair in love and war. Nothing venture, nothing have. And on the other side, the stars. . . . It was a particularly fine morning. When I removed my blouse they looked away; I sneered at them inwardly. My assistant blushed at having inadvertently touched my breast; there were tears in his eyes. What did I care? I was within reach of my goal.

TO BE GOD. THE FIRST.

And after long hours, after these slow monologues carried on near you and for you, more time is needed: time for your eyes to lose this gleam of comprehension mingled with wonder, this light of compassion, of love that is too passionate, that I recognize from having seen it in other eyes resembling ours, here and elsewhere. Now we must wait for you to stop nodding your head, saying yes, seeking my hand. I wait. I speak. You speak. We speak. Are we really speaking to each other? My child, my sister, you think we're alike, don't you? But no, you're mistaken. I wait. I wait for the tears that are blurring your vision to dry. I wait for you to hear what I'm really saying. I wait for you to understand at last that my mouth is not forming your words.

And finally you ask me, "But why do you want to go back there?"

You take my silence for disavowal. Upset at having displeased me, you drop your head. You do not understand why I am not satisfied with the universes opened to me by the Bridge. Oh, I've seen your eyes shine as I describe my journeys and the encounters with other Kathryn Rhymers filled with uncertainty or burning in their cold hell. Your old dreams are not all done with, you have many to live before creating new ones. . . . To be God, you say, not in one universe but in all universes! Not in all, Kathryn: only in those that resemble ours enough for the Bridge to be present, or almost present; those from which one can COME BACK. Don't you find this limitation strange? ... No, you are ready to credit it to a faulty technique, or some hidden fear that holds me back from the truly unknown . . . . I myself have not been able to discard this theory completely; sometimes I tell myself that perhaps I don't really want to go home, not yet, and that each journey consumes yet another dream . . . .

Why do I want to go back? Perhaps to find my place empty at last, to be confronted with what I really have been, and not with these strangers who bear my deceptive faces. But I shan't say this to you, not now. "Stranger" would wound you; you still believe that I am like you.

Round and round you revolve this question, this barrier between us. WHY GO BACK? WHY DOES SHE WANT—SHE/ME—TO GO BACK? I DON'T WANT TO GO BACK, I'M VERY HAPPY HERE . . . .

"Why did you come to Aïgna as soon as you learned I was here?"

You look at me almost reproachfully, as though the question were a betrayal. Then, as with everything I say, you accept it. You move away, arms crossed behind your back, a gesture that I know well: you're thinking it over. And I know where this question is leading you: like the other Kathryn Rhymers sent here by other Bridges in other universes, about whom I will not tell you for many a long day, like them this question will lead you one day to the great, round room; you will stand naked before the metallic sphere, a lustrous fruit in its corolla of cables and tubes, linked by these cables and these tubes to other machines; a machine, but a machine of dreams; the light bouncing off its rounded sides will metamorphose your surroundings, reflect you standing very near, round head and pensive eyes set on a tiny but perfect body, ready to be born yet once more, hundreds of times more in hundreds of universes, until the day when, at the other end of the Bridge, no one comes to meet you; when at last you find your place empty in this world, and when, for the first time, your acts are your own.

GHOST ISLAND

Pierre Châtillon
translated by Michael Bullock

At eighteen, his backpack on his back, François was hitchhiking around Quebec with no particular goal in mind. One evening after more than three months away, when he was planning to get back to Nicolet, his native village, the only driver who stopped to pick him up was a commercial traveller heading for the Sorel Islands. François accepted this slight change of direction. Once at this destination, the young man watched the sun disappear beneath the horizon, then unconcernedly crossed the little bridge leading to Ghost Island.

Unconcernedly indeed, for—being unaware of the events to follow and with the wonderful ingenuousness of his age—he had no means of knowing that soon the whole earth was going to look to him like an island, an island full of flowers and birds, to be sure, but an island lost in space, an island on which we are all wandering among the mists of mystery, an island haunted by the hideous phantoms of our terrors, by the luminous phantoms of our hopes and dreams, the desolate phantoms of our illusions and our dead loves.

Not knowing where to spend the night, he spotted, where the rows of chalets came to an end, an odd building that caught his fancy and he made his way towards it. It was in fact a dilapidated ship's cabin resting on four tree stumps. At one of its corners he saw a bell of the kind rung by sailors on foggy nights. On the doorstep an old man was smoking a pipe of strong tobacco and François greeted him, immediately put at his ease by the grey swirls rising from the pipe, which looked like the clouds of dreams that drift about the world.

"Sit down, young fella," said the old man. "Sit down. Take the time to smoke a pipe with me. There's no hurry."

François sat down, filled his pipe with the tobacco, moistened exactly right, which the old man held out to him. The old man told him about the ducks, the reeds, hunting, the weather, the channels between the islands. He revealed that his name was Phège, that he had rested on this spot over thirty years ago; then he fell silent.

"That's a nice name, Ghost Island," ventured François to break the silence.

"That's a nice name, a nice name," repeated the old man. Then he added, as though talking to himself: "Some people will tell you there aren't any more ghosts. That's because they haven't looked right. It's full of ghosts here, lad. If you sleep here, at daybreak I'll show you. If you've got nowhere else to sleep, you can sleep in my boat. I'm not worried you'll run off with it because there's no gas in the tank."

It was late, the mosquitoes were attacking them from all sides, the bats were brushing past their ears. Old Phège retired to his ship's cabin and stretched out on a palliasse filled with bulrush leaves like the one duck hunters use in their blinds, and François climbed into the old man's boat. It was a large cast-iron boat, a former lifeboat on which Phège had constructed a wooden cabin. To get into the cabin, François had to step over the big oily wheel of an old engine. Inside, he stretched out on one of the two moss-grown benches and in no time at all was fast asleep, rocked by the tiny waves of the channel.

Next day, at dawn, the island was wrapped in pink mist. Phège emerged coughing and knocked on the cabin window.

"Are you ready, young fella? C'm on, it's ghost time."

Shivering, streaming with droplets of mist, they made for the tip of the island. Away on Lake St Pierre, on the anchored freighters, sailors were ringing bells.

"I don't see anything," said François, growing impatient.

"There's no hurry," replied Phège. "They're coming, they're coming. I can feel it. But to see them right you've got to put yourself in the mood."

He took a ten-ounce bottle of gin from under his heavy woollen sweater, opened it, took a gulp, gasped, spat out the fire, then passed it to François. White butterflies were dancing over the surface of the slack water. Peacefully seated side by side on the cold sand, they drank the whole bottle in little gulps. When they had finished, Phège filled his heavy, big-bowled pipe with strong tobacco and said: "Here they are."

Then the beautiful silky phantoms rose simultaneously from the old man's pipe and from the depths of the waters; it was impossible to tell exactly where they were coming from. They took shape and assumed the elegant bearing of supple white ladies dreamily shaking out their long hair in space. They let themselves glide on the wings of the wind, returned with slow steps followed by weightless pink veils, melted one into the other, reappeared in new shapes and with new faces, exchanged bodies, breasts, dresses, hair and souls in an exquisite, milky waltz. At times they were as numerous as snowflakes; at times they all melted into a single Lady, the Lady every man is obscurely searching for beyond the many faces he loves in the course of his life.

One fairy approached the bank, barely brushing against the fine tips of the reeds. François wanted to follow her; he went into the water up to his belt and would have drowned but for Phège's strong arm that caught hold of his shirt. As he struggled to move out to sea, the old man splashed a shower of icy water in his face.

"Where are you going, young fella?" he said.

"I don't know, I felt happy ... but what are we doing in the water?"

They waded back and sat down, soaking wet, on the shore. "Look closely," said the old man, knocking out his pipe on a rock. The tobacco, no longer alight, was scattered over the sand. The sun drove away the mist.

"You see," continued Phège, "your mind was taken by a cloud of smoke, of rose-coloured smoke, to be sure, but smoke. Happy is the man who is not the victim of the chimeras of passion. But most men take a cloud of smoke and then make goddesses from it, women they love who have no more reality than those graceful phantoms you just saw whirling around, phantoms created by my magic pipe.

"Some men follow them and then wake up with a fistful of icy water in their faces and they say, bewildered: 'What happened to me?' Some men follow them and then drown without being aware of it. Some men, the unlucky ones, manage to catch a phantom and keep it—a young man like you, you see, wants to grab an intangible phantom, to bring everything to a stop and then be happy. But in cases like that the phantom weaves a kind of cocoon of cotton batting around the two of them; then the cocoon encloses them forever in a sort of comfortable tomb where they die, suffocated by the cotton batting."

"Then these phantoms are real demons," cried François.

"No, young fella, no. You're making a big mistake there. There's no treachery among phantoms. A phantom is a phantom; the white ladies are the way they are; it's you yourself that's to blame, no one else, if you meet with misfortune, because it was you that imagined them to be real. You have to love them the way they are, without asking for anything more. There's nothing wrong with loving a cloud of smoke. In fact no man can live without smoke. That's what tobacco is for: so everyone can make little clouds of smoke when he needs them. And that's why Nature created the big clouds that drift around the world. Men look at them and model them according to their desires and that does them good.

"When you've understood that, you'll sit down somewhere, you'll stop chasing after shadows, you'll send up from your pipe beautiful clouds of smoke shaped according to your fantasy and then you'll love them as we love women. You have to sit quietly and smoke."

The old man lit another pipe and then added: "But I'm not kidding myself—you're the kind who goes on chasing clouds of smoke for a long time before sitting down quietly."

They went back to the old man's cabin. They picked tomatoes and radishes in his garden and made sandwiches, which they ate with a beer. In the afternoon, Phège showed him around the island. Everywhere willow bushes concealed blinds used in hunting duck. Bustards were pecking at grain in big osier cages. The old man had once been wealthy; he had done business in the States, had had horses, mistresses, a legal wife and children. After coming to the Sorel Islands to hunt when he was in his forties he had never left. Although he had stopped working, he had nevertheless managed to live reasonably well by selling vegetables, ducks, fish and frog's legs.

When the sun had begun to go down, they dined with gusto on corn on the cob and cheese, and the old man said to François:

"Young fella, I must also talk to you about the shady freighter."

Then Phège told him that during the first few years he had spent on Ghost Island he had several times seen the shady freighter with his own eyes. This freighter did not differ in any way from the other boats sailing on the river, except that at nightfall it craftily placed itself at the exact spot where the sun was going to go down. Instead of touching the surface of the water, the sun then came to rest on the deck of the ship, where it was brutally stuffed into the hold and the ship sailed on toward the sea.

The first time he caught sight of this manoeuvre Phège had jumped into his longboat, started its big outboard engine, pursued the freighter and, taking advantage of the violet mists of evening, had boarded the vessel. He found no one on deck, but his intrusion had been quickly noted and huge black spiders, taller than a man, came up out of the hold. Phège fired his gun at them, then killed several of them with his knife. The monsters split open, giving off a filthy stench, but in the end the spiders grabbed him with their many legs and threw him overboard.

Outraged by this abduction, Phège had related his adventure to an old fisherman. According to the latter, the spiders transported the sun to the other side of the world in order to inject it with their venom. Then they set the heavenly body free to resume its passage across the sky. And it was the spiders' injections that produced the big black spots on the face of the sun observed by scientists. A day would come when the whole sun would become black and that would be the end of time. It was useless, said the old fisherman, to board the shady freighter and massacre the pirates, because there were too many of them. They even went about on land. The fisherman had seen one of these spiders jump out from behind a tree, fall upon his father and sting him. His father had turned black and died on the spot.

Phège also told François that he had often heard these spiders skulking around his cabin at night, that he had lain in wait for them with his gun but that he knew very well that they would quickly jump on him with their claws and their crowns of bloodshot eyes and carry him off to some sticky place where their nest was.

As night had fallen, they went to bed. Old Phège slept badly, because it seemed that someone was quietly trying to open his door. François too slept very badly, but he wasn't thinking about the spiders; long white shapes came and stretched out beside him; he undid the cords of their veils, caressed exquisitely soft shoulders, breasts, bellies, and his heart pounded.

At dawn, François came out into the freezing air. He drank a beer, rubbed his eyes that were red with fatigue and, without telling Phège, ran as far as the tip of the island.

He took a ten-ounce bottle of gin in his pocket, but he didn't need it. A very white mist that was wandering above the reeds took on the shape of a delicate young girl gathering handfuls of seagrass to make herself long hair, gathering drops of water from the leaves to make herself eyes. Instead of running away she came towards François, who began to tremble. He stepped back then remained transfixed. Their hands touched, they intertwined their long, sinewy fingers, then stayed like this for a long moment unable to utter a word.

Never had a woman appeared so beautiful, so much like the dream that had dwelt in him since his birth. The more he looked at her, the more he understood that he had just found love. Everything in her breathed gentleness. Everything was grace and sensibility. François felt so oppressed, his breathing became so laboured that he was suddenly afraid of dying, human nature being so little able to endure happiness. He was almost in a hurry for their emotion to resume a more regular rhythm so that he could live for a long time in the company of this woman.

A green light now stretched along the edge of the horizon. A grey seagull flew heavily through the mist. Birds sang. The sun would soon appear. "Kiss me quickly," the fairy managed to say, "otherwise I shall disappear and we shall never see each other again." And François kissed her.

Immediately he had before him, no longer an evanescent wraith, but the loveliest of young girls. He hugged her until she uttered a little cry of pain, so earnestly did he wish to make sure that she had a real body. Now they looked at each other greedily and both of them, without knowing why, began to weep. Then, through the tears, a big smile rose in their faces like the sun on the horizon.

François took his friend's hand and they walked towards Phège's cabin. The old man was sitting on his steps smoking. François was about to speak but he signed to him to say nothing.

"Don't disturb the dream by useless words," said the old man. "You're going to tell me she's the most beautiful, the most perfect of young girls, the one you've always dreamed about. I know that, because I was waiting for you. You're going to tell me you're immensely happy. I know that too and I won't conceal how moved I am."

He smoked for a long time, then added: "Yesterday I told you: 'Happy is the man who is not the victim of the chimeras of passion.' I talked to you like a sage, but today I'm going to talk to you like a man, a real man, and I say to you: 'He alone is happy whom a great passion draws to his destruction.'"

"We want to get married," said François.

"I know that too," said the old man. "We'll get into my boat and sail to Ste-Anne-de-Sorel for Mass."

Half an hour later, they reached the church of Ste-Anne. The sun was shining brightly. The trees were full of birds. The weather was so fine that all three of them, instead of entering the church, sat down on the steps and looked at the gleaming water. The young girl filled her hands with the sparkling light and made two crowns from it, which the lovers put on their heads. For the whole of the Mass, they remained there, happy, desiring nothing.

When the crowd began to come out of the church, Phège rose, made a dignified gesture in the air with his pipe and said: "I declare you man and wife."

Some people applauded, wished the newly-weds much happiness, shook François' hand and kissed the young girl, who had decided to call herself Sabine for the occasion.

"Let's all go to Rose-Irma's," cried someone. "Be my guests."

And the little troop set off. Rose-Irma ran a restaurant not far from there. In fact it was an ordinary house whose parlour served as a dining-room.

In this room, the guests sat round a big table of rough-hewn wood. The room was heated by a large stove. Rose-Irma approached, enormous in her flowered dress, her legs covered with varicose veins. She seemed happy to see the young couple and served them with bigger, thicker slices of white onion than the others. Fish stew was the only dish on the menu. Rose-Irma made it with potatoes, carrots, perch, turbot and sweet-smelling herbs. She served everyone several ladles of stew straight from the cauldron.

Some people had brought cases of beer, others bottles of spirits and in a very short time there was raucous laughter, the usual jokes, shouts, songs.

To drink you must sell.
To drink you must sell.

I sold my blonde's skirt,
I sold my blonde's skirt,
For no more than five sous,
Then I went for a booze.
I fell down flat
And lost my hat.
Hey, Momma, hey,
Let's drink and be gay.

To drink you must sell,
To drink you must sell.

I sold my blonde,
I sold my blonde,
For no more than five sous,
Then I went for a booze.
I fell down flat
And lost my hat.
Hey, Momma, hey,
Let's drink and be gay.

Then they pushed back the table, one of the guests took out his mouth-organ and another his accordion and everyone started dancing. The party lasted till mid-afternoon. Faces were bright red. Several people went swimming in Monk's Channel with all their clothes on. Then François said he would like to go to Nicolet to introduce his new bride to his parents and Phège told the lovers: "I'll lend you my boat so you can get to Nicolet across Lake St Pierre." And all the party crowd burst into a discordant chorus.

Away, away, let's sail away
Across the lake so blue and bright.
If we don't make land today

> We'll get there in the night.
> Ship your oars and hoist the sail.
> Let's hope the sun keeps shining.
> But if there's a cloud as big as a whale
> We'll look for a silver lining.

The lovers went aboard. François took Sabine in his arms and put her down on the roof of the cabin, so that no spot of grease should soil the filmy tulle of her immaculate dress. All eyes were turned towards Sabine, her face was so radiant with happiness. François, who was busy with the cables and the engine, was obviously in need of help, if only to push the heavy vessel into the middle of the channel with an oar. Two fine fellows, already pretty drunk, stepped forward from the little crowd gathered on the quay and spontaneously offered to lend the young man a hand.

"We'll stay with you, kid. We'll take you across to Nicolet. You mustn't get your hands oily on your wedding day. It's a fine day, it'll do us good to get some fresh air. My name's Valmor, he's Roger."

Filled with the emotions of this great day, François put up only a half-hearted resistance and the two men got to work, one of them casting off the cable from the iron bollard, the other pushing with the oar. François had sat down at the wheel and the ship was leaving the quay when an adorable little girl of five or six came forward with a huge bouquet of fireweed, those long-stalked plants with countless pink flowers at the tip. Sabine was so happy that François suggested taking the little girl along with them, picked her up and sat her down alongside Sabine. With the two men aft, François amidships holding the wheel and Sabine and the child on the roof, the iron-hulled craft moved away from shore. Sabine and François waved for the last time to old Phège, who was staying behind on his island.

Once the engine was running, the boat moved slowly forward along the channel, rounded several almost uninhabited islands, hugging coastlines covered with willows whose leaves dipped far out into the water. Suddenly the surface was rippled by a bad west wind veering to the south. The channel widened out: in front of them was Lake St Pierre.

Since the slow boat had to cover a distance of over thirty miles, the voyage promised to take four or five hours. Amidships, under the cabin door, to the right of François' seat, the wheezy old engine was driving a big wheel that pissed water. It was more or less a miracle that the whole thing was working and they had to handle the vessel with great care, because after a while the engine pipes became white-hot.

"François, come and have a drink with us, dammit!"

So long as they were sailing among the islands, François had not always refused his passengers' well-meant invitation; but now that the boat was venturing out into the lake the voyage was becoming a more serious matter, not to mention the fact that the waves were getting bigger and bigger.

The two men had brought a case of liquor on board and hadn't stopped drinking since they cast off. They were now completely drunk and François, realizing that the boat was heavily overloaded, looked forward to the long trip with some apprehension. Valmor, feeling unwanted, was content to empty bottle after bottle and, stretched out on the narrow gunwale aft, was roasting his belly in the sun. As for Roger, he wasn't happy-drunk and was becoming more and more objectionable. He had got it into his head that he wanted to steer and kept hassling François to let him take over the wheel. At one moment he told François he was going in the wrong direction, at another he wanted to head for a buoy, believing it to be an island full of women. In fact he was becoming more and more obsessed with women and he addressed a number of crude remarks to Sabine.

"Go on, have a drink, gimme the wheel, dammit."

And Roger rose and staggered from one side of the boat to the other, making it tilt so far over that it would have capsized but for the presence of mind of François and Sabine, who was stretched out on the roof of the cabin and kept the boat balanced by rolling to left or right.

As soon as François refused to drink, Roger's frustration had turned to hate.

"You're going the wrong way, for Chrissake. That asshole's making fun of us. He thinks he's better than us because he don't drink."

"Let him be, Roger," cried Valmor. "C'm on here and bring the rum."

"That asshole is judging us. I tell you he's judging us. I'm going to chuck him overboard."

But Roger didn't dare make a move. He was drunk enough to utter threats, but even the alcohol didn't impart energy to his flabby muscles.

Some time ago the sky had started to become heavily overcast, the wind was blowing steadily from the south-west, quite large waves were striking the sides of the vessel, making steering difficult. When they were in the middle of Lake St Pierre, Roger decided to go back to Sorel and pick up girls, and Valmor, who till then had been content to warm the hairs of his belly in the sun, was full of enthusiasm for the idea.

"Go on, François, turn her around. We gotta have some fun while our wives aren't there. There ain't no hurry. Go on, have a drink with us, dammit, we'll go and pick up some broads in Sorel."

As François didn't answer, Roger rushed over and grabbed the wheel, but the boat, suddenly swung off course, made him lose his footing and he cracked his head against the gunwale. Sabine had thrown herself over to the other side, firmly holding the hand of the little girl, who was sobbing with terror and pressing the big bouquet of pink fireweed to her heart. Roger was lying semiconscious on the bottom of the boat.

François took off his shirt, because he was sweating with rage. A freighter was heading towards them. Roger decided to approach the ship to get whisky. François had to let him take the wheel for a few moments; then he gave him a sharp blow that sent Roger crashing into the gunwale again. François only just had time to grab the wheel and turn the boat's bow into the swell spreading out in the wake of the freighter.

Exhausted, Sabine kept moving to the right, to the left, back to the right, non-stop; otherwise the boat would have capsized.

Roger slipped into the low cabin in search of gin. He knocked everything over, lost his balance and rolled from one side to the other like a bag of cement. Suddenly Roger, his cheeks purple, came up out of the deck-house, stumbled and threw François' shirt overboard.

"God damn you," yelled François, "you've vomited over my shirt."

"What did you say, asshole? Did you say 'God'? Leave God in the church. I've lived forty years and I've always managed to have fun without bringing God into it. I'm going to chuck you overboard, dammit!"

Roger seized an empty twenty-six ounce bottle and made for François, who quickly drew his sheath-knife, caught the bottle on the blade, sending it flying into the lake, and punched the drunkard in the stomach. The boat lurched violently and Valmor, who was dozing on the after gunwale, shot overboard.

He floated blissfully, unaware that he was no longer on the boat and that the current was carrying him away. François stopped the engine and hurried to lend a hand to Roger, who could only manage to keep Valmor afloat. Valmor, completely drunk, was singing.

They grabbed him as firmly as they could and managed to hoist him aboard with a single jerk; but the boat, completely off balance, swayed over and threw François to the deck while Roger, stepping backwards, was catapulted in his turn over the other side.

"Help, help me. I can't swim. I don't want to die!"

François stretched out a long oar to him, Roger managed to get a grip on the gunwale, François grabbed him under the arms and, with a great effort, heaved him on board. The boat almost capsized, François slipped, banged his head on the bottom and Roger rolled on top of him.

When François came to, he heard despairing cries. On the roof of the deckhouse, Sabine was struggling in the arms of Valmor. The little girl was crying and clutching her bouquet. François tried to get up; Roger, sitting on him, threatened him with an empty bottle. The wind was now blowing in squalls. The waves had become enormous. It was almost dark.

Suddenly the arms, chest and face of the two drunkards became covered in black hairs. Their fingernails grew into sharp claws. Their bodies were shaken by grotesque spasms and six long sticky arms sprouted from their rib-cages. Their faces became hideous things and their heads were soon crowned with eight bloodshot eyes. In extreme terror, François realized that these men were two of those black spiders who hide in the hold of the shady freighter. He grabbed his knife and drove it into the belly of what had been Roger. His legs curled up; he uttered a terrible cry and collapsed onto the white-hot pipes of the engine. There was a sizzling sound, a thin plume of smoke and a fetid stench. His skin was so burned that it shrivelled into two-inch-high blisters, rising like black flour from one side to the other.

François hurled himself upon the spider Valmor, who had just finished raping Sabine, and plunged his knife straight into his face. The spider uttered a cry, let go of Sabine and tipped over into the lake, dragging with him in his fall the little girl and her big bunch of fireweed. Then, righting himself, the monster made off at full speed, gliding over the surface like a skater-bug. The flowers from the bouquet spread out and the whole expanse of the lake turned pink. Sabine, standing on the cabin roof, turned completely black and after giving François a heart-rending look, she disappeared without a word, black in the darkness.

The sky was furrowed by lightning flashes. The wind began to rage, raising waves ten feet high. A weld had cracked and the engine refused to start. François, thrown to the deck by the vibration, held on tight and the boat was carried off by the storm.

Suddenly there was a horrible cracking sound. Water was spurting everywhere. The boat had been hurled against the breakwater formed of a chain of rocks that protects the entry into the Nicolet river. François climbed out of the boat and crawled on all fours along the great rocks battered by the waves. Finally he found himself in front of the La Batture yacht club, whose lights he could see on the opposite bank. He shouted for a long time. Finally someone heard him and came to his aid.

Wrapped up in warm woollen blankets, he slept in the yacht club, right beside the fireplace, while outside the night uttered long windy groans.

Next day, he wanted to go to the wreck of the boat, but no one had seen the big cast-iron vessel and yesterday's shipwreck seemed never to have taken place.

That same afternoon, he headed straight back to Ghost Island. He looked for old Phège and his cabin on four tree stumps. Of all those he asked, no one knew the old man and no one remembered any such cabin.

As for Rose-Irma, she existed in flesh and blood, huge in her flowered dress, supported on legs blue with varicose veins, but she got quite angry and swore she had never seen François and had never served fish stew at a wedding.

François went back to the tip of the island, where he had met Sabine. On the sand a big polythene bag full of garbage, split open, was giving off an unbearable stench. François' stomach heaved; he trod on a dead eel from which swarms of green flies rose into the air. Then, despairing of ever understanding anything about love and life, he cast a last glance at the water of the channel on whose surface puddles of gasoline created an absurd travesty of a rainbow.

COMPULSION

Claudette Charbonneau-Tissot
translated by Michael Bullock

It lacked strength and rigour. I stretched out my hand over the page, and bringing my fingers towards the centre, I quickly crumpled the sheet, which made a scrunching sound like an onion skin.

It was an ill-fated day. The livers of the birds must have been mouldy.

I rose and, although I knew that my mind would inevitably remain as tethered to the text as a goat to the stake, I went out.

And I set off towards the road leading to the village I had decided to go to, even though I knew that there were still sufficient provisions in the cupboard and that this long walk would only serve to bring me back to my starting-point, that is to say to the text on which I had not managed to make a start although I had been working on it for three weeks and had already written over a hundred pages. However, I had crumpled up the pages as soon as they were written and then thrown them over my shoulder into the room.

It might have been enough to kneel down and uncrumple these pages one by one and place them one after the other, at random, in order to give birth to a book whose spontaneous disorder and incoherence might perhaps have better conveyed the inner disorder and incoherence of the character than the rigid sequence of words I had been trying to create since the day on which I decided to go into seclusion for a while in order to get this story out of the way.

But I knew that the god that lived in me and periodically demanded of me a new story would not tolerate either facility or perfidy, just as the gods who, in olden days, demanded a holocaust of young virgins did not tolerate these sacrificial victims being chosen from girls who were weakly, sick or already dead.

And just as the fury of the gods fell upon the cunning when an odour of putrefaction rose from the hieratic pyre, so the rage of the god had fallen upon me the day when, doubting the Machiavellianism of the spirit that haunted me, I had offered up a truncated text assembled from the remnants of other texts.

I was now on my guard against his anger and only offered him faultless texts which, however, sent me into a trance. For the god that resided in me was satisfied only with obscure and bloody stories in which I was led to wallow and live immersed, since as soon as I embarked on a text I immediately underwent a process of personality splitting and metempsychosis, becoming each time not merely the author and the narrator of the text, but also its main character.

For three weeks the story which was coming to me, without, however, finally solidifying into a clear and connected text, kept bringing me back to an isolated house in the interior of which a man was demanding from me explanations of the terms of the pact that I must one day have concluded with someone who, ever since, had enslaved me and ceaselessly demanded, as his fodder, stories that absorbed my time and energy and left me empty and shattered.

But I had been inventing these stories for so long that I must have confused the truth with one of them, then forgotten it, so that I could no longer remember the author or the reasons for my yoke, being conscious only of the constant pressure put upon me and the inflexible rigour of this oppressive force.

The man, then—hoping that, if he mingled his threads with those of the fiction, the truth would one day come back to me— compelled me to create new stories in an unbroken chain.

Although this compulsion was even more cruel than the first one, I submitted; because it seemed to me too that one day, swept along by the ceaseless flow of fiction, the truth would rise to the surface again, perhaps even inadvertently, which forced us to be constantly vigilant.

Snow was piling up higher and higher at the windows and doors, but the man dared not go out for fear that at this precise moment, inside the house, the only story that might have provided the key to the impasse in which we found ourselves might have finally come to my lips. And I didn't dare go out either, for fear that at this precise moment, while I was outside, the right words might suddenly come out of my mouth only to be immediately lost in the vast fields in which the only trees that might have served as landmarks or beacons had already been swallowed up by the snow.

For several weeks now words of the story had been coming out of my mouth and attaching themselves to different parts of the ceiling, like spiders' webs, so that I had to walk about with my head and back bent in order not to be caught in these webs. For three weeks now, in the room where I was writing this story, sheets of paper had been flying about and were gradually cluttering the floor, so that I had to walk cautiously in order not to be sucked down into this accumulation of words on the floor.

On certain days, even as I was talking, I felt the need to walk, to gesticulate and almost to struggle, as if the threads of words, instead of attaching themselves to the ceiling, were falling onto me like a net. And the man, perhaps thinking that this was the price I had to pay for having allowed the threads of reality to mingle with those of fiction, did nothing to help me out.

But little by little I observed that the man took pleasure in seeing me caught like this.

When the words did not fall of their own accord to catch me in their snare, the man took matters into his own hands by putting each story that came from my mouth through a sieve, denouncing the incoherences and weaknesses and demonstrating that once again it was only a fiction, only a fresh lie.

One day, when I could no longer come up with a new story, the man took off the tasselled cords that held back the curtains, came over to me, bound my wrists and ankles and tied me to a chair.

Then began the interrogation that lasted for whole days and nights, during which the man, whom I could scarcely recognize in this role of inquisitor and torturer, brought his face close to mine under the arc lamps, which made the sweat run on his forehead as much as on mine—brought his face so close to mine that I could see the pores of his skin and feel his damp breath—and struck me over and over again, endlessly repeating the same questions regarding the pact I could no longer remember having signed, nor with whom, exactly the same questions for hours on end, as if his vocabulary were limited to these words and phrases, spraying me with saliva each time he pronounced them.

From time to time the man would withdraw his face and cool it in the shadow, moistening his throat with a little water, while I continued to dehydrate under the lights.

In the beginning I often used to beg him to set me free and ask him the reasons for such cruelty, but I soon developed a kind of progressive amnesia in which it seemed to me that this man had never been anything other than an interrogator and that I had always been in the position of a victim. So there was nothing for it but to continue in this role, refusing any admission, simply for the sake of refusal and the blows which refusal brought with it, and not for the sake of what the admission might have revealed, for in reality I didn't remember the answers to the questions the man was asking and sometimes I couldn't even remember clearly what it was all about, since bit by bit—as if the man had become caught up in a movement similar to the one that was sweeping me along—his questions became more and more general and vague, as if he too had forgotten what it was all about, retaining only the verbal formula.

Then he gradually forgot even the formulas of the questions. At this point, he switched off the now useless arc lamps and untied my bonds.

I fell to the floor, exhausted and bruised, but without any aggressive feelings towards the man who, seeing that the method of non-stop stories was ineffective, had tried another, even more draconian one, in the belief that if the truth refused to come out of its own free will, it might perhaps do so under duress.

That didn't happen, however.

The man stretched me out on a bed, washed my wounds, then gave me food and drink.

In spite of his excuses, his caring for me and the fact that he had only inflicted this torture on me with the aim of hastening my deliverance from the spell that bound me, I soon saw from his expression that he had enjoyed tormenting and molesting me.

I got up and moved away from him.

I walked around the house a bit; then, picking up the cords that had encircled my wrists and ankles, I tied back the curtains, which merely opened on an opaque darkness that prevented me from seeing the only trees that might have served as landmarks or beacons.

I curled up in a corner of the room and tried to sleep.

But as soon as my eyelids grew heavy, I was woken by something like a signal. I immediately looked in the direction of the man who, each time I started to drop off, seemed to have moved his chair closer to me, dragging it along the floor; perhaps the sound had brought me back to the surface; or else he had cautiously lifted it so as not to rouse me from my torpor.

But all the time I kept my eyes open and looked at him, the man seemed to be asleep, and I was so exhausted that soon my eyelids grew heavy again and my head fell forward.

This alternation between dropping off and waking with a start went on for a long while, and little by little I grew accustomed to this rhythm and was now scarcely concerned by the man's imperceptible movement, attributing it to an optical illusion due to an error of focus in my drowsy eyes.

But suddenly, as I opened my eyelids almost mechanically to check the man's position, I found myself gazing into his eyes a few inches from my face.

I tried to rise and get out of this corner in which he was confining me by stationing his body in front of mine; but already his gaze was taking effect on me, as if those eyes were leeches applied to my eyes to suck out all will-power and strength to struggle.

I soon felt my fists unclench, my muscles unknot and all my attention concentrate on those leech-eyes and on that mouth that had started to speak. It was articulating with such care that, with each syllable, I could see the lead in the cavities of his sharp teeth, and I suddenly felt I was looking not at a human jaw but at a metallic trap which, if I stretched out my hand, would quickly close on it.

With an effort I tried to slip my hands under my thighs. But it was useless. My fingers barely moved.

Until dawn, the man kept me in this cataleptic state and subjected me to a second interrogation which, without involving physical violence, was nonetheless a psychic rape, because whereas at the beginning of the interrogation the man asked questions about the infernal pact by which I was bound, questions to which I could only reply in a vague, confused way, he soon started questioning me in a much more personal and indiscreet manner about matters that had nothing to do with the pact.

At every reply, although there was nothing lubricious about them, I could see his pleasure at the exhibitionism in which he was forcing me to indulge.

At dawn, the effect of his eyes gradually faded and I was increasingly able to move my fingers and refuse to answer his questions.

When his eyes no longer had any power over me, the man rose and held out his hand to help me up.

I quickly turned my head away and refused to move.

Then I watched him walk away.

And I suddenly understood that it must have been with this very man that I had concluded the pact which had held me in subjection for so long. His pretenses, his interrogations to make me denounce the pact and deliver me from it had probably only been a trick to crush me still further, unless he had quite simply grown tired of the game and wanted to put an end to it in a twisted sort of way. But I couldn't understand what interest he had had in forcing me periodically to create these stories which he read or listened to only with a distracted eye or ear. Perhaps this too was only a different and subtle form of oppression.

I stood up and told the man that henceforth I would no longer be a victim.

As though he had followed the inner evolution of my thought, he did not seem surprised by this statement.

After a few moments of silence, he told me that no other relationship was possible between us.

I replied that in that case there was nothing left for him but to leave.

He said that even if he left I should remain a victim.

I didn't understand the meaning of his words but, believing that he was still trying to mystify me in order to force me to continue this morbid relationship, I told him to leave.

Without argument and without taking any luggage, he opened the door and went out.

Outside it was unbearably hot.

I closed the door and went to a window to watch him walk away.

Suddenly there was a slight explosion a long way off and I saw the only trees that could have served him as landmarks or beacons burst into flames in the summer solstice. And as though he himself had only been one more landmark in this uniform universe, I saw him catch fire and fall in ashes like the trees around him.

Dumbfounded, I opened the door and started to walk slowly, fearing that I too might be struck by the sun and suffer spontaneous ignition, towards the place where I had seen him catch fire.

But at the place where I had seen the man collapse there were neither footprints, nor burnt stumps, nor ashes.

I searched for a long time in this burning desert for a sign of his passing, a remnant of his body.

After hours of fruitless seeking, my forehead burned by the sun, I returned to the house from which all trace had also vanished of the man, who therefore was probably only one more creation of my mind, the character in a new story which I must have created under the oppressive yoke of this god who was still there and hence was not, as I had thought, the man.

To escape this infernal being, under whose spell I now lay more than ever, I went out and started to run around in this uniform universe without landmarks or beacons; I ran around for days and nights on end, hoping eventually to find the road that would enable me to get out of this despairing universe and return to the normal world of the living, a world from which the god who was subjugating me must once have drawn me by some subterfuge or enticing lie about the promised land which had soon turned out to be nothing but a trap invented to catch me and shut me up in this house from which, despite my headlong running, I could not completely escape, and from whose attraction I could not tear myself away, so that—exhausted, starving and defeated—I finally returned to it.

But when I entered this house everything was so peaceful that I wondered whether my headlong flight had not been the product of some other fantasy.

Then the days passed and no other power came to subjugate me and force me to invent stories.

I began to believe that I had finally been freed from the spell that had bound me.

To begin with, I enjoyed this new freedom that left all my time free. I was able to sleep for hours on end and eat my meals slowly. I brought in wood for the approaching fall and put new candles in the candlesticks. Then I occupied myself with needlework that calmed me and emptied me of all thought. I cleaned the chandeliers and the light bulbs, I waxed the floors, I polished the silver.

Nothing and no one was putting pressure on me and on some days I began to believe that my whole past life had been only a bad dream invented by my idle mind. On other days I believed that the god who had oppressed me had really existed, in the guise of the man, but that he had died with him on the day when, breaking the bonds that bound me to him, I had killed him by depriving him of the essential condition for his existence as an oppressor, that is to say my status as a victim.

Then autumn came and the nights grew longer and colder, and the dust gradually descended again on the chandeliers and the light bulbs, the silver oxidized and the candles melted. And everything had to be done again.

But I no longer felt like it.

I now spent all my time by the fire, beginning secretly to forget the time of oppression when I made up stories.

Soon I spent my days walking up and down in this house where I was beginning to suffocate, as if my one life wasn't enough for me, as if, in order to breathe freely, I would have to be catapulted—by some phenomenon of reincarnation—into other lives that would enlarge mine and set me free from the feeling of claustrophobia that was progressively developing in me as I was forced to live only my own life.

Then one evening the need to write was so strong that I started looking through the desk, the chests-of-drawers and the cupboards for the pen which I had so often filled with the black liquid I used for writing those stories which, even though they were often distressing or cruel, gave me access to unfamiliar worlds in which I did not know boredom.

Not only did I not find this pen, but I found neither paper, nor pencil, nor even, in the library, books of which I was the author, as if everything connected with the epoch of oppression, during which I made up stories, had disappeared with the man.

But the need to enter into a fictional life had become so strong that, even without pen and paper, I decided to create a story orally.

It took me hours to find the first sentence, then the story seemed to take off. But I soon noticed that as soon as I had uttered a word I forgot it, so that I was constantly losing the thread of the story and finding myself with words which, detached from their context, no longer meant anything.

So, in order not to lose the thread, I decided to write the words with my fingers in the dust on the furniture and the cupboards as they came to me.

But no sooner had I written the words than dust fell on the furniture and filled the furrows left by my fingers.

I tried to write with ash, or by embroidering the words on sheets with a needle, or by scratching them with my fingernail in the frost that was beginning to form on the windowpanes in the mornings.

But day after day all my attempts to project myself into another life came to nothing.

Little by little, in a sort of delirium, as if the ghost of the man or the being who had previously had me under his thumb and forced me to make up stories haunted the house, I started going into every room and invoking his power, begging him to come back and imploring him to put back on my neck the yoke which, although it wounded me, had given meaning to my life.

I went so far as to drag myself along the floor as a sign of submission, eating and drinking only repulsive things, submitting my body and my mind to all sorts of macerations, even wounding myself in order to please him, thinking that he would enjoy the smell of my blood.

But the walls remained silent, deserted by this god whom I had myself driven away, believing that I was setting myself free, whereas in fact I had shut myself up in the narrow confines of my own life.

I spent several days bemoaning my fate.

Then one morning, as I was weeping with my forehead against a window-pane, I saw a dot appear, very far away, in those vast fields in which young trees had begun to grow as though to serve as landmarks and beacons showing the way to the house to that being who was still much too far away for me to distinguish his body and his face.

The tears congealed in my eyes and for a long time I dared not blink for fear that a simple flutter of the eyelid might sweep away this vision. I was seized by an increasing euphoria and I wanted to open the door and run towards him, because it seemed to me now that it could only be the man, since it was he whom I had called and he alone knew that I was confined in this deserted spot. Nevertheless, fearing that he might burst into flames or suddenly vanish at my approach, I remained huddled up behind the window, reining in my muscles and my voice like mad horses straining to rush away. But suddenly everything broke in pieces within me when I saw that it was not the man coming back to me at all, but a woman whose long skirt and cloak I could now hear flapping in the wind and whose hair I could see flying around her head, preventing me from seeing her face and her eyes.

She walked on for a long time and I couldn't make up my mind whether I hoped she would come towards me or pass me by.

Soon she was quite close to the house and didn't seem to be about to make a detour round it. She was heading not towards the door, but towards the window where I was standing, and she came nearer and nearer until she was quite close, the same distance from the window as me but on the other side.

As soon as she stopped, her hair, which had continued to blow about, as though the wind connected with her walking had created a swirl of air around her, settled down over her back and shoulders, thereby disclosing her face, every feature of which was identical to my own.

A cry burst from my throat.

I smashed the window-pane in pieces, with my hand.

Behind the broken pane my reflection did not move.

Believing that I was once again the victim of a delirious hallucination, I quickly moved away from the window and looked for the needle, the hoop and the fabric which I started meticulously embroidering, as if this were a ritual capable of driving away phantasms.

But while I was bent over the hoop that stretched the cloth, the door—whose hinges had been in need of oiling ever since I went out of this house—the door creaked and, looking up, I saw my double enter.

She unhooked her cloak and let it slide to the floor.

Then she asked me for liquor.

Her eyes were so hard and her voice so brutal that I dropped the needle and the hoop and poured her the drink she had asked for.

But I didn't dare go towards her to hand her the glass.

She came to me, took the glass and began to walk about the room.

"You weren't expecting me."

Her voice cracked like a whip.

She continued to walk around without looking at me, casually scratching the wood of the furniture with her scarlet nails.

"It was the man you were expecting."

Her walk had brought her up to me. I remained silent, hypnotized by her eyes.

She turned away, poured herself another drink, then went over to the window.

With the tips of her fingers she caressed the twisted cords that had bruised my flesh.

"I rejoined him while you were vainly running around in the vast fields in which I was careful to burn the only trees that might have served you as landmarks or beacons."

These words released a mechanism in me and I remembered the day when, a wandering spirit in search of a body, she had presented herself to me for the first time and had spoken to me of strange worlds whose marked out roads she alone knew.

To escape the routine world in which my life was then wilting, and so that she should lead me from landmark to beacon on the way to those fantastic worlds she had told me of, I had agreed to live under her protection and had allowed her to incarnate herself in me.

But I didn't know then that this spirit lived only on stories and that I should be forced to make them up unceasingly, so that the spirit could inhabit me and bring about those metempsychoses and transfers to strange worlds which I could no longer do without.

And so that the spirit should remain in me and obtain for me the dose of unreality which I now needed in order to survive, I agreed to submit to her cruellest whims. I even went so far as to permit the spirit she once loved to be surreptitiously reincarnated in the man I then loved.

Even if I now remembered all these degrading things, I was nevertheless ready to submit afresh to her games and ceaselessly create those stories for which she had probably come back, being unable to live for long without this fleeting nourishment, just as I could no longer live by needlework and washing. I needed more and I knew that it was only by submitting to her again that I could manage to create those stories into which I must project myself as soon as possible in order not to suffocate in my own life.

She had started to walk towards me and I knew that if I didn't get out of her way she would reach me and once again merge with me.

I stood still, waiting for the impact.

Suddenly, there was a minute explosion.

She had reached me.

As I passed in front of a mirror I saw my reflection in the glass and remembered that my eyes had first acquired that hardness on the day the pact had been concluded between herself and me.

Moving away from the mirror, I took from the desk the pen and paper which, a few days ago, I had looked for in vain, and I immediately began to write a story into which I was catapulted the moment I put down the first few sentences.

For years I created those stories that enabled me at once to escape from my own life and to feed the spirit.

Then one day I could no longer start a new story.

Next day I tried again, fruitlessly.

Then she began to threaten and oppress me.

But the following days were just as unproductive.

She started to beat and torture me.

But it was no use spending hours at my desk, every page lacked strength and rigour.

Soon she began to pace up and down in me like a she-wolf in a cage.

The third week, although I knew my spirit must remain tethered to the text like a goat to the stake, I went out to escape my suffering.

When I came home she was dead.

I never again found the pen or the words that make up stories.

And in spite of my reluctance, I had to return to needlework and washing.

IN FRONT OF THE TEMPLE OF LUXOR, 31 JULY 1980

Yolande Villemaire
translated by Basil Kingstone

To G.A., who asked the question

For the last half hour I've been talking about the black pyramid I saw in my hand three years ago, about Isis and Osiris and Nephthys, a blue hippopotamus in the Egyptian room at the Louvre, Tutankhamen in all the store windows in New York in the spring of 1979, the geomagnetic forces which were in Egypt in Egyptian times 'n which apparently are coming here, 'n what my sister explained about the sphinx, 'n the sarcophagi like Russian dolls in the British Museum, 'n the pyramid reader who told my fortune on a beach on the edge of Old Orchard, 'n Akhnaton, 'n of how determiners work in hieroglyphics, 'n how they wrote the name of their god on every strip of wrapping round the mummies 'n how in my research on Egypt in Latin Elements for my ancient history course I was real surprised to learn the Egyptians didn't think the brain was important and it was the first thing they took out of a dead body, sucking it out through the nose, 'n Julien who saw two moons in Karnak when he went to Egypt, 'n Sophie who'd made a chess set out of clay with queens like Nefertiti in her visual arts course, 'n Polanski's *The Tenant*, 'n the awful nightmare I had two years ago when letters of white smoke wrote on a black background "Black forces of Egypt are my allies, I won't be scared, I won't be scared, I won't be scared", 'n the god Ptah who gives things their names, 'n the Aswan dam 'n...

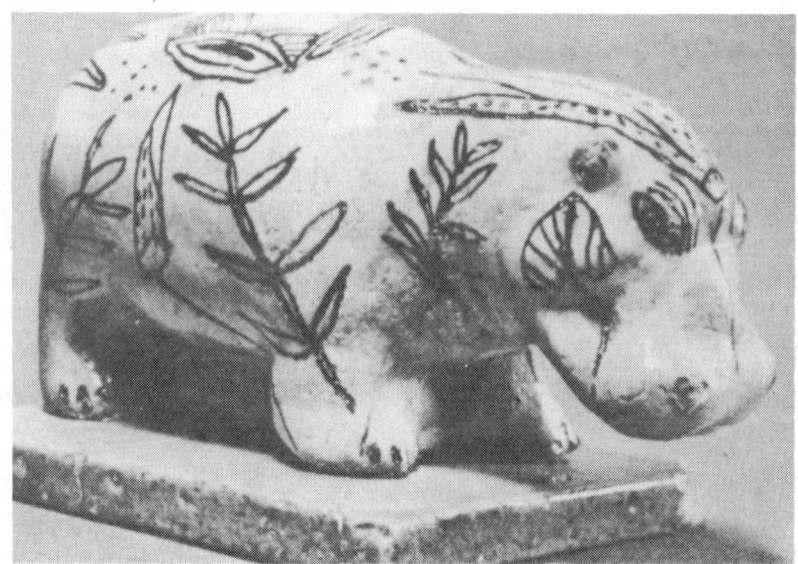

SOUNDTRACK: extracts from "In the Great Pyramid" by Paul Horn

Then you ask me, "Yes, but what *is* Egypt?"
And months later I answer: it's a *putting-off machine*. Putting you off by answering "Maybe". I mean, what would you say if I answered "Maybe" when you ask me what Egypt is?

***

Maybe it's the sun (all my friends think the sun is feminine) burning deep inside the hall of reincarnations. Fire when it sets fire to the whole dark room of memory and the living archives of the women singers in the temple of Amon, the Amazons, the witches, the madwomen, the kings, the scribes, the monks, the madmen, start whirling around in the red sands of *maybe*.
You ask me what Egypt is, and eight months later to the day I answer that it's a territory crossed by the Nile. It says in all the geography books that Egypt is a gift of the Nile. The Nile is a river of articles, nouns, verbs, personal pronouns, proper names and adjectives, born of "the Blue Nile which rises in Ethiopia

and the White Nile which comes from Uganda to join it at Khartoum, and then the true Nile flows for 3000 km northwards to the Mediterranean, creating a long ribbon of green across the desert; in the heart of a barren region it waters a long oasis which for thousands of years fed a whole civilization."

And if the word Nile—or Nil—means "nothing", so be it; on both shores of this nothing stands the imaginary territory that I am the cartographer of.

"Toda la sangre del mundo puede ser canción en el viento."

The Letter from Egypt

You asked what Egypt is, and eight months later to the day, on the sixth of the sixth month, I answer that it's the number six. Exactly, six, three and three. The sixth mystery of the path of reality; six like when the mental pyramid which has its roots in the sky coincides with the pyramid bound to the ball of fire in the earth's core. Six as a figure of junction or fissure, six or the site of a coincidence. A reference to those laser moments when the map suddenly seems to follow the undulations of the ground so closely you'd almost think you were there. Even if the whole universe were reduced to a sound or a colour, the whole universe and everything you can say and imagine about it melting into the tone of *one*, there remains and will remain the infinite sequence of the other worlds. Those we can't even imagine. The ocean of the nagual cannot be guessed at, said the redskin to his apprentice sorceress. But in the hectic interchange of the shape of your fate, you may meet it. It's a matter of seconds. If you don't grab Ariadne's thread when it goes by, you can wander for months or years or lives in the labyrinth here without even suspecting that there is a machine to differentiate the hieroglyphic side of what we call reality.

You ask me what Egypt is. And I answer that it's an image. The mage of i. The Magi of E. The Mage of I, as one says: *The Wizard of Oz*.

SOUNDTRACK: Judy Garland in "Over the Rainbow"

To journalists who said she was reputed to be difficult to live with, Judy Garland used to reply, "But you don't know how much more difficult it is to *be* Judy Garland."
    Judy is a woman's name. That's what she meant, says Galariel. Galariel is my white soul. She has something of Gaia, the earth mother, and Ariel, the Holy Spirit of mental storms. She comes from Thursday, which comes from Thor, from a choleric constellation at the other end of Iran. She records glances and can read blood. She says that at the moment she's mainly reading your Amerindian blood. And strange as it may seem, she can also read the drop of Jewish blood in your veins. But if you go on talking about Auschwitz, she is liable to remember for good the weight of the glance you gave her then, when you were dying. For she was the Aryan woman watching you die and who received the last flash of your consciousness. And this glance has crossed time and even survived the death of Elsa the She-Wolf of the SS, which was her previous name.
    Dhoran says that Egypt is dream life. That it's smoking a cigarette when you stop smoking 'n stopping smoking when you've started again. He says Egypt is somewhere between a version of the Thousand and One Nights which is faithful to the original and the thousand and one apocryphal versions which all try to be as alluring as possible. Better yet, Egypt is not finding a single cigarette in the whole house at night when all the convenience stores are closed and you've just picked up the nagual and decided that sure you have the right to cheat. Dhoran is my black soul. And he adds that it's even more Egypt when, having just written that there isn't a cigarette in the house, you remember that old dried-out pack of Balkan Sobranies which are more or less fit to smoke, plus three mental Craven A's on the time line of the life of a woman born on 31 July 1950, raped in 1970 right in the middle of the War Measures Act, and whose name was Myriam in Auschwitz. Three plus three, mystery six on the path of reality. In the bionic spider's web of reality and fiction, all roads lead to Rome, because you can't cheat with

truth. Truth, like all reality, is material. Dhoran would stake his life on it. So would this woman born on 31 July 1950, if she weren't explaining that the sphinx is linked by mental wires to the ball of fire in the earth's core to Will H. Dalst, the lawyer of willpower, who's smoking his last Balkan Sobranie ("Made in England"). Dhoran says that Will H.Dalst, in this life, thinks he's a secret agent or else Lucifer, depending on the cycle of his disguised Quebec blood. But Dhoran forgets to say that it was much worse when the man now called Will H. Dalst was a scribe at Memphis in the Old Kingdom. Because then the little lawyer of willpower thought he was the god Ptah himself. The being who gives things their names. Because when the fire flares up in the *pyramyths of the Js*, nothing is impossible any more. Dhoran is my black soul. He has something of Horus the sun god and then he's a three-year-old male child decorated with an Egyptian cross who dances around the crematorium where his father is burning. Dhoran is my black soul. He has something of the portrait of Dorian Gray and of Demian's daimon. He's a nasty little devil who says life is elsewhere, in the direction of the apparent meaning of the night of the times of things. He also says Egypt is Mickey Mouse's bland smile. That it's just a word on the map of the territory of what is called reality.

You ask me what Egypt is and Axel Forget, She Forget's brother, says the DNA chain always transmits the same message. Axel Forget and She Forget are just other characters in the actantial shape of Yvelle Swanson's journey from Montreal to Berlin on July 23-24, 1980. Yvelle Swanson is just an orienting force in the black room of memory.

No wave, no future

SOUNDTRACK: "My Mamma Didn't Teach Me How to Cook" by Annette Peacock. A few bars, then fade out. The dialogue between Dhoran and Galariel is heard in the fore-

Réjean Ducharme

ground, while in the background Annette Peacock's song can be vaguely heard.

DHORAN: Wow, what have you done to your hair?

GALARIEL: It's a nice red, eh?

DHORAN: Not bad! Boy, Galariel, you've got hair like a three-alarm fire!

GALARIEL: Those are cute. Let me see them.

DHORAN: They're cute, eh? They're golf shoes. I bought them on sale at Simpson's for ten bucks. Brand new, too. I've never seen anything so ugly. They'd be cute with my houndstooth stretch pants, but I don't know where I put those. I suppose She's put them on.

GALARIEL: Speak of the devil. Sure, look, there she is, over there.

DHORAN: Where?

GALARIEL: There, look.

DHORAN: I don't see her.

GALARIEL: Yes you do, look, beside the boy in yellowy-orange tights.

DHORAN: I still can't see her. Anyway, why does everybody here look so dumb? Just because they're no wave, they don't have to look so dumb! No wonder this place is called Ice, everybody's as cold as ice!

GALARIEL: It's the no future look. No wave, no future.

Fade in on the end of Annette Peacock's song: "I'm a woman, my destiny is to create".

Stage directions

You will have noticed that when the lighting operator puts the green spotlight on, Galariel faints. She explains to Dhoran afterwards that it's because of the kryptonite. That green light is green waves and green waves is the wavelength of hate 'n it pierces her Superman shell. That's when they both decide to leave because you never know with kryptonite. The stuff is radioactive.

You will have noticed during this scene that Galariel, under her red mane, looks more and more like Isis. And that Dhoran, staring at her golf shoes which look so funny with her no wave astronaut suit, is exactly like her sister Nephthys.

The Hall of reincarnations

FIRST LESSON IN ARCHAEOLOGY

ISIS, *sister and wife of Osiris, had great magical powers. Among her other beneficent roles, she protected children. This made her the most popular of Egyptian goddesses.*

RA, *sun god of Heliopolis, became the State god during the Vth dynasty. In certain traditions he created the human race; the Egyptians called themselves Ra's flock.*

ANUBIS, jackal god of embalming, present at all ceremonies to introduce the dead into the next world. He holds the divine sceptre wielded by Pharaohs and gods.

NEPHTHYS, sister of Isis, goddess of women. Her name means Lady of the Palace, and she was associated with Osiris' household and helped in his resurrection.

HORUS, falcon-headed god, holding the ankh, symbol of life, in his right hand. He was the son of Isis and Osiris, and most Pharaohs identified themselves with him.

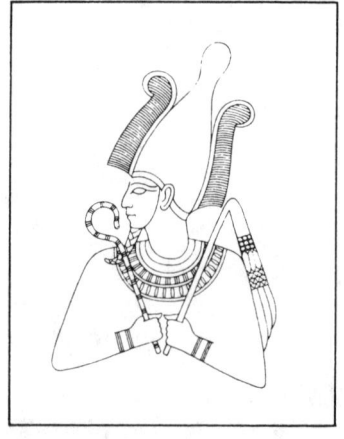

OSIRIS, god of earth and vegetation. His death symbolizes the annual drying out of the land, and his miraculous resurrection represents the Nile's cyclical floods and the growth of cereals.

HATHOR, *the cow goddess of love, also divinity of happiness, dance and music. Seven Hathors leaned over the cradle of every newborn baby and decided its fate.*

SETH, *the lord of Upper Egypt, represented as a legendary animal with long ears like a donkey. Associated with the desert and storms.*

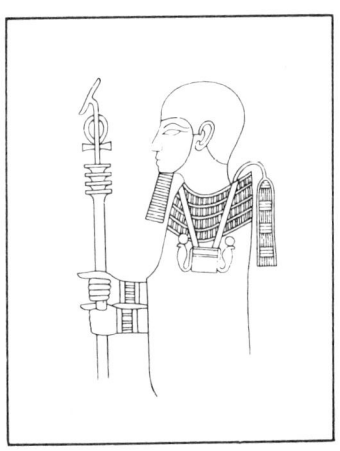

PTAH, *local god of Memphis, patron of craftsmen. Some believed that he created all the things in this world by naming them.*

GALARIEL: I found the photo.
DHORAN: What photo?
GALARIEL: The one of Yvelle Swanson in front of the temple at Luxor.
DHORAN: Oh, yeah? Show me. July 31, 1980? How can that be?
GALARIEL: Sure, Yvelle can travel in time. She had somebody take the picture of her in front of the temple of Luxor *before* she went to Egypt.
DHORAN: That s interesting. Who took the picture?
GALARIEL: Will H. Dalst. Sometimes he goes by the name of Bill. Some people know him as Billie Holliday. Solange thinks his name is William Tellier. But mostly he goes by William Rose.
DHORAN: But Will H. Dalst is his real name.
GALARIEL: No, neither. His real name is Arnartr Tagaphd but that's too hard to pronounce, nobody calls him that.
DHORAN: Oh I see, Anar whatsit is his Egyptian name.
GALARIEL: No, neither. His Egyptian name is Na-Otis, but it isn't very important because he was just a little boy of ten who lived in Hermopolis in the age of the Pharaoh Mentuhotep. Before that he was a scribe in Memphis, but an anonymous scribe.
DHORAN: Wait a minute. Mentuhotep, in the eleventh dynasty? Na-Otis, you said? Seems to me I know that name.
GALARIEL: You should do, he was your son.
DHORAN: Oh, yes? When I was Houri and you were Nefertari? Can't be, though, they were in the nineteenth dynasty.
GALARIEL: Oh that's right, I didn't tell you. I wasn't *Queen* Nefertari after all. Not Ramses II's wife whose tomb is at Abu Simbel. Ramses II is Réjean Ducharme. Darned confusing, isn't it? That's why I thought you were Réjean Ducharme when I met you, d'you remember? No, it wasn't that Nefertari. She was just a woman singer in the temple of Amon. As it said on the postcard from the Egyptian room in the Louvre that I sent you that summer, remember?
DHORAN: So how can you read Na-Otis's memory? Because you were his mother?

Axel Forget and She Forget

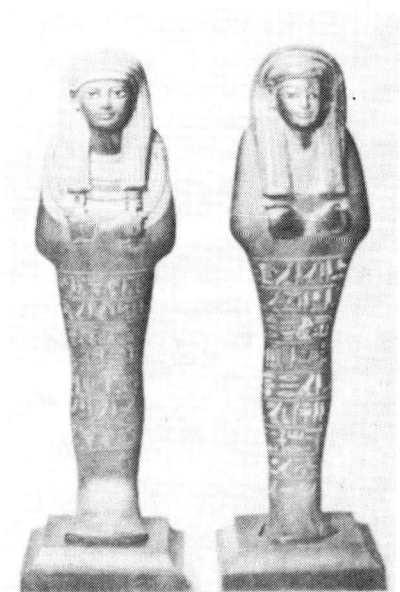

Dhoran and Galariel

GALARIEL: Not only that. I'm also his reincarnation along with Will H. Dalst.
DHORAN: Oh. All right, what can you read in Na-Otis's memory?
GALARIEL: It's a bit hard to say. In any case he understood something about Osiris. It was the 1st of May 2104 B.C. I think he'd been taken to see the Sphinx at Giza, because in the picture you can see the Sphinx. It's very very hot, there's lots of sand. And there's a golden statue of Osiris which is dazzling in the sunlight. Anyway you know all this as well as I do, since you're his reincarnation too.
DHORAN: Oh, and how d'you know that?
GALARIEL: Things you've already told me about your mother, 'n something Axel told me about you too.
DHORAN: Which mother, the one in this life?
GALARIEL: Of course, silly.
DHORAN: What is it? You've got to tell me.
GALARIEL: I can't tell you. You don't need to know anyway, it isn't your area. Memory is my problem, not yours. Besides, you were the one who taught me it's sometimes important to keep a secret.
DHORAN: So what did Axel tell you about me?
GALARIEL: The same thing. Axel was your mother before, that's why. But hey, we've got to stop, we could go crazy. It's just details.
DHORAN: All right. So Will H. Dalst 'n you 'n me are all descendants of Na-Otis. But who was Anar whatsit?
GALARIEL: That's his Atlantean name. Atlantis keeps cropping up lately. Did I tell you that in Mexico, on Christmas Eve, I met an Indian, I forget what kind but he looked like an Aztec. His name was Jean Lafleur.
DHORAN: Yes, you told me.
GALARIEL: It was really Juan Flores, of course. He was the one who told me, "Puerto Vallarta esta el paradiso del nuevo Atlantida." Atlantis is the red race coming back.
DHORAN: Yeah. But let's get back to Yvelle Swanson and Will H. Dalst.

GALARIEL: Okay. The first scene is in Berlin. In a bar called the Oui-Ja. Very ska, all black and white. Black glasses, white tables, the walls and ceiling are black, the dance floor is shiny white melamine. They only serve angel's kiss, because it's white. It sits heavy on your stomach. Yvelle has come straight from the airport. She's wearing white jeans, white running shoes and a white sweatshirt with a black Mickey Mouse on it. Will H. Dalst just got in from Rome. He's in a dark suit and wearing dark glasses, and he's carrying an attaché case with top secret documents about the "Path of Ptah" project. Yvelle looks at her wristwatch, it's ten to three in the morning. She feels sick to her stomach because she's drunk six angel's kisses. At quarter to two Berlin time she reserved a seat on Lufthansa flight 606 to Alexandria. At five to three Will H. Dalst crosses the white melamine dance floor as arranged. Just then the fire alarm goes off.
DHORAN: And?
GALARIEL: I don't know what happened then. It wasn't a fire anyway, 'cause there was no smoke. I never did dream the end of it because my alarm clock rang 'n I had to get up 'n go to work.
DHORAN: Yes, but what about the photo of Yvelle Swanson in front of the temple of Luxor?
GALARIEL: That's another story.

Stage directions

Supposedly the text works like a synergetic battery. A planned arrangement of the hieroglyphs in the sound-space is supposed to produce holograph images of the self. The self is just the code the characters use to decode the top secret message in the attaché case of the little lawyer of willpower, the former scribe, the international spy. Since the message is the same for everybody, the actants need only exchange their variable selves to activate the machine for differentiating the psychic relays in the Moebius strip. Which creates a computerized hum which decodes the black ocean of reality right down to the fire in the core of the pyramyth of the I's.

The text then supposedly narrates the endogenous movement of Yvelle Swanson variable 206 to Yvelle Swanson variable 214 via Galariel variable 29, Dhoran variable 33, Will H. Dalst variable 39, Axel Forget variable 38 and She Forget variable 390. It then discusses the dome of the Bonsecours market which can be seen from the Beaujeu Terrace. The text would then add the following information: the dome is that of the nagual. It is also that of madness, according to a novel by Agatha Christie. It lights up like a flying saucer, and inside it people dressed in white are doing tai chi.

SECOND LESSON IN ARCHAEOLOGY

French scientists measuring the Sphinx. Engraving by Vivant Denon, a member of the team of artists and scientists who accompanied Bonaparte on his Egyptian expedition. Like many of their predecessors who came to conquer, the French were amazed by the architectural splendours of ancient Egypt. "At the sight of so much majesty," Denon says of the arrival of the French in front of the ruins of Luxor in 1799, "the whole army halted and, as one man, ordered arms."

Will H. Dalst in his previous name

Postcards

Alexandria, 25 July 1980

"Der Eurythmie-Student erhält eine vierjährige Ausbildung, die neben der Eurythmie—nach einem gestuften Lehrplan—kulturgeschichtliche Fächer wie Metrik, Poetik, Aesthetik, Musikkunde, Geometrie, Anthropologie und Anthroposophie umfasst." I'm walking in the ruins of the library at Alexandria. Abyssinian cats pursue me in the souks, it smells like a fire everywhere. Justine has dyed my hair with henna. A whole afternoon with my head in mud and the dry smell. My hair is red. My hair waves above Atlantis out to you, Isis, Nephthys, my no wave no future sisters. I walk beside the her, I read papyri that have been through the fire and that haunt the memory of Hathor, the horned goddess of love and celebrations. Justine is reading the *Alexandria Quartet*. I feel I'm in a cartoon strip by Régis France, in Thailand, at the other end of the world. Or anywhere but Alexandria.

***

Rosetta, 26 July 1980

The mint tea burns my bird brain. My tongue is on fire and I speak Arabic the way Ariane speaks Martian, in other words badly. The fall of Carthage raises a smokescreen in front of the Rosetta Stone, because I'm writing to you from the Salammbo café in front of two old gentlemen writing postcards who make me think of Flaubert's scribes. It's sunny, sunny, sunny. I'm collecting information about Egypt.

THIRD LESSON IN ARCHAEOLOGY

UNLOCKING A LOST LANGUAGE

The vital clue to hieroglyphic translation is a broken slab of black basalt, shown below, unearthed by French troops digging trenches near Rashid, or Rosetta, during Napoleon's Egyptian campaign of 1799. The proclamation carved on it, praising Ptolemy V in 196 B.C., is of relatively little significance; what is important is the fact that the inscription appears in two languages. Although scholars immediately understood the value of the Greek text in decoding the hieroglyphics, as well as an Egyptian script called demotic, 23 years passed before the Rosetta Stone finally surrendered its secret with the deciphering of a single word of hieroglyphics *(opposite)*.

THE DECIPHERER, Jean François Champollion, a brilliant linguist who worked from an 1808 copy of the Rosetta Stone's inscription. He studied it for 14 years without ever seeing the original.

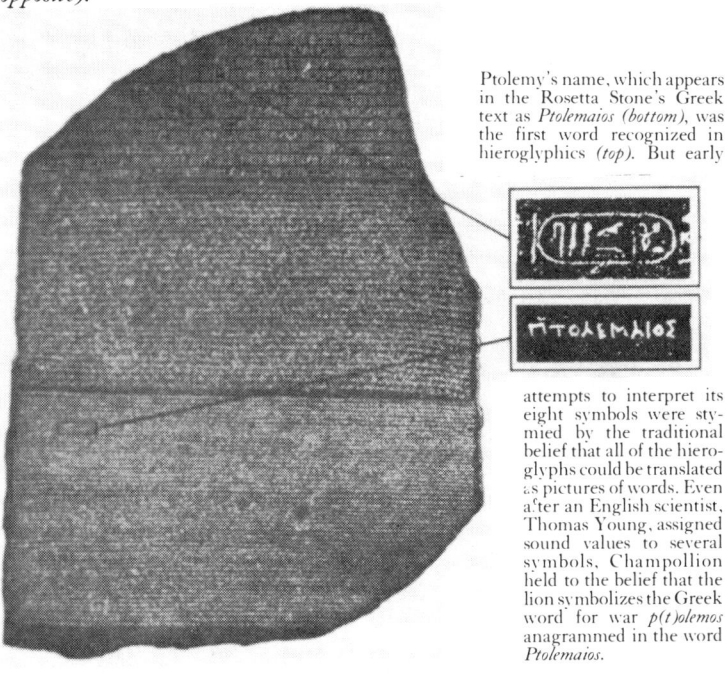

Ptolemy's name, which appears in the Rosetta Stone's Greek text as *Ptolemaios (bottom)*, was the first word recognized in hieroglyphics *(top)*. But early attempts to interpret its eight symbols were stymied by the traditional belief that all of the hieroglyphs could be translated as pictures of words. Even after an English scientist, Thomas Young, assigned sound values to several symbols, Champollion held to the belief that the lion symbolizes the Greek word for war *p(t)olemos* anagrammed in the word *Ptolemaios*.

Cairo, 27 July 1980

Millions and millions and millions of people. Cairo produces an infernal and incessant din. Mr. Muffler is conspicuous by his absence and silence, silence, silence is just half a white postcard.

FIRST GRAMMAR LESSON

CHAPTER FIVE
PRONOUNS

1. Personal Pronouns
   1.1 Independent Personal Pronouns

There are twelve forms for independent personal pronouns in Literary Arabic.[1]

	Nominative	Accusative
	/ʔana/"I"	/ʔiyyaaya/"Me"
masculine	/ʔanta/"You"	/ʔiyyaaka/"You"
feminine	/ʔanti/"You"	/ʔiyyaaki/"You"
dual	/ʔantumaa/"You"	/ʔiyyaakumaa/"You"
	/huwa/"He"	/ʔiyyaahu/"Him"
	/hiya/"She"	/ʔiyyaaha/"Her"
dual	/humaa/"They"	/ʔiyyaahumaa/"Them"
plural (m)	/nahnu/"We"	/ʔiyyaana/"Us"
	/ʔantum/"You"	/ʔiyyaakum/"You"
(f)	/ʔantunna/"You"	/ʔiyyaakunna/"You"
(m)	/hum/"They"	/ʔiyyaahum/"Them"
(f)	/hunna/"They"	/ʔiyyaahunna/"Them"

   1.2 Dependent Personal Pronouns (Single)

There are twelve forms for dependent personal pronouns in Literary Arabic.[1]

---

1. Fewer forms (around eight) are found in different colloquial dialects.

En route towards Giza, 28 July 1980
I am the black-eyed audioanimatronic sphinx dying of heat and being jolted about in the Wildabeast. Africa is the memory of sand, I don't know either the question or the answer. Something is fading away. Something like enthusiasm. I'm dying of the heat under the stimulus of the tropism of events. The bus's engine is backfiring, the pyramids are jumping, the sphinx has the hiccups. It's all wonderfully useless.

***

Memphis, 29 July 1980
The pool at the Ptah Hotel really isn't bad. I'm playing at being a swan, swimming under the little bridges. Gliding like my mother Gloria Swanson, like time off a duck's back, quack, quack. In a corner of my memory, there's a moiré blank spot, the trace of a solar self, something like time regained. I'm creating intangible artefacts and it's causing draughts. Which is lucky, because we're dying of the heat in the Ptah Hotel. There's no air conditioning. Justine's reading *Death on the Nile* and I'm looking for Agatha Christie.

***

The Valley of the Kings, 30 July 1980
It was a city of blast furnaces while Cuba sinks in flames to the bottom of Lake Geneva. The silent rooms are so cool and the frescoes are so well preserved in the queen's chamber that I completely forget what words mean. In my dreams there's always a door. On the door it says "The Path of Ptah." And I go in. And when I go in it's Hell. Paradise would be to drown completely in the blackout. I'm afraid. I'm reading *The Egyptian Book of the Dead* in the translation by E.A. Wallis Budge, Keeper of Egyptian and Assyrian Antiquities in the British Museum.

350 Invisible Fictions

FIRST LESSON IN EGYPTOLOGY

Magical Texts in the Mummy Chamber

II. SPEECH OF NEPHTHYS. Nephthys saith unto the Osiris Ani, whose word is truth:—I go round about thee to protect thee, O brother Osiris. I have come to be a protector unto thee. [My strength shall be near thee, my strength shall be near thee, for ever. Ra hath heard thy cry, and the gods have made thy word to be truth. Thou art raised up. Thy word is truth in respect of what hath been done unto thee. Ptah hath overthrown thy foes, and thou art Horus, the son of Hathor.][1]

[1] The text of Ani is corrupt here, and the words within brackets are translated from the following text:

III. SPEECH OF THE TET. I have come quickly, and I have driven back the footsteps of the god whose face is hidden.[2] I have illumined his sanctuary. I stand near the god Tet on the day of repelling disaster.[3] I watch to protect thee, O Osiris.

"I won't be scared"

BLACK FORCES OF EGYPT

"Black forces of Egypt are my allies. I won't be scared, I won't be scared, I won't be scared." In the black chamber of memory, black Isis. Black as in the black of the black of the cosmos, like the black of the black of the night of time. Isis the magician of black magic as frightening as when the labyrinthine strip of the map and the territory catches fire and it crackles right into the hall of reincarnations. Sabeth the Egyptian and Elizabethan queen practises the black arts and enters the academy of dead women, of the infinite line of dead women, the mummies, the mothers lost in the genealogical chain. And the invisible like a tree takes over their voices, haunts their great numbers and their likeness which they differentiate in the continuum, from black hole to quasar, from interruption to silence. As if in a Walt Disney film, while it sleeps peacefully in its block of ice, the Milky Way spirals like a cloud of locusts disguised as fireflies at the founding of Ville-Marie which steadily winks out in the darkness of the last black phosphene.

SECOND LESSON IN EGYPTOLOGY

"In the temple of Luxor, in the spot located in the *haty*, that is to say in the chest region, which contains the channels that animate the body with air and blood, there is an important ancient inscription which describes the ritual of the foundation and consecration of the temple.

"We are still proceeding from the proposition that everything in the architecture of the Pharaonic temple is motivated by a symbolic reasoning, which is made didactic by the strict observation of an esoteric canon.

"Just as everything in the Universe is linked by the same breath of life, so likewise it would be a mistake to consider any aspect of the architecture of the temple separately from the whole. We cannot dissociate one part of the building from the rest, since they all serve to express one thought.

"Thus we must find the link which connects the parts of the building with the Numbers, the inscriptions and the representations of the myth to create the magic of the temple of the Anthropocosm.

"These reasons lead us to seek the meaning of the joints between the stones which cut through the carved figures and the hieroglyphic signs in a manner which at first sight is disconcerting.

"In the four representations of Giving the Temple to its Master, found in four places in the temple, we have, as the joints in the stones will prove, not merely a formula of inauguration or consecration of the temple. The whole Universe is contained in

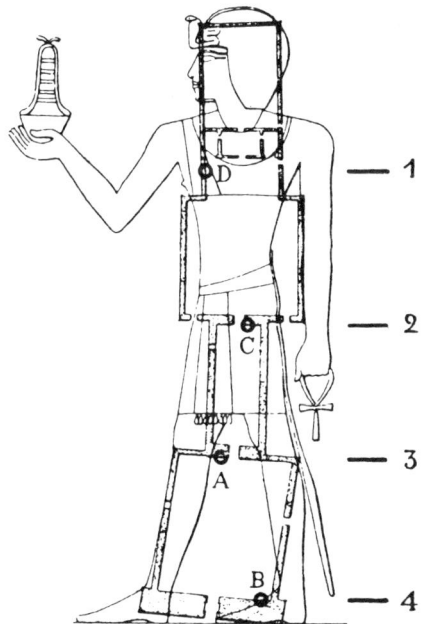

Figure 4. Location in the Temple of Luxor of the scenes from Giving the Temple to its Master. Relation of these locations to the human body represented by the projection of the King onto the plan of the temple.

a single action. Here the consecration of a temple is identical to animating the earthly body, indeed animation in general, in the direction of the greatest knowledge."

In front of the temple

You asked me what Egypt is and, eight months later to the day, on the sixth of the sixth month, I tell myself it must be a question of time.

While Dhoran and Galariel in the no wave no future Hell dream of Yvelle Swanson in front of the temple of Luxor on 31 July 1980, she watches them dreaming and wonders why her little androgynous sisters aren't content just to have children. Her mother Gloria Swanson, the son of the sign, used to say time is a Great Goddess, a sarcophagus that constantly claims new lives to ensure that the illusion will survive. Gloria Swanson, the son of the sign, used to say also that her three daughters would one day have to submit to this law of the Great Goddess. But Yvelle Swanson doesn't agree with her mother. And it's because they refuse to be mummified that Dhoran and Galariel persist in dreaming of Yvelle Swanson about to enter the temple of Luxor while the loudspeakers in the no wave bar yell "Hey Manon, come 'n do the ska".

For "the temple is not like a church, it is the magic milieu which transports the human being beyond himself. In the temple, he experiences what he is normally incapable of understanding, he becomes aware of a state of being that rational thought cannot formulate." And that's how Dhoran and Galariel wander from temple to temple, from Ice to Vol de Nuit to Oxygène to Baby Face to 5116 to Les Beaux Esprits in the hot night of the big-city Hell, pursuing their version of Yvelle Swanson, the astronaut of memory on a mission to Luxor where it is now 40 degrees in the shade.

But it's in bright sunlight that Will H. Dalst, that little lawyer of willpower, takes a photo of Yvelle with his one step polaroid just as she is about to go into the temple of Luxor. It is infernally

The cat catches its breath

sunny over Luxor, on 31 July 1980, as Will H. Dalst watches the photo slowly developing before his very eyes. And Will H. Dalst doesn't understand. He doesn't understand because the photo isn't right. Of the real side of what we call reality, right in front of him, there's only the temple of Luxor drowned in sunlight, the blue murmur of the Nile, and the persistent image of Yvelle Swanson smiling at the camera in front of the temple of Luxor.

But it's the hieroglyphic side of what we call reality which has left its mark on the film. Yvelle Swanson, her hair on fire, is walking forward on a narrow bridge of ropes and boards, red, orange, yellow, green, blue, indigo and violet. "One two three four five six seven Violet, Violet," as in a radio test. She is seen in profile, hieratic, her left foot set on a violet board, her right foot poised above an indigo board. An orange storm like a golden angel falls in a fine rain and the bridge seems to sway above an abyss of dazzling snow. Yvelle is wearing dark glasses and looking straight ahead.

And in the middle ground there is another Yvelle, on another rainbow bridge, and in the background still another Yvelle on another bridge, and so on without end as far as the eye can see.

Yvelle in her song, Yvelle in her song
And on the banks of the Nile Yvelle in her song
Yvelle catches her cat, Yvelle catches her cat
And on the banks of the Nile Yvelle catches her cat
The cat catches its breath, the cat catches its breath
And on the banks of the Nile the cat catches its breath
The breath catches fire, the breath catches fire
And on the banks of the Nile the breath catches fire
The fire catches the wind, the fire catches the wind
And on the banks of the Nile the fire catches the wind
The wind catches the sand, the wind catches the sand
And on the banks of the Nile the wind catches the sand
The sand catches Egypt, the sand catches Egypt
And on the banks of the Nile the sand catches Egypt
Egypt catches the memory, Egypt catches the memory
And on the banks of the Nile Egypt catches the memory
Memory catches Yvelle, memory catches Yvelle
And on the banks of the Nile memory catches Yvelle

This is when Will H. Dalst, alias Yvelle Swanson, throws his attaché case into the waters of the Nile. Yvelle Swanson will never know what the Path of Ptah project was. At most she will remember that it was an anagram linking the path of fire with the voice of the god. This is when Will H. Dalst alias Yvelle Swanson starts howling with rage, terror and passion while Yvelle Swanson alias Will H. Dalst walks into the half-shadow of the temple of Luxor, leaving behind her her double, the little lawyer of willpower in a dark suit who is yelling with dread because he can't find a name for his terror. And while the cry of Will H. Dalst swells like a shout in the crackling heat of the 31st of July 1980 in front of the temple of Luxor, Yvelle Swanson is walking in visions of Egyptian deities, pyramids and sarcophagi, guided by a voice that murmurs "Black forces of Egypt are my allies. I won't be scared, I won't be scared, I won't be scared." Death is only a symbol of the third circuit to describe fear, Yvelle remembers. For Yvelle Swanson is only an orienting force in the black room of memory.

***

For the past half hour I've been talking about the black pyramid I saw in my hand three years ago, about Isis and Osiris and Nephthys, a hippopotamus in the Egyptian room in the Louvre, Tutankhamen in all the store windows in New York in the spring of 1979, the geomagnetic forces which used to be in Egypt in Egyptian times 'n apparently are coming here, etc. etc. etc.

THE DEAD COW IN THE CANYON

Jacques Ferron
translated by Betty Bednarski

I

François Laterrière, the fifth son of Esdras Laterrière of Trompe-Souris *rang**, Saint-Justin de Maskinongé, came of good stock. When he was sixteen years old he already looked twenty. His father said to him:
"You're not a child any more."
"No," he admitted.

*Rang. In Ontario, a "concession". The French word, referring to the adjacent farms along a country road running parallel to a river, is typically Québécois and has been kept throughout.

The conversation went no further. Several months passed, and the old man continued:

"Well then, my boy, seeing as how you're not a child any more, have you thought what you're going to be in life?"

"Yes, Pa: a habitant like you."

A strange idea, this, coming from the youngest son! The old man made up his mind to give it some thought. A year later he asked his son:

"Hey, François, who was it put such an idea into your head?"

"What idea?"

"Lord love us! The idea of becoming a habitant."

"The priest, Pa."

The priest. Now that was a serious matter. Esdras Laterrière, his brow knit, realized the going could be tough. "Whatever I do," he thought, "I must be sure and not rush things."

"François," he said, "I have great respect for the priest. You know that. But the harder I think about it, the harder it is for me to understand. Why ever did he advise you to become a habitant?"

"Because that's what you are, because that's what your father was, and because we must preserve the heritage of our ancestors."

"The heritage of our ancestors?"

"Yes, Pa."

The old man waited to hear no more. He hitched up the old grey mare, jumped onto the cart, and with a "Giddap!" was off to the presbytery.

"*Monsieur le curé*, I've come to pay my tithe."

"There was no hurry, my friend."

When the calculations were completed and the arithmetic done, the habitant did not budge from his chair.

"And there's something else," he said.

The priest had suspected as much.

"There's my son François," the habitant continued, "he's stirring up trouble at home."

The priest expressed surprise. The habitant explained.

"But there's been a misunderstanding!" the priest exclaimed.

"François has no intention of ousting his eldest brother! The land will go to him, whole and undivided. François knows that as well as you and I do. He simply wants to follow in your footsteps and become an honest farmer himself, Monsieur Laterrière."

"He doesn't want my land?"

"No, he doesn't, I can assure you."

"Then I have to agree with you, Father. He's not a bad boy at all."

The habitant, however, was not entirely reassured. He had nothing against his son becoming a farmer, but where was he going to get his land?

"That's a mere detail, Monsieur Laterrière!"

"A detail! There's no land left in the parish, and there's none in the county either."

The priest rose to his feet.

"There was no more land in France. Our ancestors found it in Canada. There's no more in the county, no more in the province, you say? Your son won't let that stand in his way. He'll find land somewhere else!"

"Where?" the habitant asked.

"In the Farwest," the priest replied.

Esdras Laterrière had never heard of any such country. The Farwest, Patagonia ... they were one and the same to him. But no matter. His worries were over. His boy would not be setting himself up at his expense. Back home again, he said:

"François, I've found you some land."

François thanked him. The next day he set out for the Farwest. Two years later he arrived in Regina.

"*Monsieur*," he asked the first man to come along, "is the Farwest still here?"

"No," said the man, "it's moved to Calgary."

The lad from Trompe-Souris was beginning to find the Farwest a little too much for him. In Toronto they had told him it was in Winnipeg; in Winnipeg they had said it was in Regina; and now he had reached Regina only to discover it had already moved to Calgary. The land of Esdras Laterrière had never shifted an inch. True, it was very well fenced ....

"It's a strange country, this Farwest, *Monsieur!*"

The first man to come along agreed with him politely, then bade him goodday. This man was followed shortly after by a second man, but François did not speak to him, nor to any of the others who came his way. Without further pause, he continued on to Calgary.

Calgary is a city with wide avenues, where there are no longer any horses to be seen. There are, however, a great many horsemen, whose sleek boots, thick belts, steel spurs and high hats all attest to the fact that they have left their mounts at the city gates. The avenues themselves tell you nothing you do not already know, show you nothing that cannot be seen elsewhere. But close your eyes for a moment and you hear the hard jangle of spurs on the pavement. In an instant the ordinary world is abolished, for the place is surrounded by a thousand horses, impatiently pawing the dust. You breathe the air they blow from their ardent nostrils; it is the air of the Farwest. François inhaled it with satisfaction, but before long his throat was dry. He went into a tavern.

"I'm happy," he said to the landlord.

The landlord slid two glasses his way.

"Why two?" asked François, whose tastes were modest.

"In my tavern that's how it is, my boy," replied the landlord. "You have one drink because you're happy, and I offer you another because I'm happy to see you happy."

This friendliness, the beer, and the joy he felt at finding himself at last in the Farwest put the young man in a confiding mood.

His chin over the glasses, his hand in his mane, a faraway look in his eyes, he began to tell his story. The landlord interrupted him, banging on the counter with his fist. The glasses jumped, but the young man did not flinch.

"You're from Trompe-Souris?"

"Yes, *Monsieur*."

"And you want to be a habitant in the Farwest?"

"Yes, *Monsieur*. A habitant like my father, like my grandfather, like all the Laterrière, because we must preserve the heritage of our ancestors."

The landlord leaned over to Timire, his assistant. "Take off your apron," he told him. "Run and tell the Chief: the Chosen One has arrived."

Timire took off his apron and hurried out. François, however, protested that he was not the Chosen One. The landlord hastened to reassure him.

"You're from Trompe-Souris, I'm from Crête-de-Coq. You're from Saint-Justin, I'm from Sainte-Ursule. We're from the same county. Could I possibly wish you any harm?"

"No, not if it's like you say."

"If it's like I say? It's even better than I say. Why, I wouldn't be surprised if you weren't my cousin. My name is Siméon Désilets!"

"Well, how about that! My mother is a Désilets!"

"Her first name?"

"Wait now...."

"Georgina?"

"No."

"Valéda?"

"No.... Wait now.... I've got it; Victoria!"

"She's my sister; I'm your uncle."

The landlord wasted no time. He seized a glass and filled it. Uncle and nephew raised their glasses. The drinks overflowed; they were deeply moved. The beer spilled onto the counter; the landlord mopped it up, himself scarcely able to hold back the tears. When you're a French Canadian you can't possibly know all your relatives, but you're overjoyed to make their acquaintance all the same. Family spirit is strong!

When they had drunk, the landlord asked for news of the old country, then he continued:

"You're not the Chosen One, Nephew. I know that as well as you do. You're no fool and I've still got my head screwed on. But we can make the Chief believe you are."

"The Chief?"

"Yes, the Chief. One of the feathered breed, a kind of Iroquois. When I first arrived here I traded with him. Then I bought my tavern. A good-hearted fellow, but not much of a head for business. I owe a lot to him. He's right at home here. I let him drink as much as he likes. He's always paid me. If he weren't my friend, I sometimes think he'd be my best customer."

The landlord drained his glass. François did the same. With the glasses empty the acoustics were much improved.

"Why should we make him believe you're the Chosen One? I'll tell you why, Nephew. He has a daughter. Her name is Eglantine. He wants to marry her to a white man. The fellow's nuts. He says the spirits have spoken to him. The spirits, they're the good Lord's flying *curés*. When they command, you have to obey, otherwise you go mad. So there's the Chief, looking for a white man. Not that there aren't plenty of them about. You can find white men of every race and religion in the Farwest. The trouble is my friend is fussy; to him all whites are savages. He wants to obey his priests, but he doesn't want to give his Eglantine to a savage. He's in a right quandary. So what does he do? He comes to see me. 'You good white,' he says to me, and to the good white he offers his daughter. Now, if ever any man has cheated, robbed, taken advantage of the old Chief—I can tell you this, you're my nephew—that man is me. Hearing him talk like that just about breaks my heart. 'Chief,' I says 'I'm good, all right, as good goes. But that doesn't mean I'm the man to marry your daughter. I'd consider myself lucky, make no mistake, but alas, I'm old, the tavern ties me down, and then there's Beauty Rose, my Irish girl. You know her: she'd spit the fire of hell in your face if she heard of your offer.' Before I could finish my speech the Chief was in tears. It was the first time I'd ever seen him in such a state. I was touched. I said to him, 'There, there, don't cry. I'll pray to God and ask him to send you my cousin, a fine lad from Maskinongé, not savage at all, and white as milk. We'll marry him to your Eglantine.' That was the promise I made to the poor Chief, out of the goodness of my heart. Tell me, François: wouldn't you have done the same?"

"Yes, of course," replied the young man.

"Ah, Nephew, you are indeed the son of my sister Victoria, the kindest girl in the world."

And the landlord proceeded to fill the glasses.

"To your mother, to my own kind heart, to the goodness of the Désilets!"

They drank.

"After hearing my promise," the landlord continued, "the Chief went away rejoicing. I can see him now. And that was more than two years ago. He went away, but he came back. At the end of every season he'd come down from his canyon to ask for news of the promised cousin. I'd do what I could to keep him happy. The last time, at my wit's end, I promised him he wouldn't have to wait much longer. The old boy went home. The season ended. Yesterday he arrived with his Eglantine to greet the Chosen One. There wasn't a cousin anywhere I could lay my hands on. I didn't know which way to turn, I cursed my promise. But I didn't have the heart to disappoint them. They were so happy, so trusting. So I said to them, 'Come back tomorrow.' Oh, what a night I spent! And then morning brought me you, dear Nephew! Even if you're not the Chosen One, you must admit you couldn't have come at a better moment!"

The landlord paused for a moment and banged his fist on the counter. The glasses jumped. François did not flinch.

"Thanks to you," cried the landlord, "your uncle's word will not be broken!"

The young man was uneasy. He'd have liked nothing better than to help an uncle keep his word, but it wasn't for that that he'd walked for two years, crossed four provinces, worn out fifteen pairs of cow-hide boots. Besides, the Commandment that told him to honour his father and mother made no mention of any other relatives, least of all an uncle with a tavern in the Farwest, who he hadn't even known existed until one day, feeling particularly dry, he'd entered this tavern to wet his whistle.

"What's the problem, Nephew?"

"The problem, Uncle, is that I'd like very much to oblige you ...."

"I know that."

"It's also that I didn't wear out fifteen pairs of cow-hide boots and come all this way just to meet an Indian maiden from the Farwest."

"Now you're talking! Have another drink, you deserve it."
And the landlord slid one over to him.

"All the same, Nephew, what would you say if this Indian maiden, a fine-looking girl, as it happens, also brought you a canyon the size of a whole parish for a dowry?"

"A canyon?"

"A piece of fine land surrounded by mountains as high as the sky."

"Hey," said François, "then I'd ask to see her."

He saw her, found her to his liking, and the next day they went to the church. A priest with carrot red hair, not one inch a Metis, married them with a wave of his sprinkler. The ceremony continued at the landlord's tavern. After eight days of revelry, the Chief stopped drinking, pushed away his glass and said:

"It's no good."

He still wasn't drunk. His thirst was intact. So why go on drinking? This wasn't the first time he'd tried. His previous attempts had all ended in failure. He'd never managed to get himself drunk. To bring him to his senses, it had always been necessary to knock him out. With age he'd grown wiser. This time, before he lost patience, he'd cut short the drinking, thus avoiding the final fury.

"It's no good," he repeated.

The landlord, who knew his Chief, having had occasion to bring him to his senses in the past, was careful not to insist. He made haste to end the celebration and had the horses brought up. When the animals were at the door, François asked:

"And what about the cows?"

For François Laterrière, shaken though he was by the little jolts of marriage, still held fast to his resolve.

"Yes, Uncle, the cows. I cannot become a habitant like my father, like my grandfather, like all the Laterrière before them, and preserve the heritage of my ancestors, if I don't have at least one cow to put in my canyon."

"What did he say?" asked the Chief.

The landlord explained his nephew's demand.

"Pooh!" said the Chief.

"What did he say?" asked François.

"He didn't make himself very clear," replied the landlord, "but I think he has a rather low opinion of cows."

The lad from Trompe-Souris, touched to the quick, flashed an indignant glance at his father-in-law, who continued:

"Cows! Pooh! Buffalo in canyon."

"What did he say?"

"Instead of a cow he's offering you a herd of buffalo."

The young man refused. Who had ever seen a buffalo on a habitant's land? It was a cow he needed. The Chief raised his arms to heaven: a cow would never be able to climb up to the canyon.

"He's right," urged the landlord.

But François took no notice. Disdainful and proud, he remained deaf to anything that might deter him from his mission. Blood will tell. Like all French Canadians he was a descendant of Madeleine de Verchères. He was a hero. All that mattered to him was his cow. They suggested a doe: a fig for their doe! A goat: fie! and for shame! Eglantine was growing anxious, the Chief impatient. Suddenly the landlord cried:

"A heifer!"

There was some sense in the idea; our hero considered it; he hesitated. Pressing his advantage, the landlord slapped him on the back. A heifer, after all, was only different from a cow for a few months. And what were a few months to a determined young man who had worn out fifteen pairs of cow-hide boots, crossed four provinces and found his way at last to his uncle, Siméon Désilets?

"Come on, François, come on!"

François gave in at last.

"I give in," he said, "but I'm not giving up. I'll accept the heifer but I won't forget the cow. I'll give satisfaction to the Farwest, but I'll remain faithful to the traditions of my ancestors."

"Bravo!" cried the landlord. "God has inspired you. You speak like a true *curé*!"

They all applauded and everyone was happy. All they had to do now was find the heifer. The gods smiled on them: she was found at once. François took her in his arms and leapt onto his horse. The party moved off. Siméon Désilets stood alone at the door of his tavern.

"Whew!" he said.

Then he went inside and poured himself two drinks, one because he was feeling happy, and the other because he was happy to see himself happy.

"You're laughing," exclaimed Timire in amazement.

"And you would be too," replied the landlord.

II

Once they were out of Calgary François cried:

"Hallo!"

He was echoing that distant hallo that the rising mountains call to the plain.

"Hallo, plain," they say, "give up your illusion: the earth is not flat."

The lad from Trompe-Souris was astonished. The mountains drew nearer. His astonishment did not lessen, but his apprehension grew.

"The canyon isn't up there, I hope," he inquired.

They showed him, between two dazzling peaks, the pass they would have to cross to reach it. He felt no pleasure at all at the sight. Like La Vérendrye, he would gladly have turned back. Nevertheless, he continued. It was a long climb. When he finally reached the canyon he vowed never to come down. One year later he started down again. You can be sure of nothing when you've a heifer in your care.

By spring the heifer had already become a cow. She took no notice and continued to graze. However, she was gaining less now and grew more slowly. Summer came. She stopped growing altogether and was amazed.

"Why should I bother to eat any more?" she asked Eglantine.
"Eat, my girl, eat," replied Eglantine. "You'll not regret it."
Enigmatic words, which the cow was to ruminate for a whole month. At the end of the month she wanted to know more. Eglantine proceeded to instruct her. From then on, her ears aquiver, her neck strained, she lived in expectation. She forgot to eat her due. There, amid the juicy hay, hunger gnawed her, and she began to wail. It was pitiful to hear.

"What's wrong with her?" François asked.

"She claims," replied Eglantine, "that your hay tastes bad."

This insinuation was not well received. The hay was from good millet and identical in every way to the ancestral hay. How could it possibly taste bad? The cow was an impudent hussy and was lying shamelessly. To satisfy himself François went and examined her closely. When he came back he announced:

"Wife, there's nothing the matter with my hay. It could feed more than a cow; it could feed a whole herd."

"In that case," inquired Eglantine, "why does she wail, poor thing?"

"There's another reason. We must go down to Calgary and bring back a bull calf."

At that same moment the Chief emerged from the bushes. He had been gone since fall and had spent the winter hunting. His pelts had been rich; he was carrying a roll of bills as fat as a girl's thigh. The roll redoubled his valour; his children were on their way to Calgary; without pausing for breath, he set off behind them.

"Well!" thundered Siméon Désilets, "this is a big surprise!"

The Chief put his roll on the counter.

"Count," he ordered.

The landlord felt it.

"It's velvet to the touch."

"You keep," said the Chief, "if you find way to get me drunk."

Thus challenged, the landlord felt every confidence in his ability to get him drunk. He brought out his very best mixture: white lightning, beer and rubbing alcohol. One week later, the

Chief was hollow-eyed, but he still sat upright in his chair. "Wait a moment, my good Chief," said the landlord, "you won't be sitting like that for long!" And he placed in front of him the decisive glass, filled with straight rubbing alcohol.

"Just taste that now and tell me what you think."

But the Chief didn't seem the least bit curious. He didn't even touch the glass. Perhaps he needed a little encouragement. Siméon Désilets, acting out of the goodness of his heart, went to give him a friendly pat on the back .... He remained rooted to the spot, his hand upraised, extremely surprised. The Chief had spun round, lithe as a cat, and plunged a knife into his belly. No allowance had been made in the itinerary for any such stabbing. Having come down to Calgary for the sole purpose of acquiring a bull calf, François and Eglantine had intended to go straight back once the calf was acquired. They were obliged to attend the landlord's funeral, then the Chief's trial, and finally, his hanging. These family duties kept them in Calgary for more than three months.

Meanwhile, above the canyon, the sun never blinked from morning to night. In time it grew very hot; the springs stopped running, the water in the trough dried up, and in a cloud of dust drought descended on the land. The little cow soon found herself in difficulties. Whenever she took a step, thousands of grasshoppers would fly up, and with their shrill call warn the grass to flee still further. Imprisoned in a moving desert, she could find nothing at all to eat. Her skin was loose, her bones unsteady. She had grown so thin she looked as if she were wearing her big sister's coat. Ridiculous and pitiful, she wandered about, saying to herself:

"If only I could get a drink."

It was her sole concern. A hundred times a day she returned to the trough, and always came away disappointed. Above the grasshoppers, the hawks hovered; higher still, the vultures. Neither bird was a good omen. At last, her courage failing, the unfortunate cow said to herself:

"My hour is come."

And, so saying, she let herself fall onto the burning ground. After a time, however, discovering that she was not quite dead, she opened her eyes and strained her ears .... And what should she hear, but the sound of running water!

"My hour is not yet come," she cried.

And with this she struggled to her feet, poor creature, and rushed off once more in the direction of the trough. But the effort this time was tremendous; her strength gave out; she staggered; a thousand suns were spinning in the sky. To regain her balance, she stopped, but her skeleton kept right on going. She was blinded by the dust, deafened by the grasshoppers, the hawks, and the suns. A vulture landed on her head. The skeleton was still going; it was already well ahead of her; she didn't know what to think. She shook the hat and the vulture flew off; she had lost sight of the skeleton now, concluded that she must be dreaming, and continued on her hallucinating walk. She arrived at last at the water trough; on the dried up mud lay the skeleton of a cow. She was not dreaming; it was her own.

"I am dead," she murmured to herself.

Death has as a rule a most devastating effect on life. In this case, the opposite was true; the result was exhilarating; the cow felt better dead than alive; freed of needs she could no longer satisfy, harassing needs, more terrible by far than hawks or vultures, she once more took pleasure in herself. The impression was a strange one: she almost felt alive again.

At the same moment, the sun blinked and rain transformed the landscape. As soon as they were wet the grasshoppers fell silent; reassured, the grass came back, soft and defenceless. The carrion birds, lords of the drought, had disappeared; green silences replaced their harsh cries. Although she was indifferent to this renewal, the little cow nevertheless felt inside her a joy that grew with each new day. Her courage had returned, her skin fit once more. True, she still had no skeleton, but it hardly mattered; her appearance was most respectable. She wandered freely through the canyon. Every now and then she would pause to take a mouthful of grass; not that she was hungry—it was pure caprice. Sometimes she would go over to the water trough and there, occasionally, she might take a drink; not that she was thirsty—it was just a lapse; she simply wanted to see the reflection of the spectre her joy had brought to life.

When they returned to the canyon, François and Eglantine were delighted to find her, to all appearances, in the best of health. They ran to her, embraced her fondly, then introduced the male calf they had brought back with them from Calgary.

"He's a nice little animal."

There was no glow of passion in her eyes.

"Nice, he is," Eglantine replied, "but that's not all. Just wait: a year from now, burning with passion, a little bull he'll be."

The cow remained cold.

"What's the matter with you, little sister?"

"I'm dead," she replied.

Eglantine burst into tears.

"What's wrong?" asked François, who understood nothing of the language of cows.

"She says .... Oh, God! it's dreadful."

"Well, what?"

"She says she's dead."

Surprised, François walked around the animal, then looked up, skeptical. Eglantine, offended, brushed away her tears.

"How could you have the heart," she cried, "to doubt the word of a poor dead cow?"

To which he replied that he, for his part, had heard no such word.

"Is it my fault if you're deaf?"

"If I'm deaf, Eglantine, then maybe you've too much imagination."

Then she asked him if he thought she was crazy. No, he didn't think she was crazy. But he did disapprove of her listening to the blather of animals. She argued back; he refused to climb down. She called him a savage; he called her a squaw. In short, they quarrelled. When they had finished, the cow motioned to them to follow her: she led them to the water trough. The skeleton was there, irrefutable.

"Well?" said Eglantine.

François, shattered, could find no reply.

"Now do you dare to say this cow is not dead?"

He did not dare.

"But," he added, "dead or not dead, what's the difference, as long as she'll calve?"

"What do you mean?"

"Let's leave the little bull to sort things out."

A year passed. The bull calf, now every inch the animal required, began to lift his eyes in the direction of the cow. One day, emboldened, he lifted his legs instead. The cow, already suspicious, had seen him coming; she jumped sideways and the bull fell to the ground.

"You should be ashamed of yourself," she said.

He picked himself up, his forehead bristling, all ready to try again.

"If you want to know the truth," the cow went on, "you disgust me."

Round-eyed, he stared at her.

"Fool, can't you see I'm dead?"

The poor chap swallowed his saliva. He was sincere in his intentions, but, blinded by passion, he had not noticed the sad condition of his companion. In his innocence, he had wanted to serve her. Since she was dead, he did not insist. He walked away. Not for the world would he have defiled her. And his ardour, with no outlet, turned inward against him now. His head became swollen, his eyes shot with blood; he longed to crush his bones against a rock; the canyon shook with the sound of his bellowing. Until in the end the little cow took pity on him.

"After all," she said, "I may be dead, but that doesn't stop me from taking a mouthful of grass here, a drink of water there. Why shouldn't it be the same with the other little necessities? There, poor boy, don't look so sad now. You can do what you like with me. Feel quite free: it's really all the same to me."

Now it was the bull's turn to be disgusted.

"Thank you very much," he replied, "but I don't need your cold carcass!"

And with that they were estranged, estranged forever, sadly, foolishly, all because of a few thoughtless words, estranged for no good reason! For they could have been reconciled; indeed, they should have been. Love is the coming together of life and death; it is perfectly natural for one party to be cooler than the other.

Meanwhile, François himself had not been idle. Having talked at first for the sake of it (which improved his voice) he found at last the word he had been looking for. And so it was that the virtue of the race, at first inoperative, one day bore fruit. Eglantine, mysteriously touched, smiled as she grew heavier. In spite of her condition, she continued to look after the animals. Her shoulders thrust back, portly as an ambassador, she went from the bull to the cow and from the cow to the bull, mediating as best she could, but unable to make peace between them. This failure, however, did not trouble her unduly, for she had already achieved within herself the reconciliation of opposites. François, for his part, was preparing the nest. He was putting the finishing touches to a house, the perfect replica of the farm house of the Laterrière in Trompe-Souris, in the parish of Saint-Justin de Maskinongé. He had thus reconciled future and past, heir and ancestors, and was on the point of transplanting to the Farwest the traditions of the Quebec people. It was too perfect to last.

One morning, Eglantine, on one of her diplomatic missions, spied the bull, normally quite stand-offish, coming towards her with blood-shot eyes, his head low.

"What's the matter, little bull?" she asked.

He did not answer, but kept on coming. Then Eglantine, guessing his intentions, uttered loud and piercing screams. Her emotion only proved to the animal that she was indeed alive. Frustrated by a dead cow, he needed nothing more. The morphology of the two parties did not lend itself to their union. The fair Eglantine died. François, who had rushed to the scene, now furious at finding himself a widower, killed the bull, then collapsed himself on the two bodies. When he came to, he heard a wail. It was a baby girl, lying there, kicking, in the blood of her mother and the monster.

François Laterrière left the canyon that same day. It was the dead cow who moved into the house, that perfect replica of the ancestral home. She felt quite happy in it. But there were times when she would climb up to the attic and there, with her head thrust out the window, gaze nostalgically into the distance.

III

Fleeing his canyon, François Laterrière left behind him, like an absurd dream, a house built in the Quebec style and haunted by a dead cow. The chorus of ancestors tried to hold him back, but he refused to stop, thinking it was the cow. For two days and two nights he walked; after which, already much distressed by the death of Eglantine and the failure of his mission, he had completely taken leave of his senses. God guided him. At the end of the third day he reached Calgary, a city large enough to get lost in. But God did not abandon him: he found his way to the tavern of his late uncle, Siméon Désilets.

The last client had left, and Beauty Rose and Timire were in the process, she of totting up the day's cash, he of wiping the tables. Any moment now they would be closed. The door opened; a man walked in and placed on the counter a tiny bundle of soiled linen. Automatically, Beauty Rose slipped him a glass; he emptied it in one gulp. She slipped him another; he emptied it just as fast; then a third, and a fourth.... He was clearly very thirsty. Beauty Rose, her interest aroused, said to herself:

"Something tells me I know this man." But she could not put a name to him. Suddenly the tiny bundle moved.

"Lord, it's moving!"

"So what?"

"What is it you've got all wrapped up there and moving like that?" she asked him.

"Dunno," he replied.

She took pity on him.

"Come along with me," she said.

He followed her to the Tourist Rooms adjoining the tavern. She pulled off his boots and put him to bed. A maid appeared, enticed.

"Is this one for me, Ma'am?"

"No," replied Beauty Rose, "he's not for you, nor me, nor anyone. He hasn't a cent and he's sick; his own mother wouldn't want him now."

When the servant had left, Beauty Rose thought to herself: "Perhaps he really hasn't got a cent." She checked; she was right. But what should she find in his pocket but the rosary of Siméon Désilets, her late husband.

"It's my nephew, François," she said to herself. "I thought he looked familiar!"

She left the room. To the maid, she said:

"It's my nephew, François. Something terrible has happened to him."

"Poor you," said the maid.

"Something terrible. And he's changed, changed! I recognized him by his uncle's rosary."

"Poor you! What a dreadful thing to be so changed!"

Cutting short these ancillary condolences, Beauty Rose went back downstairs. The bundle was still on the counter.

"Timire," she called.

Timire arrived.

"Unwrap this bundle, Timire. I haven't the heart to do it myself."

He unwrapped it. She clutched her hands to her breasts.

"Lord Jesus! Just as I thought: it's a girl, a lovely little girl! Timire don't just stand there with your mouth open! Come on! Do something."

Do what? Timire had no idea.

"Why, baptise her, of course! Can't you see she's cold? You never know; she might have caught her death, the poor dear little creature."

Timire, beer in hand, said:

"I don't know what to say."

"Poor fool! You say: 'I baptise you in the name of the Father, the Son and the Holy Ghost'."

Timire was about to touch the baby's forehead with his glass. Beauty Rose stopped him.

"Fool! Precious fool! It's not beer you use to baptise a child! Do you have no principles, then?"

She handed him a bottle of white lightning.

"It's white lightning!"

Once the ceremony was over and the way to paradise opened

to the poor dear little creature, the widow of Siméon Désilets regained her composure.

"Now," she declared, "we must see to it she doesn't die."

Timire called the maids. They came down to the tavern.

"This," the widow told them, "is the child I've been promising you. She's my niece. Her name is Chaouac."

Their joy was amazing to behold. The child was handed over; her weight seemed to reassure them. When they had taken her away, Beauty Rose asked Timire how he felt.

"I'm very glad," he replied.

The next day, although he had fully recovered his senses, François Laterrière did not recognize the grimacing little frog he had found lying in the blood of a monster and a woman; they showed him a clean, well-fed baby, asleep on the breast of one of the maids. This breast, alas, reminded him of another.

"Aunt," he said, "Eglantine is dead."

"I'd guessed as much," replied Beauty Rose.

He told her the tragic story. She said:

"François, your daughter is my daughter. Stay here; we'll bring her up together."

At such generosity the young father lost his composure and fell down upon his knees. Seeing this, his aunt lost hers, and burst out laughing.

"Get up off your knees, you silly boy! You owe me nothing. It's a favour you're doing me letting me take your daughter."

He got up.

"There are three reasons why you owe me nothing. Just listen to them and you'll stop your genuflexions, you'll see!"

And Beauty Rose explained that she had not always been a person of staid disposition, having first been driven by wanderlust for many years. Born in Dublin, she had acquired her Irish education in haste and had left in search of adventure by the time she was thirteen years old. Her travels had brought her, by a thoroughly capricious route—via Australia, China and Russia—to Canada, where she had at first sojourned in the ports of the east. After which she had moved to the Yukon, and from there to the Farwest.

"Nephew," she went on, "I paid my own way. For a long

time I had the means. As I grew older, however, I found it more difficult to make a living from my looks, and I was soon in desperate straits. From then on travel became difficult. I have very unpleasant memories of the Yukon: men there are quite unreasonable. When I arrived in Calgary I was exhausted. Siméon Désilets came along. He needed a wife, I deserved a rest, we were married. He was a strong man, your uncle! He kept me where he wanted me and there I stayed! And I became staid, oh so staid! We lived together five years, then his friend the Chief did him in. He's gone now; but he left me his memory, Timire, his tavern and his morals. That's the first reason why you owe me nothing, even if I am helping you out."

But the inheritance was not all pure gold. There was also, in the widow's estimation, an element of wastage, understandable if one considered that Siméon Désilets had not come to Calgary via Australia, China and Russia. He had held on to certain of the prejudices of Sainte-Ursule de Maskinongé, which Beauty Rose had been obliged to dispense with after his death. On the subject of the sexes, for example. Not for anything in the world would the landlord have encouraged contact between them. He had every occasion to do so, however; beer awakens a client's generosity; after two or three bottles he very often feels the need to bestow his favours on some poor disadvantaged girl; in this case, why not help him to find her? Besides, collaboration of this nature is always profitable.

"Your poor uncle always refused."

François Laterrière had not travelled via Australia, China and Russia either.

"By God," he exclaimed, "my uncle was right."

"After his death I gave in."

"You betrayed him!"

"Precisely," said the widow, "and that, you see, is my second reason. I've been unfaithful to the principles of your uncle. I'm sorry, even though I didn't approve of them. You're his nephew. I'll help you and so make amends."

François, indignant:

"Make amends some other way. Don't count on me any more. I'll have nothing to do with your acts of fornication."

Beauty Rose, taken aback:
"Fornication?"
"Yes, fornication."
"I don't understand, Nephew. You're forgetting that I have morals."
"Morals? You must be joking!"
"Morals that I got from your uncle. If I hadn't had them, I'll admit, I'd have gone in for a brothel; but I had them, and so I made do with Tourist Rooms."
François had spoken too hastily.
"Tourist Rooms, that's different," he conceded.
"Just a modest little enterprise: ten rooms, four maids. So help me, I don't see where you get your fornication, Nephew! I employ the maids to look after the rooms; in between chores they have time to spare; I don't ask them how they spend it; that's their business. I collect the money for the rooms. What could possibly be wrong with that, Nephew!"
"Why, nothing at all, Aunt Beauty Rose."
"Besides, I'm never in the place; I stay in the tavern. There, after the second or third bottle, a client will sometimes ask me for a girl; I offer him a room, I promise him nothing; I tell him if he's lucky the maids will like his pretty face. If he still takes the room it's at his own expense, and not theirs, because he never has a pretty face. I personally select the clients; the pretty faces always go elsewhere to be admired."
"And the third reason?" asked François, who was beginning to weary of his aunt's dialectics.
Beauty Rose hesitated.
"To be perfectly honest," she replied, "when the client goes upstairs I'm not as confident as I let on to you. True, I've personally selected him; he never has a pretty face. But then, I'm not that well acquainted with my maids either; they just might have poor taste. And so, to calm my fears, I've insisted that they all have milk."
François, aghast:
"Milk!"
"Yes, milk."
"Hmm," said he.

"Of course," Beauty Rose went on, "a maid can't have milk without having previously experienced a certain misfortune and I tell myself that the milk will prevent it happening again. That's my third reason: we'll have more than enough to feed your daughter, you lend her to us, we'll care for her, and you can keep your genuflexions for another: your daughter will pay us back."

The young father, horrified:

"How?"

"By sucking," came the reply.

Having milk is not everything; what matters is being able to keep it. To achieve this end, it's best that it be drunk, since breasts are so made that they will fill up only as long as they are emptied. For a while, before the arrival of François Laterrière and his daughter, Chaouac, this generous paradox caused Timire great concern, for it was he who had been put in charge of the milk-maids' welfare. Day in, day out, morning, noon and night, he had to provide them with hungry children. He chose these children with the greatest of care; they were nevertheless always taken off the streets, where children have a tendency to be more talkative than elsewhere. And so it happened that certain parents came to hear what repast was being served in the Tourist Rooms, and they were most upset, for parents, it is well known, are always more or less corrupt; these felt obliged to forbid their children the healthiest, the noblest, if not the most humane of all foods. As for Timire, they talked quite simply of hanging him. Timire would hear nothing of it, but he was anxious all the same. He had no difficulty approving the adoption of Chaouac.

François Laterrière also approved it, but with less promptitude. First he had to listen to a debate in his conscience between his daughter, the said Chaouac, on the one hand, and his priest, Monsieur de Saint-Justin, on the other. The priest spoke first; he affirmed truths to which François listened, but which he barely heard, since the acoustics of a "tourist room" in the Farwest are hardly as conducive to such things as those of a farm house in Trompe-Souris. Then it was Chaouac's turn; her speech was short and to the point; she was thirsty. With her first cry François heard her and felt the torment of her thirst.

"Oh, *Monsieur le curé*, forgive me," he cried, handing the child to Beauty Rose, "I have no other choice!"

"Not so fast, there, Nephew!" replied Beauty Rose. "I may have my morals, but I'm not a *curé* yet!"

One of the "tourist rooms" was made available to the young father and it was suggested that he might like to help Timire in the tavern during the day. He accepted the room but refused the job, happy to be able to sleep next to Chaouac, but not the least bit inclined to get himself breathed all over by drinkers of beer. Not that he despised these drinkers; they were his brothers, exiles like himself, and for the most part of the same origin. Indeed, the tavern is the only place in America where a French Canadian can speak his language freely. But François Laterrière was not one to indulge in conversation. He was a serious lad, who had no time for idle talk and knew that, as far as essentials were concerned, everything had already been said long ago by persons in authority, and in particular by Monsieur de Saint-Justin. And so he preferred the open air.

He went to work on a ranch. No speeches there, just grass and wind, and sometimes a cloud or two, or else an empty sky and the backdrop of monotony against which simple, uncomplicated souls, inclined to melancholy, seem to thrive. François found peace there, if not happiness. They hadn't given him a lasso; he had no idea that he'd become a cowboy. The ranch seemed to him like one vast Trompe-Souris, a free and unfenced version of the lowlands of Maskinongé County. He wished for nothing more. At night he came back to sleep at the Tourist Rooms; in the morning he returned to his cows. He took care, however, never to go near the tavern, which he believed to be a haunt of the Devil. On the ranch he felt no cause for anxiety. Yet it was there that a sinister encounter awaited him. One day he found himself face to face, not with Satan, but with a white bull, an animal utterly lacking in subtlety, who was nevertheless to have a most disastrous influence on his soul.

Both parties began by examining one another coldly. The landscape was green, almost blue. Then a strange heat was felt, as a cloud moved aside, unmasking the sun, which was yellow, almost red. And in that same moment both turned coward. Each took a step forward in the hope that the other would take a step back, then keep on going, leaving fury triumphant and carrying off in his retreat the cowardice of both. But the other party also stepped forward. So there was no alternative but to fight it out. François was the madder of the two. His fury triumphed. With his neck wrung, the white bull turned coward and died. "Bulls and I," said François to himself, "just don't seem to get along!"

He had to admit that he, for his part, detested them, for the very good reason that one of their kind had forced him to leave the Canyon, where he had found his mission, where Eglantine lived, and where his ancestors and his children would together have brought about his certain happiness. But he refused to allow for the existence of any such sentiments on the side of the bulls. Yet the bulls had every right to feel this way, since they considered their brother in the Canyon to have been guiltless, laying the blame for Eglantine's death on the dead cow and responsibility for the bovine fury on François, who, they claimed, could have prevented it by removing the offending organ. In short, as is always the case, both sides had excellent reasons for carrying on the war. And the war continued. Ten more times, pitting his strength against an ever renewed enemy, François Laterrière emerged victorious, thus demonstrating the superiority of the lad from Maskinongé over the bull of the Farwest. This was not quite what the boss had had in mind.

"You'll go far, my boy," he said. "Ten bulls in one week is a mighty fine start! Carry on the good work anywhere you like, but keep off my ranch!"

So François took himself elsewhere and, at the expense of another boss, proceeded to repeat his demonstration. Before long a nasty reputation had overtaken him. Thrown out a second time, he was unable to get himself hired on a third ranch. After which, on the advice of Beauty Rose, he went to see old Jesse Crochu at the Calgary Stampede. Crochu took him on immediately, but on one condition: he was to change his name. Frank Laterreur he became.

Not long afterwards, who should arrive in Calgary but Monsieur de Saint-Justin, on an apostolic mission. He was accompanied by an academician—a ferret-faced pin-head—none other than the famous historian, Ramulot. They had come from Edmonton where, on behalf of the Committee for the Survival of the French Agony in America, they had been inspecting the few remaining houses where the French Canadian lingo could still be heard. In Calgary there was no-one to visit. And so, to the Calgary Stampede they went. There, the said Frank Laterreur greatly impressed them, both by his courage and by the extreme simplicity of his technique. Indeed, without picadors, without banderilleros, alone in the ring, and unarmed, without the aid of a red cape, or a lance, or a spear, with only his bare hands, he slew the black bull. This beat anything Europe and its toreadors could do.

"Oh my! Oh my!" exclaimed Monsieur de Saint-Justin.

"Hooray! Hooray!" cried Ramulot, his mouth watering.

After which, still hungry for more, they decided to go congratulate the champion on behalf of their Homeland and to present him, *honoris causa*, with the emblem of the fleur-de-lis. In the wings they bumped into Jesse Crochu, who asked them, "Who're you?" They gave their names and listed their titles. The Academy? Old Jesse had never heard of any such thing, but, putting two and two together, guessed what it must be. "I reckon that's what those fellas down East call their Rodeo," thought he.

"Anyhow," he said, "don't go getting ideas about taking Frank away from me. Bulls, now—that's okay. If you need some, I can let you have all you want. But not Frank. He's mine, and he stays right here with me."

Ramulot thanked him: the Academy was not in need of bulls. As for the said Frank, they had no desire to hire him. They simply wished to congratulate him and pin a fleur-de-lis on his chest. Jesse Crochu, reassured, saw no reason to stand in their way. Let them congratulate, then, and decorate, let them fleurdelisate to their heart's content!

François saw them approaching. Like most priests when they travel, Monsieur de Saint-Justin was not wearing a cassock. François caught sight of his collar. "Bah! it's a clergyman!" thought he.

As for Ramulot, he was wearing a tie, a blue one, distinctly on the gaudy side.

"You, my pinhead," said François under his breath, "you can pay for the heresy of your friend."

And drawing in his neck like a bull, he advanced towards him.

"Mr. Laterreur!" cried the Academician, "I have the greatest admiration for you. Please stop and allow me to decorate you with the fleur-de-lis!"

Now, in the Farwest, this symbol is used for branding cattle.

François: "Just you wait! I'll show you who's the calf around here!"

But Ramulot had no wish to wait. He turned on his heels and fled, and all went well until a terrible boot with a deadly aim caught him from behind, raising his lower quarters high off the ground and causing his upper quarters to plunge accordingly, so that he sailed through the air, a ferret-faced Icarus, in the direction of the nearest manure pile. There he landed, pin-head first, and sank so deep that François abandoned the fight in disgust. And turning to Monsieur de Saint-Justin:

"Mr. Clergyman," he said, "take back your shit-faced friend."

So ended the encounter of François Laterrière and his parish priest in Calgary. They met again in Saint-Justin twenty-five years later, but this time, the priest having assumed his cassock and François his real name, they recognized each other.

"So!" cried François, "the clergyman was you!"

"So!" cried the priest, "the toreador was you!"

And they burst out laughing at the memory of Ramulot. He alone had kept his identity. And a fat lot of good it had done him.

"God can't have wanted us to recognize each other," the priest concluded.

"Still, there were a lot of things I'd have liked to tell you, *Monsieur le curé.*"

"You can tell them to me, now, François Laterrière. It's never too late."

And François did. There was Siméon Désilets and his tavern, there was his marriage to the Chief's daughter, the canyon and the dead cow, Eglantine's death and the birth of Chaouac, Beauty Rose and her Tourist Rooms, and the Calgary Stampede.

"Upon my soul," thought Monsieur de Saint-Justin. "I foresaw nothing like this when I sent this boy to the Farwest!"

François also told him about the milk-maids, but out of regard for his listener, he arranged the episode in such a way that it appeared edifying.

"There you are, *Monsieur le curé*. That's the story you'd have heard in Calgary if by chance we'd recognized each other."

"Very well," said Monsieur de Saint-Justin, "but what happened next?"

What happened next, presented François with certain difficulties of narration. It had come to pass that the said Frank Laterreur, having constantly to pit himself against the bulls, had ended up resembling them in one very significant way, the consequences of which are easy to imagine when one considers that he was spending his nights in the Tourist Rooms and that more often than not the four chamber maids whom Beauty Rose reserved for her clients also slept there. He took advantage of the fact that they were his daughter's wet-nurses and insinuated himself into their company, with the result that the clients soon ceased to receive the attentions they were accustomed to. The affairs of the Tourist Rooms declined, seriously damaging those of the adjoining tavern. All of which would have given Beauty Rose cause to complain, but Beauty Rose herself had no time to think about it, being, in spite of her age and her morals, just as well served as her maids. The honeymoon lasted four years. After which business picked up again and improved from month to month. Two years later, Tourist Rooms and tavern were flourishing as before. It was the said Frank who had gone under. The bulls had stopped hating him, he himself no longer detested them, and from there it followed that everything else was changed. Jesse Crochu had fired him. Beauty Rose now did the same.

"Your daughter is six years old," she told him. "There's nothing to stop you putting her in a convent now. I'll not be able to help you any more. As it is, I've given you far more than I need have done. I've paid off my debt to the late Siméon. Farewell, Nephew!"

François Laterrière, ex Frank Laterreur, fallen champ, now not even worth his weight in beef, left Calgary, taking with him his Chaouac, his bright little flame, his only passion. In Regina and Winnipeg he worked as a butcher, in Toronto, as a gangster. When he reached Montreal, Chaouac was turning fifteen. She was well educated and beautiful. Together they opened up Tourist Rooms, and fortune smiled on them . . . .

"Very well," said Monsieur de Saint-Justin. "What happened after that?"

"After that . . . well, er . . . ." What happened after that, it seemed, presented certain difficulties of narration. Here was the gist of it.

With a sweep of his hand, François indicated, over by the presbytery, the huge black limousine, in which he had driven up like a prime minister.

"My, my!" said the priest. "What a big car! I'm very glad indeed. Then the advice I gave you wasn't so bad after all!"

"It was good advice, *Monsieur le curé*, and I thank you for it. However, I must tell you that I didn't carry out the mission you entrusted me with."

"What mission? I don't remember any mission."

"To be a habitant in the Farwest, a habitant like my father and my grandfather and all the Laterrière of Maskinongé county."

"Forget it, François, forget it! You've kept your faith. You've kept your language. And you're rich. What more could anyone ask?"

François Laterrière was sad, for he knew himself to be unworthy of the priest's approval.

"Besides," the priest went on, "even if you didn't succeed in putting down roots there yourself, the conquest of the Farwest by our people is going well."

He pulled out some photos of his trip, showing the various houses in which, twenty five years earlier, French was still being spoken.

"What do you think of this one?" he asked.

François recognized his own house in the Canyon.
"Doesn't it look just like one of our own?"
"Yes, indeed, Father."
"When we visited it, the owner was away. A cow had climbed up into the attic, and she was standing there, with her head out the window, mooing and mooing. I said to her: 'Now stop your mooing. Your master'll soon be home.' And I blessed the house."
François Laterrière took leave of Monsieur de Saint-Justin. The village around the church had not changed. In his big car he drove through Trompe-Souris. Trompe-Souris had not changed either. The parishes of Quebec took on their definitive shape in the last century. Since then they haven't budged, hardening like cases around their inhabitants and retaining always the same invariable number, the number they held one hundred years ago. François found his childhood still intact. And yet, in spite of this, he was a stranger in the village and in the *rang*; his place was no longer here. But then, had it ever been here? Temporarily, perhaps, until such time as he could grow up and be expelled to an absurd Farwest. For he belonged to that surplus humanity that the Quebec parishes have continually to reject, in order to preserve their traditional face, the one they put on for the benefit of foreigners, and exploit and sell, the grimacing face of the puritan prostitute.

When François Laterrière left Saint-Justin the first time, wearing his cow-hide boots, he wept, and could find no solace till, in a far off canyon, he had managed to recreate the likeness of his Homeland. When, thirty years later, in his big black limousine, he left the village for the second time, no tear blurred his vision. He knew then that he had never been loved. He also knew that a country that values itself more highly than its children and doesn't hesitate to get rid of them, sending them off to the cities, to the mines, to every corner of America, without thought for their fate, concerned only with the preservation of its own old togs, is a country that does not deserve to be loved. And he was perhaps sadder than the first time.

When he got back to Montreal, he sold his Tourist Rooms. No-one has ever enjoyed running a brothel, and François Laterrière was no exception. He had been driven to it out of necessity. After the death of Eglantine and the failure of his mission, with nothing left to guide him, he had understandably sunk very low, low enough to collect the wages of sin and to bounce back onto the highways in a big, black limousine, like a prime minister. This limousine he also sold. Soon he was free to go as he pleased. He returned to that absurd and unlikely canyon, which was the place in all America where he felt least like an exile. Meanwhile, at his side, with staring eyes, her head stuck out the attic window, the dead cow mooed in the direction of an unattainable Trompe-Souris.

ABC

Monique Proulx
translated by Basil Kingstone

"You're late," said Mrs McKinnon for the third time, tugging at the left sleeve of her dress.

She didn't seem to want to move from her chair. In fact you would have thought it was her favourite occupation to tug at her sleeves and tell other people they were late.

"You're terribly late," she repeated.

"Yes, ma'am. I'm really terribly sorry, ma'am, it's because of the bus as I told you ..."

"I wish I was somewhere else," Marie Bilodeau was thinking feverishly. She had to get entangled in this absurd excuse instead of just telling the truth, that a violent attack of nausea had left her limp just as she was about to leave the house; she'd had to lie down for a while, soaked in a sudden sweat that made her want to vomit. Even the principal of St Margaret's School would have understood that, despite her proverbial severity. Now it was too late. She'd stumbled over her words and this unlikely story had come out about a bus that came to a stop in the middle of its route because it ran out of gas (why not a hijacking, Marie had thought in a last moment of ironic dismay, as she bogged down in her story). It always happened like that. She could never express her ideas clearly. Whatever she said she seemed to be lying, with that uncontrollable stammering that tied her tongue like a thick straitjacket.

But the principal was finally standing up. She was very tall; beside her Marie suddenly looked like a tiny worried schoolgirl.

"You've already done supply teaching, haven't you?"

"No, I ... yes, I have."

Of course she had. But every time, a nameless anguish twisted her guts as if she was suddenly going to vomit her soul to the four winds and dumbly die of terror. She went into a class with the painful feeling of going to the slaughterhouse. Perhaps it was just the air, with its obstinate faded school smells, books, ink, blackboard, sweat; or the unpleasant tapping of heels on the wooden floors of the halls; or a mixture of all of it, built up into a frightening whole in which she recognized her own childhood governed by nuns' headdresses as black as death. But there were no nuns left at St Margaret's School, and the teachers all had the vaguely masculine air of Mrs McKinnon, who was now guiding Marie through a labyrinth of twisting staircases.

"Do you know Thérèse Dallaire?"

"No."

"Well, it's she you're replacing. The poor child's health is awful. The School Board doesn't know what to do, with all these supply teachers coming and going..."

Mrs McKinnon was hanging onto the banister and turning around to glance at Marie.

"You seem reliable."

"Yes," said Marie, not knowing what to say.

"Remember, the class ends at three o'clock. With a special first-year class, you can't go too fast."

They had reached the fourth floor; you couldn't go any higher, the staircase suddenly ended in a deserted hallway crossed here and there by sudden bursts of sunlight. Crystalline voices occasionally broke the silence, as if unwillingly, tinkles of laughter died away as soon as they had burst out. The principal listened with obvious satisfaction, and leaned against the wall for a few seconds to tug at the right sleeve of her dress.

"It's a long way up here," she sighed, "but at least it'll be quiet. Your class is right at the end of the hallway, on the corner. You'll see, nobody can hear you and nobody will disturb you."

But Marie wasn't listening. The words "special first year" were still ringing in her ears, and now she was looking at the principal with growing concern.

"It's a small class, you'll see, they're very nice," Mrs McKinnon went on, still struggling with her right sleeve. "They're very intelligent, most of them, but they have emotional or family problems, you know how it is."

She gave Marie a little friendly tap on the shoulder.

"You'll have a lot of fun with them. Miss Thibeault is with them at the moment, she'll explain things to you. Room 424."

Marie watched her disappear rapidly down the staircase. She looked like a great aircraft with its wings cut off, gliding skilfully down from one step to another, seemingly without touching the ground; the sound of her footsteps had already died away.

"Okay," Marie thought, and she walked very unsteadily down the hallway. The problem was that she didn't like children. She couldn't stand their frankness, which she felt was fake, nor the freedom from punishment which they enjoyed. The main thing, which she didn't dare admit to herself, was that their gaze made her so uneasy she came to hate them. She made great efforts to overcome this feeling for fear of being an outcast, a heartless woman whom society would stone. She tackled supply teaching in kindergartens and grade schools, but the tension was always there, as if there was no way to end their antagonism towards each other.

Miss Thibeault wasn't in room 424. She had left on the desk a large sheet of paper, carefully cut out, on which she had written in an ornate handwriting like thin tortured shadows:

> *I'm sorry, I can't wait any longer, if you need me I'm in room 420, there are exercises on the board and also on the photocopied sheets beside it.*
> *The class ends at three o'clock. Good luck.*
>
> Lisette Thibeault

The children were sitting in a semicircle behind pale desks which hid their whole bodies; only their hands showed, and their little motionless faces turned silently towards Marie. The most surprising thing was that they didn't seem to have taken advantage of being left alone for a while to kick up an almighty racket, as Marie might reasonably have expected. At once she relaxed a little, and she felt vaguely grateful to them.

"Good morning," she said, "I'm replacing your teacher."

And almost at once, feverishly, she started distributing exercise sheets to the twelve desks, without getting the least reaction from the expressionless faces raised towards her with calm curiosity. "These children are like statues," Marie thought, not without pleasure. At bottom she could stand them better this way, petrified and silent, as different as possible from the diabolical little creatures she usually got.

"You can call me Marie," she conceded, almost warmly. "Aren't you going to say hello?"

"Good-mor-ning-miss," said twelve calm little voices in unison.

They didn't grab the helping hand she was clumsily holding out to them, they had already had time to melt into one anonymous reciting mass, retreating from Marie at a hundred miles an hour. In fact she felt vastly relieved. The free children of Summerhill weren't about to reappear here, she wouldn't have to exhaust herself trying in vain to set up any other relationship between her and them but the age-old one of dominator and dominated. Yet Marie was not at ease in the role of torturer. It's true that she wasn't really at ease anywhere, and here less than elsewhere, among children who reflected like a mirror her own disillusioned weakness.

"Each of you in turn is going to tell me your name, okay?"

Everything had fallen into place, the sugary teacher's voice, the learned paternalist tone she hated so much in other people and which would be hers now, for she had suddenly realized it was the right part for her and she had to play it.

"You c'n see our names!"

Marie immediately hated the little redheaded girl who had just spoken. She was sitting in the middle of the semicircle of desks and looking at Marie with not the ghost of a smile, in fact with an air of downright hostility gleaming nastily in her eyes. Calm down, Marie told herself. The little redhead wasn't even looking at her, and indeed there were big coloured rectangles on each desk, spattered with huge letters which you could have read with your eyes shut: Catherine, Jean, Stéphane, Evelyne, Richard.... The little redhead's name was Françoise.

It was no good telling herself quietly that the coloured rectangles hadn't been there five seconds before; Marie was losing her calm, a fluid was leaking unstoppably out of her brain to drown in the surrounding air among the little freckled faces raised towards her.

I must keep cool, Marie thought, looking gratefully at a little girl smaller than the others, reassuringly blonde, and who clearly had no piece of cardboard with her name on.

"What's your name, pretty girl?"

"He's a boy, and his name's Benoît," said the little redhead with the same implacable calm.

Before Marie's bewildered eyes, indeed, the blonde girl suddenly lost her femininity and acquired broad shoulders and a hardness of expression, a whole little rigid mask which was unmistakably male. It's his hair, Marie told herself, sitting down heavily on her desk, her heart caught in a vise. His hair, she thought again, before taking off the thick glasses which hid her eyelids. The certain knowledge beat in her brain with insane force that the names were not on the desks when she came in, that Benoît had been a little girl a few seconds before, and that she desperately wanted to go home. But no, none of that was true, the children were looking at her confidently, waiting for instructions which she wasn't giving because, her hands sweaty with fear, she had once again let her sick imagination get out of hand. But the attack was past, now the class would proceed in an orderly manner.

"Take the sheet I gave you. As you can see, there are blank lines under the words; copy each word twice. Understand?"

No, they didn't understand, she had to explain it again, and again, before the puzzlement finally faded from their faces. Marie couldn't help herself, irritation and weariness were already taking over her voice, she'd have liked them to guess what she meant before she spoke, instead of hanging on her and begging for knowledge she didn't feel like giving them. She was thinking this when a large caramel-coloured eraser hit her in the back of the neck and nearly knocked her off balance.

"Who did that?"

Instinctively her suspicions focused on the little redhead, but the child hadn't moved an inch; she had her pencil up her left nostril and seemed to be lost in thought over her sheet of paper. The others, behind Marie, were all bent over their work, frowning with the effort, slowly moving their clumsy fingers in the calm of innocence.

"Whose eraser is this?" she asked, so angry she surprised herself.

The faces looked up hesitantly. An interminable silence weighed on the class, while Marie watched the dirty eraser shaking between her fingers, its four corners bitten off by nervous teeth.

"Will you kindly answer me?"

"Not mine," said little Philippe, and at once eleven voices mumbled "Not mine, miss, not mine," then burst into a wave of giggles which Marie cut short with one movement.

Nothing could be done about it. She felt alone and humiliated, but she dared not lash out at random in the blind rage that was suddenly shaking her and that common sense ordered her to bring under control.

"Get on with your work."

The twelve heads furtively hunched against their desks, and the scratching of pencils held too tightly was all she heard for several minutes, mingled with that sort of ghost whisper that seeped out of lips pursed with tension: *papa ala pipe pipo lape lelala*. Stupidity, hopeless idiocy, Marie thought, as she watched a big fat fly zigzagging tirelessly around the fluorescent lights following an itinerary it alone knew; sheer crass idiocy. But she was doing nothing to rescue these vulnerable first-graders from the bath of sterile culture they were being plunged into, drowned in, with papa and his endless pipes and pipits peeping and see Dick and Jane and see Spot run and all the bland little statements for children wound wretchedly around life like Christmas present wrapping with nothing in it, masks to hide reality, piggy banks full of bottle tops. But it was too difficult, and too dangerous, to get involved in a battle you couldn't win, and in the name of whom or what, my God? children, almost subhuman beings, whom she couldn't bring herself to like despite their playacting.

Suddenly an unusually bright spot on the floor near her desk awoke her from her reverie. She went up to it and saw shiny fragments all over the floor like a broken necklace—without knowing why, she thought of diamonds—but when she looked closer she felt a gnarled hand squeeze her stomach. It was her glasses, carefully smashed into countless tiny bits, scattered in all directions.

"Who did that?"

It was a useless, rather ridiculous question, since the faces looked at her with an unshakable serenity, then the heads quickly bent over in inborn respect for their mistress' voice, but nobody answered. In vain Marie looked at their faces, nobody was suspiciously blushing. And in that painful messy situation that was making her temples throb, she wondered how she could have failed to hear or see anything while her glasses lay there in bits.

"I said, who did that? Do you expect me to believe the angels broke my glasses?"

Marie was amazed at what she sounded like, she wasn't in control of that quavering rattle which served her for a voice now, a tide of terrible anger was slowly submerging her and would soon drown them all.

"All right," she croaked, "if that's the way you want it, I'll go and get the principal."

Marie turned towards the door amid profound silence. Mrs McKinnon, with her severe face like a colonel's, would no doubt get to the bottom of this. Seventy-five dollar glasses, Marie kept thinking, feeling tears of despair burn her eyelashes.

She turned the door handle, but the door didn't open. The handle turned uselessly. That's absurd, Marie thought, and she found she was pushing with all the strength of her arms against a solid door, then with her shoulder, then kicking it, more and more frantically, to no avail. The door wouldn't open.

Marie turned around. On the blackboard, in enormous chalk letters, were the words DEATH TO MARIE BILODEAU!

The children were watching her, motionless. Marie was sinking into a sticky swamp, her old past terrors flooded back stronger than ever, as if she had already experienced and foreseen this childish nightmare that she was now living, while other people went about their distant business, terribly unavailable, terribly uncaring, Thérèse Dallaire, Lisette Thibeault, Mrs McKinnon, mummy, MUMMY!

"Who—who wrote that?"

"Not us," said Françoise, the little redheaded girl. "We can't write."

They all stood up at once, and their combined laughter, pure and fresh, burst out in the classroom like clusters of flowers. Marie had time to see that they all wore the red armband of revolution.

METAMORPHOSIS

Claire Dé and Anne Dandurand
translated by Basil Kingstone

Men had drowned the earth in cries and horrors. Suppurating diseases flourished in everyone's lungs and crotch and skin. Their hair was falling out. Their teeth were shaky in their mouths. When they could afford it they bought twenty-four-carat gold teeth guaranteed to kill germs on contact. Every other man and woman drank tap water at their own risk, as suggested by the Minasshole for Health and Welfare. Indeed, by a curious twist of the mind, the Minasshole for Sickness and Illfare and his federast colleagues had gotten them used to accepting falsehood as truth.

"Not all of them were killed, but all were stricken." One of their free-thinking prophets had foretold it, four hundred years earlier. Men and women alike were rotting away in their houses, glued to their giant remote-controlled screens. It was their religion, a monist one, with an idiotic Manichean tendency, masticatory and anti-fever, a remedy, a leech, like a drug. The success of the programmes depended on a skilful mixture of active American ingredients: octyl-phenox-polyetocy-tiranol fear, fatty misogyny (may contain sadistic oil), and congealed consumer's paradise. The message lied, but the medium massaged them good.

While thinking about all this, her mind elsewhere, instead of following her programmed route, she pushed through the surging crowd and turned left, against the flow. The cold air tasted of crushed crystals. It never failed to flay her mucous membranes. Blood blocked her nose, so she swallowed air in great mouthfuls. As she did this she slobbered, her eyes became glazed with indifference, and her face took on the mask of idiocy. Apart from the children, who were terrified, nobody objected.

Her steps led her to the display window of an ancient fish store. Brightly coloured inscriptions filled the cracked glass, tempting and tasty-sounding: "Fresh Oysters", and especially "Live Lobsters." This "Live Lobsters" caught her eye, which squeezed out of its socket and stuck on the glass. Led on by that greedy desire which a touch of exoticism awakens in us, she took her eye back and walked into the fish store. A living salty smell overwhelmed her. Knowing only smells based on alcohol, aluminum chloride and radon, she almost fainted. Her lungs emptied themselves like pickled cucumbers emptying their brine; she recovered and felt a profound sense of well-being.

In contrast to the chaos outside, the fish were laid out on their sides in impeccable order, their eyes bright, their gills pink; they had a metallic sheen to them. Like a joyful morgue, a genuine morgue, with its refrigerators, its white slabs, its chrome, the whole store breathed a disturbing culinary eroticism, promising delights of a bygone age, suggesting forgotten pleasures.

In one corner the sea-green water of a crate was staring at the ceiling with a bored expression. Hypnotised, she went up to it. It contained a unique blue-green lobster. It was motionless except for its claws. From what oil spills had it fled? How had it escaped the slaughter?

"I'll take it," she said, not caring about the expense.

They wrapped up the lobster and very soon she was back outside, as if awakening from a dream. The lobster was definitely alive, sloshing decapodically in its plastic bag and clacking its rick-rack claw. She no longer felt the cold frosting her cheeks and freezing her drooling spittle; she was carrying her supper home and her mind was aglow with the thought of her coming feast. Behind her the fish store disappeared without a sound.

Everything was ready, the curtain drawn, the tablecloth spread, the place setting laid out, the pepper mill on the table, the pat of butter melted, the stove on. She poured her whole ration of water, five quarts, into a deep bowl. Behind her the screen was mumbling its annoying assertions as usual, but she heard none of it, she was paying all her attention to the heating water. A necklace of bubbles formed around the edge but was soon replaced by fatty globules, which in turn agitated the flat surface of the liquid with tumultuous blisters. The water was boiling and ready, it was the magic moment. She picked the quaking lobster up by the tail and held it motionless for a moment over the steaming bowl. A moment too long, because it pinched her. She dropped it. It died. She forgot the incident and had a good feed.

***

The coal-black eyelid of night grew heavy. In a moment there would be a complete silence consecrated by the federastic anthem which was fading out in a last lament. She was still digesting, blissful and mindless. As it did every night about midnight, it started raining hard, a mixture of ashy hail and acid rain.

Suddenly she was thirsty, her skin was drying out, cracking and growing scabs. She ran out into the downpour with her mouth wide open. In forty-one seconds she was soaked to the skin, but she was happy.

She had forgotten that it's illegal for a woman to walk on the street alone in the dark. She had forgotten Gisèle Giroux, shot dead between the eyes at point-blank range, and Johanne Pelletier, twenty-two years old, riddled with bullets. She had forgotten Lola Telma Pannunzio, found naked in a trunk on the edge of an empty lot, and Julie Lessard strangled by, as they said, a practical joker. The alarming rise in the crime rate was far from her mind; she was drinking the water in through every pore, with a need which had to be satisfied.

A man parked his pickup truck a little way down the street, jumped out and ran up to her. He grabbed her by her coat, pulled her hair and tore her clothes. And then—nothing. Darkness. Emptiness. In the distance, a comet exploded. Midnight, the fateful hour.

At first she didn't notice anything. Then a spiny shiver ran under her shell. She was changing, being transformed into a lobster, in a rapid, instant, motionless sloughing. She lost the sense of smell but her touch became more sensitive. She grew antennae, telescopic and swivel-jointed. Her left hand opened and a frightening claw appeared, three feet long. The man's face was contorted with terror. That was his last emotion, because the claw cut him open under the jaw with a crack like a nutcracker. The right claw tore him in half lengthwise, from the crotch up. The corpse jerked once then collapsed gurgling. She ran away with huge lobster strides. With marvellous agility she reached home via sewers and gutters and spent the rest of the night in her bathtub.

The man had gotten her pregnant. She had to organize her life around her bathtub, and she sewed a zipper into her waterbed. Her water bill went up fourfold and her salt consumption tenfold.

And so, one night, she gave birth to a thousand human male and female lobsters. She set out for the edge of the river, for the point where the fresh water meets the salt, with her anonymous colony hidden in a bucket. Thanks to a certain amount of instinct and a few brilliant ideas, she successfully raised ninety-eight per cent of her thousand eggs. A new revenge of the cradle, you might say.

The lobster men and women became known and respected for their wisdom and their calm. Males and females alike worked for a return to nature and water, they negotiated and pacified. Their mother, who became a lobster every night, the accidental mother of this new generation, lived to a ripe old age, delighted with how things had turned out.

CASE STILL OPEN

Claire Dé and Anne Dandurand
translated by Basil Kingstone

"It all started with a toothache, inspector. An obstinate ache that got worse and worse, in the wee hours of January 15th. You may remember that a whim of the weather had kept Montreal deprived of its usual white blanket. That had never happened in a hundred years. Anyway, this toothache wrapped me around itself till I couldn't think straight."
. . .
"Pardon me?"
. . .
"Yes, I knew Ariane N. At least, I've seen her in the street a few times. She has a dentist's office next door. You know, inspector, it's hard to describe her, she's so discreet, so unassertive. Anyway, on the morning of January 15th I asked her for help.

"She received me at once. She worked in her own home. A strange office, inspector."

...

"About five feet by twelve. The window was buried under the green of spiders and ice. There was pink wallpaper on the bottom half of the walls, then great masses of posters. I've never seen a dentist's office like it, inspector. Oh, and there was a governess, or secretary, I'm not sure what you would call her, who let me in. Although it was still first thing in the morning, her hair was done up in curious curls."

...

"She's disappeared? I don't know ... I couldn't tell you."

...

"It's so painful for me to tell you. After examining me, she injected me with a thick liquid. I was in so much pain that I hardly felt her long needle pierce my gum. Even the air congealed. Ariane N. stared at me in dismay and told me gently that my teeth were in very bad shape and would all have to come out. She was stroking my hand with her fingertips, it made me quiver."

...

"No, no, inspector, I believed her right away. I was so relieved, and as if deadened. She was looking at me so gravely."

...

"At the rate of two teeth a week. She began in the back of my mouth. I was surprised by her skill, inspector. It never hurt. And besides, her office smelled so good, a cross between oak and sandalwood, with something else that tickled my nose."

...

"It's hard to explain, the other woman always seemed to be waiting for me, then she disappeared."

...

"I never saw any other patients, never."

...

"The surprising thing is that every week I was drowsier, in fact I fell asleep during the extractions. The dentist didn't say much. She would examine me, her lips slightly parted. I would sink into weird delightful dreams in which I was brushed against and clawed."

. . .
"I don't know. I would get up from the chair feeling limp, as if after a night of making love."

. . .
"What can I tell you? I don't know why she would have made a set of dentures using my old teeth. Nor why she was found naked and her body was covered with bites. And I refuse to try to figure out why the bites match the dentures she made from my old teeth. Since she died, inspector, I feel weak, I'm scared, I can feel my strength slipping away."

From MONSIEUR MELVILLE

Victor-Lévy Beaulieu
translated by Ray Chamberlain

Father's given up. He just went to bed. As he passed behind me he tapped me lightly on the shoulder, saying again how wrong I was to drive myself like this. I almost answered that, being alone, I had no need to worry about how I was or what might become of me: Judith didn't need me any longer, she was holed up in Daytona Beach with Julien and the two children he'd given her. Even my own characters want nothing to do with me, they're just as happy to be rid of me. Why then should I give a second thought to my life?

So I remain stubbornly at the apple-tree wood table thinking of what I've written up to this point, not trying, however, to get any more out of myself. I'm going to sink into a dream-like state as I always do when I'm like this—so very full of desire.

Thus I imagine myself on the highway running through the Adirondacks at the wheel of an old blood-red Cadillac with big, shiny fins—and with a whale's tooth beside me on the seat. The American border guards pick it up and weigh it in the palms of their hands, pinching it with their thumbs on all sides. They have to think the tooth's hollow.

The radio's turned up as high as it will go; I'm in a trance. That's how it always is when you start out on the hunt; eyes fixed on the miles and miles of narrow highway, your body tensed as you head towards the objective. Mine is simple: to reach Pittsfield, find Arrowhead and interview Melville. I intend to offer him my whale's tooth as a present. I'm sure Melville doesn't have one like it. Old Captain Coffin gave it to me as Job J ate an apple with Blanche on the deck of The Doris. That was three or four years ago, when they were camping on a small rise in front of the gulf. At that time Job J had just begun his research on whales. For Blanche it was too late: she was preparing herself for her fatal end, it being as ineluctable as the end of Sulphur Bottom himself.

The old blood-red Cadillac with its big, shiny fins is rolling and I'm heading through the American countryside and its fugitive scenes which have become one long stream of sea-green light as rain falls all over the continent. It must be mid-October, red-leaf season. Unparalleled rainfall. In spite of it, I roll down my window and breathe what might be sea air: it tickles my nose.

It must be noon when I get to Arrowhead, now a museum such as those you find all over America. Melville's name is inscribed on a bronze plaque on the door. But ring as I might, no one answers. So I take a seat on the steps—this feeling of being in a haunted house or upon a deserted ship. I've placed my whale's tooth securely upon my knees, stroking it continuously because I've got much on my mind and could easily leave it here.

I must have dozed off. I sleep so little at night now that I catch up whenever I can. All I need do is close my eyes and I'm gone. I don't know if Melville could do as much. I'll ask him when the museum opens. It shouldn't be long. There—what I was waiting for: footsteps on the gravel. I open my eyes to see a small black man coming up the walk. He looks a bit like the rabbit with white gloves and a large dangling gold watch that Lewis Carroll liked to put in his stories. The small black man passes by without noticing me. When he unlocks the door I rise and follow him in. He takes off his hat and hangs it on the rack and trots over to the counter in the middle of the room, taking up his place behind it. Then he opens a large notebook of sorts and immediately buries his nose in it. I place my whale's tooth upon the counter.

I say, "This tooth is for Monsieur Melville. Could you give it to him? And tell him that I've come from far away to interview him." He says, "Interview Mister Melville? Give him a whale's tooth? What's this all about anyway, my friend?" I say, "It's just a present. May I see him?"

The small black man gives me a cool, not especially friendly look. He says, "What do you want Mister Melville to do with your whale's tooth? My advice to you is to go back where you came from. Anyway, Mister Melville doesn't live here any more. I'm just his memory, and memory's never much good. Maybe you'd have better luck in New York City. In any case, you'd be doing me a favour if you went to look there."

I pick up my whale's tooth and go back out the door, leaving it open behind him. New York's not at the end of the world! I've come all the way to Pittsfield, why not head for Manhattan? Once you've made Broadway, the rest is easy. You merely let yourself be carried along by the crowd. It moves you steadily towards the port. It's easy. All you have to do is blink your eyes and you're there. At this time of night I'm sure to find the man I'm looking to interview, with my friend Abraham Sturgeon's small Japanese tape recorder hidden under my coat. Here's the way it takes place now that we're finally here; I'm too tired to shake off my languid dream, so I head towards Melville to catch him before he leaves on the Acushnet this third day of January, 1841.

***

Thus, with my coat draped over my arm I stroll along the docks whistling happily as I wait for him to step out of the fog. Soon it will be dawn. Melville will appear then exactly as I've imagined him.

The dockers have got to come first though, and they do, greeting each other with loud, friendly insults and hard slaps on the shoulder. Already there are shouts and the screech and grind of pulleys, and cranes and derricks high in the sky, and huge vibrating motors; already fumes and fuel infest the air; already wide oil slicks are forming upon the water.

Spotting Melville, I advance towards him and say, "I'm Abel Beauchemin, I've come to interview you. As agreed, I've brought you a whale's tooth. It's nothing special but it's all I had for you to recognize me by. Come this way."

I lead him to the far end of the wharf after handing him the whale's tooth. He hasn't even looked at it, nor does he seem particularly surprised to see me here. So I take advantage of the fact and lead him to a small cafe across the way. As though by chance, it's called the Spouter Inn. Melville takes a seat in front of me, then removes his hat and places his cane upon the table; he glances at the wall clock made in the shape of a ship's wheel. I'd like to get rid of the whale's tooth. Now that Melville's seen it, it's served its purpose. At some point I'm going to put it in the basket on the window sill even if I rouse the big cat lying in it, staring with his yellow eyes at the spider hanging motionless in the middle of the window. Melville's looking at nothing.

I say, "Excuse me for barging into your world like this but I couldn't think of any better way. I knew you still came to the docks and I told myself that it could continue here as well as anywhere else. Don't you agree?" He says, "What do you want from me?" I say, "You remind me of Job J's grandfather." He says, "You come from Quebec, I believe?" I say, "Not exactly. From the Gaspé, at least where it begins." He says, "Do you know that the *Acushnet* sank in the St. Lawrence Gulf?" I say, "That's one of the reasons I wanted to see you so much. They found the whale's tooth I've brought you in the very spot where the *Acushnet* went down." He says, "Do you know that Lizzie and I went to Montreal and Quebec on our honeymoon?" I say, "Yes, of course. That's the second reason I've dreamed my way to you. My country is very tiny, you see, and we don't often get visitors the likes of you."

I look at Melville—there's much more than mere distance between us. It won't be easy to overcome. To keep from thinking about it, I ask for red wine. A full bottle that Melville and I begin to drink. After half a bottle nothing has changed: Melville's still staring off into space and I'm still sitting here like a dope.

I say, "Excuse me but I don't seem to be able to tell you what seemed so clear to me on the way here. Now that you're here in front of me, I'm a little lost in my dream. I don't want to waste your time."

He pours himself another glass of wine and downs it in one swallow. The cane rolls on the table when he sets his glass down. I look at his hands: they don't look like the hands of a whale fisherman. The rest, yes—large square shoulders, a broad chest, strong thighs. A build which says he'll live to be a hundred. But maybe hands die first, maybe they wear out before the rest. To hide my distress, I turn my face towards the window and the big cat lying on the whale's tooth.

I say, "Don't worry about me. What's important is that I listen to you." He says, "It doesn't help make things any clearer." I say, "That's not why I asked to see you."

He raises his hand to his neck and massages it with small, round strokes. His hair is totally white and must feel like silk. He takes a thin cigar from his pocket and offers it to me. He says, "Take it. I've others." I shiver when Melville's fingers touch mine. Such heat, how is it possible? I strike a match on the bottom of my chair and hold it out to Melville. He draws on the thin cigar, the match flame swells and casts shadows on his face. Melville's eyes are much grayer than I thought. He says, "I'm afraid you're in for a disappointment, poor friend. It's not your fault. You simply don't know that you can't expect anything from somebody whose only goal is the supreme discretion of strolling along the docks of Harlem even though they don't exist any longer. Go back to Gaspé, you'll be fine there. And give old

Captain Coffin my greetings. Sulphur Bottom was quite a whale too."

He downs another glass of wine. His lower lip trembles, his eyes merely two dark spots upon his face. He says, "In any case, it's late and I must be going. Lizzie's not as patient as before. Mind you, I don't wish to displease you. You've come this long way for me and you're the first to have undertaken such a trip since my death. I owe you that, at least, if nothing else. But you must understand that I'm in an uncomfortable position, I'm rather badly placed to satisfy your desire. It's one of the consequences of death; it deprives you of the images you entertained of yourself, but gives you none with which to replace them. There, I believe I've said most of what I have to say. I really must go." I say, "May I come with you?" He says, "We see no one now, you know. Lizzie's willing; it's I who generally refuse. She'll be quite surprised."

I leave all the money I have on the table and follow Melville to the door. Just before turning the knob he stops and stares at the big cat asleep in the basket on the window sill. He says, "My whale's tooth. I was about to forget my whale's tooth."

The big cat allows himself to be picked up and set to one side. He stretches, his claws scratch the wood. With two paws placed firmly on the basket handle, he waits for us to take the whale's tooth so he can lie down once again. Melville unbuttons his coat. Beneath it, the tooth protrudes slightly at the stomach. I close the door behind us and we walk off into the night side by side down the deserted wharves; all is quiet except for the tapping of the cane on the pavement. Melville takes my arm by way of asking me not to walk too fast. He's quite right—night's eternal return, no hurry. Anyway, a few steps and we're there. Melville and I, in the house he bought in the heart of New York City when, after 13 years of life in the country, he sold Arrowhead. That was in March 1863, long after the *Acushnet*, long after the lengthy journey to New Bedford and Nantucket, at a time when the Melvillian countryside lay in ruin.

Melville leads me into a sort of drawing room situated at the far end of the hall, then he disappears. I wait for him, seated upon a small chair covered in purple velvet. I recognize the geraniums and the red roses in the window, as well as the photographs framed in black on the walls. I realize now for the first time that no one in them is smiling, neither Melville nor his son Malcolm, not Lizzie, not Augusta. Their expressions are vacant.

I turn my eyes away. Now I see only boats. I recognize the *United States*, a man-of-war Melville served on during his return from the South Seas. But I don't see either the *Acushnet* or the *St. Lawrence*. On the other hand there is that lovely scene of New Bedford as it was at the time when Melville became a sailor. The docks are so full of goods you get the impression that the ships are mired in a sea of barrels and casks. I sit wondering what all that whale oil must have smelled like when suddenly exposed to the sun.

Melville returns to the drawing room at last. He sits down on the love seat facing my chair. His eyes run rapidly around the room without settling on anything in particular. He says, "I brought you into this room because it's the only one that hasn't been disturbed by this our final move. Elsewhere in the house things are already packed up. Here all that's missing is my small collection of old travel books. Have you read Captain Cook?" I say, "No, not really." He says, "Or Vancouver?" I say, "Not him either." He says, "Or Bougainville?" I say, "No. But I'm familiar with La Pérouse and Kotzebue. And with the life of Captain Nepos." He says, "Now, there you're in ancient history. Captain Nepos doesn't have very much to do with whales. He was after other game. He was merely a fighter who lived by ruse. He would catapult baskets full of snakes onto the decks of enemy vessels. He wasn't really an explorer. He probably didn't even like water very much. He died in bed, poisoned, I believe. But as for Cook and Bougainville—we'll come back to them. One can't navigate the South Seas without them. And that's what you intend to do, isn't it?"

Thus, he understood before I could tell him. Maybe he knew it the moment I accosted him on the docks of Harlem. That's why he spoke of Captain Cook and of Nepos' ruses. For me to get used to the dream and all it will bring in its wake.

I look at him again. He seems less old since we left the port. If his beard weren't completely white, I could easily believe he was a man in the prime of life. His eyes are bright with malice. I'd like him to speak to me right away about Bougainville and Captain Cook. As I tell him so, he raises a finger to his lips. Footsteps in the hallway. Then Lizzie appears; she is wearing a long black dress closed at the neck by a gold brooch. She smiles at me. She says, "You resemble Nathaniel Hawthorne when we knew him at Pittsfield. Can it be you, come back at last from old England? Herman said nothing about your visit."

She sits beside Melville on the love seat. Where did he pull the whale's tooth out of? He shows it to Lizzie, explaining to her who I am and why I've come. Lizzie's face hardens, fleeting but intense hostility appearing in it. She says, "Herman, hadn't you promised never to leave me again? This young man is perfectly capable of travelling alone." He says, "It won't prevent you from going to our sister Fanny's as planned. I won't be away long. A few months at most. Afterwards it shall truly be over." She says, "Weren't we supposed to go to Arrowhead next week? Since our good Allan moved in, it doesn't seem the same house we lived in. In any case, it wasn't at all the same house this spring."

Melville shrugs his shoulders. Lizzie says, "Won't you at least drink something before you go? And I want Nathaniel to tell us all about his long stay in old England." Melville says, "We won't have time for that. Nathaniel will tell us about it later." Lizzie says, "As you wish, Herman. I'll go to sleep then. Don't forget to close the door well when you leave. Last time you left it open."

Melville and I are alone once again. He seems happy. For the first time I see his white teeth between his lips. He says, "I was afraid it would be more difficult. Poor Lizzie! Isn't it strange, her mistaking you for Nathaniel Hawthorne? But it isn't such a bad idea, I think from now on that's what I shall call you. I'll feel then that we belong to the same generation. It will simplify many things. Come."

We climb a long staircase that leads to a hallway. We pass many closed doors as we thread our way through a line of enormous trunks. We arrive at a door that is open a few inches.

Melville pushes it with his foot and we enter what must be his study. There is an iron cot next to the window. It was Melville's death bed. On the table a long quill pen is still standing in an inkwell. Beside it lies a large white sheet of paper upon which are written three lines:

But, crying out in death's eclipse,
When rainbow none his eyes might see,
Enlarged the margin for despair—

I don't dare look at anything else. All I notice are Melville's feet moving about in the room. He says, "It's not so tragic. You'll see many others. Come help me here."

Melville wants to move a trunk that's blocking the closet door. I grab the large leather handle with both hands. The trunk is very heavy. He says, "There is what I leave the world, this simple trunk which no one shall even think to open, perhaps. *Billy Budd* is in it on the very bottom. I want them to find it only at the end, only once the rest shall have been finally used up." He laughs. Then he says, "I might have chosen another mania, don't you think, Nathaniel?"

He said "Nathaniel" in a strange voice. It must have been that way between him and Hawthorne at Pittsfield. I smile, aware that something very important has just happened to me. There is reciprocity between us now, all the constraints have finally disappeared, swept away by the magic of the name with which Melville has baptized me. I feel at one with him now, words seem unnecessary between us.

Melville rummages in the closet and comes up with two monkey jackets, one green, the other brown. He says, "We'll need these where we're going. Take the brown one, I prefer the green. I wore it on all my trips. The brown jacket is a gift from Hawthorne. It's got two big inside pockets."

Hawthorne's monkey jacket is a bit large for me but I imagine that with a sweater underneath it won't show. Melville says, "Now that we've got the basic equipment, let's go, shall we? It takes quite a few hours to get to New Bedford from here."

Letting me pass in front of him, he closes the door to his study. Then he rests his hand on my shoulder and we go back down the long flight of stairs. Melville's eyes have changed since we put on our monkey jackets. They're oddly brilliant. I have the feeling that if I were to stare into them for too long they would run me through. I think about the Golem of Prague, that magnificently animated figure, and say to myself that that is what Melville has become. All men's eyes become the eyes of God if you think they are the eyes of God, said Don Benito Cereno. Melville says, "No doubt. But we mustn't miss the stagecoach. There's only one we can catch in this dream. Get a move on, Nathaniel."

***

If it weren't for the cobblestones under our wheels, I'd say there wasn't much difference between our stagecoach and a train. We're just as comfortable. Melville and I are the only passengers. We're sitting side by side, though I suggested a different arrangement. He refused, I think, because of his eyes; he didn't want them to make me uncomfortable. Melville's eyes are ablaze; they became so the moment the horses took their first step. His face has changed completely. Melville is sitting upright, his elbow placed on the arm rest. He's smoking one of his countless Mexican cigars.

I make myself as small as possible beside him, my left leg slung over my right. I look out the glass in the stagecoach door. I see the port in Harlem far off behind us and the silhouetted ships, and the lamps like will-o'-the-wisps along the docks. Soon we'll be on the road that runs along the ocean into New Bedford. But we're not likely to see much through this foggy curtain that fell between us and the rest of the world the moment we left New York. So we'll manage to get some sleep. Afterwards, Melville will light a new cigar, put his large hand on my knee so I'll feel more at ease, and say, "What would you like us to talk about? We won't reach New Bedford for a long while yet."

I fill my pipe with Hawthorne's tobacco and strike a match on my shoe. We're crossing a small bridge now, we can hear the horses' hooves on the wood. I glance at the window pane. All I see is the inside of the coach. I say, "We're fine the way we are, I think. Why do we need to speak?" Melville says, "Perhaps you're right, Nathaniel."

He rests his head on the back of the seat and closes his eyes. I won't disturb him. I'm going to do as he and stick my hands in my jacket pockets. It's curious riding in a stagecoach: when you close your eyes you get the feeling you're travelling at breakneck speed. Also, it's as though you were moving out of yourself, as though that other body in you were being projected into space. I allow mine to leave the stagecoach entirely. It returns to New York City and floats above Bleecker Street just like the ghost of Doctor Sax the time that Kerouac and I were strolling along Beaulieu Street towards the murky-brown Potomac.

Everything is quiet now, which is fine with me. I feel tranquil, I'm simply happy to be here in this stagecoach with Melville on the way to New Bedford.

When the stagecoach stops we look once again out the window. On our left tiny points of light stipple the darkness. It must be Boston where old Major Melville is still on the prowl—he's wearing his knee breeches and his tri-cornered hat, and his cheeks are puffed up with air with which to keep dying fires alive. The driver opens the door. He says, "It won't be long, gentlemen. We're just changing horses. One of ours bloodied a hoof on some stones. He lost his shoe." As they unhitch them, the horses shudder and shake their heads—that slobber hanging from their lips. Melville and I still are not interested in speaking. The two worn-out horses must be in the stable with their noses stuck greedily in the feedbag. Their replacements are snorting and champing at the bit. The driver rubs and pats their noses before removing the brakes from the wheels. The whip cracks. The stagecoach takes off with a jolt. It's the middle of the night. Rain begins to fall. I glance once more out the stagecoach window. We're already in New Bedford, the capital of the whaling industry. You can smell it; with all the barrels on the docks and those fabulous three-masters rocking gently on the waves, you feel submerged in oil.

Fortunately, I'm not alone in my excitement: Melville can hardly keep still. And it's time we arrived in New Bedford. After the silence inside the stagecoach, a little excitement's not at all unwelcome. New Bedford fever takes hold of us; the town's so bright beneath that big red eye of a moon staring down on us.

Melville doesn't even wait for the horses to come to a full stop. He opens the stagecoach door. He says, "Come, Nathaniel. I'm going to show you New Bedford. It's exactly as it was when I sailed on the *Acushnet* that first trip."

I jump down out of the stagecoach, landing at Melville's side. He takes my arm and leads me along streets full of coaches and wagons and tall sailors with lined, weathered faces and shiny white teeth. Melville says, "It was night when I arrived in New Bedford for the first time. It was just as it is now—cloudy, dark and cold. Since I had little money, I walked the streets for a long while looking for lodgings. In those days boats for Nantucket were rare, and I missed the last packet leaving for there. So I had a night and a day and another night to spend in town before I could get aboard one. But look, Nathaniel, we've arrived too late also, the packet is already under way."

Because of the sunshine I shield my eyes so I can see what Melville wants to show me: far off in the distance I see something that could be a packet boat. It's about as big as a sardine can and is rolling slowly on the horizon. I grimace. Melville says, "Now, now, Nathaniel. Don't be disappointed. In New Bedford we'll find things to help us pass the time till the packet comes back. Let's go."

How could I resist? To tell the truth, I don't want to. Nantucket will be waiting for us when we arrive. So I fall in step with Melville, keeping my eyes wide open so I won't miss anything of this New Bedford through which we move as though through so much hot butter: all these Atlantic coast towns look alike with their squat buildings, their houses lined like sheep along zigzagging streets that funnel you into the port and its docks dark with people. Melville and I have to elbow our way to the Spouter Inn.

Ever since *Moby Dick* the Spouter Inn in New Bedford is famous, as it is elsewhere in the world. There's a Spouter Inn in New York City, another in Dublin, another in Halifax, another in Amsterdam. In Bombay there are two, just as there are in Cape Horn. But New Bedford's Spouter Inn is the authentic one. The reason is simple: it's because of the large oil painting that you can't miss as you enter the place. In Mattavinie, France is making me a fine reproduction of it. Like me, when she read *Moby Dick* she was fascinated by that besmoked, defaced depiction of Cape Horn in a great hurricane. You're presented a half-foundered ship weltering there with its three dismantled masts alone visible, and an exasperated whale, purposing to spring clean over the craft, is in the enormous act of impaling himself upon the three mastheads. Melville says, "It's rather impressive, isn't it—such an unaccountable mass of shade and shadow—don't you find?"

The wall opposite the large painting is hung all over with a heathenish array of monstrous clubs and spears. Some are thickly set with glittering teeth resembling ivory saws; others are tufted with knots of human hair. Then Melville calls my attention to a particularly strange whaling lance: it is sickle-shaped with a vast sweeping handle. He says, "With that lance Nathan Swain killed 15 whales between a sunrise and a sunset. One day, in the Java Sea, he flung it into a whale that ran away with it, not to be slain till years afterwards off the Cape of Blanco. The iron had entered nigh the tail, and, like a restless needle, travelled full 40 feet through the blubber and at last was found embedded in the hump."

But we can't stay in the hall all night. So we go through the low archway—cut through what in old times must have been a great central chimney with fireplaces all round—and enter the public room where on a bench presides old Peter Coffin. I notice the long, low, shelf-like table covered with cracked glass cases filled with dusty rarities gathered from the world's remotest nooks. All that's missing is the whale's tooth I gave to Monsieur Melville in New York City so that he'd recognize me. When I tell him that he unbuttons his monkey jacket, reaches into the big inside pocket and comes up with the very same tooth, which he places on the table between two cases full of bones. As he does so I look at the bar—a rude attempt at a Right Whale's head. Melville says, "How's business, Peter Coffin?" Old Peter Coffin says, "If it's a room you're wanting, why I ain't got a bed left." Melville says, "You've done this to me before, Peter Coffin." Old Peter Coffin says, "But avast, you haint no objections to sharing a savage harpooner's blanket, have ye, or I can accommodate ye." Melville says, "Just as before, Peter Coffin. Just as before! But this time I'm with my friend Nathaniel. We won't be given the business as easily as that." Old Peter Coffin says, "So long as you pay me, the rest is another man's matter, not my own." Melville says, "Well, rather than wander—" Old Peter Coffin says, "All right; take a seat. Supper's the thing to get you ready for bed. It'll be ready directly."

He disappears behind a door. Melville says, "Dumplings, Nathaniel. Dumplings with meat and potatoes. You'll see, there's nothing better. Nobody serves dumplings as good as Peter Coffin's."

They're not bad, as a matter of fact, they're just what your stomach needs. Then I say, "We should get down to business, Monsieur Melville." He says, "Soon, Nathaniel. Let's finish our dumplings first."

But I'm already nodding out. I say, "Perhaps we could go to sleep?" Melville says, "With the savage harpooneer?" I say, "With the savage harpooneer." He says, "In that case, we might stay up a bit longer. No man prefers to sleep two in a bed. In fact, one would a good deal rather not sleep with his own brother. I imagine what it must be sleeping three in a bed. I suggest we'd be better to try those wide benches."

I say nothing; Melville doesn't recall having had the same idea when he came to sail on the *Acushnet;* it's stayed in his mind. Old Peter Coffin has fun with him, saying "So you wish to bed down on the bench? Well, between it and the savage harpooneer, I'm sure I know which I'd choose. I'm sorry, I still can't spare ye a tablecloth for a mattress; it'd be almost as good as your Canadian gannet feathers." I say, "Don't go stirring up Canada any more, Peter Coffin. We've had enough of that. Show us to our room."

Old Peter Coffin winks at me, then starts off with a candle in his hand. We follow him to the room. Upon entering, Melville says "Cold as a clam!" I glance around the room; besides the bedstead and centre table, I see only a rude shelf and a paper fireboard representing a man striking a whale. Then I notice a hammock lashed up and tossed upon the floor in one corner, and a large seaman's bag which must belong to the savage harpooneer.

But I don't want to think about that yet. Later, we'll see. For the moment all that's on my mind is climbing into bed where I'll fill my pipe and wait for Melville to fall asleep. It won't take long.

I look at him; it's ridiculous, but I'd like to throw myself in his arms and roll around with him in this huge bed, and cry my heart out; I'd ask him to let us stay here and forget about Nantucket and the *Acushnet*, even to forgo the trip to the South Seas he agreed to take with me because he knows I love him, because he knows that I'm at one and the same time Hawthorne and his son Malcolm, and Jack Chase, and Billy Budd, and Clarel, all that's left, that is, of imagination for him after all these years of solitude. I'd like to press myself against him, give him my warmth so he'd have the courage to stay up with me, the courage to wait for the savage harpooneer and never think of his son Malcolm again. He's lying on his side, his eyes closed—doubtless so as not to see Queequeg's bag in the corner of the room. I don't dare touch him. I have the feeling that if I did, he would crumble. All my trouble for nothing. I'd have to get back into the old blood-red Cadillac with the big, shiny fins that is waiting by the Harlem docks and return to Quebec. I say, "Are you asleep, Monsieur Melville?" He doesn't answer. I can hardly hear him breathing. I reach for my pipe on the floor beside the bed. I intend to fill it again and light it, then suckle it like a mother's breast. I say, "Sleep, Monsieur Melville. I'll be the one to stay awake in this dream."

***

Then the savage harpooneer enters the room. I watch as he kneels and digs into his seaman's bag. Rising and coming towards the bed, he's as surprised as I am to find me next to Melville. I raise a finger to my lips to prevent one of those guttural cries of Queequeg's that frightened Melville so much the last time. He smiles at me, visibly happy at having become my accomplice so easily. Queequeg is a fine, strapping man, broad-shouldered and with beautifully developed muscles; his yellowish skin is covered with tattoos; and his roving black eyes, sparkling with mischief, stare straight at me.

The tomahawk doesn't scare me: the Montagnais of Pointe-Bleue have equally efficient ones. And then, one way or another, we all wind up getting scalped. So Queequeg's tomahawk doesn't faze me. Looking at him again, I even feel closer to him because of my miscreant nature, which explains why I'm drawn to marginal types and crackpots. I can recognize myself even from a distance. And what I recognize as I look at Queequeg has nothing to do with Melville's troubled shudders when he saw him for the first time.

Queequeg strips naked and crawls into bed between Melville and me. Now it's he who is looking at me—attentively, ignoring Melville's snores. We don't speak. Sleeping with a man has always excited me, I don't know why. It doesn't give off the same sensuality nor does it offer the same attraction as a woman's body. It always makes me extremely vulnerable and leaves me feeling warm inside. My very skin feels different, becoming a thousand times more sensitive. It was a great discovery for me to learn this when Antonin, Job J and I lived in the apartment house on the rue St-Denis. I imagine that if I had become a sailor, it would have been for that reason. Because of his upbringing, I doubt that Melville would ever be able to accept that two men, full of love for each other, should feel the need to offer themselves totally to each other.

I don't know how I'm going to broach the subject with Melville when the time comes. He's never spoken about it except here and there in his novels, and in the extraordinary love letters that make up his correspondence with Hawthorne. However, at the period of Melville's trip on the *Acushnet*, male friendship of this type was a common occurrence. To go on a four-year voyage with only a band of vigorous men for company—hearty, well-built types little given to solitude—was enough to turn your head after a while. I can imagine what it must have been like—beautiful muscular bodies, sun-darkened skin save for strangely white buttocks, male members hard in the dark, all the more prodigious and threatening since there was a moral code forcing you to see this proposal of beauty as a most hideous vice. I couldn't have. I mean to say, I couldn't have lived for long with all those men without my hands starting to roam, and widely—the wafting musky odours, how provocative it must have been!

Such are my thoughts as Queequeg sits staring at me. In no time at all I explain to him what I'm doing in the room and why I'm making the trip with Melville this time. Queequeg says nothing as I speak. He merely nods as though agreeing. Soon I'll ask him to let me touch him, to let me run my fingers over his tattoos. It's curious. Somehow I feel that Queequeg's memory is encrusted in his skin. Entirely in relief from head to toe. I touch Queequeg's body ever so lightly with my open hand, meeting the richness of the red world, its unbelievable precision, its unparalleled fullness.

Queequeg and I remain lying on our backs, our bodies so close together that I can feel the blood pulsing in his veins. He continues to smile at me, flashing his beautiful white teeth. What a fascinating double watch we're standing—it ends when I fall asleep to dream of soft moist lips upon mine and of two strong thighs closed tightly around my sex.

When I awake Queequeg is sound asleep. My head is resting on his left arm. Melville has hold of his other. There was some truth then in what Melville wrote in *Moby Dick:* "You had almost thought I had been his wife." But now there are two of us in that role, lying on opposite sides of him: the light streaming in the window makes his stark naked body seem even more imposing than it appeared last night; it's indefinably soft, discreet even, despite that member as stiff as a pike-staff.

I don't dare wake Queequeg. Melville opens his eyes, he gives me a wink. Together we free ourselves from Queequeg and climb out of bed. Queequeg groans; he brings his arms together and rolls over on his stomach. All the while Melville and I continue to dress. Melville says, "Let him sleep. He will undoubtedly join us on the docks."

We go out of the room leaving Queequeg still fast asleep. After a hearty breakfast we head down to the docks and go aboard the packet boat, on our way to Nantucket at last. It's still the third day of January, the day Melville and I are to leave for the South Seas.

NOTES ON CONTRIBUTORS

VICTOR-LÉVY BEAULIEU is one of Quebec's leading novelists. Born in 1945, he is the author of more than forty books. In 1973, with Léandre Bergeron, he founded the publishing company Editions de l'Aurore, and in 1976 he founded VLB Editeur, now Quebec's major literary publishing house. In 1975, he received a Governor-General's Award for fiction.

BETTY BEDNARSKI teaches Quebec literature at Dalhousie University in Halifax, and has most recently translated *Selected Tales of Jacques Ferron* (Anansi, 1984).

CLAUDE BOISVERT was born in Amos, Quebec, in 1945. He has had a varied career as promotion manager, translator, art professor, children's playwright, and journalist. His stories are collected as *Parendoxe* and *Tranches de néant*.

JANE BRIERLEY is a literary translator who lives in Montreal. She has published other work by Elisabeth Vonarburg and is currently translating Vonarburg's science-fiction novel *Le Silence de la cité*. She has recently published an annotated translation of Philippe-Joseph Aubert de Gaspé's memoirs *Man of Sentiment*.

JACQUES BROSSARD was a career diplomat in the Department of External Affairs. His foreign postings included Colombia and Haiti. He now teaches political science at the University of Montreal. Author of five collections of essays on political subjects, his stories are collected in *Les Metamorfaux*. He has also published a novel, *Le Sang du souvenir*.

MICHAEL BULLOCK won the Canada Council Translation Prize for Michel Tremblay's *Stories for Late Night Drinkers*. Professor Emeritus of creative writing at the University of British Columbia, he has translated over 150 books from French, German, and Italian. He has also published several collections of surreal prose and poetry.

ANDRÉ CARPENTIER was born in Montreal in 1947. His story collections include *Rue St. Denis: contes fantastiques* and *Du pain des oiseaux*. He has also edited a collection entitled *Dix contes et nouvelles fantastiques*.

ROCH CARRIER was born in a small village in Quebec in 1937. He is now a professor at the University of Montreal. His many works available in English translation include *La Guerre, Yes sir!*, *Floralie, where are you?*, *Is It The Sun, Philibert?*, *They Won't Demolish Me!*, *The Garden of Delights*, *No Country Without Grandfathers*, and *Lady with Chains*. His stories appear in *Jolis Deuils*.

RAY CHAMBERLAIN is originally from Georgia and now lives in Montreal. He has translated three volumes of Victor-Lévy Beaulieu's *Monsieur Melville*, and his *A Québécois Dream* and *Satan belhumour*, as well as poems by Claude Beausoleil.

CLAUDETTE CHARBONNEAU-TISSOT was born in Montreal in 1947. A professor at the community college of François-Xavier Garneau, she is working on a doctorate at the University of Laval. She has worked in the psychiatric department at the Montreal General Hospital, an experience which informs much of her fiction. She has written a novel, *La chaise au fond de l'oeil*, and two story collections, *Contes pour hydrocéphales adultes*, and *La Contrainte*.

PIERRE CHÂTILLON was born in Quebec in 1939. He received his degrees from the Universities of Sherbrooke, Montreal, Ottawa, and the Sorbonne, and taught at the Royal Military College at Kingston, and the University of Quebec at Trois-Rivières. As poet, novelist, and storywriter, he has published ten books. His stories appear in *L'Île aux fantômes*.

CLAIRE DÉ and ANNE DANDURAND are twin sisters who live in Montreal. Poets, fiction writers and playwrights, they often collaborate on their work. They are currently writing thirty episodes of a half-hour TV detective drama for Radio Canada. Their first book was *La Louve*.

MICHEL DE CELLES was born in Montreal, and has lived throughout Quebec. He holds degrees in physics from the University of Laval and the Sorbonne. He has written over a dozen scientific papers and now works for the Quebec Ministry of Education. His short stories have appeared in many Quebec literary magazines, among them *Possibles*, *Liberté*, and *Les écrits du Canada français*.

RAY ELLENWOOD is from Toronto and teaches at York University. He has translated Jacques Ferron's *The Cart*, *The Penniless Redeemer*, and *Quince Jam*, as well as Claude Gauvreau's *Entrails* and the complete 1948 automatistes' manifesto, *Refus Global*.

JEAN FERGUSON was born on a MicMac Indian reservation in Quebec, but lived a decade in Brazil. He graduated from the Universities of Ottawa and Montreal, and now lives in Val D'Or where he writes novels, theatre pieces, and essays. His stories first appeared in *Contes ardents du pays mauve*.

JACQUES FERRON was born in 1921 and died in 1984. By profession a physician, he was also a novelist, essayist, playwright and short-story writer, as well as the founder of the satirical political group, the Rhinoceros Party. In 1964, his collected stories (most of them available in translation as *Selected Tales of Jacques Ferron*: Anansi, 1984) won a Governor-General's Award.

MADELEINE FERRON is the younger sister of Jacques Ferron. A well known journalist, novelist, and storyteller, her works include *Coeur du sucre*, *La fin des loup-garous*, *Le Baron écarlate*, *Le Chemin des dames*, and *Histoires édifantes*.

SHEILA FISCHMAN has become well-known for her translations of many Quebec classics, including novels by Anne Hébert, Marie-Claire Blais, Michel Tremblay, Yves Beauchemin, Roch Carrier, Victor-Lévy Beaulieu, and Jacques Poulin. She has won the Canada Council's Translation award for Roch Carrier's *They Won't Demolish Me!* and Marie-Claire Blais' *The Wolf*.

CLAUDE GAUVREAU was born in Montreal in 1925 and died in 1971. A pioneering poet, playwright, and polemicist, Gauvreau influenced an entire generation of writers. He was one of the original signatories to the famous manifesto, *Refus Global*, which introduced instinctive dance, theatre of the absurd, surrealism, free verse and non-figurative painting to the conservative Quebec of 1948.

ROLAND GIGUÈRE was born in Montreal in 1929. He is one of Quebec's leading poets and graphic artists. His publishing company, Erta, specialised in limited editions featuring poets and artists. Through the group known as Phases, he participated in the international surrealist movement. For his poetic achievements, he has received many prizes, including the France-Canada Prize, the city of Montreal prize, and the Quebec Prize. In 1974, he refused a Governor-General's Award for poetry.

ALAIN GRANDBOIS was one of Quebec's major literary figures. Practically unknown in English Canada, he wrote thirteen volumes of poems and short stories. His work and career form the basis of over a dozen literary studies. A world-traveller, he contributed to the formation of the Académie canadienne-française. He died in 1975.

FRANÇOIS HÉBERT teaches at the University of Montreal. He is now editor-in-chief of *Liberté*, one of Quebec's leading literary magazines. For six years, he was literary director of Éditions Quinze, and he is now literary consultant and critic for *Le Devoir*. His three novels include *Holyoke*, *Les Rendez-vous*, and *Histoire de l'impossible pays*. With Gilles Marcotte, he has co-edited an anthology of Quebec literature. He has also written a story collection, *Histoires*, and a book of essays, *Triptyque de la mort: une lecture des romans de Malraux*.

LOUIS-PHILIPPE HÉBERT was born in Montreal in 1946. He has published a wide range of poems, stories, essays, and radio plays, as well as broadcasting book reviews for the CBC radio network. His prose fictions appear in several collections, among them *Le Roi jaune*, *Le Petit Catéchisme: La vie publique de W et On*, *Le Cinéma de Petite-Rivière*, *La Manufacture de machines*, and *Manuscrit trouvé dans une valise*.

GEOFF HANCOCK, editor-in-chief of *Canadian Fiction Magazine*, has edited many anthologies of contemporary Canadian fiction, including *Magic Realism* (1980), *Illusion: Fables, Fantasies, and Metafictions* (1983), *Metavisions* (1983), *Shoes and Shit: Stories for Pedestrians* (1984), and *Moving off the Map* (1986). He has also published a series of interviews with Canadian writers, *Canadian Writers at Work*, and is writing a study of contemporary Quebec fiction.

M.G. HESSE is chairperson of the Department of Modern Languages at the University of Lethbridge, Alberta. Her translations of Yves Thériault and Gabrielle Roy have appeared in many literary magazines and she is the author of a recently published book on Gabrielle Roy.

BASIL KINGSTONE is a professor of French at the University of Windsor, Ontario. He is a translation teacher as well as a translator himself, and has received an MA in translation from the University of Ottawa. He is currently translating a book on André Gide from the Dutch.

ALBERTO MANGUEL is from Buenos Aires, and now lives in Montreal. His many anthologies include *The Dictionary of Imaginary Places*, *Black Water: An Anthology of Fantastic Literature*, *Other Fires: Stories by Latin American Women*, *Black Arrows: Chronicles of Revenge*, and *Evening Games: Chronicles of Parents and Children*.

PAUL PARÉ participated in the founding of the publishing house, Le Biocreux. His works include a novel, *L'Improbable Autopsie*, a "quasi-novel", *L'Antichambre et autres Métastases*, a novel, *La Vengeance du couteau à mastic*, and *Ils: essai-fiction*. His short stories appear in *Les Fables de l'entonnoir*.

THOMAS PAVEL was born in Rumania in 1941. A professor of linguistics at the University of Ottawa, his stories are collected in *Le Miror persan*.

Notes on Contributors

MONIQUE PROULX was born in Quebec in 1952. She has written scripts for TV and radio including the CBC's "Beaux Dimanches," as well as theatre pieces and screenplays. Her first collection of stories was *Sans coeur et sans reproches* (1983).

LARRY SHOULDICE teaches English at the University of Sherbrooke in Sherbrooke, Quebec. His *Contemporary Quebec Criticism* won the 1981 Canada Council Translation Prize and he has translated Alain Grandbois' *Avant le Chaos* as *Champagne and Opium*.

MARIE-JOSÉ THÉRIAULT is the daughter of novelist Yves Thériault. For many years she was literary director of the publishing house, Editions Hurtubise HMH. Poet, storyteller, novelist, and professional singer, she has twice been nominated for a Governor-General's Award. Her stories are published as *La cérémonie* and *L'envoleur de chevaux et autres contes*.

YVES THÉRIAULT was one of Quebec's great novelists and storytellers. Author of more than fifty novels and story collections, he has won most of Canada's and Quebec's literary awards. His best known works are *Agaguk* and *Ashini*. Thériault died in 1983.

MICHEL TREMBLAY is one of Canada's foremost playwrights and novelists. His eleven plays are considered Canadian classics. He is currently working on an eleven volume novel cycle, the last novel to end at the point where the first play begins. His short fictions appear in *Contes pour buveurs attardés*.

YOLANDE VILLEMAIRE was born at Saint-Augustin-des-deux-Montagnes in 1949. Theatre critic and performance artist, as well as poet, storyteller, and novelist, she has taught literature at the community college in Rosemont. Her short fictions are published as *Que du stage blood, Du côté hiéroglyphe de ce qu'on appelle le réel* and *Devant le temple de Louxor de 31 juillet 1980*.

LUISE VON FLOTOW-EVANS is from Windsor, Ontario. She is currently working on her doctorate in Quebec literature at the University of Michigan at Ann Arbor.

ELISABETH VONARBURG was born in France in 1947 and moved to Quebec in 1973. One of Quebec's major science-fiction writers, she was founding editor of the sci-fi magazine, *Solaris* in 1979. She also organized the first science fiction conference in Chicoutimi in 1982. Her stories are collected as *L'Oeil de la nuit*.

ACKNOWLEDGEMENTS

We would like to thank the copyright-holders for their kind permission to reprint the stories which appear in this collection:

Roland Giguère, "Miror", translated by Sheila Fischman, originally appeared in a collection published by Press Porcepic; courtesy of the author.

Madeleine Ferron, "The Weaker Sex", translated by Basil Kingstone, from *Le chemin des dames;* originally appeared in *Canadian Fiction Magazine;* courtesy of Les Editions La Presse.

Marie-José Thériault, "The Thirty-First Bird", translated by Luise von Flotow-Evans; courtesy of Sogides Ltée.

André Carpentier, "Birdy's Flight", from *Du pain des oiseaux;* translated by Michael Bullock; courtesy of VLB Editeur.

Yves Thériault, "Nuliak", translated by M.G. Hesse, originally published in *The Malahat Review;* courtesy of VLB Editeur.

Alain Grandbois, "The Thirteenth", translated by Larry Shouldice, originally published in *Champagne & Opium* (Quadrant Editions); courtesy of the translator.

Thomas Pavel, "The Persian Mirror", from *Le miroir persan;* translated by Michael Bullock; courtesy of Les Quinze Editeur.

Jacques Brossard, "The Metamorfalsis", from *Le metamorfaux;* translated by Basil Kingstone, originally appeared in *Canadian Fiction Magazine;* courtesy of Editions Hurtubise HMH Ltée.

Roch Carrier, "The Bird", "Steps", "The Ink", from *Jolis deuils* (Editions du Jour); "The Wedding" appeared in *Etudes françaises*, vol 5, no. 1; "The Room" originally appeared in *Ecrits du Canada français* 25, 1969; all were translated by Sheila Fischman and appeared in translation in *ellipse*; courtesy of Les Editions Internationales Alain Stanké.

Louis-Philippe Hébert, "The Hotel", from *La manufacture de machines*, and "A Text Concerning Strawberries", from *Le cinéma de petite-rivière* (Editions du Jour); translated by Alberto Manguel; courtesy of the author.

Michel Tremblay, "The Hanged Man, The Eye of the Idol, The Ghost of Don Carlos, The Octagonal Room", translated by Michael Bullock, originally appeared in *Canadian Fiction Magazine*, and in *Stories for Late Night Drinkers* (Intermedia); courtesy of John Goodwin et Associés.

Michel de Celles, "Recurrence", translated by Basil Kingstone, originally appeared in *Liberté #146* and *Canadian Fiction Magazine*; courtesy of the author.

Paul Paré, "Five Fables", translated by Basil Kingstone, originally appeared in *Canadian Fiction Magazine* and *Les fables de l'entonnoir* (Le Biocreux).

François Hébert, "Prowling Around Little Red Riding Hood", translated by Basil Kingstone, originally appeared in *Liberté #146* and *Canadian Fiction Magazine*; courtesy of the author.

Jean Ferguson, "Ker, the God Killer", from *Contes ardents du pays mauve*; translated by Basil Kingstone, originally appeared in *Canadian Fiction Magazine*; courtesy of Editions Leméac.

Claude Gauvreau, "The Dream of the Bridge" and "The Prophet in the Sea", translated by Ray Ellenwood, originally published in *Entrails* (Coach House Press); courtesy of the translator and of Pierre Gauvreau.

Acknowledgements 437

Claude Boisvert, "A Slice of Nothingness" and "The Prophet", from *Tranches de néant* (Le Biocreux); translated by Michael Bullock; courtesy of the author.

Elisabeth Vonarburg, "Cold Bridge", from *L'Oeil de la nuit;* translation copyright © Elisabeth Vonarburg and Jane Brierley; courtesy of Le Préambule.

Pierre Châtillon, "Ghost Island", from *L'Île aux fantômes;* translated by Michael Bullock; courtesy of Les Editions Internationales Alain Stanké.

Claudette Charbonneau-Tissot, "Compulsion", from *La contrainte;* translated by Michael Bullock; courtesy of Editions Pierre Tisseyre.

Yolande Villemaire, "In Front of the Temple of Luxor", translated by Basil Kingstone, originally appeared in *les herbes rouges;* courtesy of *les herbes rouges*.

Jacques Ferron, "The Dead Cow in the Canyon", translated by Betty Bednarski, originally published in *Selected Tales of Jacques Ferron;* courtesy of House of Anansi Press.

Monique Proulx, "ABC", translated by Basil Kingstone, originally published in *Sans coeur et sans reproche;* courtesy of Editions Québec/Amérique.

Claire Dé and Anne Dandurand, "A Metamorphosis" and "A Case Still Open", translated by Basil Kingstone, excerpted from *La Louve;* courtesy of Les Editions de la Pleine Lune.

Victor-Lévy Beaulieu, from *Monsieur Melville*, Vol. I: *On the Eve of "Moby Dick",* Chapter 12, pp. 143-167, published by Coach House Press; translated by Ray Chamberlain; courtesy of the translator.

Other Anansi books from Quebec

Non-fiction:

Voices of Deliverance: Interviews with Quebec and Acadian Writers, Donald Smith (Larry Shouldice, translator)

Practical Handbook of Quebec and Acadian French/Manuel pratique du français québécois et acadien, Sinclair Robinson & Donald Smith

Reality and Theatre, Naïm Kattan (Alan Brown, translator)

Fiction:

Hubert Aquin, *The Antiphonary* (Alan Brown, translator)
Jacques Brault, *Death Watch* (David Lobdell, translator)
Louis Caron, *The Draft Dodger* (David Toby Homel, translator)
Roch Carrier, *La Guerre, Yes Sir!* (Sheila Fischman, translator)
  Floralie, Where Are You? (Sheila Fischman, translator)
  Is it the Sun, Philibert? (Sheila Fischman, translator)
  They Won't Demolish Me! (Sheila Fischman, translator)
  The Garden of Delights (Sheila Fischman, translator)
  The Hockey Sweater and Other Stories (Sheila Fischman, translator)
  No Country Without Grandfathers (Sheila Fischman, translator)
  Lady With Chains (Sheila Fischman, translator)
Jacques Ferron, *Selected Tales of Jacques Ferron* (Betty Bednarski, translator)
Jacques Poulin, *The "Jimmy" Trilogy* (Sheila Fischman, translator)
Jacques Poulin, *Spring Tides* (Sheila Fischman, translator)

Jl